MOONSHINE MELODY

A MYSTERY

GARY W. EVANS

Copyright © 2019 Gary W. Evans.

All rights reserved. No part of this book may be reproduced, stored, or transmitted by any means—whether auditory, graphic, mechanical, or electronic—without written permission of both publisher and author, except in the case of brief excerpts used in critical articles and reviews. Unauthorized reproduction of any part of this work is illegal and is punishable by law.

Library of Congress Control Number: 2019917632

ISBN 978-1-7331826-4-5 Paperback
ISBN 978-1-7331826-5-2 Ebook

1

THE WOODS WERE OMINOUSLY QUIET THIS MONDAY NIGHT IN May. In fact, if it hadn't been for the insistent whine of mosquitoes, David Freeman wouldn't have heard a sound. The cloud canopy was outlined in silver, a result of the full moon, and partially hidden. David crept quietly along the path in the heavily wooded Trempealeau River bottoms, clutching a rifle in one hand and a large bag of yeast in the other. His brother Justin trudged ahead of him, a bucket filled with corn in each hand. David paused every few steps and checked over his shoulder to make certain no one was following. In spite of the cool night, sweat trickled down between his shoulder blades. After a half hour of stop-and-go progress, they arrived.

Justin set his buckets next to the still. A twig snapped behind them, and both brothers whirled around. David pressed a finger to his lips, set down the bag of yeast, and began to slink down the path they had just traveled with his rifle pointed in the direction of the noise. He'd only gone a hundred feet when he nearly bumped into a figure wearing black.

"Who are you?" He grasped the figure by his shirt, spun him around, then shoved the butt of the rifle into the person's chest. When he didn't move, David pressed the button on his flashlight and shone it in the guy's face. "Byrle, what the hell are you doing here?"

The intruder pushed aside the flashlight and smiled. "So this is it, huh? The place you make the stuff. Been trying to find out ever since I first met ya, and my impatience finally paid off."

"You mean you've been following us for a while?"

"Yep. Your operation was driving me crazy, so I decided to try and find out more a coupla weeks ago."

David stared at him. He and Justin had met Byrle Oldendorf, owner of the Handy Corner Bar, at a mutual friend's party just over a year ago. Everyone had been drinking the Freeman brother's moonshine, and Byrle had commended David on how good it was.

Oldendorf had rubbed meaty hands together over the fire as he looked at David. "Mighty fine stuff you brought."

"We like it," David had replied. "We learn as we go, but we're pretty happy with how things are going."

"How much of the stuff do you make?"

"A few gallons a week." The two sat down at a nearby table, and David propped an elbow on it. *Why is this guy so interested?*

"Ever thought of selling the stuff?"

"No; why would we? Hell, it's not that good. Besides, we only make enough to satisfy our thirst. We're still learnin'."

Oldendorf turned from the fire to look him in the eye. "I disagree. It's damn good. In fact, it's a helluva lot better than most of the shit I sell in my bar. I'll tell you right now, I could sell 15 gallons of it a week, no sweat."

David blinked. "You're joking."

"Hell no. 15 gallons at a minimum. In fact, assuming the price is reasonable, I'll commit to 20 gallons a week, right here, right now."

David laughed and started to walk away. Oldendorf grabbed his shoulder and spun him around. "Listen, Freeman, I'm serious. Twenty gallons a week. And if you can make more, I'll sell that, too."

David shook off the man's hand and took two more steps away from the fire. Oldendorf grabbed him again. "Any idea what it'd sell for?"

"None," David told him. "Heck, we haven't even thought about selling it."

"Well, if you can supply stuff as good as what's here tonight, I'll pay you 80 dollars for every gallon you can deliver."

David's eyes widened. The music was loud. Obviously, he had misunderstood. "Eighty bucks a gallon? Did I hear that right?"

"You did. I'll take as many gallons as you can deliver, and I'll pay 80 dollars for every one of 'em."

David shook his head. "I'll... give it some thought."

The other man slapped him across the back. "That's all I ask."

In a daze, David moved across the park area, nearly stumbling into Justin. David caught a whiff of rum and frowned. Justin never knew when to stop. He grabbed his brother by the elbow and led him toward the parking lot.

"Guess what?" David let go of Justin as they reached their truck. "I just bumped into a La Crosse guy who says he'll pay us 80 dollars for every gallon of shine we can deliver."

His brother appeared to sober instantly. "Eighty bucks? Sure you heard that right?"

"I asked him. He confirmed it."

"Hell." Justin ran shaking fingers through his already disheveled hair. "We better get into the liquor business. More money in that than workin' at Wolverine." He grasped David by the arm, turned him around, and planted a hand between David's shoulder blades to shove him forward. "Go talk to the man. Get him to sign on the dotted line."

So, David did, and that night a business was born. Over the next summer, the brothers refined their craft, producing moonshine that they sold to Oldendorf for the agreed-upon 80 dollars a gallon. Although he had no actual figures to back it up, David figured in his head that they could produce a gallon of shine for about eight dollars, so they were clearing 72 bucks a gallon. They began by meeting the bar owner's initial request of 15 gallons of shine each week, clearing a little over a thousand dollars, which gave the brothers plenty of walking-around money.

It wasn't enough to satisfy them for long. The lure of a good thing had the brothers talking about the potential of growing the business. Oldendorf wasn't helping, constantly telling his young vendors that he could sell ten times as much liquor as they were sending him.

Visions of clearing almost 11,000 dollars a week stoked the brothers' dreams.

"Do you realize," Justin said to David one night as he fed wood to the fire beneath the still, "that's more than a half million a year?"

David nodded. "Yeah, I run the numbers too, all the time. But do you think it would be worth the risk for us to up the total 10 times?"

Justin frowned. No doubt his head was full of ideas about how to spend his share of more than a half million a year. He shoved more wood into the fire and stirred it with the poker. "I don't know. But David, if we were makin' that kind of money, we could quit our day jobs. We're killing ourselves now, working five nights a week and all day Saturday and Sunday at the still. And I wouldn't mind going on a date once in a while. No chance of that now."

David studied his brother in the glow of the fire. He and Justin were often told they looked a lot alike, except David's hair was long and dark, and Justin wore his reddish-tinged hair short. At 23, David was three inches over six feet. Justin was a couple of inches shorter, but while David did pretty well with the opposite sex, Justin had to fend them off. His face looked as if it had been chiseled from limestone. A motorcycle accident at 17 had left him with a long scar down his right cheek. Rather than detract from his looks, the scar only seemed to make him more attractive to women. He'd always spent a lot of time in their company, and the forced hiatus had to be killing him.

"That's a fact." David tossed an empty paper coffee cup into the flames. "And we aren't getting any younger. Yeah, I've been thinking about dropping out of Wolverine, too. The company's on its last legs. The number of employees is down to about an eighth of what it was when we started twelve years ago. Won't be long before the whole place shuts down."

"You're makin' my point, David. Why not do liquor, make some real money, and get out before we get caught?"

Since then, they'd supplied the bar owner with a small amount of the fiery stuff every month and hadn't heard any complaints. So what was he doing out here now?

"I told you when I met you it was great stuff." The man swatted at the ever-present mosquitoes as Justin walked up and joined the two men. "In fact, I could get rid of a bunch more of it at my bar, if you were interested. I just wanted to check out the operation for myself, first. Confirm that you were really making it yourselves. Problem was, I've had the darndest time finding it. I got to that little burg of Dodge and thought I had lost you 'til I crossed the river and saw your lights off to the right. You guys are pretty good at covering your tracks. Tonight's the first time I've actually been able to track you here."

"Well, you scared the hell out of us. I damn near shot you, you idiot. Why follow us? Why not just ask us if we're able to make more?"

"Yeah." Justin tapped the barrel of the rifle. "David coulda killed ya."

"I damn near did." David lowered his weapon. "You're one lucky guy, Byrle. And I don't appreciate you not trusting us." He scowled.

The three men stood there staring at each other. Byrle, shifting from foot to foot, finally broke the silence. "Well, I'm here. That should tell ya I'm pretty damn serious. How about showin' me around?"

David threw a look at Justin, who shrugged. The two of them had never shown anyone their still. Could they trust Byrle? It really did seem as though the man was serious about giving them more business, but it could be a way to land them both behind bars. Still, it could finally allow him and his brother to get out of their crappy assembly-line jobs at Wolverine Machine in Winona. Although that would mean they'd have to pay for the metal they needed for parts for the still, and the time to make them, instead of sneaking both from the factory. Exhaling loudly, David waved to his brother to walk back the way they had come.

When they reached the still, David moved closer to the various containers that made up the fermenting and distilling operation. Pointing from one part to another, he said, "It's a matter of science, Byrle."

He nudged a tank with his boot. "Propane gas is used to fuel the stove, here. As pressure builds in the still, alcohol begins to evaporate, turning to steam. We force the steam through this pipe." David pointed to a copper pipe coming out of the top of the still. The arm led to what appeared to be a modified beer keg.

Oldendorf walked to the device, looked it up and down, then touched the pipe as he bent down to inspect the keg. "Ah!" He yanked back his hand and shook it.

"Shoot, you got burned pretty good." David reached into a nearby metal chest. "Here's some ointment. Slap some of this on."

Oldendorf nodded as he backed away from the apparatus and took the ointment from David. "You get that from my place?" He pointed at the keg.

So that was part of it. Oldendorf wanted to confirm that they weren't stealing from him. "No sir, we bought that from the Schott distributorship in Winona."

Oldendorf applied ointment to his hand and tossed the tube back to David. "You guys have any idea how good your liquor really is? Let me tell you. Ever since I began sellin' the stuff, my bar has been the most popular place in La Crosse. Do you know what a change that is? From a sleepy little watering hole on the north side to having the parking lot filled every night? I could sell three times as much hooch as you get me.

"And that's not all. Lately, I've got bar owners coming in and begging me to get them some of the stuff. You have a potential gold mine in this little still,"—Byrle nudged the keg with the toe of his boot—"and you don't seem to know it. If we join forces, we could make a bundle."

David rubbed his forehead with the side of his hand. *Join forces?* Hadn't they already done that? What more did the man want from them?

"Listen, you guys, I think I could get 20 bar owners to buy from you. Think about it. At 10 gallons a week—minimum— that's 200 more gallons. And I think I can get at least 90 dollars a gallon for it. Cut me in for ten, and we'll all be able to retire in a few years."

Wow. Two hundred gallons more a week. And at 90 dollars a pop. Wow. His legs a little weak, David stumbled away from the hot barrels and sank onto a worn lawn chair. Justin and Byrle came out behind him. Byrle took the other lawn chair, and Justin sank down on an overturned bucket. The three men sat, the sounds of the swamp closing in around them as if to emphasize their silence. The soprano sounds of the mosquitoes harmonized with the bass emissions from the bullfrogs.

After a few minutes, David took a deep breath. "We're gonna have lots of expenses if we ramp up this business, you know. This still isn't going to produce 185 gallons more a week, so we'll need another. How about we pay you five dollars a gallon to start? When we reach 200, the pay per gallon goes to 10."

Oldendorf rubbed his chin. "Tell you what, give me a day to consider your proposal. That'll also give me time to contact a few bar owners to check my estimates. You'll be bringin' in 15 gallons tomorrow, right? I'll give you my answer then. Fair enough?"

"Fair."

David's mind was already exploding with thoughts of all that would be necessary to ramp up production. Could he and Justin handle that much more business? Was it worth the increased chance they'd get caught and tossed into jail? David did the calculations quickly in his head and his mouth went dry.

Eighteen thou a week. Minus Byrle's cut, of course. Still...

He bit his lower lip. If they were caught in possession of the stuff, they'd spend a few months in prison and have to pay a fine of a couple thousand dollars - which would be pocket change to them at that point. He managed a grim smile. Of course, if they got stopped while transporting it, the punishment would be much steeper. More like one to six years in the clink. His smile faded.

David thought about it for about three more seconds before shoving back his shoulders. Well then, they'd just have to make damn sure they didn't get caught, wouldn't they?

2

WHEN MORNING BREAK ROLLED AROUND THE NEXT DAY, David and Justin met at a picnic table in the Wolverine yard. Justin's face was red and sweat ran down his face.

"I'm killin' myself lugging steel. Let's get the hell out of here."

"Oldendorf says he can sell everything we send him, but before we quit our jobs, I'd like to have an exact number. In writing. How about we hear what he has to say tonight?"

His brother rubbed his palms of his thighs, leaving damp streaks on his work pants. "I'm nervous. What if he backs out?"

Then we're screwed, because he knows where the still is.

"He won't back out. He's got as much to gain from all of this as we do," he said instead. David picked up his gloves and headed back to his welding station. The Wolverine work was routine and boring, the liquor business risky and exciting. *Why not? Why the hell not?*

He picked up a piece of metal and began to weld it to

another panel, anxious for the day to end. The rest of his shift passed with agonizing slowness, as thoughts of expanding the liquor business dominated his thoughts.

As they walked out of the plant at the end of the day, David glanced back over his shoulder just in time to see Justin step into a small hole and stumble. He grabbed his brother's arm. "Whoa, easy there, boy. Can't have you falling and hurting yourself if we want to become millionaires."

As they got into the truck, David studied his brother in the fading daylight. "Justin, do you realize how much risk we'll be taking if we expand the booze business?"

"How much?"

"About a hundred times more than now. Hell, the minute we hire people to help us—and we'll have to—the risk rises exponentially." David drummed the steering wheel with one hand as he shoved the key into the ignition with the other. "We'll really have our asses on the line. For one thing, we won't be able to keep getting by with just one still. We'll need another. We've got this one operating at capacity as it is. So we'll need another place. And if we have two stills, you'll have to supervise one and me the other. That means we each need someone to help us. That's two more mouths—at least—that can blab about what we're doing."

"Well, we just gotta hire good people. Shouldn't be too hard."

"Hell yes, it's gonna be hard." David scowled. "How many good people do we work with?"

Justin looked out the window as the truck moved along the Mississippi to the central part of Winona. "Yeah, I guess you're right. It won't be easy."

"Damn right it won't. To keep 'em quiet, we'll need to give 'em a piece of the action. That cuts into profits."

"Don't you wanna grow?"

"Yes, I wanna grow. And yes, I wanna get the hell out of

Wolverine. But I don't have a real good idea right now about the best way to do it."

"Let's start with what you suggested. We can ask him to commit to a deal for a certain amount of booze, right? Then we'll know what kinds of numbers we're talking about." Justin patted the dashboard. "Let's get goin'. I'm hungry for one of his hamburgers, anyway."

David shrugged as he turned the pickup toward La Crosse. Justin was right. They'd head to the Handy Corner and try to work out a deal with Byrle that would allow them to go into the moonshine business full-time. While they were at it, they'd have one of the best burgers in the area.

3

DAVID DROVE ACROSS THE MISSISSIPPI NORTH OF LA CRESCENT and headed into North La Crosse and the Handy Corner. When they entered, some kid was tending bar. Byrle was nowhere to be seen.

"Where's the boss?" asked David, after ordering a couple of taps. One for him and one for Justin.

"He's due in a few minutes." The kid aggressively polished glasses with a less-than-clean, formerly white towel. "He had some errands to run and he left me in charge for a few minutes."

Justin smacked a hand on the bar. "Is the kitchen open?"

"Yep." The kid nodded and kept wiping.

"Can I get a cheeseburger and fries?'

"And I'll have a California burger." David leaned a hip against the bar.

With an exaggerated sigh, the kid set the glass down hard on the shelf, tossed the towel onto the bar, and strode toward the back.

David's eyebrow rose. "Guess that saves us a tip."

Justin snickered. "I'll grab us that table in the corner."

David followed him across the room and they settled onto wooden chairs across from each other. The white-and-red-checked plastic tablecloth looked a little worse for wear, but relatively clean.

"Well, look who's here." A familiar voice boomed as the back door opened to admit Oldendorf, who was carrying a box that appeared to be full of buns and condiments. "Had some shopping to do," he explained. He set the big box on the kitchen counter just off the bar and walked over to their table. "Ready to talk, are you?"

David leaned back in his char. "Thought we should have a chat. Firm up some things."

Oldendorf pursed his lips as he pulled out another chair at the table and lowered his considerable bulk onto it. "All right. Let's do it."

The kid who'd been working the bar carried over the plates with burgers and fries and dropped them in front of David and Justin with a thunk. Without a word, he turned on his heel and strode back to the bar.

Oldendorf grimaced. "Sorry about that. My nephew. Absolutely useless, but I promised my sister I'd put him to work."

David shrugged. "It's fine." He popped a fry into his mouth and chewed and swallowed. "Justin and I are workin' harder than we want. We make good money off the liquor we sell you, but it's not enough to allow us to quit our day jobs. If what you told us last night is true, we might be able to do that - go into the business full-time. But we need hard numbers. You talk to your friends to see if they want in?"

"Yep. Fact is, my buddies in the bar business know I have somethin' goin' on. They've had some of your hooch. They love it. They want to buy some."

"How many of 'em are there?" Justin spoke through a mouth full of burger, leaning over his plate.

"Five for sure, maybe as many as nine."

David almost choked on the sip of beer he'd just taken. He returned his glass to the table and cleared his throat. "They'll all want 15 or 20 a week?"

Oldendorf grabbed a napkin and scribbled on it with a pen from his pocket. "If more bars are handlin' the stuff, it'll thin out the traffic some, I suppose. But for openers, they pretty much all committed to 10."

"Ten." David rolled the numbers through his head. "That'd be a total of 105 a week, assumin' nine of 'em and you'd stay at 15. In round numbers, that'd make about 8,500 a week in sales. Byrle that's nowhere near the 200 you mentioned last night."

Oldendorf tapped the pen against his chin. "If I'm gonna take care of sales and distribution - be the front man, so ta speak - I'm gonna need at least 10 a gallon for my time. If you want 200 gallons, that'll take some effort."

"At 90 a gallon?"

Oldendorf stopped tapping and scribbled some more on the napkin. "We might be able to get 90 or 95 bucks a gallon."

David held out his hand. Byrle handed him the napkin and pen. After figuring out their costs, gross sales, and what they'd owe, he said, "That's 18,000 a week at 90 and 19,000 at 95. I like 95 better. Is that doable?"

"If I get 10 for me."

"We can go as high as 7.50 a gallon." David was in full selling mode now, leaning halfway across the table toward Oldendorf. "Everything over 200 gallons, we'll pay 10."

Oldendorf shook his head. "Too little for the work involved. I gotta bar to run too, ya know."

David paused, then shoved back his chair. "Thanks

for your time. We'll find ourselves someone else to be the middleman. Let's go, Justin."

A look of panic crossed the big man's face as he lifted both hands in the air. "Hold on now, hold on. Let's not be too hasty. We're just in the middle of negotiations."

David lowered himself slowly back down to the chair. "Well, we're ready to wrap them up. There are plenty of other people who'd be willing to work with us for five a gallon." He had no idea who, but Byrle didn't need to know that.

The bar owner's jaw tightened. "Tell ya what. Make it 10 at 150 and we got a deal."

David glanced at his brother. The trace of a smile crossed Justin's face, and David turned back to Oldendorf. "Deal."

The two men shook on it. Then Justin shook Byrle's hand, too.

David picked up his burger. Even at that rate, he and Justin should clear about 8,400 a week, or roughly 215,000 dollars each in a year. Of course, some of that would be eaten up by wages for two other workers, say as much as 100,000 a year, but that'd still give him and his brother more than 150,000 each.

David swallowed a bite, wiped his mouth, took a gulp of his beer, and looked at Oldendorf, who'd been watching him silently.

"Any chance we can get more than 95?"

"Geez, more'n 95. Man..."

"At 95, by the time we hire help and buy supplies, there's not as much left as I'd like."

The bar owner studied him, frowning. "We might get as much as 105. But not until the owners see how well it sells. I think they could price it with 105 in mind, which would let us move up a little easier. How about 95 for the first two months, and then we'll see about raising it?"

"I think that's fair," David said.

"You know," Oldendorf picked up a fork and twirled it between his fingers, "if we could get some variety into the stuff, we could sell a lot more. If you added fruit, say, produced a raspberry or peach-flavored product, that might go over real well. Bring in the female market. Could increase the customer base by as much as 70 percent."

David reached for the pen. The napkin was nearly full, but he turned it over and found a small open space in one corner. After a moment, he held the napkin in Justin's direction. "That would mean our take'd be around a mil, give or take a few dollars."

Justin's mouth dropped open, and a French fry fell onto his plate.

"I like those numbers better, Byrle. How about checkin' with your guys. See how many you can get to commit at 105. Tell 'em we'll add some flavored stuff—assumin' we can figure out how to make it. But make sure you tell each one to keep their mouths shut. The wrong people hear about that still we're running and it's all over. We'll check back with you next week."

Byrle nodded.

David pushed back his chair. He'd been too excited to eat all of his dinner, but his brother's plate was empty. Justin followed him out to the parking lot.

In the truck and driving toward downtown La Crosse, neither of them spoke for a few minutes, until Justin shifted in his seat. "Good deal?"

"I think so, little brother... assuming we can quickly expand our operation and figure out how to make fruity-flavored liquor to please the women. Then, if Byrle can come through, we'll be on the gravy train."

"That sounds good."

"Yeah. But ya gotta understand there's a helluva lot of risk. If we get caught, it's off to prison for a long, long stay."

"Well, we ain't got caught yet, have we?"

"No, but now there will be more than ten times as many people who can squeal."

Justin appeared to ponder that. "Where we gonna put a new still?"

"I've got half an idea, but I'm not ready to say yet. It needs to be a very safe place, because we are going to need one big still, that's for sure."

"Will we make it at Wolverine?"

"I hope so. But that means we'd have to do it while working for at least a couple more months. I'd like to quit now but we don't have the money or the tools to get the job done if we don't do it there."

Justin lifted his shoulders. "We can handle a few more weeks there, knowing we'll be able to quit soon and start working for ourselves. Won't that be great?"

"Sure will. But we have to find a place for a new still and see how big we can make it." *And then we have to pray that no one finds it, or all of this comes crashing down on our heads.*

4

"**YOU AREN'T GONNA BELIEVE IT.**" THOSE WERE THE FIRST words out of Oldendorf's mouth when the brothers walked into the Handy Corner the following Friday night.

David forced himself to walk calmly over to their table in the corner, sit down, and nod at the chair beside him for his brother to join him. Appearing too eager would give the bar owner the upper hand, and that was the last thing David wanted. He picked up the menu and pretended to peruse it.

Oldendorf had followed them to the table and stood behind a chair. David nodded at him. Byrle sat down. He was grinning like a hound dog with a meaty bone. "What is it?"

"The first 10 folks I talked to after speaking with you committed to 10 gallons a week at a hundred and five bucks a gallon. And my phone has been ringing off the hook since word got around to others."

David blinked. "That's pretty good. How soon will they be ready to go?"

"Pretty good? What the hell do you mean? That's pretty damn great and you know it." Byrle's voice rose as he talked.

"Sssh." David looked around, trying to see how many people might be listening. Satisfied that they were pretty much alone, he asked again, "When will they be ready?"

"Now."

David closed the menu and set it on the table. "Well, that isn't gonna happen. We gotta build another still, hire a coupla people, find more suppliers for sugar and corn... There's a lotta work to do. How does three months from now sound?"

"Disappointing," was Oldendorf's flat response. "But they'll wait. There ain't no alternatives, ya know?"

"Well," David lifted a hand, palm up, and looked at Justin. "Seems like we gotta bundle of work to do."

Justin shrugged. "Good stuff, though."

David looked at Oldendorf. "How many others do you think there are?"

"Hmmm, that's a tough one. I still have four or five to talk to that I'm pretty sure about. And when I told one of the men that you were thinking of fruity flavors, that's when I heard from two women and signed 'em up. There are several more women I haven't talked to."

"Okay then, me and Justin have gotta see what we find for a second still site. And based on what you're saying, Byrle, we might have to think about a third, even."

"Let me know what you decide. In the meantime, you got today's delivery?"

David and Justin hauled in the week's supply of liquor and stored it in the room set aside for it. When it was done, David shook Byrle's hand. "We'll keep in touch."

"Sounds good."

The trip home was alive with discussion. The brothers debated stealing materials for another still from Wolverine.

Finally, David shook his head. "I think it's too risky. No sense getting caught for some small infraction and missing out on the big payback. Maybe we can snatch the small stuff, but we'll buy the copper sheeting and piping we need."

"Good idea."

David stared through the front window at the road. "Ya think Hummer down at Boomer's could get us what we need for copper?"

"Hell yeah. I bet he'd get us whatever we need."

They hatched a story to tell the plumber. Justin would ask his friend about two 4 by 8 foot sheets of copper, telling him the boys wanted to build a backsplash for a new fireplace they were installing in their basement.

"He'll bite." Justin crossed his arms over his chest.

David shot him a sideways glance. Confidence was good, but cocky crossed a line that could cause them trouble. And trouble was the last thing they needed at the moment.

5

TWO DAYS LATER, AFTER WORK AND BEFORE LEAVING FOR THE still in Buffalo County, Justin was sitting on the front steps of the house he and David had inherited from their parents when Emily Whetstone came home from work at Wolverine. Five women lived in the house next door, all of them young and pretty, but Emily, to Justin, was special. At 5 foot 5, she had icy blue eyes, strawberry blonde hair, a stunning figure, and the greatest smile Justin had seen. He watched as she drove up, parked her car in front of the brothers' house, and jumped out.

"Hi, Justin," she called after digging her coat out of the back seat. "Nice day, huh?" She walked around the car to the sidewalk and stopped to visit.

"Sure is. Busy day at work?"

"Not too bad. It's pretty slow. You must see that, too. Not much going on. Worries me, to be honest."

"Me, too. Do you think the plant is gonna shut down?"

"It could, but I'm also a student at Winona State. I'm a junior and right now I am working on marketing. So, if

Wolverine goes down, I have that to fall back on. But I love the work. To be honest, I'd like to get a job there."

"Really?" Justin stayed where he was, sitting on the porch steps, afraid to move in case she decided to head into her house. "I bet you'd do a bang up job," he told her.

"Nice of you to say that, but it's a tough assignment. I'm learning a lot, that's for sure."

"Say, Emily." Justin stood and wandered down the walkway to be nearer to his neighbor. "I was wonderin' if you'd ever have time to go out to eat. I see you going back and forth, and you always seem so busy. I was thinkin' maybe a nice night out would be good?"

"Why, Justin, I'm flattered. I'd love a dinner out, but do you have time? You guys are always gone, and I assumed you were either attached or too busy at work."

"Yeah, I guess we're both busy, but ... Wait." His head jerked up. "You'd like to go? Great! How about Saturday?"

"Yeah. That would be terrific."

Justin leaned a hip against the hood of her car. "Around six o'clock, then? Be thinkin' about where you'd like to go. I'll check with you on Thursday. That way I can make a reservation."

"I really don't need to think very hard." She had the cutest dimpled smile. It took everything Justin had not to reach out and pull her to him. "I love Sullivan's. I hear the places in La Crosse are great, too, but I haven't been to any of 'em. Surprise me. I'll be ready at 6:30, okay?"

"Perfect."

As Emily turned to leave, she gave him another of those killer smiles. Heat flooded Justin's cheeks. He couldn't believe he had actually asked her out. And as unbelievable as that was, the fact that she said yes was even more astounding.

He wasn't sure if he walked into the house or just floated. When he told his brother about his date, he expected a tongue-lashing. His brother was a quiet guy and rarely had time for friendships, especially with women. And right now, with everything going on with their new business, it likely wasn't the best time to bring someone new into their lives. To his surprise, David clapped him on the shoulder and grinned. "Good for you, Justin. That's great. She have a friend who's free? We could double."

Justin blinked. "Gosh, David, I don't know. All those girls are really good lookin'. You want me to ask her?"

"Only if an opportunity comes up. Right now, we'd better get somethin' to eat. We've got lots of work to do tonight."

A couple of days later, Justin was sitting on the steps again when Emily arrived home. She waved when she saw him, and he strode down the walk and stopped in front of her. "Say, Emily, when I told my brother we were going out to dinner, he suggested I ask if one of your roomies would like to go out; he said we could double."

"He's David, right? Tall? Dark hair? Good looking, too?"

Too? Did that mean she thought Justin was good looking? Warmth crept up his neck. "Yup, that's him. He's my brother, and smart as a whip."

"Justin, I just love it when you blush." She smiled. He could think of no good response, but she saved him. "I've got three roommates who drool over David whenever they see him. But I think you're cuter. What kind of girl does he like?"

"Gosh, you're all pretty," he stammered. "Umm, he likes tall girls—really tall girls."

"One of my roommates is 6-foot-1 and plays basketball. She has dark red hair, auburn really, and she's extremely pretty. Also the only one who is actually unattached, besides me."

"David was a great basketball player at Winona High. He could have gone to college on a scholarship, but both of us wanted to get to work as quickly as we could."

SAVE
the
DATE

for the wedding of

Elizabeth Schwanke &
Zachary Miner

May 23, 2026
Stewartville, MN

Formal Invitation To Follow

zola.com/wedding/minerschwankewedding

"Would he like Madison—the tall one—do you think? Her last name's Danielson."

Justin knew the roommate she was talking about. "She's gorgeous—almost as pretty as you. Yeah, I think he'd like that."

"You realize that I'm gonna have friends who are jealous when I ask her."

"Well, if it's too—"

Emily laughed. "It's fine. They all have men in their lives. They just like looking. I'll ask her."

"That'd be great."

"Gimme your cell number. I'll call you."

Justin rhymed off the number, and she added him to her contacts. "Is Sullivan's still okay?"

"Great." She turned and left. Sorry to see her go, Justin went into the house. Twenty minutes later, she called him to say that Madison was thrilled and, as predicted, her other roommates were jealous.

"Maybe next time," he said to her.

"I'm not telling them that." Her thrilling laugh drifted through the phone line. "I'm not gonna create any false expectations."

Justin grinned. "Fine. I wouldn't want you to get into trouble. See you Saturday?"

When he told David about his date, his brother was happier than Justin had seen him in a long time.

"We better get at it, then," said David. "We need to get a big batch going if we are going to be off on Saturday."

Justin didn't mind the extra work at all. Not if the reward at the end was a night out with a couple of very beautiful women.

6

MA'S CAFÉ WAS BUSY, AS USUAL. LA CROSSE CHIEF OF Detectives Al Rouse settled onto a seat across the table from County Chief Deputy Charlie Berzinski. Al had a matter of some urgency he wanted to discuss with his buddy Charlie, and from the way his friend bounced in his seat, Charlie obviously had something he wanted to talk to him about as well.

Al repressed a grin. "So, how's life these days?"

"Al, it's a bitch. And that's bitch with a capital B."

"That bad, huh? Fact is, mine sucks, too."

Charlie set down his menu. "Since you're payin', why don't you vent first?"

Al opened his mouth, but before he could speak, Ma Olson, proprietor of the café, called to them from the counter. "You guys know what you want?"

"The usual for me," replied Al, glancing at Charlie.

Charlie hesitated just long enough for Ma to break in. "Okay, okay, let me get a pad and pencil. When Charlie gets a hitch in his get-along, I know it's gonna be a menu buster."

The big deputy, 6-foot-five and 300 pounds, didn't disappoint. "Four eggs over easy. Four strips of bacon, two slices of ham, four slices of toast, an order of hash browns... Oh, and a waffle on the side."

Ma looked up from her notebook. "Charlie, how many sides is that? Four eggs take up one plate. Then we got the meat, the toast, and the waffle." Charlie started to protest, but she held up her hand. "Stop. I know you're just a growin' boy. I heard it before."

"Shucks, Ma, you're no fun at all. Besides, that's the truth. I am just a growin' boy."

"Yeah, just like my late husband was a boy when he died at 65, four years ago."

"Aww, Ma, you know I like to eat. And you know I'm partial to your cookin', right? So, ease up and let Al spend his money buyin' me a big breakfast. How about it?"

Wheedling as he was, Charlie had everyone in the restaurant laughing. Even Ma had to hide her face behind the notebook to cover her chuckle.

"You got me, Charlie. When you tell me that you like my cooking, you hit me in the sweet spot. You'll get your big breakfast."

With a wide grin splashed across his face, Charlie cocked his head and looked at Al. "Ain't nothin' you can tell me that'll break this mood. I believe my day is about to turn around, Al. I'm walking out of here with a full belly."

"Now that we have established that you'll have a fully belly and I'll have an empty wallet by the time we're done here, maybe you'd be good enough to hear about my problem. Or is that asking too much?"

"Al, today you get what you want. Fire away."

Al tucked his menu into the metal holder. "Someone's pushing illegal liquor in La Crosse, and the chief is on my butt to find 'em, and find 'em fast."

"Illegal booze?"

"Yep. Someone's bringing booze here that they've either made or bought from someone who's making it."

"So, like moonshine?"

"Yeah, like moonshine."

"Man, have we gone back in time? It's startin' to feel like the Wild West around here. You ain't gonna believe this, but I'm chasing rustlers who are stealing cattle from farmers south of here. Not havin' much luck with it, either."

"Moonshine and rustling. Amazing. It like we stepped back into the 1800s."

An hour later, as Al had predicted, Charlie's belly was full and Al's wallet considerably lighter. They hadn't solved their problems but, as always, talking things out with his buddy had gotten the wheels turning for Al. He left the restaurant newly motivated to track down whoever it was that was producing and selling moonshine in his territory. No way La Crosse County was going to become the new Wild West.

Not on his watch.

David pulled the truck into the shed in the marsh near Dodge and he and Justin began to work, the weather thankfully cooperating. The brothers moved through their tasks quickly, starting a new batch of moonshine and then carefully bottling the supply to deliver.

While they worked as if they had four hands and one body, David said, "Justin, we can't get so mesmerized by our dates that we forget there's a lot to do to get ready for expansion."

"Geez, we've been so busy I haven't had time to think about that."

"Well, you'd better start thinking. The clock is ticking, and I'm worried." David finished filling a quart jar and handed it to Justin to cap. "I'm having a hard time coming up with names of people I'd either trust to help or want around. "You have any ideas?"

Justin removed his cap and swabbed sweat from his forehead. "No good ones." He restored the cap to his head and reached for the next quart. "None of our friends are that trustworthy, and we need people we can trust, like you said. What're we gonna do?"

"Well, we need to get the new still built first. We can give it some thought while we're doing that." David handed off the last jar of moonshine and peeled off his gloves. "Better head home if we want to pick up the girls on time."

They made their way across the property to their truck. They'd already decided they would take their new SUV that night; an Acadia Denali. It was the fourth Acadia they had owned, and this one was the best, especially as it had come equipped with everything. A rich black cherry metallic, it was a handsome vehicle and, when freshly washed, sparkled in the sun. It also fit nicely in the two-vehicle garage with their older GMC Sierra, which they used for work.

The Denali was the only thing the brothers had splurged on. They had inherited their house free of debt when their dad had died. They worked hard, saving much of the money they made at Wolverine. And the sale of moonshine had fattened their savings account.

Once home, they continued to talk about where to place the still. "Tell you what," said David as he paged through an issue of Motor Trend, "Maybe tomorrow, before we go to Wisconsin, we can check on some sites I've been considering."

"Sure." Justin grabbed a towel from the closet and headed to the shower.

A few minutes before six, David backed the SUV from the garage. After parking it in front of the house, the brothers walked to the neighboring house and Justin rang the bell.

Emily opened the door, smiling. Behind her stood an

auburn-haired beauty who towered over her companion. Both women wore spring dresses, their hair was done, and their makeup had been applied perfectly. The scent of some kind of floral perfume drifted on the air, and Justin breathed deep.

Emily grasped her roommate's arm and tugged her to her side. "Madison, this is Justin Freeman and his brother, David. David and Justin, Madison Danielson."

"Good to meet you." Justin nodded at Madison. When his brother didn't speak, Justin elbowed him in the ribs.

"Uh, nice to meet you."

Justin almost laughed. His brother was usually the articulate one. Clearly he was overwhelmed by his date for the evening. "All set?" Justin held out his hand and Emily took it. The two of them started down the pathway. David and Madison followed.

Justin and Emily climbed into the back seat. David held the passenger door open until Madison had settled on the front seat. He closed it, rounded the front of the truck, and slid behind the wheel.

Madison turned slightly to face him. "Emily tells me that you were quite a basketball player in high school, David. You sure look like an athlete."

"Th... thanks," stammered David. "I did play, but I wasn't all that good."

"That's a lie," shot Justin. "David still holds the all-time scoring record at the high school. He started as a sophomore and played three years. He was the leading scorer each year, and his senior year the Winhawks went to state. Shoulda won it. Got beat by one point in the championship. If David hadn't fouled out, it woulda been easy."

The ride to Sullivan's along the Mississippi in Wisconsin, south of Winona, was fun. The girls loved the Acadia and

David seemed to relax as they drove, proudly showing off the vehicle's features to Madison.

In the back seat, Justin and Emily talked without stopping. "You know, Justin," she reached for his hand and squeezed it gently, "I have to tell you that you and your brother have caused a lot of trouble at our house."

"How so?"

"Do you have any idea how catty five women can be when they argue? Let me tell you, it's not a pretty sight."

"You live together and you argue?"

"Yes, and it's all your fault. Well, yours and David's."

David glanced into the back seat. "What do you mean, it's our fault?"

Emily chuckled. "Do you want to tell them Madison?"

"You got yourself into this, Emily. I think you'll have to get yourself out." Her roommate laughed.

"Well, whenever we see you guys either outside or through the window, the fighting starts about how handsome you are and which lucky woman will win your hearts. Isn't that true, Madison?"

"It is," said Madison. "But, of course, I'm never involved."

Emily reached over the seat and lightly tugged a lock of her friend's hair. "You never involved? Don't you guys believe it. She's always drooling over you, David."

Madison's face turned red. "Well," she sputtered, "maybe I participate once in a while."

"Oh please. Madison, you are the ringleader."

"Emily, quit exaggerating. I participate, yes, but the fight is always over David because you picked Justin for yourself. And after he asked you out the other day, you became impossible."

Emily smiled contentedly, squeezed Justin's hand, and remained silent.

She'd picked him out a long time ago? Justin's heart rate

picked up as he leaned toward Emily and lowered his voice. "I've wanted to ask you out for a while now."

"What took you so long?"

"Wish I'd known what you were thinkin'. If I had, I'd a done what I was thinking."

For a few miles, conversation quieted. As they turned off Highway 35-54 to head for Sullivan's, Madison tucked a long strand of hair behind one ear. "Where are your folks? I mean, you guys are pretty young to seem so well fixed. House, new car, truck—heck, you've got it all."

"Not quite." David rested his arm on the back of the seat. "We were raised in the house we live in. Mom died when I was eight and Justin was seven. Dad never really got over losing her. He was wonderful. Then he got lung cancer three years after mom died.

"At first, he did well. He fought it for six years, even kept working at Wolverine all that time. When I was a junior, the cancer got really aggressive. He worked for a while, but after a time he couldn't handle it, so he went on disability. By that time, both me and Justin were working at Wolverine after school and on weekends. At first it was nice to have the extra money, then it was necessary. The disability helped, but our incomes were essential. Dad died when I was a senior, so when I graduated I started to work full-time. Justin followed sort of naturally, I guess. Now we're veterans, but the business isn't doing well and we soon might be out of work."

Madison tilted her head. "I'm so sorry. I had no idea. I didn't mean to pry. Please forgive me."

"Nothing to forgive." He pulled his arm from the seat and returned both hands to the wheel. "It is what it is. Justin and I are getting by just fine. Sure, we'd love to have Mom and Dad back, but that isn't going to happen, so we just deal with it. And look at us tonight - on our way to dinner with two beautiful women."

Smiling at him, Madison said, "We were both excited by your invitation. But David, next time maybe you could ask in person?"

Even in the dim light of the cab, Justin could see the tips of his brother's ears turn pink. "Do you have any idea how hard it is to ask out a beautiful girl?"

Madison laughed. "I can't say that I do, but I'm just giving you a hard time. It's not a big deal, but please don't be afraid to call, okay?"

He nodded and Justin breathed a sigh of relief. So far the evening was going even better than expected. The food at Sullivan's was terrific. The view from their table by the window as night fell over the valley was breathtaking - the yellows turning to orange, then purple, before darkness settled in. The whistles from the tugboats pushing barges on the Mississippi added to the charm.

After exiting the restaurant, they drove through Perrot State Park on their way home, narrowly avoiding two young deer that hurried across the road in front of them.

"Bet their mama wasn't happy about that move," said David, chuckling. "Good thing the speed limit here is 20. I don't think I was even going that fast."

"You weren't," said Madison. "I'm not anxious for the night to end, either, so you can go as slow as you want."

The mood in the vehicle was light and joyous. When they crossed the bridge on their way back into Winona, Justin reached for Emily's hand. "Would you guys like to come over for a drink?"

She grinned and Madison shrugged. "The season is over, so I guess I can have a drink."

Ten minutes later, David pulled the truck into their driveway and the four of them piled out. "Wow, this is nice," exclaimed Emily when they walked into the house. "You guys must do really well, huh?"

"We do okay," agreed Justin. "And there's just two of us, so we keep things as neat as we can."

The four of them strolled into the kitchen. David pulled open the fridge door. "So what can I get you? We have beer and booze."

Madison shook her head. "We're not beer drinkers. What kind of liquor?"

"Our kind." David smiled as he produced a gallon of clear liquid from the refrigerator. "We make it."

"You make it? Can I smell?"

He handed her the bottle and she held it to her nose. "That's strong, isn't it?" She passed it to Emily, who sniffed it and wrinkled her nose.

"It's got a little kick," David admitted as he took the bottle and carried it over to the counter.

"Well, we have to try it, don't we, since you made it. Shall we both have a mild drink, Em?"

Emily nodded. "I'll have cola in mine, if you have it."

"We do." Justin reached into the fridge and grabbed two bottles.

"That'll do. Just a little of the liquor and lots of cola and ice."

David mixed two drinks and handed one to each of the girls before pouring a small glass of straight whiskey for himself and Justin. The two couples headed back into the living room. Emily and Justin settled on the sofa and Madison and David took the armchairs opposite them.

Emily gingerly tipped her glass to her lips, took a sip and smiled. "This is good. It's smooth, but it's potent. And you make it yourselves?"

"Yep." David strode to the record player. In minutes, the voice of Adele filled the room, lending a gentle touch to a soft night.

"This is wonderful." Madison held up her glass. "It may

be the smoothest liquor I've ever had. Where and how do you guys make this?"

"We have a small operation on some land we own in Wisconsin." Justin's chest puffed out a little. Maybe his brother didn't want to brag, but he wasn't shy. "We pride ourselves on the quality. This is some of the best we've made, and we keep a few bottles on hand for special nights like this."

"So you bring lots of women here for drinks, do you?" Madison nudged David in the arm with her elbow.

"No, no, you've got it all wrong." Justin slid an arm around Emily's shoulder. "We only bring very special women here. We've had a hard time finding 'special.' So no, we don't bring lots of women here."

"You had to settle for us; is that what you're saying?" Emily stuck out her lower lip, but her blue eyes twinkled. "I bet you tell all the women you bring home how special they are."

"You're the first, scout's honor." He held up three fingers to mimic the Boy Scout oath.

David rescued him. "Justin's right. We rarely have people over. Heck, we never have people over. We're just glad you agreed to come in for a drink."

For the next three hours, the conversation flowed as freely as the moonshine. It was as if the brothers and the two women had known each other for years. At one a.m., after Emily had yawned for the third time, David and Justin walked the two women to their door. David and Madison stepped into the house, but Justin lingered on the porch with Emily.

"I had a good time tonight." He brushed a strand of hair back from her face.

She smiled up at him. "Me too."

Neither of them moved for a moment, until she tapped him on the chest lightly. "Aren't you going to kiss me?"

Justin happily obliged, then stepped back as David came out the front door. A smudge of lipstick at the corner of his mouth suggested he'd had the same satisfying conclusion to his date as Justin.

Madison followed him out and touched him on the arm. "Want to have dinner again tomorrow night?"

Emily giggled. "Tonight, you mean?" She winked at Justin. "Us too?"

His cheeks warmed. "Sure."

"Okay." David clapped Justin on the shoulder. "Tonight it is. Why don't you come over, we'll put something on the grill, listen to music, and have a couple of drinks. Sound good?"

"Perfect," agreed Madison. Emily nodded.

Justin grinned all the way back to their house. It had taken him thirty years, but he'd finally found the perfect woman. "Oh, m'god, I think I found *the one*."

David grinned. "Actually, we might have just found *the two*. And right next door. Who would have thought?"

7

UP AT SUNRISE THE NEXT DAY, JUSTIN FELT GREAT—NO TRACE of a headache, and pleasant memories of the night before flooding his mind. He and David reached the still just as the sun peaked over the bluffs, and by a little before noon, they had bottled 100 more gallons of clear, sweet shine. They would deliver the bottles Monday night, using both their vehicles to transport it to Byrle Oldendorf.

A good day's work done in fewer than six hours, the brothers headed home. Justin slumped against the passenger door, perfectly content with his existence and looking forward to another evening with their next-door neighbors.

He crossed his arms over his chest. "They are perfect, aren't they?"

"They are. Absolutely perfect."

"What're we gonna feed 'em?"

"How about those six lobster tails we ordered from that outfit in Maine?" David glanced over at him. "Good food for a celebration, don't you think?"

"Perfect. Do you know how to fix 'em?"

"They came with instructions. We can just follow those."

"Sounds good." Justin closed his eyes and daydreamed about Emily for a few minutes, before he straightened. "David?"

"Yeah?"

"Do you really like Madison?"

"Much as I can, I guess. I only met her last night. I'm not about to jump off the diving board just yet."

"I really like Emily. Geez, I can't get her outta my mind."

"They're both great girls. I could really get into Madison, for sure. But she's younger; still in college. I'm not ready to commit to anything at the moment."

They drove in silence the rest of the way home, Justin contemplating his brother's words. As usual, his older brother was right. He shouldn't jump into anything with Emily too quickly either, especially with everything else they had going on at the moment. Still, thoughts of her consumed him until David pulled the truck into their driveway and they both climbed out.

After the brothers had showered and shaved, David retrieved the lobster tails from the freezer, set them in the sink, and tended to the grill, filling it with coals and stacking them to be lit. Justin was setting the table when he walked back into the kitchen. "How much shine do we have left?"

Justin held up a jug. "More'n a gallon. Should be lots. It's really good stuff, isn't it? I didn't have a trace of a headache this morning."

"Me neither. You know, I think we could get a lot more money for it than we are."

"Ya think? 105 dollars a gallon is a pretty good price."

"That's 20 dollars a fifth. Good booze sells for more than that. We should be able to get as much as good booze sells for, don't you think?"

"I s'pose, but I don't wanna get greedy. We're doin' all right, aren't we?"

Just as David was about to respond, a knock sounded on the door. In spite of his earlier words to his brother, his heart rate picked up a little. "C'mon in," he called.

Emily and Madison walked into the room and, in spite of himself, he couldn't stifle the whistle that formed on his lips when he saw them. Each was wearing shorts, and although they were not scandalously short, they emphasized two pairs of tanned, shapely legs. Madison wore a gentle yellow top to go with her teal shorts. She was barefoot. Emily had on red shorts, a low-cut white blouse, and a pair of white flip-flops. Justin greeted her with a warm hug.

"Can't you do better than that?" She leaned forward and kissed him deeply.

When she stepped back, David almost laughed. His brother's face had gone completely red. Still, he slid a hand behind Emily's head and pulled her to him, kissing her until David and Madison started to laugh. David nudged her gently with his elbow. "We may have to throw water on them, don't you think, Madison?"

Justin broke off the kiss, his face growing an even deeper crimson. Emily bailed him out by saying, "Well, we haven't seen each other for almost 17 hours. That's a long time without a kiss."

All four laughed, and Justin pointed to the kitchen table. "David's got supper on the grill, and it should be ready soon. Would you like to sit down and have a drink while you're waiting?"

"If you have any of that stuff you served us last night, I want some." Madison clapped her hands. "That was the best booze I've ever had. Are you sure you didn't buy it somewhere?"

"Nope." David shook his head. "It was made with our own

hands, a lot of corn and sugar, the purest water around, and as much love as we can bestow on a batch."

"You oughta be in the liquor-making business," suggested Emily. "I bet we could sell a thousand bottles a week to WSU students."

Justin looked at David and they both laughed.

While his brother mixed drinks for their dates, David lit the grill. After a few minutes, Madison joined him out on the patio. It was a little dangerous to leave Justin and Emily alone in the house, but David was too interested in a little alone time with his own date to do anything about it.

Justin handed Emily her drink and held out his hand. She took it, got up from her seat at the table, and followed him into the living room. He sat on the couch and tugged her down beside him. Just as his arm encircled her shoulders, David yelled from the backyard, "Justin, could you and Emily make the salad, please?"

Damn. I was just getting to where I wanted to be. His big brother had always had spectacularly bad timing.

"C'mon, Justin, we'll have fun with it." Emily grabbed his arm and pulled him from the couch.

Justin groaned.

"Don't be a grouch. We'll have time for that later. Promise." She winked at him and Justin melted.

It was a festive dinner. The lobster, for a first-time effort, turned out perfectly, and the salad Justin and Emily had tossed was good, too. All four ate until filled, then David pushed his chair away from the table and mixed more drinks while Justin and the women cleaned up the kitchen. The four moved to the front porch after Justin found some easy-listening music to stream.

All four sipped drinks and talked about themselves. By that time, the moonshine had begun to affect its drinkers to the point that Emily had grown giggly, Madison was slurring her words a bit, and Justin was slightly dizzy himself.

Madison held up her hand when David reached for her glass. "That booze packs a wallop. I think I better cool it a bit. I'm sorta having an out-of-body experience."

"Me too," Emily giggled. "It's a good thing we live next door, or I may have had to stay here tonight."

"Where did you say you make the stuff?" Madison propped her elbows on the steps behind her and leaned back.

Justin shot David a look. His older brother shrugged. "In Wisconsin."

Emily rested her head against Justin's arm. "Will you show us?"

"Sure, one of these first days." Justin didn't look at his brother this time. Likely David would not approve of him agreeing to Emily's request, but with her body warming the side of his, there wasn't much he would deny her. "Not tonight, though, that's for sure. The mosquitoes would eat us alive." His fingers trailed up and down her legs - the smoothest he had ever touched. David had wrapped his arms around Madison too, and was holding her close.

"Oooh, I hate to call it a night." Madison sat up, breaking the clinch. "But I'm tired and this home brew has gotten to me."

Emily straightened. "Justin, if you don't take me home right now, I'm gonna fall asleep on this swing."

Justin already missed the warm softness of her pressed against him. "It would be wonderful to wake up tomorrow and find you here. You're more than welcome to stay."

"I'm guessin' that will happen someday." Emily tripped over her words, obviously also affected by the liquor. "But it prob'ly shouldn't happen tonight. After all, what would you think of a girl that made it that easy that quick?"

She flashed him a smile that suggested she knew exactly

what he was thinking, before she slid to the edge of the seat and stood. Reluctantly, Justin took her hand and walked down the stairs and across the lawn to her house. David and Madison followed behind them.

One of their roommates, a petite, dark-haired woman, flung open the door as Emily reached for the handle. "When do I get to taste that stuff Em and Madison are raving about?"

Emily squeezed Justin's hand. "Justin, this is Andrea. We might have mentioned how good that booze is that you've been serving us. Hope that's okay."

"Sure. We'll bring some over for everyone to try one of these days," Justin promised. As Emily and Madison went into the house, David moved to stand beside Justin. "Maybe tomorrow," he suggested.

"Tell you what," said Andrea, "how about we make dinner for you guys tomorrow night? The price of admission will be a bottle of the stuff."

"I don't know. We—" began David.

Before he could refuse the invitation, Justin cut him off. "Sure; that'd be great. What time?"

"Dinner's at 6," shot back Andrea. "I'm cookin'. Get here about 5:30 so we can have a couple of drinks."

"Sounds good." Before his brother could protest, Justin grabbed him by the elbow and pulled him back over to their house.

At Maple Grove, southeast of La Crosse, Al and his wife JoAnne, along with Charlie and his wife Kelly, were finishing dinner. It had been a festive evening in celebration of Kelly and Charlie's sixth anniversary, and as the waitress delivered cake and ice cream, Al took advantage of the break in conversation to ask Charlie, "Any luck catching those rustlers?"

Kelly groaned. "I sure wish he could. That's all he talks

about, day and night, even in his dreams. I sure as heck hope he finds whoever is doing it, and quick."

JoAnne rubbed a hand over Al's back. "Al's the same. He's almost as obsessed with finding these moonshiners as he was when he was searching for Genevieve Wangen."

Al shook his head. "It's true, I'm afraid. Since misery loves company, I'll tell you that I'm getting nowhere on the case, either. What's worse, it's spreading. We keep hearing that lots of bars are selling it now, but we haven't been able to put the collar on a single one."

"The rustling total is up to 346 head of young stock." Charlie set down his fork, something he didn't do often when there was still food on his plate. "I don't have a solid lead to follow. Sheriff Dwight is none too happy about it. First it was a joke. Now it's no laughing matter."

"I hear you. The chief is gonna have my head if I don't hit something soon."

Charlie picked up his fork and stabbed at a bite of cake, his appetite clearly restored. "How about we get together Monday and see if we can put together a plan for each of us? I'd appreciate bouncing a few ideas off of you."

"Great idea." Al tugged his wallet out of his pocket as the server set the bill down on the table. "I'm fresh out of my own ideas. Maybe yours will trigger something for me."

Charlie waved him off when he reached for the check. "Just so you know I ain't cheap, Al. It's my turn to buy."

8

DAVID WAS AWAKE AND READY TO GO EARLY THE NEXT MORNING, but Justin was slow and sluggish. "C'mon, bro, we've got booze to make if we're gonna get done in time to make cocktail hour next door."

With the prospect of seeing their new friends again, work passed effortlessly. David and Justin got the cooker ready to go. David set the propane burner to come on at ten and cook the mash for exactly four and a half hours before turning off. That would prepare a new batch of liquor that the brothers would put through the beginning distillation process the next night.

"This should get us what we need for next week." David set the timer. "That corn we got from Hank Chappell up at Gilmanton is great, and I really like the new yeast you convinced me to try."

"I knew it would be good. I read up on it and thought we should try it. It's almost magical in its qualities."

Finished at their hidden operation by two in the

afternoon, the brothers walked back to their truck. As they were about to climb in, a gunshot echoed across the valley.

David ducked instinctively, rounded the front of the truck, and pulled his brother into the reeds.

"What the hell was that?" Justin shoved the long grasses out of his face as he crouched beside David.

"It was gunfire. I'm sure of that. Even though I don't think it was aimed at us, better hang out here for a while to see what's up."

Two minutes later, another shot sounded. The brothers stayed where they were, afraid to move. Two more minutes passed before they heard another shotgun blast.

David laughed. "Baby brother, I think we've been had by one of those shotgun alarms people use to scare crows and other intruders off their property."

"You think so?"

"Yeah, I'm sure. The space between shots is too exact." David stood and brushed dirt from his knees, "Hurry up. Let's get the hell out of here - we have time to make up."

As they drove back to Winona, David gripped the steering wheel. "We're going to have to step up our progress if we want to meet the new demand for the shine."

Justin shifted on the seat to face him. "Have we taken on too much, do you think? Maybe we should just get out."

David frowned. "Why the hell would we do that? We're making damn good money, and Byrle says there is more to be made. If we just buckle down for a few weeks, we can get to the point where leaving Wolverine is a real possibility. That'll make things a lot easier for us."

"I'm willing to work my ass off, David, but I've found something else I like, too. Emily is pretty great."

"I know, Madison is, too. But we need to figure out exactly how to make everything work together."

Justin rested his head on the back of the seat and closed his eyes. "Maybe we should make the girls our partners."

He tensed, as if bracing himself for the negative reaction he was sure to get from his brother, but David smacked the steering wheel with his palm. "Justin, that's a helluva good idea. You know, baby brother, once in a while you come up with a real gem."

Justin's eyes flew open. "Really? You'd consider takin' 'em on?"

"Damn right. 'Course we don't know what kind of workers they are. They're young, but they'll be around a coupla years, I guess. I think it's a great idea. We should think about it."

"I'm stunned," admitted Justin, "but I bet they'd be great. They're serious. They prob'ly can use the money. And how nice would it be to have them around while we work?"

"Of course there's a downside to that. Would we get anything done?"

"Sure we would. We'd have to. Gotta meet our commitments, don't we?"

"It's an idea worth thinking about. But don't go mouthin' off to them about it yet, okay?"

"Not a word." Justin pressed his lips together.

Rather than going straight home, David drove them to Wolverine, where the brothers spent an hour and a half working on the second still, which would be much larger than the first.

When David finished welding, Justin stepped back and pursed his lips. "It looks like a still. Where the hell we gonna hide it?"

"I think we'll have to take it home. We've got the truck, but we need to cover it. Is there something around we can use? We can finish it in the garage, then cover it again to take it to wherever we're gonna put it."

"What about that spot off County Road 25?" Justin

studied his brother as he made the suggestion. "That logging trail that leads back from the stone quarry as you start down the hill toward Minneiska?"

"Hmmm, interesting thought. Yeah, we need to take a look. There are 80 acres back. Have to see if we can buy it, then post signs to keep people out. The area is part of a game refuge, which is good. Hell, it'd be overrun with hunters if it wasn't." David tapped a finger against his chin. "Could work."

They loaded the still into the back of their truck then found an old tarp and tugged it over top, securing it with a couple of frayed ropes. Now they just had to hope no officers pulled them over on the way home and started nosing around.

A couple of hours later, the still safely stowed in their garage, David clutched a paper bag with a gallon of moonshine tucked inside one hand as he started across the lawn to Emily and Madison's place - his brother at his heels. The women met them on the porch and kissed them warmly, then Emily carried the bag into the house, returning a few minutes later with tall glasses of liquor and ginger ale for the brothers, and cola and whisky for herself and Madison.

Andrea, wearing an apron, emerged from the house a few minutes later with a drink in her hand. "I didn't believe it when Em and Madison told me about this stuff. But man, it's great. Did you guys really make it?"

"With our own two hands." David held out his hands and smiled. "Glad you like it, Andrea. Looks like you're working. Anything we can help you with?"

"Not a thing. Dinner may be served at 6, like I said, if this stuff doesn't get to me first. Hope you like pasta."

"We sure do," said Justin.

"And seafood?"

"That, too." David rubbed his hands together. "Sounds like we're in for a treat."

"Nothing as fancy as you cook. When Madison and Em told me you grilled lobster for them, I was pretty jealous. Wish I'd met you first."

"Well, you didn't," shot Madison. "So keep your hands off our guys, okay?"

"Yes, Mother." Andrea laughed as she turned and headed back into the house. "You two don't have another brother somewhere, do you?" she flung back over her shoulder.

"No, sorry," Justin replied.

Emily waved a hand through the air. "Don't mind her. Andrea likes to flirt, but she's just teasing. She's taken. Didn't you see the rock on her finger? She's getting married next summer."

"Even if she wasn't, I wouldn't be interested. Honest." Justin winked at her.

"Good. Now you guys better come in and meet the other two. They're helping Andrea."

David took Madison's hand and they followed Justin and Emily into the house, where Emily introduced them to Chelsea and Liz.

Justin's eyes widened. "God, do you have to pass a beauty test to live here?"

"Sorry guys, we're all taken." Andrea displayed her left hand. "Liz, Chelsea, and I are all engaged."

"Where are your men?" David asked them.

"Mine's doing a tour with the National Guard in Cuba," said Andrea.

"My fiancé, Rick, is in our hometown, Kenyon," offered Liz.

"And my guy is gone with the WSU golf team." Chelsea waved the knife she'd been using to slice tomatoes through the air.

"So we have five beautiful women all to ourselves." Justin slid an arm around Emily's waist.

Andrea laughed. "Well, for a month. The three of us are seniors. We're graduating in a few weeks and then we'll be gone."

The dining room table was set for seven. "David and Justin," said Andrea, "you take the ends. Emily, over there. And Madison, you there. Liz made the Caesar salad, Chelsea made the dessert, and I, as you know, made the main course. We didn't let Em or Madison touch anything."

The food was as good as anything Justin had eaten, and the dessert that followed was equally delicious—a light cherry cream filling in a graham cracker crust topped with almond-flavored whipped cream.

With dinner over, Andrea mixed another round of drinks and brought them to the living room. The banter went on until almost ten, when Andrea, Liz, and Chelsea excused themselves to clear the dishes and clean up the kitchen. Emily, Madison, Justin, and David decided to take a walk through the Winona State campus, quiet now that the end of the semester was nearing.

When they reached the gazebo at the center of campus, Justin and Emily settled on a bench. David and Madison walked a little farther before finding a spot to sit on a cement wall outside the library. Perhaps it was the food, maybe the weather, or just the entire mood of the evening, but Madison seemed particularly amorous. Their kisses grew urgent, and when she finally pulled away, David let her go with great reluctance. He contemplated Justin's suggestion about hiring the two women. Maybe they wouldn't get a lot of work done, but they'd sure have fun doing it.

All too soon, the clock approached midnight. David and Madison retraced their steps, collected Justin and Emily, and walked back to the women's house.

They stopped on the front porch, and David faced Madison. "Can I see you early next week?" Even that seemed too far away, but David didn't want to sound too pushy.

"For sure," whispered Madison, hugging him. "Absolutely."

David kissed her and forced himself to walk down the stairs and across the front lawn. The words he'd said to Justin the night before, about not wanting to jump into anything too quickly, mocked him now.

Ready or not, he was already in.

9

JUSTIN WENT STRAIGHT TO BED, BUT SLEEP CAME STUBBORNLY. His thoughts were too full of Emily and their evening together. Finally he got up, went to the fridge, opened a soda, and drank most of it. He was about to head back to his room when David walked in, looking as frazzled as Justin felt.

"Can't sleep, either?" asked David.

"No. Too wound up, I think. God, I like Emily, David. I can't wait to see her again. I've never felt like this about anyone before."

"I can relate. Madison is incredible. Nice, intelligent, gorgeous, warm—everything a guy could want. I think she likes me, too."

"You know, David, I really think we should take them on as partners."

"As I said before, it's helluva good idea. I already trust Madison more than any guy I know—except you. I think asking them might be a great idea. But they're still in school, and Madison plays basketball, too. Do you think it's too much?"

"I'm not sure. What if one says yes and the other says no. Then what?"

"That's something to think about, all right. Let's invite them to go along to Wisconsin. See what they think. If they seem interested in what we're doing, maybe we can ask them. Besides, it would be fun to have them along, wouldn't it?"

"It would. Hey, now I really don't know if I'll be able to sleep."

"I probably won't, either, but we better try. We've got lots to do tomorrow."

The boys headed back to bed, where Justin tossed and turned, thinking about Emily and how nice it would be to have her with him when they were making the moonshine. When the alarm sounded at 6:15, he was slow getting out of bed. Thankfully, they had enough time to stop at Caribou for their customary lattes before barreling up the highway to 54th Avenue and their turn off.

Work didn't help much. Orders were slow. The winter rush of work was behind them, so they spent the day in boring tasks like cleaning the shop, inventorying materials, and organizing hand tools.

Although Justin was certain the quitting whistle would never sound, it did—right at four pm. Although, by the time he heard it, he and his brother were nearly at their truck. No one seemed to mind them skipping out a few minutes early, as long as the work assigned had been completed, so the Freemans took full advantage of the privilege to get out early.

"I'd like to spend some time on the new still," David said as they climbed into their truck.

"Okay," said Justin, "but we have a long night at the old one ahead of us, too."

When they reached the house, David went immediately

to the garage to do more welding. Justin showered, changed into his second set of work clothes, these dark in color, then took a nap before waking up in time to fry burgers before the two set off for the Trempealeau River swamp.

Work that night passed quickly. While David readied a new batch of mash for the cooker, Justin carefully filled bottles and boxes to make sure 105 gallons of liquor were ready to be delivered to La Crosse.

Done before ten, and happy with their accomplishments, the two checked everything before deciding all was in order. They headed back to the garage at the entrance to the property, Justin pulling a wagon carrying bottles of booze. *Hopefully, the walk to the new bottling set-up, wherever that ends up being, will be less stren*uous. Thankfully, it had been a dry spring and the wagon pulled fairly easily across the hard ground.

After showering and changing into better clothes, Justin and David relaxed for a while on the front porch with drinks. The lights were on next door and Justin was tempted to go see Emily, but before he could, she came out on the porch. Seeing the brothers, she called into the house for Madison, and the two of them walked over.

Soon the four of them were snuggled on the swing and loveseat. It was a perfect ending to what had been a busy evening for the brothers, and Justin was grateful for the wind-down time.

Beyond noting that they had been away making another batch of liquor, nothing was said about the brothers' intention to ask the women if they were interested in jobs in the operation.

As the girls were preparing to leave a little after 11:30, Madison nuzzled David. "One of these days you're gonna have to show us where you make liquor."

David shot Justin a look. "I think we can make that happen."

Emily sat up and turned to face Justin. "Really? When?"

"Maybe this weekend."

Madison yawned and stood up. "This weekend. We'll hold you to that."

Her tone made Justin a little uneasy, but when Emily rose too, he got up and the four of them walked over to the girls' house.

They saw their neighbors most evenings that week, and on Friday Emily and Madison walked over to join them on the porch again. Madison settled onto the love seat beside David. "So are you going to take us to the place where you make that great liquor tomorrow?"

"Okay," agreed David. "We'll take you if you really want to go. But you'll have to be up at dawn. We get an early start on Saturdays so we can get home with plenty of time to enjoy the day."

"What time?"

"We like to be on the road by seven."

"We can make that work, can't we, Em?" When Emily nodded, Madison threw her arms around David. "We'll be over before seven and ready to go. Should we pack a lunch?"

"Tell you what, if you're willing to help a little, we should be done in time to get something on the way home."

Justin watched the two girls head back to their house. Well, it was done now. Whether or not it was a good idea, he and David were about to share with Madison and Emily one of their most closely guarded secrets. Hopefully, they wouldn't end up regretting it.

The next day was cloudy and cold, but when David opened the front door and stuck his head out at 6:45, Madison and

Emily were seated on the porch. Each of the women wore baseball caps, light jackets, and Winona State sweatpants.

"That cold?" asked David, looking them up and down.

Madison unzipped the jacket a little to show him the sweatshirt she wore underneath. "It is now, but we're wearing layers so we can remove things and enjoy the sun if it peeks out later."

"C'mon in," said David, opening the door wider. "Justin's still dressing."

Emily laughed. "Hmm, maybe I should go up and help him."

Madison giggled. "I'm sure David wants to get going. If you head upstairs, no telling what time we'll see you again."

When she winked at David, his heart skipped a beat. Her words seemed gilt-edged and dripped with innuendo.

He swallowed hard. "Well, he better get down here soon. I'm hoping we have time to stop at McDonald's on our way out. I like their breakfast sandwiches."

"They make great coffee, too." Emily strode to the bottom of the stairs. "Justin, better get your butt down here, or we're gonna leave without you!"

David heard his brother before he saw him. "Coming!" Justin shouted, bounding down the stairs two at a time. He stopped at the bottom, grabbed Emily around the waist, and kissed her soundly.

"Mmm, freshly scrubbed and minty," she teased. "Almost like kissing my toothbrush."

"Colgate fresh. Let's go; I'm starved."

A quick trip through the McDonald's drive-through and they were over the interstate bridge and into Wisconsin. Before David turned the truck south on Highway 35-54 for the short drive to County Road P in Buffalo County, they had finished their breakfast and were sipping their coffee quietly.

In spite of the cloudy skies, David was thrilled to have

Madison beside him. The light scent of some kind of flower drifted from her, and he breathed it in.

When David turned onto County Road P, and the road eventually turned from blacktop to gravel, Madison leaned forward to peer past him and out the window. "This is amazing." She waved a hand at the passing scenery. "I never knew places like this existed so nearby. It's beautiful."

"Full of mosquitoes, too," said Justin. "You two smell great, but you're gonna have to put on bug spray or they'll eat you alive."

"C'mon, Justin, we're both farm girls." Madison winked at David. "I think we can handle a few mosquitoes."

"They grow 'em as big as mallards over here," joked David. "Hope those sweatshirts and pants are thick."

"If they keep boys out, they'll keep mosquitoes out, too." Madison elbowed him in the ribs.

"Hmm, is that a challenge?"

"David!" Madison sounded shocked, but her blue eyes twinkled as her cheeks turned pink.

Soon David turned onto their property and activated the remote control gate and garage door. He pulled the pickup into the garage. "Here we are. Now we'll see what kind of moonshiners you are."

"Ah. I wondered if it was brewers or moonshiners. I guess now we know."

David's smile faded. "It's shiners, Madison. And what we do is illegal, so we'd appreciate you keeping everything you see today to yourselves."

Madison lifted her shoulders. "Em and I assumed what you were doing wasn't exactly legit. No one knows where we are, only that we're out for the day. We told our roomies we were going for a hike."

"Terrific." David reached for her hand and squeezed it. "We were hoping that you'd understand and help us out."

"Well," teased Madison, "if it means we get free booze, I think we're in, right, Em?"

"Damn straight."

"Let's get at it so we can get our work done and do some playing." Justin shoved open the back door of the truck.

David conducted a quick tour of the garage, informing the girls that it was the bottling center. "We don't keep booze here for very long, though. The garage is too near the road for comfort, so we generally bring the stuff to be bottled here and take care of it right away. Ready for a walk?"

The women were quiet as the four walked through the bottoms - David ahead and Justin bringing up the rear. The weeds and reeds grew thicker as they made their way along the path. After several minutes of walking, David stopped and shoved aside a weed patch. It swiveled to expose a dirt pathway. The four walked through, Justin pushed the patch back into place to conceal the path, and a few minutes later they emerged into the clearing that held the still, the pump, and a shed.

"Here we are." Justin swept an arm through the air. "This is where we make the stuff." Madison and Emily wandered around the clearing, touching the still as they passed, then peering into the shack.

"Look at that," said Madison. "It's a wagon with a big tank attached. Is that how you get the booze to the garage by the road?"

David nodded. "It is. And it works like a charm."

Emily lifted a hand. "So what can we do to help?"

Justin inclined his head toward the pump. "Since you're so eager, you can help me pump water."

"And while they're doing that, Madison, we'll go inside and get the mix ready for the cooker." David pushed open the shed door.

The women proved to be fast learners and great helpers.

In less than an hour, David was totally impressed by how quickly Madison had picked up on the things he was doing. In fact, when they had the first batch in the cooker, she pointed out that she thought the fire might be too hot.

"Fix it," he told her. And she did, dialing the propane flame down slightly to ease the temperature in the cooker.

When he went outside to check on the other two, his brother appeared equally pleased with Emily. She had taken over the pumping, and as soon as both pails were filled, she hurried over and picked them both up, working her way back and forth from the pump to the still and then to the shed.

In record time, the Freeman brothers finished their Saturday work. What normally took six hours, with the help of Emily and Madison, had been accomplished in under four hours.

As they walked back to the garage, the two women remained silent, but once they were in the truck, Madison rested her head on David's shoulder. "I can't remember ever enjoying a morning more than this one. What fascinating work you do. I love watching the two of you work."

David smiled down at her. "You did a lot more than watch—both of you. So, thank you."

"I'm not sure we did that much." Madison shifted closer to him.

Justin reached over the back seat and grasped her shoulder. "Not only did you both do a lot, you shocked me with how hard you worked. The pumping and carrying is not for sissies, and both of you were great at it."

"We had a great time, didn't we, Emily?"

"Sure did," said Emily, "but the company was pretty darn good, too. Don't you think, Madison?"

"Extraordinary. Watching your muscles ripple as you worked was a huge turn on. I almost tackled David."

David grinned. "If I'd known that, we'd still be back there."

"I looked for a good spot," Madison tilted back her head to look up at him, "but unless you have chairs or couches stashed away somewhere, there wasn't really any place to be comfortable. By the way, do you ever see any snakes there?"

"Yep, we've seen a few. They like to come around the still when the weather turns cold. Seem to like the heat." Justin let go of her shoulder and sank back against his seat.

Emily shivered. "I hate snakes. 'Course, if I have a big, brave, handsome man around to protect me, it might not be so bad." She squeezed Justin's arm. "I do have a question, though," she said. "I pumped a helluva lot of water. What do you do with it all?"

"I think a better question is, what the heck do you do with all the moonshine?" Madison's eyebrows rose. "Seems like you make a ton of it."

David took a deep breath. "Actually, we've decided to talk to you about that. Why don't we get some lunch? Afterwards we can take a ride, and Justin and I can let you know what we've been thinking."

Madison nodded and leaned her head against his shoulder again. David turned off Highway 61 toward Rollingstone. A few miles later, he pulled up across the street from Bonnie Rae's Café and turned off the engine. "Great omelets. And I'm hungry."

Everyone was hungry, it turned out, and the omelets, as advertised, were great. By the time David paid the bill and they were ready to leave, all four plates had been scraped clean.

"Best omelet I've ever had." Madison pressed a hand to her stomach as they walked across the street.

"Me too." Emily pulled open the back door of the truck. "Where to now?"

Justin slid a hand through the crook of her elbow and guided her to the front passenger side door. "We're looking for a site for another still. I found one I think might work the other day. David doesn't know where it is, so I'm gonna drive. Join me up front, mademoiselle!"

Emily attempted a curtsy. "Don't mind if I do, monsieur." He held the door until she had climbed onto the seat. When he slid behind the wheel, she shifted over until she was pressed against him. "Is this too close, dear sir?"

"Ummm, not quite close enough, to be honest."

"But, sir, if I get any closer, I'll be sitting on your lap."

"Yep, that's what I had in mind."

"Listen, you two," said Madison from the back seat, "if you can't behave, we're gonna have to switch seats again. And since I kind of like the fact that David's hands are both free now, that's gonna make me mighty angry."

"Okay, okay," agreed Emily, laughing. "I'll leave him alone so you two lovebirds can smooch. But you better take it easy, or I might have to tackle him anyway."

Justin, one arm wrapped tightly around Emily's shoulders, drove through Rollingstone and out County Road 25, steering the truck up the hill when they were about a mile outside town.

"Whoa," said Emily, "I've never been this way before. Just where are you taking us, sir? Not to a place where you can take advantage of us, I pray."

Justin pressed a kiss to the top of her head. "I guess you'll have to wait and see."

10

After the truck crested the hill and began to descend, Justin slowed the vehicle, and then turned right into an area that looked as if it had been widened for a road construction crew. All that was visible in the clearing was a huge pile of gravel. Justin carefully steered around the pile and, once past the gravel, headed for a two-rut road that seemed as if it hadn't been driven on for ages.

"Is that where we're goin'?" Emily peered ahead then moved away from Justin a bit, as if to give him more room to drive.

"Yep. I wanna show David something I found when driving around the other day."

"Justin Freeman, were you up here with a girl other than me?"

He shot her a look. She'd crossed her arms and stuck out her lower lip, but her eyes twinkled with mischief. He elbowed her gently. "Absolutely not. I was alone. Besides, it was before I'd even met you."

"Okay. Is this road maintained?"

"Not sure," said Justin. "Not sure I want it to be."

"Why not?" She uncrossed her arms. "You like me bouncing against you every few seconds?"

He grinned. "Well, yes. But I meant that I don't really want strangers driving along this road, given what we plan to do on the property. So it suits me that it's not at all inviting."

She slid closer, bumping against him. The truck swerved left, rocking out of the ruts before Justin corrected their course. "Hey, cut it out," he said. "I'm gonna be black-and-blue. And we're gonna take a wild ride down the hill."

"Ohh, pooooor boooy. Soooooo sooooooooooory to have hurt the itty, bitty boy."

"Just cut it out if you want to be safe."

"Fine, I'll move over here." She slid across the seat to lean against the passenger side door.

"Hey, I wasn't that upset. Besides, I like how you smell and feel, so move back over here, will you?" Justin held out his arm.

"Say please."

"Pleeeeeeeeeeeeeze."

Emily slid back across the seat, ramming him hard when she reached him.

"Okay, okay, easy. No need to wreck the truck, is there?"

"Absolutely not. After all, it's my truck." David leaned forward, his hands on the back of the seat between Justin and Emily. "I'd just as soon any fights occur outside moving vehicles, okay?"

Just as he said that, the truck hit a deep rut, and both Madison and David bumped their heads on the roof of the cab.

"Little brother, do I have to do the driving?"

Justin gripped the wheel and met his brother's gaze in the rearview mirror. "No, sir, but you could get this tiger up here to ease off a bit."

"It's okay; I'll be good." Emily relaxed demurely at Justin's side. After they had driven another mile across the rocky, rutted road, they emerged into a clearing.

"This is it." Justin stopped the truck and rammed the transmission into park. He grabbed his cap and opened the door. "Let's take a walk."

Jumping out of the truck, he pulled Emily after him. "Don't worry, it's not far."

David and Madison climbed out of the backseat and followed them. They walked along what Justin presumed was a deer trail through a dense wood before breaking out into the sunlight.

"Great, sun." Emily tipped back her head. "It feels great, doesn't it?"

"Pay attention to where you're walking." Justin reached for her hand. "There's a steep drop-off up here a little, and I don't want to have to retrieve anyone who isn't careful."

Just as he had claimed, another few feet and they were atop several large, flat rocks that formed the edge of a cliff. While the drop was some 200 feet or more into what appeared to be a dormant stone quarry, the view was spectacular.

"Wow. How did you find this place?" David gazed around then looked at his brother and smiled. "Not sure if this is the right place for a still, but it's one helluva view."

Justin studied the sight for a few moments. "I was up here a few weeks ago. Remember that day that you had to work late and I got out early?" When David nodded, he said, "Well, I took a drive through Rollingstone. I like this trip, because County Road 25 comes out at Minneiska, and I like the burgers at the Eagle View. Anyhow, I had a little time, and I've always been intrigued by this clearing. I wasn't sure there was anything behind the gravel pile, but I drove in to look and found the path. I had my own vehicle, so I thought I could take a chance.

"Anyway, I drove up the lane, stopped at the trees, and walked through the wood. And I found this. Best part was, when I got behind the gravel pile, there was a 'For Sale, 350 Acres' sign tacked to a post. On the way back, I wrote down the number and called the guy."

"Seriously?"

"Yep. The land belonged to a fellow from St. Paul who inherited it from his grandpa. He sold off the farmland, donated a few acres to John Latsch Park, and this is what was left. Now," his arm swept from left to right, "I own these 350 acres. When he told me he'd sell it for ten dollars an acre because it was worthless, I jumped at it. Figured for 3,500 I couldn't go wrong. Whadda ya think?"

"I think it's spectacular. How come you didn't tell me?" David's eyebrow arched.

"Thought you might get mad. Then I thought, what the hell, I can always sell it and make a mint if David doesn't like it. I've been up here a coupla times, and I've always seen deer. Could make a great deer-hunting plot—and those go for big bucks. Guess the guy didn't know that." He laughed. "Big bucks for big bucks. Excuse the pun."

"Well, it was a genius move. And for you, that's amazing. Where do you think the still should go?" David wandered around the clearing, peering around rocks and trees as he strolled.

"Big brother, you ain't seen nothing yet. Trust me." He walked over to David, took him by the arm, and began to lead him, nodding at the women to follow. "Over to the south, there's a little holler. At the back of the holler is a springhead. And beside the springhead is a cave. It's pretty big, too—big enough to hold a still. I've made a fire in there and the smoke must go out a natural chimney, because I haven't been able to trace it. And I had the water tested and it's as good as the water we have in Wisconsin—100 percent pure, WSU says. I think it's perfect. Couldn't wait to show it to you."

Justin glanced back to make sure the women were okay. Emily stopped at the edge of the woods he'd been about to lead them into. "Won't there be a lot of bugs in there?"

Justin shook his head. "I've been down here a coupla times, and I haven't seen so much as a mosquito."

Emily nodded, and she and Madison followed them into the trees. Justin found another deer trail and took them down an incline of a couple hundred feet. "The creek is just over here," he told them. "Watch your step."

He picked his way along the rough trail carefully, stopping when the sound of the gentle burbling of water reached him. Another fifty feet and he caught a glimpse of the silver-white swirl of fast-running water.

"Best part is, the creek goes back underground after about eight feet, so there's no real place for mosquitoes to hatch." When they reached a wall overgrown with vines, Justin pulled back a couple of them to reveal a hole. He tugged a flashlight from his pocket and handed it to Emily, then pulled the vines farther apart to admit her, Madison, and David. When they'd passed through the opening, he joined them in the cave.

"It's at least 400 feet deep," Justin told them, "and it gets larger as you move toward the back. If we walk a ways, you'll see where I started a fire, and even though I hiked all over the hillside above, I couldn't find any trace of smoke. I wanna take some time to explore thoroughly in case there's a back exit. It'd be great if there is, 'cause getting' the booze outta here'll be tough."

"But it's wonderfully secluded." David clapped a hand on Justin's shoulder. "Guess we're going to have to take up deer hunting, baby brother. As for a site to make shine, this is perfect."

Justin beamed at the praise his older brother was lavishing on him. "I brought a flashlight for everyone in case you wanted to look around the cave."

"Great idea," said his brother. "How do you want to go about it?"

Justin gave out flashlights to Madison and David. "Let's walk back through and see what we find. I haven't been all the way to the end."

All four activated their lights and they entered the cave, Justin leading the way. "My god, how far does this thing go?" David shone his light around the space.

"No idea, but it's way more than 400 feet. We're not there yet."

Another 100 feet or so into the cave, they came to a V with one branch seeming to head into the hill and another toward the river. "Which way do you want to go?" Justin aimed his light down the passage that seemed to wind toward the river, then brought it back to illuminate the larger opening that projected farther into the hillside.

"Let's go left." David waved an arm in that direction. "See where that goes."

The branch to the left projected downward at a gentle pace before abruptly turning left at a sharp angle. When they turned, they found themselves at an opening in the rock. After walking out into the sunlight, Justin glanced back. The opening they had just come through was a well-masked gash in the limestone, about 150 feet above Highway 61. Had they not known about where the opening was, they wouldn't have seen it.

"Perfect." David slapped his brother's back. "We're right on the edge of a meadow. Wonder who owns this land?"

"Not sure, but I can find out." Justin switched off his flashlight. Some time we should take a look and see if we can find the property line stakes. The owner of the piece I bought told me his dad had the property surveyed and staked."

"How about we go back the way we came and take the other passage?" David slid an arm around Madison's shoulders and guided her back toward the opening. "As long as we're here, let's take a look."

They trudged back through the cave, uphill this time, and took the passage that appeared to lead back into the bluff. That branch, too, led a few hundred feet then dead-ended at a rock wall that appeared solid, until Madison picked her way to the side of it and found a narrow opening. After stepping through the opening, she poked her head back into the cave and gestured for the others to join her.

Emily followed her. "In here. Take a look." She bounced up and down on the balls of her feet.

Justin went through the opening, clambered up a couple of boulders, and poked his head out a small hole. "I think we're atop the bluff," he called down. "Has someone got something I can use to mark this opening?"

Madison stripped off her purple sweatshirt, revealing a T-shirt beneath it. "I'm roasting, so you can use this." She handed it to Justin. "I would like it back, though, so take a good look around the area where you put it."

After another long walk, they arrived back at the spring. Justin tugged the keys from his pocket. "Let's walk up the bluff. When we get to the top, hopefully we will have plenty of light left to look for Emily's sweatshirt. I don't know if the opening is at the top of the bluff, so we'll have to look carefully so we don't miss it."

Once at the top of the bluff, they reconnoitered before spreading out to walk through the woods in search of the sweatshirt. Forty-five minutes later, Emily pointed to a spot ahead of them. "There." A short walk led them to the sweatshirt, lying beside an overgrown opening into the hillside. "Good eyes, Em." Justin picked up the sweatshirt and glanced around. Was there something more permanent he could use to mark the cave opening? Something inconspicuous?

Justin and David dragged a couple of fallen birch trees to the area, crossed them over the opening, then attached an orange plastic bag to one of the limbs in such a manner that it could have been blown there by the wind.

They tramped up the hill to the top of the bluff. Justin held a hand above his eyes to block out the sun. "We're about a quarter mile from the clearing and the truck. Should be a relatively easy walk since there's a wider trail here that might have originally been made by loggers." He whirled toward his brother. "You know, we could camo the opening to the trail, improve it a little, and be able to drive the truck down it to the back opening. You think we could use that opening for the liquor?"

"We'll have to look at that closely when we're here next." David pursed his lips. "It might work. Sure would be better than dragging the booze up the hillside."

"That's for sure." Justin lowered his hand. "I think this really could work David. I did good, right?"

David laughed and slapped him on the back. "Yes, little brother. For once I have to agree with you. You did good."

11

AS THEY DROVE FROM THEIR NEWLY PURCHASED PROPERTY back to County Road 25, David gripped the back of the front seat. "Madison, Emily, there's something Justin and I want to talk to you about. We're wondering if you'd like to help us with our liquor business."

Emily twisted around in the front seat, her eyes wide. "Help you with your liquor business? What does that mean?"

"When we start using the second still, Justin and I will each need a helper. We like you and we trust you, so we thought we'd ask you first. If you don't want to, that's fine, but we do hope you'll keep our secret." David studied Madison's face. *What is she thinking?* They were taking a huge risk, asking these women they barely knew to join them, but he felt they knew them well enough to be sure they would be good partners. If she didn't agree, he wasn't sure where the two of them would go for help.

Madison covered his hand with hers. "When would we start?"

"We've got quite a bit of work to do at this new site."

David worked to keep the enthusiasm from his voice, not wanting to bias the women. "And we have to keep the other site running, too. What do you think, Justin? Three, four weeks?"

"If we really crack it."

Madison bit her lip. "There's lots to think about."

"We'd sure love it if you'd join us." Justin half-turned from his seat behind the wheel.

David held up his free hand. "While Justin's right, we don't want you to feel pressured. As Madison said, there is a lot to think about, and we want you to be sure that you understand what we are doing is illegal. You'd be taking a big chance if you worked with us, although the payoff could be huge."

"I'd still love it," insisted Emily, "but you need both of us, right?"

"Well, each of us needs a helper. Looks like Justin's found his." David shot a sideways glance at Madison. "Do I need to keep looking?"

Madison pulled back her hand. "Look, it's a big decision. First of all, as you said, it's illegal. We get caught and all four of us are going to jail. Secondly, we have to think about next year. With our three roomies leaving, we either have to find three new women to join us or find a smaller place. And if we're involved in something illegal, we'd have to choose our new roommates pretty carefully. I'm pretty sure I want to do it, but I'd like to take the night to think about it. Okay with you?"

He laughed. "I was only kidding. Of course, you can take the rest of the day." He reached for her hand again. "But we really do have to make a decision soon. Yes, take the night, but can you let us know tomorrow? If you don't want to, we've got to find other people who do. And we have to do it quick."

Madison squeezed his fingers. "Emily and I will talk

about it tonight. My guess is Liz, Andrea, and Chelsea will go to the bar. They've been doing that a lot lately." She tilted her head, her big brown eyes searching his. "We'll let you know first thing in the morning, okay?"

David swallowed hard. When she looked at him like that, there wasn't much he wouldn't agree to. "Sure." He lifted her hand and kissed the back of it. "We're heading to the old still tomorrow. Do you want to come with us?"

"Sure, I'd like to." Madison smiled at him. "How about you, Em?"

"Absolutely."

"Great," said David. "Let's stop and pick up some hamburger and buns on the way home and I'll grill burgers for dinner."

It was a festive night. In spite of the serious talk they'd assured the men they would have, the women seemed in no hurry to leave the Freeman house, and it was after midnight before final kisses were exchanged and the brothers walked their neighbors home. David was about to suggest they come in for a nightcap when a cab pulled up to the curb and deposited Liz, Andrea, and Chelsea on the sidewalk. Before another party could start, Justin and David excused themselves and headed home.

"Do you think they'll agree?" Justin pulled open the front door and held it.

David stepped into the kitchen and turned to face his brother. "Honestly? I have no idea. But I really hope they do, because I have never wanted anything so badly in my life."

12

AL ROUSE AND CHARLIE BERZINSKI WERE RUNNING OUT OF hope. Neither had had any luck trying to get a lead on the criminal activity that was affecting all of La Crosse County, including its largest city. On this morning they were sitting in Ma's Café on the south side of La Crosse. It was a beautiful spring day, the kind that makes you happy to be alive, and though the lawmen were dour, they approached the day with cautious enthusiasm.

"Charlie, I'm beside myself." Al tossed an empty sugar packet onto the table and reached for his spoon. "Reports of illegal liquor are coming to us from all sides now, and I still don't have anything. I'm beginning to think I don't know the first thing about detective work."

Charlie stared into his coffee cup. "I have the same problem. Cattle rustlers continue to decimate herds in the south of the county, and even though we've concentrated our entire work force patrolling the areas they've been hitting, we haven't managed to see or hear a thing."

"I know damn well that we've heard from every bar that

isn't selling the illegal booze. They're screaming for action. At the same time, I'm pretty sure most of them would make a deal with whoever's bringing it in if they knew who it was."

Ma stopped by, her order pad at the ready. Having her move from behind the counter was a rarity. She planted one fist on her ample hip. "Can I help you boys? You look like breakfast is the last thing on your mind."

Charlie exhaled loudly. "You know, Ma, I am almost too upset to eat. Better go light this morning."

Shaking her head—likely at the absurd thought of Charlie being too upset to eat—she tugged the pencil from behind her ear. "So, two plates then instead of the usual four?"

Al snorted and Charlie threw him a dark look then jabbed at the menu with one beefy finger. "Let's just make it three eggs, bacon, ham, and four slices of toast. Skip the waffle. Like I said, I'm not very hungry."

"Whew, that's a relief," said the older woman, pushing a tuft of gray hair back behind her ear. "For a minute, I thought you were really sick."

"On a normal day, you know I'd have more food. Just haven't got much of an appetite right now. Things aren't good. Might have to take up waitressin' one of these days."

"If you decide to do that, apply somewhere else, will ya? I couldn't afford to have ya on the payroll here. You'd eat me out of house and home."

"Aww, Ma, that ain't fair. You know I'm one of your best customers."

"That's just it. I want you on that side of the counter, where I can bill you." She waited a beat then shook her head. "You guys used to have a sense a humor. Now it's like a wake when you're in here."

"That's a fact, Ma," agreed Al. "Neither of us has made any progress on the cases we're looking into, and we're frustrated. You're just going to have to put up with us until we get a break and make some progress. In the meantime, I'll take the usual."

"Got it." She turned and wended her way around the tables toward the kitchen. When she was gone, Al and Charlie got down to business.

"Here's what I know, or think I know." Al fished a small notepad out of his shirt pocket and flipped it open. "I have a hunch that the booze is coming in from north of here. The reason I say that is this guy Byrle Oldendorf, who runs the Handy Corner in North La Crosse, seems to be a key. Best I've been able to find out is that he's suspected of distributing the stuff. But we've been watching his place, and he hasn't walked an inch over the line."

"I know him." Charlie drummed his fingers on the table. "Actually, I know him pretty well. I think he's a good guy. Much as I hate to say it Al, bar owners today have a heckuva time makin' a living. The laws have really tightened up, fewer and fewer people seem to be drinking, and those who are ain't drinking nearly as much as they used to, likely because the stuff is taxed so heavily. At least that's my view."

"I think you're right, Charlie. And I suppose that if some guy comes along selling illegal booze for a decent price and you can avoid paying the government those higher taxes, it must seem like a good deal."

"I guess. And if it makes you feel better, I ain't havin' any luck with the rustlers, either. If they're selling the cattle they're stealing, it's not around here, or else everyone I been talkin' to is lyin'. I don't have a lead. I actually think that the rustlers must be penning up these cows and they're either doing it a long ways from here or in a pretty remote, out-of-sight place."

"Wouldn't it be something if these two cases had a connection? I keep thinking that if this were the 1800s, they likely would." Al sighed and settled back in his chair.

Neither spoke for a few moments, until Ma came out and set a plate in front of each of them. She clapped Charlie on the shoulder. "I'll be out with the rest of yours in a minute, but this should get you started."

He grinned. "Thanks, Ma."

Still consumed with thoughts of his investigation, Al popped a forkful of scrambled egg into his mouth, followed it with a bite of toast, and reached for his knife so he could cut up the ham on his plate. After a couple more bites, he set down his fork. "Charlie, I'd like to scare the crap out of this Oldendorf guy, and I'd love for you to help me."

"Whadda ya have in mind?"

"I think we squeal up to the Handy Corner, lights flashing, and rush inside. Then we'll put the strong arm on Oldendorf. Shake him up good. I'll station a few watchers near the bar to see what happens."

"Sounds okay to me. I better tell Dwight, just so he don't get his boxers in a bunch. When do you want to do it?"

"Soon as we can. I'm tired of sitting around waiting for something to break on this case. It's time to make something happen."

13

JUSTIN HAD JUST CRAWLED OUT OF BED THE NEXT MORNING, when Madison and Emily rapped at the door. David was brewing coffee, and soon all four were settled in the kitchen over doughnuts and steaming mugs.

"Did you guys find time to talk last night?" David tapped his hand on the table as if playing the drums.

"We sure did," replied Madison, winking at Emily. "And we actually have a proposition for you guys. Want to hear it now or later?"

"Are we gonna be happy?" asked David.

"Gosh, I don't know," said Madison, frowning. "What do you think, Emily?"

"Not sure." Her friend grinned impishly at Justin. "Maybe they don't like us as well as we think they do."

David stopped tapping. "The suspense is killing me. Maybe you could just let us know?"

Madison looked at him, a smile dancing at the corner of her lips. "Listen to Mr. Impatient, will you, Em? He wants to know and he wants to know now. Well, Mr. Right Now, what if I tell you it all depends on you?"

His eyebrows rose. "On me?"

"And Justin," said Emily.

Justin rested a hand on her knee. "In what way?"

"Should we tell 'em, Em? Or should we let 'em wait a while longer?"

"Listen, Ms. Danielson." David cupped her chin in his hand and gently turned her to face him. "Could you please just tell us? Or do I have to drag it out of you?"

Madison pulled away from his grasp and stood up. "If you think you're strong enough, big guy, come and get it."

David rose and moved toward her. Madison backed toward the doorway between the kitchen and the living room. David kept moving toward her and she kept moving backward, until her legs encountered the sofa and she fell backward. He immediately climbed on top of her, tickling her ribs. She screamed, shrieked, fought like a tiger. David hung on for dear life, until at last they both collapsed, laughing.

"I wasn't kidding you," he said, through tightly clenched teeth. "Out with it!"

"Okay, okay!" she gasped. "Just let me catch my breath."

David clambered off the couch and held out a hand to help her out. Back at the kitchen table, Madison clasped her hands in front of her. "Here's the deal. We think we should accept your offer, but we do have a condition."

"A condition?" David's forehead wrinkled.

"Yes, if we're gonna be involved, we'd like to be partners. And if we're gonna be partners, then we think we should move in here and live with you, too."

David's mouth dropped open.

"You... um... you..." sputtered Justin.

"... wanna move in here?" David finished.

Madison shrugged. "We seem to really like each other.

We've spent every evening with you since we've met. Our roommates are leaving, and we either have to find new ones or a new place to live. Why not here? If we're gonna help you, be partners with you, we think you should put us up, too." Madison sat back and crossed her arms over her chest, a smug look on her face as she gazed at the brothers.

They just stared at the women across the table, until Emily's shoulders sagged. "You don't like the idea, do you?"

"Let them speak for themselves," suggested Madison. "I want to hear what they have to say."

Justin glanced over at David.

David realized his mouth was still hanging open and closed it with a snap. "Wow, I sure as hell didn't see that one comin'. Not in a hundred years. But you know what? I think it's a great idea."

Madison flung a hand into the air. "Now don't get the wrong idea."

"Oh sure, a catch. Just when I was getting excited, she's gonna pull the rug out." David winked at her.

"What I was gonna say before I was so rudely interrupted, Mr. Freeman, is that we don't plan to be freeloaders. We expect to pay our own way. We'll pay rent and help with the other expenses like food and heat, too. But like I said, our roommates are leaving in a few weeks, and we don't have anyone to replace them. And that makes the house next door too expensive for the two of us. Besides, we'll be spending an awful lot of time together, won't we?"

"We will." A smile spread across David's face. "But we only have one more bedroom. Will you be okay to room together?"

Madison grimaced and elbowed Emily in the ribs. "Oh, my god, Em, listen to him. I guess you guys don't want to share your rooms, then?"

"Now wait a minute." Justin straightened in his chair so

quickly it nearly tipped backwards. "I didn't say anything about not sharing my room."

David held up both hands. "Let me start over. We like the idea of you being our partners. We like the idea of you being roommates. And we have no complaints about sharing our rooms with you, either. Is that clear enough?"

"What do you think, Em? Share rooms with them, or room together? Maybe we should take another night to think it over."

David grinned sheepishly. "I'm sorry. I'm a little slow sometimes. I don't blame you if you want to forget the whole—"

Madison leaned across the table and stopped him with a kiss. When she pulled back a moment later, a satisfied look crossed her face. "I think we have a deal."

He half stood and kissed her again before sitting down. "I think we do. And let me be the first to say how happy I am with it."

Justin smacked his palm on the table. "So, when can you move in?"

Emily laughed. "We were thinking that it would be best for us to move after graduation. We have the house until the first of June, so we should probably wait until Andrea, Liz, and Chelsea leave. They'll likely be gone the week after commencement."

"So we have to wait nearly a month for you to move in?" David slumped against the back of his chair.

"I don't know about Em, but I'm open to an overnight here and there."

"I am too." Emily reached over and grasped Justin's arm. "Maybe we could start tonight?"

He grinned. "Sounds good to me."

David's head was spinning. Was all of this moving a bit too fast? "Tomorrow is Monday—a work day for us and a school day for you. Is that going to be a problem?" Madison squeezed his knee under the table. "I guess that means we'll have to get to bed early, doesn't it?"

Heat crept up his neck. "I guess we will." Madison pulled back her hand and flashed him a knowing smile. David swallowed. It was going to be a long day. "Well, it's time for us to get goin'." He rose and reached for his jacket, which hung on a hook behind the door to the back porch.

Emily tipped her head to look up at Justin. "You said it was all right for us to come too, right?"

"Sure, if you're ready for some hard work."

"Always." She and Madison scrambled off their chairs and followed the men out the door. The sun was peeking over the marsh as David parked the truck in the garage and led the group to the still. The world that morning was fascinating - dewdrops glistening in the sunlight on spider webs woven from reed to reed.

"It's beautiful, isn't it?" Madison clapped her hands.

"It sure is. And quiet, too." Emily stopped walking.

David stopped too. They had a lot to do, but it wouldn't hurt to take a minute to enjoy their beautiful surroundings. Maybe that would be another benefit of having the girls with them—they'd take more notice of the breathtaking sights around them. A red-winged blackbird swooped down from overhead, balanced gingerly on a reed, and then flew to a more substantial perch in a nearby oak tree.

As if in response to its flight, a flock of red-winged blackbirds rose as one from the swamp and headed away from them, squawking as they flew. The lone sentinel waited a moment before leaving his perch to join the group.

"So much for silence." Justin chuckled at the squalling coming from nearby trees.

David started off again, the rest trudging behind, until they reached the shed. "Here we are. I think we should work in pairs. Madison and I can begin another batch of moonshine. Justin, you and Emily can take what cooked off yesterday, reduce the batch by adding water, and take it back to the garage for bottling. Okay?"

Justin nodded. "Sure. And when we're done here, why don't we head over to the new site?"

"Great idea. We can try and figure out a way to use the back door for liquor transportation." David held his hand out. "Madison?" She followed him to the pump to get water for a new batch. Four hours later, they were done.

"Wow, how smooth was that?" David wrapped an arm around Madison's waist. "Thanks, you two, for helping again."

"We're partners now, aren't we?" Madison poked him gently in the ribs.

David pulled her to his side. "Now that we've seen what the two of you can do, you bet you're partners. Tonight at supper we can talk about the terms."

Justin nodded. "I agree. Should I drive us to the other property first?"

"Good idea. I'm not sure I could find the place." David waited until his brother and the two women had started back toward the truck before following them. Madison walked in front of him, and he couldn't help admiring the view as they made their way to the entrance of the property. *Yep. This new partnership might just work out fine.*

After a stop at Hy-Vee to pick up salads, sandwiches, and soda, Justin piloted the Ford F-150 to the spot in the hills north of Rollingstone.

"Let's see if we can find that back door." Justin took Emily's hand and led her from the clearing into the woods beyond. David and Madison followed. It took them twenty minutes, but they finally found the crossed birch trees, which the men moved.

David, on his knees, pulled away the grass from the opening and peered into the hole in the ground. "The first thing we need to do is widen this enough to get into the place. Then we're gonna have to figure out if we'll be able to haul the liquor out this way. If we can do both those things, that'll be a good afternoon's work."

As he began to strip the weeds from the hole, Justin handed him a short-handled spade he had brought from the truck. David dug into the ground around the hole. "I was thinking, the next time we come up here, we should bring some 'No Hunting Or Trespassing' signs and post them as the law requires to keep people off the land. Prob'ly easier to drive the stakes now before the ground dries out."

"Good idea." While David worked widening the opening, Justin spread out a tarp to hold the dirt and grass he was removing. Emily helped him straighten out the edges before brushing off her hands. "What can Madison and I do?"

Justin gave the tarp a last tug and stood up. "If you want, you can go to the truck and grab the sheet of plywood from the back. Do you think you could carry it here?"

Emily bent her arms and flexed her muscles. "Of course we can."

Justin laughed. "That would be great, if you don't mind."

"No problem." Madison started back down the trail. "Come on, Em."

Justin selected a small tree near the widening hole that David was creating and began to pull items from the bag he had brought from the truck. He fastened two metal straps around the tree near the ground, then cut two 2 by 4s into the proper lengths.

As he was finishing, the women walked up to him, lugging the 4 by 8 sheet of plywood. Justin jumped up and helped the two of them lower the sheet to the ground. The three of them then helped David clear away the grass and dirt he'd dug around the edge of the hole, which was now wide enough to admit a good-sized man into the cave.

That done, Justin and David fastened the plywood sheet to the 2 by 4s with screws. They attached metal devices to the platform and bolted that into the two pieces of metal projecting from the bottom of the tree.

"I'm gonna climb down and see what we have to do to make the hole manageable." David grabbed a length of rope and fastened it around his waist. "You guys hold the other end to keep me from falling, okay?"

Once the three of them had a good hold on the rope and had braced themselves against the ground, he backed into the hole, a flashlight stuck in his back pocket. Justin, at the end of the row, gradually played out rope as his brother descended.

"Hey, Justin?" came David's voice from the opening, "did you bring that 100-foot tape with you?"

"Sure did."

"Toss it down here, will you? But keep hold of one end, okay?"

Still holding the rope, Justin worked the bag closer to him with his foot, bent down slowly, and let go of the rope with one hand long enough to grab the measuring tape out of it. He tossed it to Madison who was at the edge of the hole. She held the rope with one hand and the end of the tape with the other as she lowered it down to David until he hollered up for her to stop.

"Whadda we have?" came the voice from beneath their feet.

"Fifty-five feet, eight inches," she shouted.

"Okay, I'm comin' up," called David.

Justin dug the side of his foot into the dirt, holding the rope steady as his brother climbed back up. When David flopped onto the ground, he looked up at Justin and the women. "Anyone have a pencil and paper?"

Justin shrugged. "Not me, sorry."

Madison dug around in the pocket of her jacket and produced an old receipt. "Here's some paper. I don't have a pen, though. Em?"

"Here." Emily tugged something from the back pocket of her jeans and tossed it to David.

He picked it up and examined it. "What is this?"

"Eyeliner. It'll work."

He shrugged and pulled off the lid.

Justin grinned. "You carry eyeliner around with you in the woods?"

Emily looked a little sheepish. "You never know when you might need it. Like now." She inclined her head toward David.

Madison dropped down beside David, who had settled on a stump. "What would you do without us?"

"Not sure, but isn't that what partners are for?"

He began to draw. When he was done, he got up and handed the paper to Justin. "This is what I'm thinking." The drawing depicted a stair arrangement with two platforms. "I figure we can go up twenty feet to a platform," he said, tapping the drawing, "then up another twenty feet to another platform over here, and then the final eight feet or so to the opening. We'll need a third platform at the opening. The one we just constructed will do nicely. Any ideas what we can use to hide it and the opening?"

Justin pointed to the tree and the assembled platform that extended from it on the 2 by 4's. "I've been working on something over there. Want to see if you think it's sturdy enough?"

David approached it, easily moved it back and forth, then climbed onto it and jumped up and down.

"Easy." Justin held up a hand. "Don't break the damn thing."

"It's sturdy, all right. Perfect." Swiveling the platform, the two of them maneuvered it until it covered the hole. David smacked his gloved hands together. "It's great. Should we cover it with brush?"

"That's the plan." Justin walked over to a felled tree he'd been eyeing while working on the platform, and grabbed hold of a couple of branches to drag it over to the opening. "First a couple of big trees and then a bunch of brush and leaves."

The other three leapt into action. David helped Justin move the tree over the opening, and the women filled in the spaces with branches and leaves. The job was accomplished in a few minutes. When they finished, Justin stood back and studied the spot. Even though he knew it was there, it was impossible to see either the opening or the platform.

David clapped him on the shoulder. "Great job!"

"Let's see how it works," said Justin, moving to the far side of the brush and pushing with his foot. The brush-covered platform swiveled to the side, revealing the opening. David walked to the other side and pushed it again, covering the hole back up.

"It's perfect." Emily clasped her hands in front of her and gazed at Justin as though he had just created the cure for cancer. "You're amazing, Justin!"

Warmth flooded his chest. It wasn't anything more than he did at work or most weekends at the still, but he had to admit her admiration felt pretty good. Justin cleared his throat. "Yeah, well, I had a good crew."

She flashed him a smile that weakened his knees a little. The four of them cleaned up the area until it looked as if no one had been there for ages, then Justin slung his bag of tools over his shoulder and they headed back to the truck. When they reached the vehicle, David stowed the tools while Justin slid behind the wheel.

Emily slid across the front seat until she was pressed up against him. Justin draped an arm over her shoulders as the truck bounced down the rutted road. She felt warm and soft against him, and he smiled with contentment. Yep, suggesting to his brother that they ask Madison and Emily to work with them might just have been the best idea he'd ever had.

14

A COUPLE OF DRINKS HAVING LIGHTENED THE MOOD considerably, the four of them dove into a large pizza, delivered steaming hot.

David pulled open the fridge door. "Beer anyone? I prefer it to hard liquor with pizza."

Everyone agreed, and David took four Leinies from the fridge, opened them, and passed them around.

After-dinner-clean-up amounted to throwing a cardboard box into the recycling with four paper plates. Glasses and silverware went into the dishwasher. Emily helped Justin with that as David and Madison retreated to the living room to watch TV.

Justin wiped off the counter with a dishcloth, then tapped it on Emily's nose. "I believe we were going to call it an early night?"

Pink tinged her cheeks. "If you really want me to stay, I'd love to. But you have to promise to be gentle. I haven't done this before."

His eyes widened. "You've never been with a man?"

"Nope. Never met anyone before that I was interested in sleeping with. But I've met one now."

"Good." He pressed his lips to hers before pulling back. "You did mean me, right?"

Emily laughed. "Of course it's you, silly."

He kissed her again, then placed his hand between her shoulder blades and gently guided her to the stairs. When they passed the living room entrance, he thought about telling Madison and David they were heading up, but the two of them were locked in such a tight embrace Justin doubted they would hear him - or care. With a wry grin, he continued up to his room and opened the door for Emily.

His chest tightened as he followed her into the room. As much as he wanted to be with her, he'd have to move very slowly, especially if this was her first time. Both their business relationship and their personal one had suddenly become very important to him, and he didn't want to do anything to ruin either one.

When Justin walked out of the bathroom into the attached bedroom, Emily was already beneath the covers. Her hair fanned out on the pillow. *She is so beautiful.* He bit his lip.

Emily watched him walk toward her, his towel low around his waist. He stopped and tilted his head. "What are you grinning at?"

"I was just wondering what you'd do if I pulled off that towel?"

"Fine by me. I'm not shy." He let the towel drop to the floor.

She slid over a bit as he crawled under the sheets with her and nuzzled her neck. "Mmm," he mumbled, "you smell good."

Slowly his hands explored her body, which tensed under his touch. Justin drew back. "Are you nervous?" he whispered.

"No... well, kinda. I want to do this, but I don't know what to expect."

"Don't worry, we'll go slow," he assured her. "You let me know what you like and what you don't, okay?"

"I will," she whispered, reaching for him. "But so you know, there probably won't be much that I don't like."

David led Madison to his bedroom, where they helped each other disrobe. Grabbing two towels from the closet, he took her hand and led her to the bath. He reached into the shower, turned on the water then used both his hands to turn her around.

"You're beautiful." He talked to her almost in a whisper, not because silence was required but because he was in awe.

His early impressions had been wrong—very wrong. She was a tall girl, yes, but her legs were extraordinary, slender but not skinny and well shaped. Her butt was maybe the most incredible part of her body. Rounded and full, it projected from her hips as though sculpted from alabaster. So white and almost translucent was her body, that it reminded him of the fine ivory carvings his grandfather had brought home with him after World War II.

"I'm not sure I want to shower." He stood back and gazed at her. "I think I just want to stand here and look at you. I've never seen anything so gorgeous."

She flushed and turned away from him. He turned her back face to him then bent to kiss her. As their lips met, she began to tremble and to dance on her toes.

"David, I'm cold. C'mon, let's shower."

Soon they were under the steady stream of hot water, soaping each other, laughing and exploring as they lathered each other. A half hour later, he extinguished the water, reached outside the shower, and picked up the towels.

Handing one to her, he went to work drying her body tenderly with the other.

When each area of their bodies had been dried thoroughly, they went to bed, rolled to meet each other, and began what would become a night to remember.

15

AT THE OLD STILL, JUSTIN COOKED A NEW BATCH OF MASH while Emily watched the cooker. David and Madison bottled up alcohol in the garage and loaded it into the truck. On Tuesday night, the men would deliver the 150-gallon weekly supply to Byrle Oldendorf in North La Crosse.

As they worked, Emily said, "Justin, can I ask you a question?"

"Sure, what's up?" He glanced over at her and smiled.

"I was wondering... You know last night, I was so anxious to have you in bed with me that I never asked about... about..."

"About what?"

"About protection. Did you use anything?"

He planted a fist on one hip. "Well, this is a fine time to be askin' about that, isn't it?".

"Well, I... I just... never thought..."

"Yeah, I know, you were so overcome with passion that you forgot all about it, right?"

"Umm..."

He chuckled. "You can relax. Yes, I used protection. I would never have made love to you without using protection."

Her shoulders slumped and a twinge of guilt shot through him. He hadn't realized she was so concerned or he wouldn't have teased her.

"You're so great. I was sure you would have known about that stuff, even if I didn't."

He frowned. "Are you suggesting that I have a different woman in my bed every night?"

Her cheeks flushed. "No, of course not. I didn't mean it that way. I just assumed you had more experience than me."

"I've had a little experience, I guess, but not a whole lot."

She closed her eyes. "Don't tell me. I don't want to know. I'd like to be your only girl. I know that's not very realistic, but let me have my little fantasy, okay?"

"So you don't want to know about those fourteen women in Texas, four in California, six in Washington, and—"

He ducked to avoid being hit by a steel bucket heaved his way. Emily grabbed another bucket and was about to launch it at him when he charged her, knocked the pail aside, and tackled her, easing her fall onto the ground. He rolled her over until he was straddling her.

"Stop it." Her fists pounded at his chest. "Justin, stop it. Damn you. Get off me."

"Not until you calm down." By now he was quaking with laughter. She tried to knee him between the legs, but her aim was off and her knee crashed into his butt. "Cut it out." He leaned down and tickled her in the ribs. Although she fought like a banshee, he had her pinned. As she wiggled beneath him, someone poked Justin in the side with the toe of a boot.

"What the hell is going on here? We can hear you guys all the way to the garage."

"Oops, sorry, David. We were having a tiny spat, and I guess it got a little out of control."

"I'd say." David nudged Justin with his boot again. "So what were you fighting about?"

Justin rolled off of Emily and stood up. He held out a hand to her.

"Justin," Emily whimpered as she took his hand and allowed him to pull her to her feet. "Don't. Please."

He winked at her. "Nothing. Nothing at all. Just a little disagreement, is all."

"Well, keep it down, will ya? It sounded like you were trying to wake the dead."

"Nope, just tryin' to keep the not yet alive not yet alive."

Emily hit him in the ribs. "Justin, keep your mouth shut."

"Sorry." Justin leaned closer to his brother and spoke in a conspiratorial whisper. "I'm gonna have to wait to tell ya."

"Justin!" Emily's face was bright red as she adopted a fighting stance.

Justin burst out laughing. "Or maybe not." He held up both hands and slowly backed away from his brother.

"Oh." Madison's eyes widened. "I think I know what this is all about." She grabbed David by the arm and pulled him toward the path. "C'mon, David."

"Madison, please don't say anything." Emily looked stricken, and Justin wrapped an arm around her shoulders.

"I won't." Madison reached for David's hand. "Let's get back to work." The two of them headed toward the still.

Justin squeezed Madison's shoulder and let her go. "Better get this mash cooked."

"What we need out here is a radio. If we had a little music, it would make the time go faster, wouldn't it?"

He pursed his lips. "Never thought of it. A little "Moonshine Melody," maybe? Is that what you're thinking?"

Her eyes widened. "Is that a real song?"

Justin chuckled. "Not that I know of, although it definitely should be."

"Some easy-listening music would be good."

"I've got a small transistor. Remind me, and we can bring it along tomorrow. You're right. Music would be great."

The two went back to work. Emily was uncommonly quiet and finally, bothered by her silence, Justin stopped what he was doing. "Em, is something wrong?"

"Not really."

Why don't I believe that? "Okay, what is it? Did I do something?"

"You're not happy with me, are you?"

Justin blinked. Where had that come from? "Emily, I'v never been happier than I have been since we started talking to each other the day you came home from classes. You're incredible, and last night was the most awesome night of my life." His tone was gentle, soothing.

Her lips slowly turned upward. "I love that, but do you really mean it?"

"Every word. I can't wait to spend more time with you. You take my breath away, to be honest. I hope you'll believe it when I tell you I've been thanking God since the day we first spoke for bringing you into my life. I feel like I'm walking on air."

"Oh, Jus..."

Before she could finish, his lips covered hers - gently at first and then more firmly.

"Mmmm." She moved into his body. "I can't wait for tonight."

"Neither can I, but right now, we better help David and Madison. We have a lot of shine to load for delivery tomorrow evening."

They finished up their work, and the four of them headed home. After dinner that night, Justin showered then joined Emily in bed. It was another sweet night. Finally, Emily whispered, "Justin, you are incredible. Thank you for making me feel so special."

He rolled over and pulled her along until she lay on top of him. "It's my pleasure, darlin'. Believe me."

16

DAVID STEERED THE TRUCK OVER THE INTERSTATE BRIDGE. A half-hour later, he, Justin, Madison, and Emily drove into North La Crosse. They continued along Highway 35 to George Street then turned right into the parking lot behind the Handy Corner Bar.

When the four of them walked inside, the room was sparsely populated. Three men sat at the bar, and two tables were filled. The man sitting at the end of the bar smiled, swiveled toward them, and held out his hand to Madison. "I'm Byrle."

"Madison. And this is Emily. Happy to meet you." The women shook his hand and settled onto stools at the bar.

"Me, too. When David told me last week that he and Justin were taking on partners, I wasn't prepared for them to be beautiful women. My goodness!"

David cleared his throat. "The chicken here is to die for." He held up a menu. "The fish is great, too. I'll have chicken and fries. Justin?"

"Fish and chips, for me."

"Justin and I have a little work to do outside, and then we'll join you, okay?" David tossed the menu on the bar and headed for the back door, Justin behind him.

"I'll take good care of 'em," promised Byrle, "but we might not be here when you're finished."

When the men returned, the food was up. "We brought you 105." David handed Byrle a sheet of paper.

"Great. When can you increase?"

"We need to get some new equipment in place." David leaned against the end of the bar. "We hope to do that this week. How much more can you take?"

"At least double."

"210? You sure you can handle that much?"

"Easy. We could do more, but no sense flooding the market. There have been a few questions. In fact, there's something I want to talk to you about."

David's stomach tightened. Questions? What kind of questions? He and Justin inched closer. Byrle glanced around the room and lowered his voice. "I was tending bar here yesterday evening when two cops swaggered in, got up under my nose, and told me they heard I was selling moonshine. I denied it, of course. They stayed for about an hour, grilling me. I was as cool as could be, answered their questions honestly, and when I had to lie, I think I did it perfectly."

The hair on the back of David's neck prickled. "We've been trying to stay under the radar. Guess that's over now. Damn."

"I wouldn't be too upset if I were you. In fact, it's best to do business as usual," advised Byrle.

"That's probably good advice, but I think we're gonna switch things up a little. We'll have Madison and Emily do some of the deliveries. How about we start bringing the loads to the shed up near Stevenstown every other week?"

"That's smart. Good to make a few changes to throw

them off the trail." Byrle grabbed a cloth from under the bar. "Time for me to get busy." As the group was finishing their meal, he returned with the check and handed it to David, along with a bulky envelope.

"Thanks." David stuffed the envelope in his back pocket and tugged out his wallet to pay the bill.

As they were driving home, Madison nudged him with her shoulder. "So what was in the envelope?"

"Eighty-five hundred cash." David leaned forward to pull the envelope out of his pocket and hand it to her. "That's what we get each week."

"Wow." Emily sounded impressed. "That's a lot of money."

"Should be enough for the four of us to live on, anyway." David glanced over his shoulder into the backseat. "But when we get the other still running, we'll be able to double that. And we'll have enough capacity to serve others, too. Have to be careful, though. We know the law is snooping. Wish I knew who it was."

Emily bit her lip. "Gosh, 34,000 a month. Say it costs us something around a thousand to two thousand to produce the stuff, that's 32,000 or more to split. Pretty good, I'd say. Worth the risk, even if a cop or two is sniffing around. We'll just have to be careful."

"Yes, we will." Justin pulled Emily to him and kissed her.

David rolled his eyes before returning his attention to the road.

The next week was crazy busy. David and Justin rushed home from work each day to meet Madison and Emily. They spent Wednesday, Thursday, and Friday in Wisconsin, ensuring an ample supply of moonshine to deliver to Byrle the following week. With four of them working, they pushed the still to its capacity, and by the end of the work day on Friday, they had 105 gallons in jugs in the garage.

They cleaned the still, and David shut and locked the door. "Probably best to close down the operation until Monday. I don't think anyone is paying attention, but just in case, it might be good to take a couple of days off so we don't establish a pattern. And this batch goes to Stevenstown, remember."

"Agreed." Justin rubbed his hands together. "Do you think that we can get the other still set up in two days?"

"It depends how much we get done at Wolverine tomorrow." David started down the path toward the garage. "If no one is working, then yeah, we should be able to get it done. I think I can get the rest of the welding and piping ready tomorrow. Sure helps that we have the spring near the cave. We can set the still up right there, which makes piping water easy. We've gotta get the steps in place. That means building the platforms. I'll be happy if we get that done on the weekend. I've still got some welding to do on the second still."

"Wish I could weld." Justin ducked under a branch hanging over the pathway. "That would cut down on the work you have to do."

"It would, but it'd take twice as long to teach you as it will to weld the still myself. Maybe someday. Hey, what do you think about camping out at the second still this weekend? It would be a nice change, and we'd probably get more done."

"Great idea. If we take the little welder along for the finishing work, maybe you could give me a lesson?"

"Yeah, maybe." Or maybe they'd quit their jobs at Wolverine, make a fortune in the bootleg business, then retire in style - and neither of them would have to weld anything ever again.

Saturday dawned bright and warm. "Gonna be a hot one." Justin lifted the coffee pot.

David nodded and slid a mug closer to his brother. "Is Emily still sleeping?"

"Yep. Like a rock."

"Good, so is Madison. Let's head over to Wolverine and get our work done first thing, before anyone else wanders in."

At work, David focused on the steps. Justin ran to Menard's to buy the lumber for the platforms. Although the brothers did most of their business at Kendell O'Brien's in town, David theorized it would draw less attention if they got these boards at Menard's.

"Must have some heavy work to do," said the guy working in the yard at Menard's.

Justin grinned. "Sure do. Wanna come along and help?"

"Wish I could. I'm stuck here all day. Saturdays are as boring as it gets around here. Only a few do-it-yourselfers like yerself come by for lumber, so I sit here and twiddle my thumbs."

"Sorry, pal." Justin took the slip and headed for the cashier to pay. That done, he returned to Wolverine to find David nearly finished welding the second set of steps.

"Better take the cover off the truck." David pulled on a pair of work gloves. "When I'm done here, we can load the steps and the pilings. We put the welder from home in already, didn't we?"

"Last night."

"I almost can't remember doing it, I was so damn tired. When I went upstairs, I just crashed. One good night kiss and I was asleep."

"I had a little more time than that." A smile crept across Justin's face as he remembered the gentleness with which he and Emily had made love.

"Next time you get the bottling... and I'll have the smile."

"Sure." Justin stared, mesmerized, as sparks arced from

the welder. "Didn't realize how fast you were aging. 'Course, you are much older."

"It's not that I'm older," snapped David. "It's that I work a helluva lot harder."

"My, oh my, touchy this morning. Guess this agin' thing is botherin' you."

David tipped up his welding helmet, glared at his brother, flipped him the bird with a gloved finger, and, with Justin laughing, returned to his welding.

When the steps were done, Justin backed the pickup into the shop. He had removed the cover so the steps, although heavy, went in with ease. They wrestled the pilings on top of the stairs, then borrowed a tarp from the shop and covered everything - tying it down securely. Justin studied the load as David cleaned up the work area and put the welder and materials away.

When his brother came back out, he lifted one hand. "What's wrong?"

Justin moved a board from one side of the truck to the other. "We talked about camping out, but I don't think we have room for a tent and sleeping bags."

"No problem. You and Emily can take the truck, and Madison and I will bring everything we need for camping in her SUV, including the food and beer."

Justin nodded. "Can't forget the beer."

They were back at the house by ten. The four of them quickly packed the SUV with everything they would need to stay on the property a couple of nights, and before long the two vehicles were heading north. They passed through Rollingstone, and climbed the County Road 25 hill on their way to the cave.

Arriving at the first clearing, David jumped out to open the camouflaged gate they had built. Justin idled the truck as he waited. After a couple of minutes, David appeared at his window. Justin rolled it down. "How about Madison and I set up camp? Justin, you and Emily can work on the path to the cave. We need to clear enough brush to enable the truck to be backed into place. When the path is widened, you and I can expand the opening into the cave so we can put the stairs in place."

"Sounds like a good plan." Justin looked at Emily and she nodded. "We'll do the path."

They parked both vehicles on the side of the laneway. Justin and Emily found the ground wet enough to enable them to pull out all but the most formidable of the bushes. Returning to the campsite shortly after noon, they discovered that David and Madison had set up the tents and made lunch. The four of them ate sandwiches and then got ready to begin the construction project.

With David directing, Justin backed the truck down the path to the cave. The men then unloaded the stairs and pilings, followed by the lumber. The sun was now directly overhead, and both men were dripping with perspiration. David tugged his shirt off and tossed it over a bush.

Madison sighed. "Look at those muscles, will you?"

David and Justin used ropes to lower themselves into the hole. Once on the floor of the cave, David took out a tape measure. He marked four spots with little flags used by contractors. "That's where the posts to support the steps will go." He and Justin then cleared spots for the pilings and Madison and Emily helped them push the lengths of steel into the openings, letting the heavy metal beams fall into the spaces.

"Great job." From the floor of the cave, David looked up and flashed the women a thumbs-up. "There should be four pieces about eight feet long up there. Can you drop those next?"

The women complied, and soon they were ready for the next step. "There are two step ladders on top of the lumber. Can you please tie the rope around one and lower it? Then do the same with the second?"

When the ladders were lowered, David and Justin, wearing hats with lights attached, set them up then wrestled one of the eight-foot pieces up to the top of the piling. Before long, they had the cross pieces in place and were ready to assemble the first platform.

It was hard work. When they finished and emerged from the hole, it was late afternoon, and the brothers were grimy and sweaty.

"Yuck." Emily wrinkled her nose and stepped back as Justin approached. "You look like you've been in a coal mine."

"We've been workin', Emily. What'd you expect?"

"I suspect it would be good for you to take a dip in the pool beneath the spring. I think you should use this, too." Emily handed him a bar of soap. "Take David with you."

"Sounds great," admitted Justin, grabbing her elbow when she tried to move out of his reach and kissing her. "But why don't the two of you come with us?"

She laughed and pretended to wipe her mouth with the side of her hand. "Might as well now."

Ten minutes later they arrived at the spring. All four of them dipped their feet into the pool, allowing the cold water to soothe that part of their bodies and acclimate them to what was coming next. When they shrugged out of their clothes and entered the pool, Emily began to shiver uncontrollably. Justin held her close to him to warm her up. No one spent more than a few minutes in the water —just enough time to scrub off their bodies—before jumping back onto dry land, toweling themselves off, and donning fresh clothing.

As they began their climb to the campsite with David in

the lead, a whirring, rattling sound suddenly filled the air. David stumbled backwards into Justin.

Justin stopped him with both hands on his back. "What the hell...?"

David turned and pushed him back toward the women, then leapt to the side of the path and snatched up a thick stick. David slammed the stick onto the ground, then picked it up and slammed it down again, this time holding it in place. "Snake."

The other three had been standing several feet away, but when he said that, they backed up even farther.

"It's a rattler—nearly impossible to kill the damn things. I'd like to scare him far away, though. He's damn mad."

With the other three watching carefully, David picked the dazed rattler up with the forked end of the stick, then took about five steps off the path and, making sure the others were far away, flung it down the bluff. The last he saw of it, it was slithering through the weeds.

As the four began their trudge back up the bluff, David shot the two women a quick look. Madison had gone quite pale, and Emily appeared to be checking under every branch and behind each stone as they walked. Both kept to the middle of the path, which likely wasn't a bad idea.

When they reached the campsite, David waved them both toward the makeshift table they'd set up using a sheet of plywood and a couple of stumps. "You two relax, Justin and I will make supper."

Neither of the women spoke as they sank down on lawn chairs.

"Now for food. God, I'm hungry." Justin started the barbeque, unwrapped a package, and soon the smell of grilling pork chops wafted through the clearing. As he worked, the other three put together everything needed for the meal.

After they had eaten, Madison helped David gather wood for a fire. They built a campfire, found four sticks, and broke out a bag of marshmallows. He nudged her gently in the side. "You okay?"

She offered him a weak smile. "I think so. The snake kind of threw me. Not sure I've ever seen one live before, and I'm quite sure I don't ever want to again."

"We don't see them often. It's not a bad idea to keep your eyes open when walking through the woods, but otherwise I wouldn't worry too much."

"Okay, thanks." She stood on her tiptoes to kiss him on the cheek. "It was pretty impressive, the way you got rid of it. Like some kind of superhero."

David smiled. *Superhero, huh?* He could live with that. Still smiling, he went to get logs for them to sit on. The four of them sat up watching the flames until just after ten, when David stood up and stretched. "Madison, I'm ready for bed. How about you?" When she nodded and pushed to her feet, he took her hand and led her to their tent. Time to show Madison Danielson just how much of a superhero he really was.

All four awoke early the next morning, well rested after a night of deep sleep. David emerged from his tent with Madison right behind him. Birds chirped in the branches overhead, and he stretched and drew in a deep breath of fresh, forest air - reminded of why he had always loved camping so much.

Justin and Emily had put the coffee on the fire and broken out packages of pastries, and the four of them enjoyed a light breakfast around the fire pit.

Then followed another day of hard labor as the supports

and then the second platform went into place. The second set of stairs followed until, shortly after noon when the group stopped for lunch, the new entrance to the cave was all but finished.

"Great job." David examined their handiwork, a hot dog in his right hand and a beer in the other. "This should make it easy to get in and out of the cave."

Justin nodded. "When we leave today, all we have to do is build a pile of brush over the entrance to the path in case anyone comes by for a hike."

They cleaned up the campsite after lunch, careful to totally extinguish the fire before leaving.

"That was a great weekend of work." David tossed his toolbox into the back of the truck. "It won't be long before this still is up and running too. Then we'll really be in business."

17

TWO DAYS LATER, MADISON AND EMILY STAYED HOME TO STUDY while David and Justin delivered another 105 gallons of liquor to Byrle. When they walked into the bar, Byrle rubbed his hands together. "How soon you ramping up? Got bar owners clamoring. Don't wanna keep 'em waiting too long or they'll run out of patience."

David sat down at the bar and accepted the mug of beer Byrle handed him. "We're about ready. We'll put the new still into place this coming weekend and test it. If all is well, we should be able to quickly bring our weekly load up to 300 gallons. What have you done about drop-off points? I don't think it's a good idea to bring it all here—too many people coming by."

"I've decided that it makes more sense to drop it in an area less traveled. What would you say to putting it all in my shed up near Stevenstown? That's closer for you and easy for me to get at, too."

David pursed his lips and nodded. "It's back a logging

trail, as I remember. That right?" He could picture the place; he just wasn't totally sure how to get there.

"Tell you what. Next Tuesday, you meet me at the Hilltop Bar and Grill. The shed's about a mile from there. We'll have a beer, then drive over to the shed and unload next week's supply. I'll have a key for you, so you can make the drop there each week without anyone else being around."

David held out his hand. "You have a deal." Byrle shook it and David and Justin toasted the arrangement with their mugs of beer before draining the last drops. When they walked out of the Handy Corner into a cool, sweet evening, everything seemed perfect.

"It's all falling into place, little brother." David tossed the truck keys into the air and caught them. "Won't be long before we're rolling in dough."

"Agreed. I'm anxious to tell the girls. I hope they had a productive night. Emily said she was a little behind and really wanted to catch up."

David nodded. As they drove out of North LaCrosse, he rested a wrist on the wheel. "Madison and I had a long talk last night. She's not sure, with everything going the way it is, that she wants to continue to play basketball."

Justin frowned. "But she's good. You don't think she should quit, do you?"

David stared out the front window. After a few moments of silence, he glanced over at his brother. "It's her choice. Once the second still is up and running, it would be good if all four of us were around to help. I'm sorta countin' on her, but I can't tell her what to do either."

They drove the rest of the way in silence. As they pulled into the driveway, David blew out a breath. He didn't want to keep Madison from doing something she loved, but all four of them were going to have to make sacrifices if this business was going to take off. He just hoped Madison didn't start feeling as though she was being asked to give up more than he was giving her in return.

The next Saturday morning, the four of them drove the still to the site outside Rollingstone. The copper kettle was too large to secret in the back of the pickup, so they used a large box they'd taken from Wolverine. When they got to the site, Justin was relieved to see that the brush pile appeared to be untouched.

"I'll get it." He jumped from the truck. When he found the spot he was looking for, he shoved aside the brush. David drove the truck through the opening, and Justin pushed the brush pile back into place.

When they got to the cave, it seemed the best of all mornings. The sun penetrated the clearing through openings in the leafy canopy overhead, birds sang to them from the branches, and robins scurried around the short grass, hunting worms and various bugs for breakfast, filling themselves up before delivering to their young in nests in the trees. The air smelled sweet and the temperature was warm enough that they didn't bother to don sweaters or jackets before piling out and getting to work.

Justin again pushed the swivel to move the pile of brush concealing the hole into the cave. That done, he looked at David for direction.

"I think we should get the piping down first since we need to get that into place. Think we can get the still into the cave?"

"It's not that heavy." Madison bent and lifted a corner of the box. "But it's awkward. We'll need to use the rope. Emily and I can go down and guide it into place if you and Justin lower it."

"That should work." David smiled at her.

The two brothers maneuvered the box holding the still

to the back of the pickup. Then, with Emily and Madison pushing, they wrestled it to the ground. They turned it on its side and tipped the box upside down, freeing the heavy copper object from its prison.

Once it was out of the box, David and Justin worked a rope through the openings around the top of the still, knotted it, then all four moved it to the edge of the hole.

"Let's get it over the side. Then Emily and Madison can go down the steps and guide it down." Slowly, ever so slowly, Justin pushed the big kettle over the edge of the hole until it was teetering. "David, tighten up the rope. I'm gonna push it in."

David tugged on the rope while the women went down the stairs. Justin peered over the edge. "Maddie, you and Emily try to guide it from the steps, and keep it away from the sides of the cave. A few dents won't hurt, but try to limit them. Okay?"

Justin bent his shoulder to the still, moving it enough that it dropped into the hole. "Careful now, we don't want to break any seams."

He and David slowly lowered the kettle, inch by inch, until it rested on the platform at the end of the first length of steps. Then they joined Madison and Emily on the platform and repeated the process until the still finally landed softly on the floor of the cave.

When everything was in place in the cave, David straightened and stretched his back. "We'll also need the smokestack. Justin, can you grab that while I re-check the measurements to make sure it will fit through the hole I dug last week?"

Justin made three trips to get the things his brother had asked for. After they'd fitted the pipes together, he watched for it to come through the ground. Finally, he saw it. Cupping his hands around his mouth, he leaned over the hole and yelled, "Got it!"

The brothers retrieved the stove from the truck and lowered it into the cave, using the rope. When it reached the bottom, they wrestled it into place on the floor of the cave beneath the still and did the final set-up before attaching the propane tank.

"Let's give 'er a try. Hand me that igniter, will you, little brother?"

All it took was one click and the flame was ignited and fueling the burner beneath the large copper kettle.

"Perfect. Next time we'll bring sugar and corn. Then we'll be ready to test a batch."

Everyone was in a happy mood as David drove them back toward Winona. "That went well. Hopefully everything will go as smoothly at the other still tonight."

Emily grasped Justin's arm. "I don't think I better go tonight; I have a lot of homework to do."

Maddie shifted to look back at them. "Me too."

Justin shrugged. "No problem. David and I can handle it. We'll really need you when we get the new still up and running, but until then we can do the work on our own."

"Okay, thanks." Emily slipped her fingers through his. "Maybe we'll have a nice surprise waiting when you get home."

Justin's eyebrows rose. "Surprise? What surprise?"

"If we tell you, it won't be a surprise. Guess you'll just have to wait to find out, won't you?" The teasing look was back in Emily's eyes. "Now no more asking or there won't be one."

18

FOR JUSTIN AND DAVID IT WAS LIKE OLD TIMES. AS SOON AS they arrived at the marsh, the two set to their chores with no wasted effort. David got the burner going while Justin measured the corn and sugar. That job done and the new batch started, they returned to the garage and bottled the gallons of moonshine they needed to deliver the following night.

Justin looked at his watch. "It's only 8:30."

David nodded. "You know," he said, "we could pop down to Stevenstown and deliver this batch to the shed. The key's in the truck, so there's nothing to stop us. Want to?"

"Aren't we supposed to meet Byrle there tomorrow night? Besides, don't forget we have a surprise waiting for us when we get home. I'm kinda anxious to find out what it is, aren't you?"

"Damn, that's right. How the heck could I forget that?"

"I don't know. Personally I've been counting the minutes." Justin elbowed him in the ribs. "We could load the truck though. Then, after work tomorrow night, we can head straight to Stevenstown. That will save us some time."

"Sounds good."

The two loaded the boxes into the truck. When they finished, David slammed the back closed and leaned a shoulder against it. "We're doing the right thing, aren't we?"

Justin frowned. "Whaddya mean?"

"You know, getting ourselves so deep into this moonshine business, and now involving Madison and Emily. You think we should keep going, or consider getting' out now, before it's too late?"

Justin blew out a breath. "We can't keep goin' over and over this. We made the decision to jump in 'cause it's the best way for us to actually do something with our lives, get off the path we've been on since high school. The girls didn't have to get involved if they didn't want to. It was their choice."

David mulled that over for a few seconds then pushed away from the truck. "You're right. Thanks. I needed to hear that."

Justin held out his hand and David grasped hold of his forearm. "Got your back, bro."

His brother grinned. "And I've got yours."

It was a familiar mantra, one they had repeated to each other often since both their parents had died, leaving them on their own. Whenever life got tough, it helped when they reminded themselves that neither of them was alone in the world, and that they could always count on each other.

David let go of Justin's arm and they headed for the front of the truck. They drove to Highway 35 and from there back to Winona, traveling at a leisurely 55 miles an hour. When Justin started tapping his hands on his knees, David grinned. "I know you're anxious to get home, but no sense attracting attention from the police."

"Ah." Justin stopped tapping. "I knew there must be a

good reason, because poking along when there's a surprise waiting didn't make sense to me."

After they crossed the bridge, David made a right. "I want to come into the alley from the west so we can drive right into the garage. Best we get this truck under cover right away. We don't want anyone wondering what's in it, now do we?"

"Absolutely not, but could you at least go 35? No one's gonna pick you up for five over."

"Look, if you're alone, you can take all the chances you want, but why should we gamble on losing a load of booze and earning some jail time? Besides, we're three minutes away."

When they pulled into the alley and drove toward home, Justin cocked his head. The house was totally dark. "What's with that? They weren't going anywhere, were they?"

"I don't think so. They said they'd be waiting for us. Maybe they went to bed early."

Justin's stomach tightened. Had the girls forgotten they'd promised them a surprise? After parking in the garage, they walked into the house. There wasn't a sound.

"Anyone home?" David tossed the truck keys onto the table. Silence greeted his question.

The two walked toward the living room. Justin turned to his brother. "What the—"

"Surprise!" The yell startled him and he jumped, then blinked when the lights came on. People filled the living room and dining room. "Happy birthday, Justin!"

"What the hell?" Justin's jaw dropped. There had to be forty people in his home. He shot another look at David. When he saw the look on his brother's face, he realized he'd been had.

"I wondered why you didn't say anything about my birthday today. It isn't like you to forget. I was disappointed about Emily not mentioning it, too, but I figured no one had told her. Wow. Where did you find all these people?"

Emily came up and wrapped her arms around him. "Happy birthday, sweetie. And just in case you are wondering, this isn't the surprise I promised you. You'll have to wait for that."

Warmth crept up his neck. "You've already done a damn good job of surprising me. It's quite a crowd. Where did all these people come from?"

"I have my sources, you know. You're not quite as secretive as you think you are. You have a lot of friends. And maybe, just maybe, I had a few confidential sources who tipped me off to some of them." She handed him a glass of moonshine.

Justin tipped it back and drained half of it. Probably not the best idea to serve it to all these people, some of whom he didn't even recognize, but what the hell. It was his birthday.

Emily held up a bottle. "I'm going to refill some glasses. There are several bowls of chips on the kitchen counter if you want to grab a couple and bring them out."

Justin watched her for a couple of minutes as she circled the room, filling glasses and laughing and talking to everyone. *How did I get so lucky?* Although he was enjoying himself, part of him hoped their guests didn't stay too late—he was very interested in finding out what Emily's surprise for him entailed. Heat rushed through him and he swallowed. Better get himself another drink while he was in the kitchen.

An attractive brunette stopped him as he was about to go through the doorway. Judging from the empty glass in her hand, she was looking for more moonshine. She swayed a little and he grabbed her elbow to steady her. "Hey, big guy. You're the guest of honor, right? I'm Ava."

She towered above him. "Nice to meet you, Ava."

"I'm a friend of Madison's. We play basketball together." She bent down and kissed him gently on the lips. "Not sure where Emily got the booze, but it's wonderful. I rarely drink, but this goes down like silk. I can't stay away from it. Good thing Coach isn't here."

Justin wasn't surprised to find her slurring her words, but as she turned to go into the kitchen, she tripped and stumbled into his arms. As he was trying to get her back to her feet, Madison came to his rescue.

"Here, let me help. Ava's never been able to hold her booze. Let's take her up to David's room. She needs to sleep a while."

"Who needs to sleep? I'm having too much fun to sleep. If you want to help, get me a little drinkie, will you Maddie?"

"No, I won't. You've had too much already. A little nap will do you good."

With Justin on one side and Madison on the other, they managed to get Ava up the stairs and guide her to David's bed. Madison tugged off Ava's boots, and the tall woman rolled onto her side. Before Madison and Justin left the room, she was snoring gently. They tiptoed away and Madison closed the door softly.

"Too much of a good thing." Madison shook her head as she and Justin entered the living room. As he scanned the room, Justin's heart sank. Several of their guests had passed out on the couch or floor. The few left standing swayed to the music blaring from the stereo, couples draped around each other as though they would drop to the carpet if they let go.

He sighed. "Looks like we might have a boatload of house guests tonight."

Before he could say anything more, David rushed up and grasped Madison's elbow. "Quick, you gotta come with me. One of your friends is outside and throwing up on the lawn. It's not a pretty sight, and I'm afraid one of the neighbors might complain."

Justin mingled with the guests, uncertain that anyone knew him and pretty sure no one cared that he was the guest of honor. The party was in overdrive, the Onkyo HT-7800 system spitting out Beyoncé, Madonna, and Justin Bieber at such a high volume that any guests still coherent were trying unsuccessfully to talk over the music.

As he finished making the rounds of the room, David grabbed him and pulled him into the kitchen. "I'm worried. This is the kind of party that brings cops calling, and we've got open gallons of moonshine on the table in the kitchen and a truck full of it in the garage. It's a dangerous combination."

"I agree—there are a whole lot of drunks out there. Wouldn't be pretty if the police came by. Let me talk to Emily."

Two minutes later he had hunted her down and hustled here out to the back porch. "Em, this is a great party and I really appreciate it, but I'm worried that things are getting out of hand. There's a bunch of drunk people here, and we've got open moonshine jugs on the table. If the cops come by, we're in a world of trouble."

She blew out a breath. "You're right, it's madness around here. I'll get 'em out. You cut the music, and I'll start the exodus."

Justin ran to the stereo and snapped it off. Apparently troubled by the lack of music, most of the guests stopped talking, too. Emily clapped her hands to get their attention.

"Justin and I are so grateful you stopped by to help him celebrate his birthday, but he and his brother need to be at work early, and both Madison and I have eight a.m. classes tomorrow. We hate to end the festivities, but it's time. Thank you so much for coming."

She began to work the room, talking to people as she ushered them to the door. Fifteen minutes later, the house was quiet. Ava leaned heavily on Justin as he walked her to the curb. "Do you want me to call you a cab?"

She shook her head as she pressed a hand to his chest. "No, no, I'm fine. I just live a few blocks away."

Justin wasn't convinced, but before he could protest she turned and lurched her way toward the corner. He watched her for a moment before heading back into the house.

"Whew, I'm sure as hell grateful we escaped without a visit from the police." David wiped his brow with the sleeve of his shirt. "We need to get that moonshine out of the kitchen and out of sight under the back porch."

As he and Justin gathered up the gallon bottles from the kitchen table, Madison filled the dishwasher. Emily grabbed the wastebasket and began to pick up the empty beer cans that littered the front rooms and porch.

She brought a full wastebasket into the kitchen, dumped it into the recycling bin and headed back for more. Twice more she emptied cans into the recycling canister on the porch. "That's the last of it. My guess is we went through four cases of beer. How much booze?"

"I'd say three gallons. There'll be a few sore heads tomorrow," David predicted. "I'm just grateful we got away with serving moonshine to everyone. The cops watch this area like hawks."

As he slumped onto a chair at the table and helped himself to a piece of cake, a siren shattered the late-night silence of the neighborhood. With the Law Enforcement Center just three blocks away, hearing sirens was not uncommon. But this one grew louder, until flashing lights could be seen reflecting off the walls of the living room.

"Damn, guess I spoke too soon."

Justin strode to the front window and watched as the police car stopped at the junction of Sanborn and Johnson Streets, half a block away. Two officers got out of the car and walked to the boulevard just outside Winona State's Maxwell

Hall. The tension left his shoulders. They weren't coming here. "Wonder what that's about?"

Madison, David, and Emily joined him at the window. "Looks like someone might have fallen on the sidewalk." Emily gripped his arm. "I hope it wasn't one of our guests."

Justin reached for his jacket, hanging on the hook by the door. "I'll head over there and see what's going on."

He walked down the front steps and strolled toward the corner where the officers were crouched, talking to someone on the ground.

His chest clenched as he stopped walking. Ava. Even from thirty feet away, Justin could hear her talking about a party she'd been to and the liquor she'd been served.

Not waiting to hear any more, Justin spun on his heel and, heart pounding, forced himself to meander home, even though he wanted to sprint the last hundred feet.

"We're in trouble." He closed the door quietly behind him. "It's Ava and she's talking a mile a minute. The police will be here any minute. We need to get a bottle of regular booze on the table. Have to lead them away from thinking about moonshine."

David rushed to the pantry, grabbed a bottle of Grey Goose vodka, poured a quarter of it down the sink, and set the bottle on the table.

"I'll get those empty beer cans from the recycling bin. Help me, Em." The women rushed out the back door. While they were gone, Justin searched the fridge. He managed to find a couple of full cans of beer and a half-empty bottle of wine. The girls came back in, arms loaded with empty cans. They tossed a few onto the table and the rest into the living room. Justin added the wine and beer cans to the growing collection of containers on the kitchen table.

"Sit down everyone." David waved an arm at the table, his tone an order, not a suggestion. When they complied, he said, "We're having a quiet beer after the party, got it? No empty shine bottles in the trash, right?"

"No, we washed them and put them in the garage so we could take them to the still with us to be filled." Madison started to rise. "Should we hide them better?"

David shook his head. "No time. We'll just have to hope—" A sharp rap at the front screen door cut him off.

"Let me get it." Justin stood and moved toward the door. Gripping the knob, he took a deep breath before opening the door. A uniformed policeman stood on the front porch, and he inclined his head. "Hi, Officer. You're here about the party, I imagine. When we realized it was getting loud, we shut it down and asked everyone to leave."

"You won't mind if I come in and take a quick look around, will you?"

"Of course not." Justin backed up a couple of steps and pushed the screen open. "C'mon in."

The tall, muscular officer walked into the living room, looked around, then followed Justin to the kitchen.

"Officer..."

"Sgt. Bronk," responded the visitor. "Who are these people?"

"My brother David, and these are our friends Emily Whetstone and Madison Danielson. It's my birthday and these guys threw a surprise party in my honor. I'm afraid it got a little out of hand."

"Well, it couldn't have been too bad—we didn't get any calls about rowdiness. The only call we did receive was from someone saying there was an unresponsive female at the corner of Johnson and Sanborn. She's not unresponsive, but she's extremely drunk. Probably shouldn't have been walking alone. Said she got tired and laid down to rest." He scanned the room, his gaze coming to rest on the bottles of alcohol on the table. "Do you happen to know if this woman was at the party?"

David shrugged. "Did she say her name?"

"She was a little hard to understand, but it sounded like Ava Reynolds."

"Oh, then yes. She was here." David nodded at Madison. "She's a friend of my girlfriend's."

"She's one tall lady," said the Sergeant.

"Yes, she certainly is," agreed Madison. "She and I play basketball for the university. The season's over, but training rules are still are in effect. Ava would be in big trouble with Coach if he found out how many beers she'd had tonight."

Justin's eyebrows rose. *Very smooth.* Madison had turned on the charm and Sergeant Bronk was clearly eating it up. He sat down at the table with them and leaned back, studying the table.

"Must have had a heckuva good time."

"We did." Justin's stomach tightened. Was the officer planning to stay awhile?

"How many people were here?"

"I suppose 50 or so." Madison batted her eyelashes at the handsome officer.

Sgt. Bronk cleared his throat. "We really should take that woman to the hospital. Unless, of course, you'd be willing to take responsibility for her. That would sure save us a ton of paperwork. And save you some trouble, of course." He shot a pointed glance at the empty bottles on the table.

Justin's throat tightened. Did he suspect them of having illegal booze? What was he saying? That he suspected them of having moonshine around somewhere, but he'd drop the matter if they took care of Ava themselves?

"We'd be happy to do that, Sergeant." Madison rested a hand on the officer's arm. "How about we bring her here, put her to bed, and then, when she's able, we'll take her home. How does that sound?"

Justin and David pushed back their chairs and stood at the same time.

"Sounds perfect." The officer also rose, straightened his holster, and started for the front door. David and Justin followed him out onto the porch.

The three of them walked to the corner where Bronk's partner had helped Ava to sit up, propped against a tree.

"These folks are going to take responsibility for this young lady." Sgt. Bronk nodded in their direction. "It'll save us some time if we don't have to write this up."

Bronk's partner was much younger, possibly a trainee. "Sure." The younger cop didn't sound convinced, but he clearly wasn't about to disagree with his superior.

"Let's get 'er up," said Bronk. He and his partner worked to lift Ava to her feet. Then, as she began to giggle and spew comments that Justin knew could be problematic, he and David slipped her arms over their shoulders and guided her toward their house.

"Thank you, Officers." Madison had joined them at the scene. Her voice was low and sultry, and it had the desired impact. Both men tipped their caps before walking to their squad car and driving off.

When David and Justin had managed to wrestle Ava into the house, they dropped her onto the sofa. Madison removed her boots and covered her with a throw.

"Let's go to bed before anything else happens."

Emily slid her arm around Justin's waist. "That sounds good to me. I still need to give you your surprise."

He wasn't about to argue with that. Justin followed her up to their room. After closing the door, he reached for her and pulled her close. "That was damn close, Em. Guess we'd better not plan any more parties. And if we do, we don't serve homemade liquor, okay?"

She nodded and rested her head on his chest. Justin stepped forward, guiding her to the bed, just as a knock sounded at the door.

He groaned. "Don't move; I'll be right back." Striding to the window, he shoved the curtain out of the way and stared down at the dark front yard. A police car was parked at the curb in front of the house. Justin let go of the curtain and spun around. "Damn. They're back. God, I hope this doesn't mean trouble."

19

AFTER PULLING ON HIS JEANS, DAVID HEADED FOR THE PORCH. Sergeant Bronk was waiting on the front steps.

"Hope I didn't disturb you."

David ignored the leer on the officer's face. "Nope, I was just heading for bed. Did you forget something?"

"I did. As John and I were driving away, I remembered a note we got from La Crosse P.D. yesterday. Apparently there is a lot of illegal booze flowing into La Crosse County, especially into La Crosse. You folks don't by any chance know anything about that, do you?"

David forced his features to remain neutral. "No, I haven't heard anything about that. Actually, I wouldn't know illegal booze from legal booze. I buy all mine in the liquor store."

"Well, just thought I'd ask. That woman ..."

"Ava?"

"Yeah, Ava. She was mumbling about the best booze she ever drank. Sounded kind of funny. Then, as we were driving away, I remembered that report, so I thought I better check it out."

"No. Never heard of it. Not since studying the prohibition in school, that is."

"All right then. Sorry to bother you, but thought I'd ask. Didn't think you'd be in bed yet."

"I understand. And I appreciate your diligence. If someone is distributing illegal booze around here, I sure hope you catch them. I'd like to believe we live in a law-abiding neighborhood."

"We're certainly going to try."

David feigned a yawn. "Well, tomorrow's a work day, you know. Good night, Sergeant."

"Good night."

Although the officer hadn't moved, David closed the door and returned to bed, pretty sure there would be no sleep that night.

David was silent as he drove to work the next morning, lost in his thoughts. Justin smacked him gently on the arm with his ball cap. "What's up, big brother? Are you still thinking about the police coming by last night?"

"Of course. I'm worried. That sergeant asked if we'd heard anything about illegal whiskey. A few weeks ago, Byrle got a visit from the cops. Now this guy said they'd gotten a note from the La Crosse P.D. about illegal booze flowing into the county. Scared the hell out of me."

"Didn't say anything about us directly, did he?"

"No, but I doubt he would have come back if he didn't at least suspect we could be involved. I'm not anxious to go to prison. Don't imagine you are, either."

"No, I'm not. But I'm not going to shoot the golden goose, either. David, do you know what a good thing we have going? Dude, we're making real money here. And soon we're going to be making a whole lot more. Stop worrying—we just need to be more careful."

No matter how hard he worked that day, though, David was haunted by thoughts of Bronk's visit and his message. Justin's admonition did nothing to help.

After work that night, they picked up Madison and Emily and left in the new truck, carrying the first expanded shipment of moonshine. David was driving and, try as she might, Madison couldn't get a word out of him. Finally she shifted on the passenger seat to face him. "David, what the heck is the matter? You haven't said a word since you got home from work."

Before David could respond, Justin leaned forward. "He's been this way all day—ever since that return visit from Bronk last night. And he really needs to get over it, or it will ruin everything we're working toward here."

Madison rested a hand on his knee. "David, I'm with Justin. If you let this get to you, you are going to get us caught. You need to let it go."

David snapped on the turn signal and they crossed the Black River and shifted onto County T, traveling through Stevenstown on their way to the shed. After they'd rounded two more bends and driven down a long field road and through a patch of woods, the shed loomed ahead on a knoll.

"I'm pretty sure this is it. Byrle was supposed to meet us, but he wasn't expecting us to be here yet. The key's in the glove box, Maddie." David handed the key to his brother. "Give the door a try, Justin."

The key opened the padlock. Justin pushed the door open, turned on a light, and David backed the pickup into the opening. They offloaded the 21 boxes, stacking them carefully along one side of the shed, then drove back the way they had come. As they drove into Stevenstown, Justin pointed at a pickup parked in front of the Hilltop Bar and Grill. "Isn't that Byrle's truck?"

"I think it is. We were early. Maybe he stopped for a beer,

thinking he was ahead of us." David turned into the parking spot beside the truck. "I guess we're having dinner here."

They walked in and found Byrle seated at the bar, a beer in front of him. He swiveled on his stool to face them. "Well, look who's here. Good to see you. We've got work to do, right?"

"Nope, all done." David leaned on the bar and told the bartender, "I'll have an MGD tap. And a round for the bar." He waved his arm around the room. Besides the four of them and Byrle, there were five others.

Byrle slapped the back of the man on the stool beside him. "David, I'd like you to meet Don Stephens. Donnie, this is the guy I've been telling you about, David Freeman."

Donnie stuck out a meaty hand. "Good to meet ya. Byrle says you guys are the best."

David shook the man's hand firmly then turned to his party. "This is Justin, and these beautiful women are Madison and Emily. Byrle tells me you serve great prime rib here?"

"Yes, we do. Don't mind if I say so myself." Donnie wiped his hand on the grimy white apron tied around his waist. "Prime for all four of you? How do you want 'em done?"

The order taken, Donnie went through the door at the end of the bar. Then he leaned through the opening. "Gonna eat at the bar or do you want us to set you up in the dining room?"

"This'll be fine," David told him, since the other three had already settled themselves on stools. "Byrle, you eatin'?"

"Nah, gotta get back to work. You say you're done?"

"Yep, wanted to see if I could find it. We had no problem. Backed in and unloaded. No one around that we saw."

"Well then, I drove a long way to have a beer. You get to pay for it, David."

"No problem."

Byrle got up, shook hands with David and Justin, hugged Madison and Emily, and left.

"Good guy," said Donnie. "I'd do anything for that guy."

An hour later, a great dinner eaten, the four headed home. This time David drove at a steady 62 all the way to the turnoff into Minnesota.

As they proceeded across the dike road, red lights flashed behind them and a siren triggered, then went silent.

"Damnit, now what?" David pulled the truck to the side of the road, reached in his back pocket for his wallet, and jerked his head toward the glove box. "Grab the title and proof of insurance, will you, Maddie?" He drew in a deep breath, trying to slow his racing heart, as he rolled down the window.

"Hi, Officer."

"Good evening. May I see your license, please?"

David tugged the laminated card out of his wallet and handed it through the window, the chilly night air seeping into the cab.

The officer was young, probably in his 20s. He removed his "Smokey-the-Bear" hat and bent to look David in the eye.

Then he examined the license in the orb of light from the small flashlight he clutched in his hand.

"Mr. Freeman, would you mind stepping out of the vehicle, please?"

David opened the door and obeyed the command.

The officer backed up and waved to David to follow him into the space between the patrol car and the pickup. Once there, he stopped and planted his feet shoulder-width apart. "Mr. Freeman, have you been drinking?"

The question—and the trooper's face—was devoid of emotion.

David's chest tightened. "Sir, I had one beer with dinner in Stevenstown. That's the honest truth."

"You do seem fine." The trooper glanced down at the

license he still clutched in his hand. "The reason I stopped you is that I clocked you at seven miles over the posted 50 mile per hour limit. I have been following you since you crossed the railroad tracks about four miles south. You also crossed the centerline twice and your speed was 62, also seven miles over the limit, which was 55 there."

"I don't question anything you say. We were driving leisurely back to Winona and visiting, and I probably was not as attentive as I should have been. At the same time, sir, I surely don't think the one beer I had was responsible for my crossing the centerline."

The officer cocked his head, studying him. "Mr. Freeman, I believe you. We'll chalk this one up to experience. No ticket. But before I let you go, could I check out your truck, please?"

David's heart rate picked up again. *What did we leave back there that could be incriminating? Are there bottles or other items that could tip this guy off?*

"Do you want my brother and our girlfriends to get out of the truck?"

"Unless I find something of interest in the back of the truck, that won't be necessary." The officer's voice was friendly, and David relaxed slightly.

"Okay, let me grab the keys out of the truck and open the topper, okay?"

"Just a minute." The officer moved past him and stationed himself just beyond the open driver's side door. "Okay, one arm inside only."

David grabbed the key ring, found the right key, and strode to the rear of the truck. His fingers shaking slightly, he unlocked the door, opened it, and stepped back.

The officer waved a hand through the air. "You can return to the cab. I'll let you know when you are free leave. Better give me your keys, too. Just being cautious, you understand."

David handed him the ring, climbed into the truck, and

closed the door. Madison opened her mouth to speak, but he lifted a hand.

"Not now, darlin'. I think it's best if we all keep quiet. Feel free to pray, though, that we get out of this situation unscathed."

20

DAVID WATCHED THE TROOPER IN HIS REARVIEW MIRROR. THE officer used his flashlight to explore the bed of the truck, the light illuminating the cab in an eerie fashion that suited David's mood perfectly. After what seemed an interminable time, the truck swayed as the officer climbed into the back and began what was likely a deliberate search of all the items they'd left there. The clunking and scraping went on and on. Madison reached for David's hand and held it tightly, but no one spoke.

What's he doing? Did we leave anything back there? Is there anything that can tie us to moonshining... bottles, corn, sugar... anything at all? God, he's been back there for what seems like an hour. Are we all going to jail tonight?

With David at the end of his patience and ready to flee the scene, he jumped when the officer tapped on the window.

David rolled it down again. "Yes, sir?"

"Sorry for holding you up, Mr. Freeman. You've got quite a load back there. Took me a bit to get through everything. Clean as a whistle, though. You're free to go."

David started to roll up his window, but the officer gripped the top of the glass and he stopped.

"I should tell you, the reason I took such a close look is that we are on high alert these days because of illegal liquor that's flowing into Wisconsin. We're looking closely at all trucks, anything that could be used to haul the stuff. We're especially alert to anything with a closed bed or box. You're the fifth truck I've searched tonight." He let go of the window and touched the brim of his hat as he stepped back. "Have a good evening."

The officer returned to his blue-and-white SUV, turned off his flashing lights, made a U-turn, and sped off.

"Damn," said David, exhaling loudly as he signaled and drove back onto the road for the short drive back to Winona. "Not sure about you, but that scared the living hell out of me. I'm even more scared now than I was before he stopped us. You heard him. Illegal liquor. If we're going to keep going with this business, we'll need to be extra careful to stay off the radar."

Justin reached over the seat to clasp his shoulder. "We'll use the old vehicle next time, right? Keep switching them up so neither of them becomes too familiar?"

David nodded. "Good idea. But I think even better than that is getting the second still producing to its max as quickly as possible. Staying out of Wisconsin as much as we can might be a good idea." He rubbed his forehead with the side of his hand. "Man, I don't think I'm gonna be able to sleep tonight."

"Of course you will, honey." Madison moved over until she was touching David. "I'll make sure of that. Promise."

The feel of her next to him and the sweet vapor of her perfume eased the tightness in his chest a little, and David slid an arm around her shoulders. "I'll look forward to that..."

"I think this is the night." Emily leaned over the seat and spoke to Madison. "Don't you agree?"

"Good idea. Tell you what, David, why not drop us off at the house first and then maybe give us a few minutes, okay?"

David's eyebrows rose. "Why?"

"Just because."

He shrugged. "Okay, if that's what you want."

"Trust me. Emily and I want to do our part to relax both of you."

Justin tapped the back of David's seat. "Let's drop 'em off and head to the Lakeview. I'll buy milkshakes."

Madison glanced back at him. "Now wait a minute. We like milkshakes, too, you know."

"We'll bring one for all of us."

A stop in front of their house and a quick trip to the Lakeview later, David parked the truck in the garage. "Wonder what's going on in there? Did you see any lights?"

"Nope, but I'm looking forward to whatever is behind that closed door. Quit being such a skeptic, old man."

The two walked into the house. Candles flickered on the kitchen table and the island, giving the place a soft, cozy glow. David set the tray of milkshakes on the counter. *What is going on?*

Madison and Emily strolled into the kitchen, both clad in silk robes.

David sank onto a chair and tugged on Madison's sash, drawing her closer. "So this was the big mystery?"

"No mystery. We're setting a mood, aren't we, Em? But before the next act, let's enjoy our milkshakes."

Justin handed Emily one of the milkshakes as she sat down on the chair next to him and propped her bare feet on the rung. "You didn't specify what kind, so I took a chance. This is rum raspberry."

"Yum." Emily leaned forward and pressed her lips to his.

When she sat back, Justin grinned. "You can do better than that. Although I suppose that's good enough for now."

David watched them as he handed Madison her shake. How could his brother be so calm? Didn't it bother him at all that they could have gone to jail tonight? That they could have dragged the girls into their troubles? Repressing a sigh, David concentrated on his ice cream treat, trying to get his tight muscles to relax. When slurps indicated everyone's milkshake container was empty, David pushed his cup away and propped his elbows on the table. "I hate to break the mood, but we need to talk. I can feel trouble coming. We've gotta figure out what we are going to do."

"Tonight, David?" Madison frowned. "Do we really have to do this tonight?"

He covered her hand with his. "Yes, we do. If we don't, I'll be up all night. We've had two close calls in two days. The last thing I want is to see any of you behind bars, and it feels as though that's becoming more of a possibility with every day that goes by."

Justin scowled. "For starters, if we all act like convicts, we're gonna get caught for sure." A vein throbbed in his forehead. Emily and Madison had clearly planned something special, and David was putting a damper on the evening with his doomsday scenario.

"Well, if we don't take threats seriously, we'll make a stupid mistake and go to jail."

"I told you we would be careful, and we will be." Justin's hands clenched into fists. "So we got stopped? So what? The guy was satisfied that we were clean. Why do you have to presume trouble is going to drop from the sky?"

"Didn't you hear him? They're paying special attention to trucks. They're stopping them and searching them. What'd he say, five tonight? There are only so many ways to go to Dodge. Any one of them is risky now."

"We don't have to use the trucks," piped up Emily. "Both Maddie and I have cars. We can use those."

Justin unclenched his fists and held up both hands, palms up. "There, see? Problem solved. Now that that's settled, I'd like to get to bed."

"You brush everything off as unimportant, Justin. I wish you'd realize how serious this is."

"You know what, David? I'm not sure if it's serious or not, but I do know that whether or not we talk all night, the problem will still be there in the morning. Why don't we save it for tomorrow?"

Justin got up, reached for Emily's hands, and pulled her to her feet. "Spend all the time talking that you want. Em and I are going to bed."

Upstairs, Justin danced around the room like a boxer. "God, that was terrible. The original glass-is-half-empty guy. His worrying drives me nuts."

Emily stopped in front of him. "I thought we weren't going to talk anymore." Her smile was coy, and his neck muscles relaxed.

He reached out and tugged on her sash. "I've been wanting to do that since you walked into the kitchen."

As her robe fell open, Justin's eyes widened and he lost the power of speech. After a few moments, he recovered enough to stammer, "Oh, my god, where did you get that?" He sank down onto the bed, legs weak. "It's... you're gorgeous."

"You like it?" She pirouetted.

She was dressed in a red demi bra with black lace in a few critical areas that offered a peek at sensitive spots and allowed her breasts to jiggle. She also wore red panties decorated with delicate black lace.

"My god, woman, you are an angelic vision."

"I thought you might like it."

"Like it? I love it; it's perfect for you. I want you in it. And I desperately want you out of it." He reached for her.

Backing up a step, she posed, hands on her hips, one leg cocked to the side. "Well, which is it? Should I stand here all night while you decide, or do you want me in bed with you?"

"I don't need to answer that, do I?"

Emily laughed. "I guess you don't." She sat down on the bed beside him. "I think you should do the honors, Mr. Freeman."

Justin knelt behind her. As he began to fumble with clasps and snaps, he rested his chin on her shoulder. "There's only one rule tonight. No more talk about dangers and threats, okay?"

"Mmmm. Uh-huh."

The straps parted. And so it began.

Downstairs, David had finally stopped talking. Madison yawned, took his hand, and led him to the bedroom. Behind closed doors, he embraced her, nuzzled her neck, and said, "Madison, I just can't conquer my worries. I'm very scared. Mostly I'm worried that if Justin and I go down, we'll take you and Emily with us."

"I know you're worried, my darling, but let me see if I can relax you."

She backed away from his embrace, pulling on the sash holding her robe as she moved. Suddenly her tall, trim body was cloaked in a wisp of white lingerie that left little work for his imagination. Her promise to relax him was soon met and, to his great surprise, David found himself sinking into a deep, satisfied sleep.

When the four assembled for breakfast the next morning, the brothers were dressed for work. The women were back in their silk robes.

David felt lighter, as though the heavy burden he'd been carrying around the last couple of days had been lifted from his shoulders. If they were careful, maybe everything would be okay. He smiled at Justin over his cup of coffee. "Is Emily hiding a surprise under her robe, too? Madison overwhelmed me with hers last night."

"Sure is... or at least was last night. I've never seen anything like it."

"Madison, too. Took my mind right off our moonshine problems."

Justin tilted his head. "Looks like you managed a good sleep too."

"I did." David reached for Madison and pulled her down onto his lap. "Wore me right out, this one did."

Justin lifted Emily's hand to his mouth and kissed the back of it. "Emily wore me out too. Just talkin' about it makes me want to head back to bed."

She giggled. "You may be delighted to know that there is more to come. But I think we'll save coming attractions for when you least expect it."

"Good idea." Madison ruffled David's hair. "They'll just have to wait."

His girlfriend's words ringing in his ears, David practically floated out the door. And, with memories of the night before in his head, the workday sped past. In fact, the rest of the week seemed to disappear in a flash.

Then Friday arrived and his euphoria vanished.

As the brothers left work, David took his brother by the arm. "Justin, I'm concerned about trouble—at least in Wisconsin. I'd like to steer clear of Dodge this weekend."

"I'm pretty sure you're making too much of this, but, okay, we'll go to Minneiska."

Justin tugged his arm from David's grasp. "So you know, when Sunday evening comes, Emily and I are going to Dodge to check on things. To ease your worry, we'll drive her car and go through Pine Creek."

David nodded.

At home, the four again packed the truck for a stay in the woods above Minneiska. Tonight was the first night they would fire up the still for real production, and David fervently hoped that the new cooker would be as effective as the still in the Marshland swamp near the little town of Dodge

Justin, Emily, and Madison chattered as they drove. David stared silently out the front window, drumming his fingers on the steering wheel as he drove.

Madison poked him in the ribs. "Earth to David - come in, please?"

"Oh." David blinked. "Sorry, just thinking."

"About?"

"About how after we park the truck Justin and I should walk in ahead of you and Emily and check everything out. From this moment on, we are going to have to be extremely careful, or this whole thing could blow up in all of our faces."

21

WHEN THE TWO BROTHERS WALKED UP THE ROAD AND PASSED through the first gate, there was no evidence that anyone had visited since they'd left the previous Sunday. Justin shoved aside the brush piled used to camouflage the path, then waited until David walked back and drove the truck through the opening. Justin pushed the brush into place before joining the others for the short drive to the still. After reaching the opening to the cave, the four unpacked the truck and set up camp. Besides a tent for each couple, they'd brought a fold-up picnic table, camp stove, cooler, and a second container that protected snacks and dry foodstuffs from prying predators.

Justin opened the mouth of the cave by swiveling the brush pile. The two brothers descended into the hole. Each carried a heavy sack, one of corn, the other sugar. Emily and Madison followed with other needed supplies.

Justin and David carefully measured corn and sugar and dumped them into the cooker. Justin opened the tap to water while David activated the propane heater.

The four climbed out of the cave and returned to their campsite. David rummaged in the truck, found a deck of cards, and a spirited game of 500 ensued. Justin and Emily bid crazily and won almost every blind. But when it came to scoring, they didn't fare so well. David and Madison soon reached 500 to win the game.

As they ate lunch, something whistled past Justin's ear, so close he felt a breeze. He whipped around and his gaze landed on an arrow stuck in the ground a few feet away. "What the ..." Justin spun back around, his eyes meeting his brother's. "Someone just shot at us."

David leapt off the bench. "Quick, let's tip this up to use as a barrier." The rest of them jumped up too and helped him turn the table on its side.

Furious at how close they had come to someone being seriously injured, Justin clenched his fists. "You guys stay here; I'll see if I can scout out who shot that arrow." Leaving the others crouched behind the table, he took off in the direction the missile had come from, running from tree to tree and peering out behind each one before advancing.

Arriving at the boundary fence, Justin found himself staring into the eyes of a guy who looked to be about sixteen. The kid, dressed head to toe in camo, had bulging muscles and clutched a bow in one hand, a quiver slung over his shoulder.

The kid blinked. "Where did you come from?"

Justin's eyes bore into him. "The better question is, where the hell did you come from, and what gave you the right to shoot toward our property? You just about hit me, did you know that?"

The young archer's face blanched. "I was just out having fun. I shot at a mark on this tree here." He tapped a knot on a nearby oak with the bow. "I missed. I just about hit you?" He ran a quivering hand over his head. "I'm sorry... really sorry."

"If I were you, I'd make damn sure that what I'm shooting at doesn't have anything beyond it that, if hit, could get you in a whole lot of trouble. I'll get your arrow, then you're going to get your butt outta here and you aren't gonna come back. This is private property, understand?"

When Justin returned with the arrow, the young man was fidgeting near the fence. "I'm really sorry, man." He took the arrow then turned and started back across the field.

Justin cocked his head, amazed at how quiet the woods had become, as if every living thing had sought shelter from the young hunter. *They say silence can be deafening. This must be what they mean.* The animals must have sensed someone in the area. He and his friends would need to work on developing that sense as well.

When he reached the picnic table, familiar noises started up again. A squirrel chattered somewhere overhead. A jay squawked and a cardinal sang. Were those all-clear calls? Movement to his right caught his eye, and Justin pressed a finger to his lips and signaled to the others. Two deer emerged on the far side of the clearing and, apparently unafraid of the four humans, began to graze.

"Quite a place." Justin crossed his arms and watched them for a moment, entranced by the beauty and serenity and the wildlife that shared it with them.

David walked up to stand beside him. "So where did the arrow come from?"

Justin uncrossed his arms. "Some kid pretending to be a big-game hunter. He apologized profusely for nearly killing one of us."

David shook his head. "I guess we should just be thankful he didn't."

Because the temperature had climbed in the sunshine, the four headed into their tents for a nap. David set his phone to wake them at 3:30 when the mash would be ready for the yeast.

Two hours later, David and Justin headed to the still. Justin measured out the yeast and tossed it in. With the heat turned up to nearly 200 degrees, it wouldn't be long before the mash would begin to emit alcohol, in the form of steam, which would travel through the pipe projecting from the top of the still into a heated keg.

As he sat on the stairs to the cave, a soft hand landed on his shoulder and he jumped. Emily laughed and sat down on the step beside him. "So tell me how you guys got started in the liquor business?"

Justin thought back. "One night when we were out with friends, talking about our property along the Trempealeau River, one of them told us a story her dad had told her about all the moonshiners that distilled liquor in the area during prohibition. Apparently, one time the area moonshiners, fearing a raid by federal agents, dumped all their alcohol into the river and a herd of cows drank it. They were drunk for days, but people liked the milk. Later, when David and I were recounting that story, we got wondering if we could make liquor like those guys had. David did a little research on the Internet, found a step-by-step guide to making the stuff, and next thing you knew we'd put the equipment together at work and were pumping it out. Of course it's taken a lot of trial and error, but we've pretty much got it perfected now."

"Yes, you have." Emily squeezed his knee. "Beer is still my drink of choice, but the stuff we make is terrific."

Justin laughed. "We actually tried making beer, but it was a disaster. Booze is easier and much more lucrative."

She rested her head on his shoulder, and he gently rubbed her back. "If business takes off with this new still, it's gonna take Madison a step closer to decision time. Does she stay in school and keep playing basketball, or does she drop out and concentrate on the business? I'm staying in school. I want that degree, and my parents are gonna insist on it."

"I agree. And whether or not she keeps playing ball, Maddie should get her degree too. It will be a lot of work for both of you, but if you drop out now, you'll regret it for the rest of your lives.

David lifted the last burger from the box and set it on the grill. Madison leaned against a nearby tree, watching him. She sighed. "I think it would be best if I stayed in school, and I really want to try to keep playing basketball, too. See if I can handle all that along with the work we're doing here."

David pulled a package of sausages from the cooler and tore off the plastic wrap. "I think you should too, Maddie. At least try it and see how it goes." He dropped the sausages onto the grill. "I really hate to ask you to sacrifice something you love."

She pushed away from the tree and walked over to slide her arm around his waist. "You know I'd rather be with you, right?"

He set down the spatula and faced her. "I sure hope so. I've sort of gotten used to having you around. I hate the thought of you not being with me—even for a few days."

Madison nodded. "That's how I feel, too. It's nice having a warm body to snuggle against at night."

A sly smile crossed his face and Madison swatted him gently on the chest. "Just what is going on in that head of yours?"

"This vision of white pristine lacy sleepwear just popped into my mind." He lowered his head, kissed her, then whispered in her ear, "Am I going to get to see that again anytime soon?"

Her eyes twinkled mischievously. "If you play your cards right."

He thought about kissing her again, but at the sound of branches snapping beneath feet he let go of her and stepped back. Justin and Emily walked into the clearing, hand in hand.

"How long before supper's ready?" Emily tipped back her head and sniffed the air.

"Soon." David slid the spatula under a burger and flipped it. A sudden hiss from the grill indicated a bratwurst had ruptured, sending grease onto the coals and an intoxicating aroma into the air.

"Good." Justin sat down at the makeshift table. "I'm hungry as a bear."

Emily glanced toward the woods. "Could you please not say things like that out here?"

He laughed and pulled her down beside him. "Don't worry. If any bears come around here, I'll protect you."

"Maybe we'll have time for a game after supper." Madison sat down across from them and picked up the deck of cards, idly shuffling them.

"How about strip poker?" Justin suggested, waggling his eyebrows.

Emily elbowed him in the ribs. "One track mind."

He wrapped an arm around her and tugged her close. "Can you blame me, after that outfit you paraded around in the other night?"

David set a platter of meat down on the table. "Sounds like a good game to play before bed. Right now, how about we eat?"

After dinner, as darkness began to settle in, David built a campfire. When the wood began to snap and crackle, he and Justin spread a blanket on either side of the fire and the two couples settled down on them.

They laughed and chatted for an hour before the crackling of the fire and the warmth of the flames got to them. Justin stood and held out his hand. "I'm ready for bed, Em. You coming?"

She took his hand and he pulled her to her feet. "Definitely."

After the two of them disappeared into their tent, Madison helped David douse the fire. Before long, the two of them had retreated inside their tent as well. Exhaustion trumped desire, and David wrapped arms around Madison and closed his eyes. Shortly after he had drifted off, a piercing scream shattered the peaceful stillness of the campsite.

He and Madison bolted upright. She turned to him, eyes dark with terror. "What the hell was that?"

David unzipped the sleeping bag and flung the top back. "I have no idea. But I am damn well going to find out."

22

SECONDS AFTER THE SCREAMS WERE HEARD, DAVID WAS creeping through the woods, a flashlight clutched in one hand and a pistol in the other. In spite of his efforts to be silent, he stepped on a branch and it snapped. He froze, pressed against a large oak. Where had that scream come from?

It came again, blood curdling and lengthy, finally dying out only to have similar sounds come from farther away.

Concerned that every step could reveal his presence, David crept quietly toward the source of the noise, sweeping the ground in front of him carefully with the side of his boot to clear his path of any sticks that might snap.

As he moved, another scream sounded. Closer this time, so he was moving in the right direction. Overhead, the moon peeked from beneath a cloud—a tiny slit of light in an otherwise inky sky. Even so, he huddled next to a tree in an attempt to conceal his body from prying eyes.

When the moon disappeared a few seconds later, he set

off again, his eyes on the path in front of him as he searched for any object that might break or trip him up.

As he neared the edge of the woods, he stopped and peeked around a tree. A barbed wire fence lined a farmer's field a hundred yards away. He crept forward, finally reaching the fence and dropping down to lie on his stomach in the dark. His gaze swept the fields. There it was, silhouetted against the moon that had again crept out from behind a cloud—the perfect shadow of a large animal that looked like a dog. As he watched, the animal threw back its head and howled a mournful cry.

Was that a wolf? He'd heard that some had been sighted in Winona County. A trapper had caught one last winter, so they were around.

The animal again brayed a mournful, long-lasting howl. Definitely a wolf. With a slightly nervous laugh, David saluted the animal before turning and walking back through the woods, this time making no effort to be silent.

When he reached the clearing, he made his way over to the table, following the beam emitting from his flashlight, and sat down. "Ever hear a wolf?"

Justin's eyes widened. Madison and Emily just stared at him.

David put his fingers to his lips. They sat in silence until the night was against rent by screams. Two were relatively close, several farther away. "Those are wolves," he said. Madison and Emily nodded, then pulled their blankets tighter around their shoulders and gazed into the fire. When more howls came, both women shivered. David didn't blame them. Even though he knew what the sound was, and that the likelihood of wolves attacking humans was slim, the sighting was a good reminder that dangers lurked everywhere. They needed to always keep their guard up, whether the threat to their safety had four legs, or two.

They sat for half an hour, watching the sun's rays begin to peek through the trees and listening to the sounds of the night. More wolf howls, farther away now, the hoot of an owl, the buzzing of mosquitoes. Finally Justin tossed off his blanket and stood. "We need that new still on line to make us all rich. And I'm damn ready to stop bending metal and building heavy equipment for a living. There's a ton riding on this. Let's get going."

Madison touched David's arm. "How about Emily and I make breakfast? The two of you need to get down to the cave and look at the mash."

David smiled at her as he stood and followed his brother over to the hole in the ground. A few minutes later, he and Justin were at the still and working with the mash. Then came the initial test—tasting.

"It's sure as heck sweet and smooth," proclaimed Justin after tipping the tin cup to his lips. "Smoother and sweeter than what we make at Marshland, even. The water here must be incredibly pure."

David took a sip, swished the liquor around his mouth, savored the liquid for a moment, swallowed, and then smacked his lips. "You know, little brother, I think you're right. This is as good and maybe even better than the stuff across the river. Hand me that kit, will you, please? Let's see what kind of alcohol content we're getting."

He took three devices from the kit. The first test confirmed that the liquid was the correct temperature. The second determined the actual alcohol content of the liquid, and the third measured the potential alcohol content.

"Holy cow, this is hard to believe—150 proof or 75 percent alcohol the way it is. That's much stronger than Wisconsin. Can you believe it?" He looked at the other tester. "Wow. Just shy of 175-proof. Almost as high as the meter goes; any higher and it turns into grain alcohol. We can cut it by 40 percent and have great stuff... and great volume."

"God, David, this is terrific news. What do you think about broadening our markets?"

"If we can keep it our business as opposed to taking on other employees. Doing that means staying relatively close to home. I don't think it's a good idea to go with communities smaller than La Crosse. Eau Claire, maybe. Hastings. Twin Cities' suburbs, perhaps. I don't think we should get too aggressive. Every time we increase something or add something, we're also increasing the risk factor, so we need to be very sure that we take any step forward very carefully."

23

David was thrilled to see Madison attacking her new responsibilities with enthusiasm, including making trips to Eau Claire and Wausau in Wisconsin. There she found customers eager to purchase their moonshine, thanks to introductions made by Byrle Oldendorf. While David and Justin concentrated on the stills in both Minnesota and Wisconsin, Emily kept the books. In addition to her sales role, Madison also collected payments and helped Emily identify suppliers in the Twin Cities.

With August nearly upon them, the four sat down to talk.

David poured drinks for everyone before settling on a chair at the table in the kitchen. Emily was practically bouncing in her seat, and he smiled at her. "Go ahead, Em. Give us an update."

Words tumbled out of her mouth as she informed them they now had more than 200,000 dollars cash in the bank, and they had invested close to half a million in stocks and bonds. "You could say we're rich—at least as a group."

David, Justin, and Madison exchanged wide-eyed glances.

The group was now selling 345 gallons a week and taking in 110 dollars a gallon.

"We're clearing about 34,680 a week. Do you guys have any idea how much a year that is? We're talkin' almost two million. That's a ton of money!" Emily clapped her hands before reaching for her drink.

David had been figuring in his head. Now he told them, "Right now we're delivering 180 gallons to La Crosse every week. We're sending 85 gallons to Eau Claire and 80 to Wausau. We're working our butts off, too. Everyone think it's worth it?"

"Absolutely." Justin reached for Emily's hand and she nodded. David's eyes met Madison's. Hers were shining as she nodded too.

David exhaled. *We're ready.* "Then I think it's time for the Freeman boys to quit their day jobs. Emily and Maddie, we want you to keep up with your class work to get your degrees. But Maddie, you're going to have to make a decision on basketball."

"That's already made. Talked to coach the other day and he said his plan is for me to be a substitute. We've got two transfers and a red shirt ready to play. I will be seventh or eighth on the roster. I told him that I thought it best for me to drop the sport. He understood. I kinda think my decision took him off the hook, 'cause he knows I want to play and he sorta promised me I would. He probably could use my scholarship money, too. And I don't need it."

David reached for her hand. "Are you sure?"

Madison nodded. "Yes. Completely sure. I'd far rather be working with you than warming a bench."

He squeezed her fingers. "All right then. Justin, I suggest we give our notice. Two weeks to a month seems fair, depending on what Wolverine wants. I also think we need to buy a couple of new trucks. If we free up our days, we should be able to divide up the work a little better, too. Save the women some driving, maybe."

"What should we do about those cops that have dropped by Byrle's a few times? He says he thinks they're trying to catch him selling illegal booze. When I saw him last, he was playing it cool, but I could tell he was scared." Justin set down his empty glass. "What are their names? Rouse and Bertinski?"

"It's Berzinski," David told him. "Those guys are good. They brought in that old lady who killed all those guys two, three years ago. Remember?" He tapped his fingers on the table. What should they do about those two? After a moment, he stopped tapping. "Justin, you and I need to make the next delivery to Byrle so we can talk to him about this Rouse guy and his partner. We really have to be careful."

"Sure," answered Justin.

Madison rested a hand on David's arm. "Can we go along? I'd like to hear what he has to say."

He covered his hand with hers. "Of course. You and Emily are as much at risk here as we are. You have every right to hear just how close these guys are to finding out that we're the ones they're looking for."

The ride to La Crosse four days later, in a truck loaded with 180 gallons of moonshine, was a quiet one. David's words, about how they needed to find out if the authorities were on to them, had sobered them all. None of them wanted to give up the business, but they didn't particularly want to land up in jail either.

They sat at the bar in the Handy Corner and had a round of drinks. David's shoulders relaxed a little when Byrle told them he hadn't seen the two cops for a while. "I'm sorta thinkin' it might have been routine. I'm pretty well known, especially on the north side, and they mighta sought me out because of that. But they knew what they were looking for, and I made sure they didn't find it here."

Byrle wiped his hands on his apron before disappearing into the kitchen and emerging a minute later with four plates filled with burgers and fries that he delivered to patrons farther down the bar. When he walked back to them, he pressed a hand to the bar and leaned in close, lowering his voice. "Rouse told me they knew someone was dumpin' moonshine into the market. He's got a look about him, that guy. Like a dog with a bone he's not about to let go of. I picked the other bar owners pretty carefully though. I'm sure none of them are about to give anything away either."

Byrle might have been confident about that, but David wasn't. He left La Crosse that night with a sense of foreboding.

How serious is the inquisition? Was Rouse just fishing, or does he know something? He was a great detective, and David had heard that the guy working with him was tough as nails. They would have to be careful. Very, very careful.

24

TRY AS HE MIGHT TO SETTLE, SLEEP THAT NIGHT WAS A MISSING commodity for David. He tossed and turned until Madison grasped his arm and gently shook it.

"David," she whispered, "I know you're worried. Want to talk about it?"

He sat up and leaned back against the headboard. "Oh, sorry. I didn't realize you were awake." He rubbed his eyes, stared down at the bedspread for a few seconds, then blew out a breath. "You're right, Maddie, I am really worried about those guys in La Crosse."

"You mean our customers?"

"Well, them, too, but mostly Rouse and Berzinski. They have a reputation for being very, very good. And they don't give up, either. I worry about getting caught and going to prison. If it were just me and Justin, that would be one thing, but now you and Emily are involved. You both are very special—good friends and good partners. I couldn't stand it if we got the two of you into trouble."

"So what do we do about it?"

"That's the issue, isn't it? What to do about it? That's what's keeping me awake."

"Want something to eat? Something to drink, maybe?"

"That might be good. What've we got? Anything sweet?"

"Why don't we see what we can find?" She climbed out of bed and grabbed her robe.

When they got to the kitchen, David found cookies in the cupboard and Madison poured them glasses of milk. They sat at the table and she listened as he told her everything he'd been thinking and feeling. David had no idea how much time had passed before he met her eyes and smiled. "You're very good for me, Maddie. You know just what to say to get me over the hump. You're right, I've got to let this go. We'll be careful, take a real cautious approach to things, and I'll put this crazy feeling behind me. Sound good?"

"Sounds wonderful." She took his hand and kissed him gently. "Let me do the worrying for a while. You just do what you do best. Think of ways to make us more money."

She stood up and led him back to bed, and for the first time in days, David slept soundly and without dreaming.

At the La Crosse Police Department the next morning, Al Rouse sat at his desk, a cup of coffee growing cold at his elbow as he stared out the window. The sun was still an hour away from its daily appearance. The night was dark, and Al's mood was darker. The euphoria associated with finally capturing Genevieve Wangen, the notorious serial killer, was long gone. He was again in the position of detective with a conundrum.

He reached for his phone, aware of but willing to disregard the time. The phone rang once, then twice.

"Little early to be callin', ain't it?" Charlie's voice was thick with sleep.

"It is," admitted Al. "I've been at work for a while tryin' to understand this moonshine thing, and I'm gettin' nowhere. Thought breakfast at Ma's might help."

"Great idea. Give me a half hour. I'll meet you there at ... 7. Cripes, Al, it's Saturday, for god's sakes."

"I know. 7 it is," Al said, and then, feeling guilty about the day and time, he added, "I'll buy."

"Then get off the line," snapped Charlie. "If we're gonna eat, I gotta shower."

When Al met Charlie outside the restaurant, the big guy was ebullient. He rubbed his huge hands together. "Breakfast at Ma's on you. Almost as good as stayin' in bed with Kelly."

"Better not say that," Al cautioned, "or Kelly'll cut you off."

Charlie grinned at him like a Cheshire cat. "But I'll have last night to remember..." He pulled open the door and held it as Al went into the restaurant.

"Too much information," Al chuckled.

"But, Al, it was great. We ..."

Al threw up a hand. "How about we concentrate on work?"

"Yeah, sure, if you insist."

Al was still laughing as the little bell above the door to Ma's tinkled again. The place was already half full and more people were arriving every minute.

"What the hell is goin' on here?" asked Charlie. "It ain't huntin' season. It's Saturday mornin', fer chrissakes. Somethin' going on that we ain't heard about?"

The two men took a seat at a table near the rear of the café. As soon as they were settled, Ma yelled at them from behind the counter. "Do I need a pad and pen or are ya gonna order sensibly, Charlie?"

"Jeesus, Ma... you, too?" Charlie glanced around the room. "I was lookin' for a nice quiet breakfast, and now I got a whole room full of Jack Bennys. Look you guys, I'm tired. I'm hungry, and I'm on a diet. How about easin' up?"

With everyone in the room laughing, Charlie yelled back

at Ma, "I want two eggs, sunny side up, no meat or potatoes, and one slice of rye toast."

The room quieted. This was a very different Charlie Berzinski.

Al smiled wryly. "And I'll have the usual."

A few minutes later, he finished slicing up his ham and loaded up a fork with meat and eggs. Charlie was already done.

"This diet's killing me, Al. Now what the hell is so urgent that you got me up at dawn on a Saturday?"

"It's this moonshine thing." Al set his cup down on the table. "The rumors have really grown. The chief's upset, and I'll bet Dwight is, too."

"Yeah, the sheriff talked to me about it last week. Said he's gotten several calls."

"It's the real deal, I'm convinced." Al tugged a napkin from the metal holder and wiped his fingers. "And I'm somewhat at a loss as to where to go from here."

"You can't figure out where it's comin' from?"

"If I could, would I be shelling out for your breakfast?"

Charlie took another sip of coffee and set the cup down. "Ya got any snitches can help ya out?"

"No one knows anything."

Another silence, more coffee, then Al tossed the napkin on the table and lifted his hands. "I think this thing is pretty widespread. I believe there are lots of bars involved—including some in the county."

"Aah, Christ, don't say that. I got enough on my hands with the cattle rustlers."

"You still chasin' those guys?"

"Yep. Not getting' anywhere neither. It's like those cows disappear into thin air."

"I think it's time to talk to Brent and Dwight to make us teaming up on these two cases official. What do you think?"

"Now, there's a helluvan idea. I'm all for that. And today would be a good day to talk to 'em, too, if they're in."

"Brent's in for sure. How about the sheriff?"

"He told me he'd be working on the budget in his office."

"Great. I'll call Brent and see if he can meet us at Dwight's office in fifteen minutes. We need to get going on these cases now; I want these guys behind bars and for life in La Crosse to finally settle back down to normal."

Al took the hard plastic seat next to Chief Whigg in front of Sheriff Dwight Hooper's desk. The second he sat down, Charlie, seated on his other side, flapped a hand in the air. "Al and I were talkin' and we got an idea. He wants to tell you about it."

Al shot him a look. When had it become his job to sell their bosses on the team-up? He sighed. It *had* been his idea. He took a deep breath and outlined the two cases, filling the chief in on Charlie's challenge with the rustlers, and the sheriff in on his case. "So what we'd like to do is team up, work together to try and bring both groups of criminals to justice."

The sheriff frowned. "Does that make sense? Charlie's case seems to be south of La Crosse. And, Al, if I'm hearin' you right, you think your case is north."

"That's right, Sheriff, but the illegal booze is also flowing into bars south of La Crosse, and my thought is that it might be easier to get those guys to talk if Charlie's involved."

"Might be." The sheriff nodded. "Charlie does have a way of convincing people to cooperate, I'll give him that."

Al glanced at his friend. The man's bulk was intimidating, no question. Of course, if suspects had any idea what a big teddy bear he actually was, they wouldn't be the least bit cowed by him. Thankfully, they never saw that side of him when Charlie was working a case. "I agree."

The sheriff clasped his hands on the desk. "What do you think, Brent?"

"There's no denying Charlie and Al work well together." The chief shrugged. "It might be worth a try. We've each got a big case here, and we haven't had much luck. I'd be in favor."

"Me, too, I guess," said the sheriff. "When would this effort begin?"

Charlie rubbed his massive hands together. "We'd like to get at it today."

"Today?" echoed the chief. "Can you really get going that quickly?"

With Charlie nodding, Al reassured their bosses. "We'll spend the morning catching each other up. This afternoon we'll take a field trip. Charlie can show me where the rustling activities have occurred, and I will introduce him to the bars owners who believe their competitors are selling illegal booze."

When Brent nodded, Dwight said, "Okay, let's give it a go."

"Thanks Sheriff, Chief." Al shot out of his chair, tossing the words back over his shoulder as he went. Charlie was right behind him. Neither of them wanted to give their bosses the chance to change their minds.

Near Dodge, Wisconsin, David and Justin were finishing up bottling a batch of moonshine. Justin rinsed out the cup he'd used to measure the yeast and set it down. "What's up, David? Someone do brain surgery on you?"

His brother shot him a look over the top of the still. "What are you talking about?"

"You seem lighter, almost as though you're having fun. Like you used to in the old days, before we took on all this new business."

David nodded as he loaded the gallon jugs into a case.

"Long talk with Maddie. Exactly what I needed to get over my downer. I'm gonna try and do better, Justin, not to worry so much. Let me know if you see me slumping."

Justin reached for the broom. "I will."

"Things are going darn well, and we're starting to make some real money. Maddie and I agreed that we're not gonna ease up, but we are going to be cautious."

"Makes a lotta sense." Justin ran the broom over the floor. "We've got a great thing here. At the rate we're going, it won't be long before we can retire. Wouldn't that be something? Retired before we're 40."

"It would. I like the thought a lot. We've just gotta be sure to keep those La Crosse cops off our tail. They're tough, Justin. We can't underestimate them. We'll have to be real careful we don't get caught."

His brother stopped sweeping. "Who says we're gonna get caught?"

"I didn't say that. What I said is we have to be careful. If we want to retire early, we just need to be cautious."

"David, you're my hero. You're my older brother. We can be as cautious as you want, but we're making big money, so let's keep our foot on the accelerator."

David nodded as he closed the lid on the still absently. The talk with Madison had helped a lot, enough that worries were no longer a constant part of his thoughts. Now he could concentrate on making money.

25

THAT AFTERNOON, WITH CHARLIE DRIVING, THE TWO LAWMEN moved through southern La Crosse County. Charlie showed Al where cattle had been stolen. After they had toured the sites, Al said, "All of these are near major highways. Six of the seven are within a couple miles of I-90. The other one is right off Highway 14. Does that mean they're moving the animals out by truck?"

"Could be. But I've talked to meat processors along those two routes, and they swear they haven't seen any animals from people other than their regulars."

Al thought about that for a minute. "Maybe it's one or more of the regulars who are doing the stealing. You think?"

"Possible, I suppose. I've talked to people in Vernon, Monroe, Crawford, and Richland counties and come up empty-handed."

Al pondered the statement. "Sounds like these guys are out-of-the-box thinkers, Charlie. We're gonna have to try to put ourselves in their shoes and consider what we'd do if we were grabbing livestock. Any idea how old these cows are?"

"Most are young. You think they're hanging onto them?"

"Could be. I think we need to consider that possibility. As long as we're out here, let's stop at Buck's in Barre Mills. That's one of the places reported to be selling that illegal booze. If we have time, we can also hit up Ridge View at Middle Ridge."

Twenty minutes later, Charlie pulled to a stop. Two vehicles were parked in the lot—a beat-up pickup and a new Dodge SUV. "This is Buck's place. And I think that's his truck." Charlie nodded at the pickup.

Inside, the bar was dead and dark. A few lights illuminated the bar area, but the hanging fixture over the pool table at the south end of the bar hadn't been turned on. The bartender was an old guy with a long and scruffy beard. He wore a pair of overalls and a faded flannel shirt. A wide-brimmed straw hat completed the ensemble.

"Help you guys?" Then, as though he'd just recognized Charlie, a smile crossed his face. "What brings you out here, Berzinski? Not much happens this way. You lost?"

"Nah, just thirsty," joked Charlie, looking at his watch. "Oops, too early for a beer. Not quittin' time, yet. Guess it'll have to be a pop. Pepsi for me."

"Same here," offered Al, sitting down at the bar, "and a little of your time, if you're willing."

"Sure. Ain't much else happenin' here, as you can see." Buck popped the caps off two bottle of Pepsi and set them on the bar.

"We're following up on reports of illegal booze flowing into La Crosse County," began Al. "Visiting folks to find out what they know."

The man's eyes flicked around the room before settling down around Al's shoulders. "Got me. Ain't seen or heard nothin' about that."

"You sure? Someone said they thought they had some here."

The man slammed the second bottle of Pepsi down. "Well, they thought wrong. We run an honest business here. Don't know nothing about any illegal booze."

Al fished for a business card in his shirt pocket and set it on the bar. "If you do hear anything, give us a call, would you?" He glanced around the room. "We'd hate to have to shut down such a booming enterprise."

The bartender didn't move to pick up the card. "If there's nothing else, I have work to do in the back."

Al nodded, and the man disappeared between the swinging doors that led to the kitchen. He and Charlie picked up their bottles and headed back to the parking lot. Al pulled open the passenger door and slid onto the front seat. "That's one guilty guy."

"I agree." Charlie shoved the key into the ignition. "He'd be a small-time player, though. I've been through here at all times of the day and night, and I've never seen more than three cars in the lot. How he makes it, I don't know."

The two found roughly the same thing at Middle Ridge. Although the tavern owner was an older woman who lived in the back of the bar, she was just as nervous as Buck had been. She too insisted she knew nothing.

"Sure wish I could have been in those two bars after we left," said Al. "I think we would have learned something helpful."

"You know, Al, if we turned up the heat on those two and offered them some sort of immunity, I bet they'd sing like wrens."

Al pursed his lips. "You could be right about that, Charlie. It's definitely worth a shot."

26

Although David remained upbeat and positive, the four moonshiners sat down frequently to talk about steps they might take to lessen the chance of detection. One night, as they sat around the table after dinner, Justin said, "I've been thinking a lot about red herrings."

Madison tilted her head. "You mean like taking action to throw someone off the trail?" "Exactly." Justin piled up the four empty plates. "I've been reading a book by Charlie Noble called *Red Herring*. It's about a private investigator searching for a man who is plotting to bomb an oil refinery. It's pretty darn good."

Emily frowned. "What does that have to do with us? We're not planning to bomb anything."

David had a pretty good idea where his brother was going. "A red herring is something that leads people away from the truth. I think Justin is suggesting we use some sort of decoy to throw the police off our scent."

"That's right." Justin carried the plates over to the sink and set them down. "Remember all that rough country out from

Gilmanton. You know, up the road toward Independence?" David nodded. "What if we set up a phony still there? Well, a real one, but not ours." Justin leaned back against the counter. "We could stash a few gallons of booze there, make it look as though something's going on."

David picked up a spoon and tapped it absently on the table. "You know, it just might work. Won't be cheap, but it just might work."

Justin strode back to the table. "What if we take the still from Dodge and set it up out there? Then we can build a new and bigger still for Dodge - the size of the Minnesota still, say. That would allow us to make more moonshine, too."

"Now that is a brilliant idea." David could picture the whole thing in his head. "Could really throw that Berzinski and Rouse off the trail." He clapped his hands. "Well done, Justin. You might just have found a way to keep us out of jail. For a little longer, anyway."

The next weekend, the four of them climbed into the truck and took a ride. David drove them north in Wisconsin on Highway 35. After passing through Alma, he turned to the right onto Highway 37 and followed it to a county road that led them into Gilmanton.

As they passed through the little town, David said, "All right, now we keep our eyes open for a good spot for Justin's red herring. Up here a little ways, we'll turn off the highway onto another county road, and then we all have to be on the lookout."

"Pun intended? Be on the lookout at Lookout," cracked Justin.

The women were in the backseat, and David caught their puzzled looks in the rearview mirror. "There's a little burg up here a ways called Lookout. That's what Justin means."

After another 15 minutes of driving, David made a left

turn onto a road labeled County H. "Okay, now all eyes looking for spots," he instructed. "Justin, you and Emily take the right. Madison and I will look left."

After they traveled up a steep hill and crested the apex, Justin shouted, "Stop. That's it. Right there."

"Where?"

"Back up a little, David. There's a tree across the road."

David reversed until he could see the tree, partially blocking a road that veered off to the left and angled sharply upward. "There?"

"That's it," said Justin, shoving open his door. "Let me see if I can move the tree so we can drive up there."

"What if we run into someone down the road? Maybe they have it blocked off for a reason."

"Then we just tell 'em we're lost and looking for directions." Justin hopped out and closed the door.

David joined him and the two of them dragged the tree just far enough to one side so they could drive around it.

David jumped back into the truck, maneuvered around the trunk, then climbed back out and helped Justin move it back in place. "Better hope no one's up here," he told his younger brother. "If someone put that tree there deliberately, I doubt they're gonna be real happy to see us come along."

He drove cautiously up the road, rounding two corners before they came to a plateau atop the hill. The area they drove into was about 40 feet wide. On another plateau about 20 feet higher than the one they were on stood a log cabin. The farmyard was filled with rusting machinery, but the cabin looked cared for.

"I'll bet they have this place buttoned up for the year," speculated Justin, pointing at the building. "Look at the plastic covering the windows. Bet it hasn't been used in while."

"Could be," agreed his brother.

"I think this is it." Justin glanced over his shoulder. "What do you think, Em?"

She lifted her shoulders. "It doesn't seem as though anyone's around, that's for sure. And the road isn't terribly accessible, which is good. I think it could work."

Justin reached for the door handle. "Let's see what's down there." He inclined his head along the plateau past an old barn that was weathered and slope-roofed and looked about ready to fall down.

"All right. Probably a good idea to check the place out." David drove past the barn. A little ways farther and the road ended at a field. Off to the left were woods.

"Perfect," pronounced Justin. "We put the still in those woods, hide it, and then tip the law after it's been there for a couple of weeks. What do you think?"

David clapped him on the shoulder. "I think, little brother, that you are an absolute genius."

27

It was a happy group that returned to Winona that afternoon with a viable plan to throw off the law in place. On the personal front, Justin and Emily and Madison and David were becoming better friends each day. Love had blossomed as the summer wore on.

As they sat around the table on the deck after dinner, Justin absently piled the plates on top of each other. "What's up for tomorrow?"

"Em, how about goin' with me?" asked Madison. "I have to make deliveries to Eau Claire and Wausau. Great shopping in Wausau."

"Eau Claire, too," agreed Emily. "Sure, love to."

"Guess that leaves you helping me at the big still." David handed Justin his plate. "And speaking of the still, where are we going to build it?" He held a notebook on his lap and appeared to be drafting plans.

Justin leaned closer to look. "Do you think they would let us use Wolverine on a Saturday if we brought our own material and paid them for the welding material we use?"

"Or how about we ask them if we can borrow a welder for a weekend? That way we can build it in the garage over there."

"That's even better. No one can see us move it then. Great idea."

Madison yawned. "David, I'm tired. I'm thinking it would be nice if we went to bed." She gave him a big wink, easily visible to the others, and grabbed him by the hand to pull him inside.

"I see," said Emily. "Justin, let's us go to bed, too. No sense letting them rattle around upstairs. We might as well make our own noise."

In no time at all, the house was dark... and quiet. Or mostly quiet.

28

MADISON AND EMILY LEFT THE HOUSE ABOUT 11:15 THE NEXT morning. Emily drove the pickup, the bed of which was filled with cases containing whiskey they planned to deliver to several bars.

They drove ten minutes with Madison sitting in silence, her forehead pressed to the window, until Emily couldn't take it anymore and slapped her lightly on the arm. "Geez, lighten up. We wanna have a good day, right?"

"I know, I'm sorry." Madison straightened. "I guess some of David's habits have rubbed off on me."

Emily steered the truck along the road toward Durand, finally turning northeast to Eau Claire. They pulled into Ole's Bar on the western outskirts of Eau Claire. She wheeled the pickup into a side alleyway, stopping in front of a small shed. Madison took a key from her purse, opened the padlock on the door, and the two women offloaded 25 four-gallon cases, stowing them neatly in the shed. That done, Madison walked to the bar while Emily returned to the truck and drove around to the front. Madison emerged a few minutes later, a white paper bag in one hand and two bags of potato chips in the other.

"What's in the paper bag?"

"Mmm, doughnut holes. Ole Sanderud, the owner of the bar, gave them to me." She opened the bag, held it out to Emily, and waited while she extracted one of the sugar-covered pastries, popped it in her mouth, then reached for another. "Although I don't think it was me he was trying to impress."

Emily stopped with the doughnut hole halfway to her mouth. "What do you mean?"

"He was watching you out the back window while we were working. Told me he thought you had the nicest butt he'd ever seen on a woman. I would have thought he was just being a creepy old man, except that he sounded pretty respectful, almost reverent, when he said it."

"Oh brother." Emily popped the doughnut hole into her mouth and moaned with pleasure. "If he's going to give us these every time, I guess he can look all he wants."

Brushing sugar off her hands, she slid behind the wheel of the truck and the two of them traveled along Highway 29, a relatively straight thoroughfare, at a steady 55 miles an hour. The day was sunny and bright, and the women rolled down the windows to let the late-summer breeze blow across their faces.

"Next stop, Katie's Tavern," said Madison, pushing her blowing hair out of her eyes. "When we're done there, we'll have 11,000 dollars cash. That always worries me, because it's a lot of money for a couple of women to be carrying around. Turn left at the next corner."

Emily made the turn. "Sure is a lot of money. Now you have me worried, too."

"I've been trying to find a bank that will take that much cash twice a week and not become curious, but I haven't found one I think might work. Maybe we'll spot one on the way home. I've gotta find something soon, because we've got way too much cash in the safety deposit boxes at Merchants and Winona National. That money could be earning interest, but depositing that much would be like waving a red flag at a bull."

The two rode in silence for a few miles. Finally Madison said, "You know, Em, maybe we ought to open an off-shore account?"

Emily mulled that over in silence, long enough that Madison screwed up her face. "Lousy idea, right?"

"Absolutely not. It's got me thinking."

"About what?"

"About what opening an off-shore account might require," replied Emily. "I think it's a fabulous idea. I'm going to look into it." She applied the brakes. "Is that Katie's we just passed?"

"It is. My bad."

Emily made a U-turn at the next corner, drove back to Katie's, and parked where Madison directed her, near a shed at the back of the lot. "Only five cases here." Madison pushed open her door. "When we have it in the shed, I'll run in and get the money."

Twenty minutes later, they were back on the road to Wausau. Madison rested her head on the back of the seat until they passed a crossroads that told them they were 10 miles from Wausau. "Almost there," said Madison. "I'll tell you where to turn, Em."

Soon they were at Halverson's. This time, Madison unlocked a window in the side of the building and climbed down inside. Emily shoved 50 four-gallon cases down a chute into the basement, where Madison caught them and stacked them at the side of the room. When the last of the cases slipped down the slide, Emily closed the window and locked it, then returned to the truck to wait for Madison.

After twenty minutes, she became worried. She left the truck, locked the door, and walked into the bar. It took her a few minutes to become accustomed to the dim light, but when she did, she saw Madison immediately.

Her friend was seated on one side of a booth, a swarthy-looking guy on each side of her. Across the table were two more tough-looking men. Madison looked frightened.

Emily stalked over to the booth and planted her hands on her hips. "What's going on here?"

"Just havin' a little chat," said one of the men, his gray hair proclaiming him the oldest of the group.

"And we're done now. It's time for us to go," said Madison, clearly trying to inject more bravado into her voice than she felt.

The big guy in her way slid off the end of the bench to let Madison out of the booth. As the women turned to leave, the older man called after them, "Think about it, little lady. We'll need an answer next week."

As they exited the back door of the bar, Emily grabbed Madison, who had hurried ahead of her, by the arm. "What the hell was that about, Madison?"

"Let's get out of here, okay?" Madison shook free of Emily's grasp and jogged toward the truck. "Hurry. I'll tell you as we drive."

Madison got them to Highway 51, where they turned south. After a few miles, she looked at her companion and said, "That was terrible."

"What did they want?"

"They were demanding payments."

Emily frowned. "Payments? For what?"

Madison slumped down on the seat, her head against the window. "Can we talk about this later? I need a few minutes."

"Sure." Emily reached over and squeezed her hand.

They reached Stevens Point, and Emily steered the truck westward on Highway 54, then turned again, this time onto Highway 95. They drove steadily for more than a half hour. Then, with the truck pulling into Hixton, Emily pulled off near a ball field and said, "Okay, sister. Time to talk. What's up?"

Madison shuddered, and Emily reached for her hand. Her friend drew in a shuddering breath. "Those guys were real mean, Em. I'm worried they're going to kill me." Emily's head jerked. "Kill you? What do you mean? That's not going to happen, Maddie, trust me. Those guys are not going to harm one hair on your head. I won't let them and neither will David and Justin."

Madison exhaled. "I guess you're right."

"Let's get home and tell them what happened, okay? Maybe they can talk to the bar owner, figure out what's going on. If they threaten to stop production, I'm sure the owner will do everything he can to handle those guys." When Madison nodded, she shifted the truck into low, pulled onto the highway, went through the gears as they turned through the town, and traveled back into the country. It was a beautiful day. Fresh breezes carried odors that ranged from alfalfa to the zoo-like smells of the small dairy farms along the route through the open windows.

After a few minutes of silence, Emily glanced over at her friend. "What exactly did those guys say to you?"

"They're with the mob—the Chicago Machine they said. They want us to pay them two thousand a week to deliver to Eau Claire and Wausau, or they promised me I would be dead." Her voice quivered.

Emily reached over and gripped her forearm. "Look Maddie. We knew there would be risks when we agreed to work with David and Justin, right?"

Madison nodded. "Of course."

"Well, this is what we signed on for. We can't freak out when stuff like this happens. If we're going to, we might as well quit now. Do you want to do that?"

Madison shook her head emphatically. "No. Definitely not."

"Good. Me neither. So we have to take the bad with the good. All that money doesn't come with no strings attached, you know. But we don't have to deal with this alone. The four of us will discuss it and find a solution. Okay?"

"Okay. Thanks, Em."

Emily pulled back her hand. "No problem. We all have to have each other's backs."

A half hour later they were in the house, the truck parked safely in the garage.

"I need a drink. Bloody Mary?"

"Make mine a bloody-shiny." Madison pushed back her shoulders as she asked for a drink she had concocted that substituted moonshine for vodka with the spicy tomato sauce.

"Good idea. I'll have one of those, too. Wonder where the guys are?"

The women sipped and nibbled celery sticks, each of them lost in thought. When the drinks had disappeared, Emily rose and mixed another. No sooner had she sat back down than noises in the alley indicated the men were home.

David walked in, looked at the half-filled glasses, and said, "If that's a bloody, I'll have one, too."

"Mary or shiny?" Emily held up a jug of moonshine.

"Shiny."

"Me too." Justin followed him through the door. He kissed Emily and went to the sink to wash his hands.

David looked exhausted as he slumped onto a kitchen chair with a thud. "Man, what a day. But we got a lot done. We put together enough mash for 200 gallons. We worked damn hard, let me—" He frowned and straightened up. "Madison? What's wrong?"

She blinked. "What makes you think something's wrong?"

"You're holding that glass hard enough to break it."

"Oh." She glanced down at the glass and let go of it.

"Plus I can see in your eyes that you're upset. Did something happen today?"

"I guess I am a little upset."

Madison sighed and told them about the men in Wausau. Emily watched David as Madison talked. By the time she had finished, he was holding his own glass so tightly his knuckles were white. He tugged Madison's chair closer to his and slid an arm around her shoulders. "I'm really sorry that happened, Maddie." David pressed his lips to her temple. "They said they were with the Chicago mob?"

Madison nodded.

"This is not good. Not good at all." David took another drink. "I think we're in deep shit."

Justin leaned forward. "But they said 2,000 a trip and we're safe, right?"

Madison bit her lip. "That's what they said."

He shrugged. "So how about we look on the bright side? Of course they want money, since we're encroaching on their territory. But we can afford to pay the price, so why don't we see what they have to offer? What does the 2,000 a week get us? They say safety, okay, what's the offer? Expanded markets? How big are they talking? Before we dive off the deep end here, how about we talk to them? At least find out some things?"

"Crap. I knew it… too big too fast." David tipped back his glass and took a big swig.

All four of them started in, talking over each other for several minutes, until Justin slammed a palm down on the table and the other three fell silent. "Enough, dammit, enough!"

Emily reached for his hand. Justin was incredibly attractive when he took charge, but she didn't want him getting too worked up either. He squeezed her fingers. "We can sit here talking about the sky falling. Or we can contact these guys and then prepare ourselves for a critical meeting with them. You do what you want to, but I'm gonna be ready when we do talk to them. And the conversation ain't gonna be one-sided, either."

"You're right, Justin." Emily reluctantly let go of his hand. "We need to discuss this calmly. Working with these guys is probably our best bet. Why don't I order us a pizza and we can decide what our next steps should be."

When the pizza arrived half an hour later, they all grabbed slices to go with their drinks and kept talking. By the time the box—and the jug of moonshine—was empty, they had a plan. If the other group were amenable, David and Justin would make the trip to Wasau on Saturday. Their first job would be to find out the details of any agreement. What was in it for them if they agreed to pay? If they were satisfied with the benefits plan, the next job would be to negotiate price. They would play good cop/bad cop. Justin would handle most of the talking, and David would be the bad cop.

Still thinking about Justin taking charge of the meeting and reining everyone in, as soon as the discussion ended, Emily took his hand and led him up to the bedroom. When she screamed in ecstasy a while later, Madison and David laughed loudly.

Justin jumped out of bed and charged over to the door. He opened it a crack. "Just because you didn't have as much fun as we did doesn't mean you have the right to laugh."

Emily laughed herself when David called back, "Just let us know if you're planning on another round, because we would really like to get some sleep."

29

Now that they had their bosses' approval, Al and Charlie dove into their cases headfirst. A little after 9 on Monday morning, Al jumped into the passenger seat of Charlie's black-and-white SUV, and the two drove south out of La Crosse, headed for Newburgh Corners.

Joe Wise was a tall, lanky man with a wide smile and a weathered face dusted by wisps of hair cut short on his head. They found him using a skid steer to move large round bales to the farm's feedlot. He stopped the loader when the SUV entered the farmyard, then removed worn leather gloves from hands that were gnarled and brown.

"Hi, Charlie," he said, smiling and offering a hand to the deputy. "Been waitin' for you guys."

Charlie introduced Al to the rancher, who gripped his hand tightly before nodding at the house. "Let's go inside. I need a cuppa coffee. Bet Diane's got a treat for ya. She was whippin' up somethin' when I finished breakfast."

The two men followed him inside. The kitchen was homey but spacious, bright with natural light, and presided over by a woman of medium height who wore an apron over her dress and a warm, wide smile.

"Hi, fellas. Joe said you might be coming by today, so I threw together some blueberry cobbler. How about a piece?"

When Al started to protest that they had just finished breakfast, Charlie quickly jumped in. "Ma'am, we did just have breakfast, but we saved room for cobbler. Al, you've never had Diane's baking. You're in for a treat."

The big guy was right. The light and fluffy fruit dish almost floated to their mouths and, in spite of thinking he was full, Al found he had room for two helpings.

Joe only picked at his food. Finally, he set down his fork. "I sure appreciate you two coming out. Lost two more head of livestock yesterday. This keeps up much longer and I'll be outta business."

Charlie swallowed the bite of cobbler he'd just shoved into his mouth. "Sorry to hear that, Joe."

Al wiped his face with a napkin. "Me too. Believe me, we want to catch these guys as badly as you want us to."

"When you're finished there," Joe shoved back his chair, "there's something I'd like you both to see."

Al and Charlie finished up quickly and Al carried their dishes over to the sink as Charlie gave Diane a hug. "Best cobbler ever," he proclaimed as he let her go.

Her cheeks flushed as she shooed them out the door with a dish towel. "Go on now."

Al touched the brim of his hat before he stepped outside. "Ma'am."

He and Charlie crossed the yard to Charlie's SUV. Al slid into the back seat so Joe could direct Charlie to a spot at the rear of his farm.

"Careful now," he cautioned as they approached a field gate. "Stay to the right. What I want to show you are tire tracks in the mud over there."

When they exited the vehicle, Joe led them to an area where they could see a distinct tire track displayed prominently in the mud from a rainstorm the day before. "I keep young stock in the pasture back here. As I said, I lost two of 'em last night. But that track there, which looks to be from a trailer, is as unusual as I've ever seen."

Al studied the treat marks. They *were* different, featuring a tread comprised of crossed-X markings.

"Thought you might be able to run this one down since it's so unique," offered the rancher. "Especially if he happened to get these wheels from some local shop."

"We're sure gonna try," Charlie assured him while taking photos of the tread. Al retrieved a work kit from the truck and mixed a plaster compound that he poured over the tread. The mixture hardened quickly, and when Al picked it up, he showed them a perfect cast of the tread.

"That'll help." Charlie slid his phone back into his pocket. "It's different, that's for sure."

After they had delivered Joe back to the farmyard, they dropped him off with assurances that they would pursue this lead and let him know what happened. The two of them then headed straight to an implement dealer in Middle Ridge.

Al showed the plaster cast to the dealer, who called for his shop foreman. The man examined the tread closely and shook his head. "I ain't never seen anything like this. Gotta be something special. I'd check with the folks at Frenchville Trailer up near Ettrick."

Charlie and Al thanked the men, got back in the truck, and Charlie pointed them north. "Let's stop at Buck's again, see if we can pressure him a little about the illegal booze. When we've done that, we can drive up to Ettrick to talk to the trailer guys. Sound good?"

"That'd be great. Thanks." Al drummed his hands on his knees, impatient to get there. Now that Charlie could officially use his influence in the area to try to ferret out information, would they finally get somewhere? The two men drove in relative silence until they pulled up at the ramshackle bar in the rural area. There were only two vehicles in the lot. "Good, not too busy," noted Charlie. "Let me take the lead, Al, okay?"

Al nodded and the two headed into the dimly lit interior of the bar, the familiar smell of stale beer and fried foods greeting Al's nostrils.

"Well, lookee here!" announced Buck through the beard that covered the lower half of his face, only a tiny round circle indicating where his mouth was. "What can I do for you boys?"

"Few questions for you, Buck," said Charlie, clasping his hand. "You remember Al Rouse of the La Crosse Police Department?"

"Sure. You guys was in the other day."

"That's right." Charlie settled onto one of the red-topped stools, ripped and patched with a variety of duct and electrical tape.

The jukebox offered a selection of classic country tunes in the background while the two officers went at Buck with everything they had. After about 15 minutes, they had the bartender sufficiently flustered to hit him with the heavy questions.

"C'mon, Buck." Charlie smacked a palm down on the bar. "We know you're sellin' illegal booze. Enough of your regulars told us so that we know it for a fact. I can go get a warrant while Al stays here to make sure you don't dispose of anything. If I do that and we find anything, you're outta business. You want that?"

When Buck looked down at the bar and shook his head, Al knew they had him. The older man had lost all his bluster. He looked as though he was ready to cry.

"If you help us out," Al leaned over the bar and lowered

his voice, "we might just look the other way, so you can keep operating. Of course, we might expect you to testify if there are any arrests, but that's kind of a long shot."

That did it. Buck caved. He glanced around the bar before blowing out a long breath. "All right, you got me. I've been buyin' two gallons a week of moonshine, pourin' it into empty whiskey bottles, and selling it across the bar. It's real good stuff—the customers love it."

Al frowned. "Where does it come from?"

"I get it from Byrle Oldendorf up in La Crosse. One of his guys comes by here every Tuesday."

"You always sell out?" Charlie cocked his head.

"Always. Folks love it. Smoother than anythin' else I sell. Women like it, too. They take it with Coke or 7-Up. Doubled my business since I started handlin' it."

After a few more minutes of conversation, and with the bar beginning to fill up with folks looking for burgers and fries, Al stood up. "We appreciate your cooperation Buck. We'll likely be back to see you, but for now we'll need you to keep quiet about this conversation. We suspect you blab to anyone else and all bets are off."

Buck threw his hands in the air. "Who'm I gonna tell? Don' wanna spoil a good deal, now do I?"

Al threw one last warning glance at him before following Charlie out of the bar.

"I think we've got it, partner," said Charlie as he piloted the truck north. "Now let's see if we can have as much luck up in Ettrick."

The day was beautiful, sunny and fresh as only summer can be. Both men rolled down their windows, and the drive passed quickly as they turned north on Highway 53 at Galesville then grabbed Trempealeau County T before getting to Ettrick.

They pulled into Frenchville. The only thing that

distinguished it from the rural country they had been passing through was the implement dealership, which sprawled across several acres.

"Damn, must be 10,000 trailers here." Charlie ran a hand over his head. "Guess we know why they sent us up here."

Walking into the dealership, they were met by a man displaying a wide smile and dressed in a plaid shirt and chinos.

"Gentlemen," he said in a booming voice that echoed across the spacious showroom filled with trailers and small tractors, "how can we help two of La Crosse's finest? I assume you're not here to look at trailers."

Charlie and Al shook hands with the man, whose nametag identified him as Bob Barton, then Charlie explained they were looking for a particular and unusual brand of tire. "At least, we think it's unusual."

Al showed Barton the photos. "We have a cast of the treads in the truck if you want to see it."

Bob nodded. "Why don't you go grab it and then I'll take you to the stock room where you can talk to LeRoy Olson, our parts manager and chief mechanic."

Al jogged out to the truck and retrieved the cast. When he came in, Olson was studying the pictures Charlie had taken. As soon as he saw the cast, he said, "That's an Otani. Made in Thailand. Don't see many of 'em. There's a small trailer maker over in the Appleton area, Decker Trailers, that uses 'em. Prob'ly haven't seen four of 'em in 10 years."

Al shot a glance at Charlie. Decker Trailers. He made a mental note as Olson handed the cast back to him. "Thanks for your help."

Olson nodded. "Any time."

Charlie and Al headed back to La Crosse. Al leaned back in the passenger seat and crossed his arms over his chest. "Well, we've made some progress today, at least."

"For sure. But we've got work to do now." Charlie signaled and changed lanes. "We gotta see that Oldendorf guy and head over to Appleton for a chat with the folks at Decker Trailers. Which one do you wanna do first?"

"Not sure." Al pursed his lips. "I'm biased to the liquor case, and I imagine you're partial to the cattle case. Should we flip a coin?"

"Fine with me," agreed Charlie, "but I wanna see the coin before you flip."

Al fished a quarter from his pocket and held it up. "Heads it's Decker, tails it's Oldendorf, okay?"

When Charlie nodded, Al sent the quarter soaring to the top of the cab, caught it, slapped it down on his wrist, and moved his hand to reveal the image of George Washington. "Decker it is!" Charlie smacked the steering wheel. "When should we go?"

"Let's strike while the iron's hot. Since we've both cleared our plates and only have these two cases, let's not wait. We can hit Ma's first thing tomorrow, get an early start, and be back in time for supper."

"Sounds good to me," agreed Charlie. "How about we take the girls out for dinner when we get home; that way they won't be waitin' on supper if we're late."

Al tapped his fingers on the armrest. Now that they had leads to follow up on, he'd be happy to head right over to Appleton tonight. He'd made the mistake of letting a case consume him in the past, though, and he wasn't about to do that to his wife again.

30

ON SATURDAY MORNING, DAVID PULLED ON HIS JACKET AND clapped his brother on the back. "Ready?"

Justin shrugged. "As ready as I'll ever be to meet up with the mob, I guess."

"We're coming too." Madison grabbed her coat from the hook by the door as Emily tugged on her sneakers.

David frowned. "Are you sure? I didn't think you'd want to be anywhere near those guys again."

"I don't, but I don't really want you near them, either. Em and I can wait in the truck and listen in on my phone. If things turn ugly, we can call the cops."

David pulled open the door. "That'd be the end of our business."

"Right, but better the business end than your lives."

He couldn't argue with that. The four of them piled into the truck and drove to Wausau. David pulled around the back of the bar and they unloaded a hundred cases of booze. When they'd finished, he drove around to the front and parked. He pulled the phone from his pocket and dialed

Madison's number. When she answered, he slid the phone back into the pocket of his coat. Leaning across the seat, he kissed Madison. "Wish us luck."

She grimaced. "Good luck." When he started to pull back, she grabbed his arm. "Be careful, please. Those are not nice men."

"Got it." He smiled at her and pushed open the door of the truck. When he and Justin walked in, a group of men at a table in the corner all turned to stare at them. The rest of the bar was empty, and David rubbed his damp palms on his jeans. Had they told everyone else to leave? Or had other customers come in and, seeing the table filled with clearly unsavory characters, turned around and left? Would that be the smart thing for him and Justin to do?

Before he could move, one of the men, mean looking with a scar that ran from his right ear to the corner of his lip, shot a hand into the air. "Mornin'." His nasty-sounding voice boomed across the deserted room. "We been waitin'. Shoulda seen us before unloadin' the booze. Now you might have to load it back in the truck before you head home, aye, Franco?"

"Right," another of the men answered him. David's eyes narrowed. Franco was the name of the man Madison said had tried to scare her with his threats. His fists clenched, but he forced a neutral expression onto his face as he crossed the room, his brother at his heels.

"Ya ready ta make a deal?" Franco, a bull of a man with broad shoulders and the build of a fire hydrant, kicked an empty chair away from the table.

"We came to tell you that if you want to make a deal, last week was the last time you scare one of our partners," said David. In spite of his sweaty palms, he was angry enough at their treatment of Madison that his voice came out clear and his tone firm.

"Listen ta the young fella, will ya?" Franco nudged his neighbor and laughed. "Thinks he's in charge er somethin'."

"C'mon, Justin." David spun on his heel and started back for the door. "These guys don't wanna talk, they just wanna sound tough. Let's get outta here."

No more than a second had passed before Franco called out, "Get yer asses back here! Can't cha take a little kiddin'?"

David's eyes met his brother's. Justin nodded slightly. Exhaling loudly, David whirled around and stalked back to the table. It helped to know that the girls were listening in and would call for backup if needed.

"Whad'll ya have?" asked Franco, clearly the mouthpiece of the group.

"Wouldn't be much of a businessman if I drank anything but my own booze, would I?" David dropped onto the chair Franco had pushed away from the table.

Justin pulled out the one beside him and sat down. "I'll have mine with some bloody Mary mix."

David nodded. "Me too."

Franco tipped his chair back on two legs and hollered toward the bar, "Bring us two special bloodies, will ya, Beth?"

No one spoke until a woman in an apron came over and lifted their drinks off a tray, setting them down in front of David and Justin with shaking fingers before scurrying back to the bar. Franco picked up his own glass and held it in David's direction. "To coming to a mutually beneficial arrangement."

David didn't lift his glass to meet it. "We'll clink glasses if a deal is made."

Franco studied him for a moment before shrugging and setting down his glass. "Then let's make a deal."

For the next half hour, the discussion went back and forth. Franco crossed his arms over his massive chest. "Like we told your friend last week, our fee is 2,000 dollars a week - cash."

David clutched his glass tightly. "That's a lot of money. What does it get us?"

"Your lives, for one thing." The other men around the table all laughed. "Plus we'll allow you to continue to deliver booze in Eau Claire and Wausau every week."

David shook his head. "For that kind of money, we'll need more than that."

"If yer talkin' expansion, there ain't much for towns around here," Franco waved a hand through the air. "Mosinee is one—not much of a town but a heckuva busy area. Town's only a couple thousand, but the area is huge into recreation because of the water around there. Must be a hundred taverns in the region."

"Yeah," the man who had hollered at them when they came in, nodded. "It's all because of the boatin' and fishin'. Lots of booze sold in that area. We can get'cha in there. Right, Franco?"

"Maybe." Franco lowered the front two legs of his chair to the floor with a bang. "Look, you guys agree to the two thousand a week and here's what we can do—we guarantee your safety and get you enough of them deals to drop another 200 gallons a week in the Mosinee area. We can handle distribution," said Franco. "'Course, it'll cost ya."

David shook his head. "We can distribute it ourselves."

Franco stared at him until David's shoulders slumped. "Okay, twelve-fifty a week."

That elicited an evil-sounding laugh from Franco but no other response. David gritted his teeth. "Fine. 1500."

They went back and forth for a while, finally settling on 1800 dollars a week.

"We were too generous," Franco picked up his glass and drained it, "but we got much bigger plans for you folks."

David shoved back his chair. "I think that's enough plans for one day."

"Suit yourself." Franco held up his empty glass. "To a lucrative partnership."

It really could be. Reluctantly, David scooped up his own glass and clinked it to Franco's. "And to everyone keeping their word."

Franco scowled. "You keep up your end of the bargain, and we'll keep up ours."

"For that kind of money, I certainly hope so." David stood up. "Let's go, Justin."

His brother followed him to the door. Neither of them looked back as they headed out of the bar and into the parking lot. David squinted in the bright sunlight as they strode across the lot to the truck.

As soon as he opened the door, Madison shoved her phone into her bag. "How did it go?"

David shoved the key into the ignition and started the engine. "Let's get out of here. We can talk on the way."

Five minutes down the road, Justin leaned forward and smacked him lightly on the arm. "You did great, bro."

"So you think it went well?" asked Madison.

David lifted his shoulders. "You heard it, right? We gave up something and we got something, too. Under the circumstances, I think it was the best we could have done."

"I agree." Justin sat back on his seat. "I think they got what they wanted, but we did pretty damn well, too."

Emily spoke up from the back seat. "Sounds like you committed to a lot more production, though - at least a third more. Can we handle that?"

"Good question." David's gut twisted. Could they handle that many more gallons? What if they weren't able to produce that much? Would these guys come after them? Visions of big, burly men showing up at their house and threatening to break their legs drifted through his mind and he repressed a shudder. "Once we have the new still working, I'm sure we can. And actually, after today, we really don't have a choice."

31

WHILE THE GROUP IN WINONA WAS THINKING ABOUT THEIR growing business, Al was accompanying Charlie to talk to the folks at Decker Trailers in Appleton. Charlie had made a call the day before to ensure that the right people would be around when they arrived, even though it was the weekend.

"Really nice guys," he'd told Al as they walked out of Ma's and got ready for the drive. He opened the door of his SUV, then farted loudly enough that Al was pretty sure the patrons left in the restaurant had heard. "Damn good breakfast," he said with a satisfied smile as he slid behind the wheel.

Al frowned. "Close that door, will you? I don't want the smell in the truck, 'cause it will linger there for the whole damn trip. We've got a long ride ahead of us, you know?"

"'Course I know," said Charlie, complying with Al's request.

Shaking his head, Al climbed into the SUV and buckled in.

Charlie shifted the vehicle into gear. But before he took his foot off the brake, he shot a look at Al. "Ya know, yer one damn sourpuss this morning. What's the matter, didn't JoAnne treat you nice last night?"

Al didn't respond, so Charlie began to drive, heading toward I-90. From time to time he glanced at Al, who stared straight ahead without comment.

Charlie fidgeted on the seat. Finally, he looked at his friend and said, "So what the hell's eatin' you? Yer like a frickin' wet blanket. You weren't that way at breakfast. What the hell did I do?"

Al exploded in laughter, elbowing his buddy in the ribs. "I was just seeing how long it would take before the silence drove you crazy." He glanced at his watch. "Three minutes—might be a new record."

"Okay, ya got me." Charlie scowled. "Ain't very nice to treat a friend like that, though."

Al pressed his lips together to keep from laughing as Charlie, dour and determined, floored the gas pedal and the Ford SUV roared onto the freeway.

"Geez!" Al gripped the dashboard with both hands, "If you're gonna drive like a maniac, you better turn the lights and siren on so it looks like we have somewhere to go in a hurry."

Charlie reached down and snapped on the emergency lights and activated the siren. The SUV screamed down the highway, cars scattering out of the way, until they cleared Bangor and the road freed up ahead of them. He then eased off the accelerator, killed the lights and siren, and settled into a steady 75, the cruise control set.

"Better," said Al, releasing his grip on the dashboard. "At least I don't feel like I'm about to die at any moment."

"For cripes sake, ya were like a mummy fer a while there. Had ta do something to get ya back on track. Otherwise, it was gonna be a helluva long trip."

Al shifted on the seat to face him. "Things goin' well for you and Kelly?"

"Perfect." A smile spread across his friend's face. "You know, Al, I sure as hell wasted a ton of years with that witch of a woman. Charlene was a bitch, you know that?"

"Although I never saw her as a 'bitch,' I saw her at some pretty bad moments," agreed Al. "But you have to look at the bright side, Charlie. You're happy now. Kelly is a remarkable woman, that's for sure, but in your eyes she's a total angel. She's a good woman, and compared to Charlene she *is* an angel."

"That's true. How you doin' with yer love life?"

"Things are great. JoAnne is wonderful. After that bad spell three years ago, our relationship has grown really strong again. All I can say is, I'm truly blessed. I thank God for that every day."

Charlie drove on in silence, steering the truck through Omro and into Oshkosh before swinging north on I-41 toward Appleton. Not long after turning north, Charlie followed his GPS unit and swung east on West Wisconsin Avenue for just a little way before going south on North Lyndale Drive. Four blocks later they saw Decker Trailers on the left. Charlie turned into the parking lot, and he and Al got out of SUV, stretched, and walked into the business.

A beautiful woman, tall and slender, who looked phenomenal in the tight-fitting jeans and top she was wearing, approached them. "I'm Rhonda," she said. "How can I help you gentlemen?"

Al and Charlie dug out their shields and showed them to her. "To be honest, ma'am," Charlie propped an elbow on the counter in front of a receptionist with a blonde ponytail and freckles, "we're lookin' for rustlers we believe might be using a trailer with Otani tires. Folks in our area say you are the only Otani dealer in this area."

"I know just the guy you're looking for," said the woman, turning and walking back toward her desk and motioning for them to follow. She led them into a beautifully appointed office. The nameplate on the desk said, "Rhonda Murphy, Owner."

She held out a hand to the two leather chairs in front of her desk, and then walked over to a filing cabinet and pulled out a drawer. After digging around for a moment, she pulled out a file folder and strode around to the other side of the desk, her heels clicking on the tile floor. "Can I get you gentlemen something to drink?"

Al sank down onto a chair. "I'd appreciate a coffee, if it's no trouble."

"And I'll take a soda, whatever kind you've got." Charlie removed his hat and settled on the seat beside Al. Rhonda pressed an intercom button and someone, likely the young woman at the reception desk, answered. Rhonda asked her to bring the drinks, and then she opened up the folder she'd set on her desk.

"Pardon me, ma'am," said Charlie, "but how the heck did you get into the trailer business?"

"Death," she said bluntly. "My husband started the business 20 years ago when this area of Appleton really hadn't yet developed. "He ran it for 14 years, made it into something big, then dropped dead of a heart attack six years ago. I knew nothing about trailers—or business, for that matter—so I had to learn quickly, all while grieving my husband and trying to raise five kids alone."

"My sympathies." Charlie tugged off his hat and clutched it in both hands. "I'm very sorry."

"No need to apologize, Charlie," said Rhonda, smiling at him a little longer than Al felt was really necessary. "Decker Trailers is doing quite nicely. In fact, now that Appleton has grown to surround us, last year's profit was 14 times higher than my husband's best year. He'd be proud."

Was she flirting with Charlie? Kelly would definitely not be impressed with that. Al cleared his throat. "Congratulations. That's quite an accomplishment."

Rhonda tore her gaze from Charlie and looked down at the file. "I doubt you came here to talk about my business success, so let me tell you who I believe you're looking for."

She rifled through a few papers, then pulled out a piece and stared at it for a moment, nodding. "Here it is. René Boulon. I'm pretty sure this is the guy. He's the only one who has purchased a trailer with Otani tires in the last year. Those tires are excellent quality, but a little high-end for most of our local customers."

She showed the paper to Al, who studied it before handing it to Charlie. On it was a picture of a swarthy man with long black sideburns stretching down from his oily hair. His face seemed twisted into a permanent grimace. Altogether, it was a photo of a highly-suspect person. Where would a guy like that get the money to purchase such an expensive piece of equipment? Beneath the photo was the description of the oversized covered trailer he had purchased.

"Can you tell us anything about him, ma'am?" Charlie set the paper down on the desk.

"In a word, disgusting." Rhonda bit her lip. "The photo doesn't do him justice. He's much more sinister in person. He talks as he looks: rough and lewd. One of my female salespeople talked to him, and he came on to her so strongly she came in pleading for help. I took over the discussion. He was terrible. Undressed me with his eyes before I had said a word, didn't listen to anything I said, and then asked me out for dinner." She shivered. "He wanted a trailer large enough to carry up to 20 head of cattle. He wanted it covered and air-conditioned, with enough space in front to live in. Where the heck was I to find a trailer like that? It had to be specially built. I insisted he pay me half down to even order the damn thing. He was so unsavory I couldn't take a chance."

Al glanced at the photo. "Do you have an address for him?"

Rhonda pulled a second sheet from the folder. "Yes, here it is, René Boulon, W40789 Hidden River Road, West Salem, Wisconsin." She stopped reading and looked up. "I should tell you, I'm not sure any of this is believable. He paid cash. Wasn't very happy about having to provide personal information. He did have an I.D. card with that address on it but said he'd forgotten his driver's license."

Al scribbled the information into the notebook he'd pulled from his shirt pocket and looked up. "No phone number?"

"Unfortunately not."

Charlie pulled a business card from his shirt pocket and handed it to her. "You've been a big help, thank you. If you think of anything else, or if this gentleman comes in again, could you please give me a call?" He rose, and Al followed suit.

Rhonda stood and came around the desk. She shook their hands, and then said, "I've enjoyed the visit, gentlemen. I actually remembered more than I thought I would. We don't get many law officers in here."

Al nodded. "We're grateful for the help."

She walked them to the door. Just before they went out, she rested a hand on Charlie's arm. "Would it be too much trouble to ask you to let me know what you find?"

Charlie replaced his hat and inclined his head. "We'd be happy to do that, ma'am."

Al followed him to the truck and climbed onto the front seat. As Charlie pulled the vehicle out of the parking spot and headed for the road, he looked over at Al. "Nice lady. Helpful."

Al snorted. "Of course she was."

Charlie frowned. "What's that supposed to mean?"

"She was totally coming onto you. Didn't you notice?"

His friend's eyes widened. "She was not. And even if she was, I'm a happily married man."

"And don't you forget it. I don't want Kelly coming after me asking why I didn't put a stop to whatever was going on between you and the lovely Mrs. Murphy back there."

A red flush crept up Charlie's neck, turning his ears bright red. "Nothing was going on, that's what, and don't you be telling Kelly otherwise, you hear?"

Al waited a beat, until his friend shot him a heated look, then he grinned. "Of course not. I'm just giving you a hard time again. To make up for it, let's find a place to have lunch. I'm buying."

32

THE DAY AFTER THEIR MEETING WITH THE GUYS FROM CHICAGO, David, Justin, Madison, and Emily were all up and eating breakfast early. David pushed back his trepidation about the deal they'd made. Those types of things were just the price for doing business—illegal business, anyway. They'd done what they had to do, and now they needed to make the best of it and move on.

And David had plenty to keep his mind occupied. Today was the day the Minnesota still would be pushed to full production, and all four of them would be required in order to bring it up to capacity. Since the day was nice, David suggested a picnic lunch. When the women agreed, he and Justin put it together.

They reached the still site about 8, but with summer approaching, the sun was already up and casting its warming rays over the clearing atop the bluff. While David and Justin opened and closed the various "gates" that hid the road and cave, Madison backed the truck up the lane. When they reached the cave mouth, all four participated in unloading corn and sugar. The women moved the sacks to the back of the pickup, where either David or Justin tossed them onto their shoulders and then disappeared down the stairs and into the cave. The big task today was cooking enough mash to generate the still's capacity of 'shine. They had brought another cooker with them, and soon Justin had both working. That done, he and David prepared the still for work, then emerged from the cave and joined the women, who had rigged up a canopy between two trees. Mosquito netting kept winged pests at bay.

"Pretty sweet." Justin inspected the shelter before wrapping an arm around Emily and pulling her close. "We've got a few hours to put in. How about a game of cards?"

Soon a spirited game of 500 was underway. Justin, as was customary, consistently overbid his hand, until Emily had finally had enough. She playfully pushed him onto his back, straddled him, and wrapped her hands around his neck. "Cut it out, will you, please? We are now 1,500 in the hole with no hope of ever getting out. Can't you just let someone else have a bid if you don't have the cards to outbid them?"

"Hey," Justin laughed. "If you're going to sit on me, could you move back a little, please?"

Emily let go of his neck and shook her head. "Why can't you think of something other than sex?"

"You started it. We were just having a quiet little card game when you jumped me."

Her cheeks pink, Emily started to get up, but Justin grabbed her hand and pulled her down beside him. "I think it's time for a little nap."

David tossed his cards onto the table. "A nap sounds good, actually."

He led Madison over to a clear spot under the tree and the two of them stretched out, side by side.

Quiet descended over the glade. A couple of hours later,

David stirred. *What time is it?* He pulled his phone out of his pocket and checked. Three p.m. As happy as he would be to lie here all day with Madison, they really needed to get back to work.

He woke up his brother, and he and Justin climbed down into the cave. By the time the sun was setting, the work was done. The still had operated perfectly and at capacity. With the second cooker also operating, they would soon have another 100 gallons of moonshine ready to bottle.

Justin drew in a deep breath and wrinkled his nose. David almost laughed. As good as the moonshine tasted, it didn't smell that great in the production stage. "How's the Wisconsin still operating?" His brother asked.

"It's at full capacity too," answered David. "I can't squeeze another drop out of it, to be honest."

"So we're pretty well locked in at 800 gallons a week?"

"Yup, that's it—unless we build another still and hire more people."

"That would be a mistake at this point, don't you think?" Justin carried a stainless steel pail over to the still.

David nodded. "Yes, more people would mean more headaches. And more liquor would bring more scrutiny. I think we stay where we are for now. We get Byrle 200 gallons a week for the La Crosse area, bring the Chicago boys their 200 in Mosinee, and drop the other 400 gallons in Eau Claire and Wausau."

Justin stood there, draining the moonshine into the large stainless steel pail to be poured, with the aid of funnels, into the gallon jugs that covered the floor of the cave near them. "You know, we're only working three days a week. What if we added two? That would increase output, right?"

"We might get another 200 gallons." David shrugged. "But think about the other end—about having the mob dump another 200 gallons of shine into their markets. Don't you think that would raise questions about where the stuff is coming from?"

"S'pose so. Just seems like a normal work week would do wonders for our take."

"Sure it would, but it would mean other changes, too. Either we make several trips a week to Eau Claire and Wausau, or we buy a bigger truck. Either one promotes more visibility and more questions. I think it's a sure way to trouble."

Justin worked away filling the gallon jugs. When that job was finished, the brothers put the jugs into cardboard boxes then began the arduous job of moving them up the stairs to the glade, where Madison and Emily loaded them into the truck.

The work finally finished, and with darkness closing in, David followed his brother up the ladder, happy to find that Madison and Emily had cleaned up the site, taken down the canopy, and packed it in its canvas bag. Then, with Madison driving and the two brothers walking ahead to get the gates, the four began their trip home.

As they traveled toward Rollingstone, Justin again brought up the subject of increased production. "I asked David about adding two work days to the schedule. He thinks it would increase our chances of being caught. But just think what another 200 gallons a week would do to our take—even with a cut for the mob."

Emily tilted her head as though doing some quick calculations. "Big bucks - for us and them. We could do it. If we got another pickup, we could alternate drops in Wisconsin, maybe even get the mob to meet us partway or something."

"But is it worth the money?" Madison glanced over at David. "There'd be lots more risk, right?"

David nodded. Why was his brother pushing this?

Emily leaned forward and gripped the top of the front

seat. "We'd be careful. Maybe we could drop the booze at some out of the way spot, let the mob deal with it from that point?"

David twisted to face her. "They'd want a bunch more money for that."

"I'm sure they would," agreed Emily. "But it might be worth it."

David wasn't so sure. "Do we want to get in deeper with that mob, though? Those guys aren't playing here. They mean business. I don't trust any of them, especially that Franco."

Madison's cheeks paled, and David reached over and squeezed her arm. She gave him a weak smile. "David's right. Those guys are creepy—I don't trust them either."

"Look." David let Madison go so he could turn around and see all three of them. "I know it's tempting to go all in here and really rake in the bucks, but every additional dollar means additional danger. Let's give it some thought before we jump into anything, okay? That's all I ask."

33

THE LIQUOR DROP THE NEXT SATURDAY WAS MADE IN THE normal fashion, but this time David insisted that he and Justin accompany Emily and Madison. When the two-truck caravan reached Wausau, David and Justin found Franco, looking every bit as ominous as the previous week, waiting in the bar. They greeted each other with handshakes before sitting down to talk.

"How much ya bring us?" The swarthy hoodlum stared at David with inky eyes that never seemed to blink.

"We've got 200 gallons for here and 200 for Mosinee, like we promised."

"You dropped 200 in Eau Claire?"

The brothers nodded. Franco stared at them for a moment then raised his glass of beer. "You guys make damn good stuff. We want more—lots more."

"We talked about it," David told him, "and we think we can add 200 gallons to our output if we work more days in a week."

"Need more than 200."

David frowned. "How much more?"

"Double what you gave us this week."

"Double?" David leapt to his feet. "Impossible! We'd need more people, and that increases the risk."

"Find more people. Yer sitting on a goddamn gold mine. Take advantage of it. You give us what we want, and we'll make you wealthy beyond belief." The hoodlum set down his glass and stared up at David.

"We could, but if they aren't blood, they aren't trustworthy."

"How about some of ours?"

That's a truly terrible idea. The thought of mobsters milling around the still sites, watching their every move, sent chills ripping up David's spine. "Why are you so set on more booze?"

"Chicago boss thinks it's great. He'd like a thousand a week."

David's chest tightened. Talk about too big too fast. What had they gotten themselves into? "A thousand a week? That means another entire operation. We'd need a whole 'nother crew. Not sure we want that."

"Not sure what you want matters. I want what the big boss wants. Another thousand a week."

David understood that Franco was in the same bind he was. Both were between a rock and a hard spot. *Damn, it's uncomfortable.* "Franco, we had a deal, but I also understand your problem. You have a boss, and he has a mind of his own, right?"

"Absolutely right. I haven't let him down yet, and I don't plan to. Can you handle the increase?"

"We'll have to make some changes, but yeah, if we do, I think we can handle it. We'll do our best."

"Your best better be good enough," said Franco.

They talked for another hour, going over all the details

of increasing production. David appealed for time to think it through. Franco wanted a hard answer. Every time David raised an obstacle, Franco said he would remove it. He offered materials, people, money, whatever they needed.

When David told him he would have to talk to his partners, Franco was understanding, but insistent that he and the "big boss" could handle any problems.

"One week, no more." The mobster stared at him, those inky eyes unblinking. "Want your answer next week."

"I understand. I'll know by then."

"Good. Promise made." He reached into his suit coat and laid a small pistol on the table. "Never break a promise. Understand?"

His throat too tight to answer, David nodded, rose from the table, and forced himself to walk slowly from the bar.

When he and Justin joined Madison and Emily in the truck, there were more questions than answers—lots more. David's head was jammed with thoughts about how to double production in a manner that wouldn't quickly lead to a jail cell. The group finally agreed to discuss it over lunch in Stevens Point.

Less than an hour later they were gathered around an outdoor table at the Lazy D Pub and Grill.

Unable to focus on the words, David set down the menu. "How much money's in the bank, Em?"

"Roughly a million. If you want an exact number, I'll get it when we get home."

"Hmm. Not enough to retire on, in my opinion." David drummed his fingers on the table. "Which means we can't just run away. We have to figure out how to add a thousand gallons a week to our production. And we can't move and set up shop somewhere else, either. The mob's eyes are too big—they'd find us in a hurry."

Justin nodded at the server as she set a glass of beer down

in front of him. "What do you think about asking Liam to help us, David?"

"Hmm." David swiped at a drop of condensation on his mug. "Not a bad idea."

Madison nudged his arm. "Who's Liam?"

"Liam Richards. He's a cousin of ours in Iowa. Good guy. We can trust him, and he's a great worker. He lives on a big farm. His place might be a perfect location for a third still."

Justin nodded. "I'll call him when we get home, see if he'd be willing to meet with us."

Emily dipped a fry in ketchup. "Madison and I have been talking, and we have a couple of friends we think might be interested too. If you want, we can ask them."

"They're not basketball players, are they?" David lifted his mug to his lips and took a sip. "It wouldn't be good to steal any more people from the team."

"No, it wouldn't, and they're not." Madison dabbed at her lips with a napkin before tossing it onto the table. "One is a liberal arts major, who studied theater. The other is a real brain. She graduated from the engineering program. Both are free at the moment. Neither is attached. Couldn't be better."

David pursed his lips. "Her training might be helpful. She might find some process things that we can do better."

Madison frowned. "Do we have quality problems?"

"Not yet, but I'm worried about what might happen when we begin to ramp up production. Do you think they might be willing to move to Iowa if we set up a third still there? That's where we could really use them."

"For what you'd be paying them, and given their student debts, I'm pretty sure they'd be willing to move just about anywhere."

David set down his mug. It made him a little nervous, bringing in a bunch of new people. But they would need help if they were going to meet the demands of Franco's boss and become, as Franco had promised, rich beyond their wildest dreams. And he definitely preferred to hire people they knew and not have any of the mob's picks come join them. As long as they swore everyone to secrecy, hopefully it would be okay.

The load lifted slightly from his shoulders, and David relaxed and enjoyed the rest of his lunch.

34

DAVID AND JUSTIN SET OUT FOR IOWA EARLY THE NEXT morning. As the two men headed south on Highway 61, it was a beautiful day, the cloudless sky the blue color that only late summer can produce. The trees were leafed out now, and the smells of flowers wafted through the cab of the pickup as they drove. The Mississippi on their left, was a placid, friendly river this morning.

"God, it's beautiful." Justin rested his head against the window.

"It is," agreed David. "If we can solve our production problem, it will be a perfect day."

"Emily said she and Madison are going to talk to their friends today, too. Their names are Tiffany and Myren, apparently. She told me a bit about them last night and they sound like they might fit in well."

"Good." David watched the river out his side window, sunlight sparkling across its surface like diamonds. It really was a beautiful day—the kind of day that drove away thoughts of mafia bosses and quality control issues and production problems. Maybe all of this was going to turn out okay after all. His shoulders relaxed as he drove.

Once across the border, they drove south along the river until turning west. An hour later they were at the Richards farm. Justin had called Liam the night before, and as soon as they parked in the yard and hopped out of the truck, he came out of the house - the screen door slamming shut behind him.

"Glad you're here," he said, grasping both of their hands and clapping them on the shoulder. "I've got tons of field work to do, but your phone call has me intrigued. I'm anxious to hear what you have to say."

David and Justin followed him up the steps to the wide, wraparound veranda. Liam waved them onto the white wicker furniture arranged in a circle. "I'll grab us some iced tea."

When he returned with a tray loaded down with three frosted mugs, the brothers swore him to secrecy and then filled him in on everything they had been up to.

"You guys are making liquor?" Liam's eyes had grown huge. "That's incredible."

"Yeah." David set down his mug. "We've been doing it for awhile now, but it's suddenly taken off. We've already got our girlfriends helping out, but we could use a few more pairs of hands if we're going to keep up with production."

"Are you thinking of setting up another still in this area?"

"That's the idea," said David. "You have forest land at the back of the farm, don't you?"

"Yep. We've got 800 acres here, 35 of them woodland that borders the Yellow River Forest. It's rough, that's for sure. Except for the bear and deer, not sure anything has been back there for years. We used to camp near the creek, but that's years ago now."

David shot Justin a look. "Sounds perfect."

Justin nodded.

Liam took a long swig of tea and wiped his mouth with the back of his hand. "So, you're thinking you'd help me set the still up on our back 40, show me how to operate the thing, and leave me to run it?"

"That's the plan, if you're willing. We just installed our second one, so we've got it pretty much figured out. Shouldn't take more than a couple of days to set it up, especially if you happen to have a welder on the premises."

Liam inclined his head toward a large shed in the yard. "We do. Plenty of scrap metal too."

"Excellent." David clapped his hands. "Should be easy to put it together then. And we'd provide a couple of people to help you run it and to deliver it where it needs to go, so we'd only need you to supervise the operation, Liam."

"And for that I'd make 2,000 bucks a week?"

Justin had tipped his chair back on two legs, resting it against the porch railing, but he brought the chair down now with a thud onto the wooden porch. "Yep. It's good money, but that's because of the risk - which we'd want you to take into consideration. Cops in our area have already been nosing around a bit, but so far we've been able to keep things hidden. You'll be even safer, this far from the center of the operation, but we still want to make sure you understand what you're getting into."

"I get it, but that's a chance I'm willing to take to help out family and make a bit of extra income. It's always needed around here, believe me. Why don't we go and take a look at that back 40 and see what you think."

David and Justin followed him down the steps. Liam waved them onto the back of his ATV and they bumped their way across recently plowed fields. When they reached a grassy area and passed through another gate in the fence, David looked around, examining the area closely. "Wow, this is back there, all right. How far are we from the road?"

"About two and a half miles. But wait until you see the spot I have in mind."

They drove for another half mile or so. Then the land curved sharply downward. Liam stopped the ATV, jumped out, and motioned for them to follow. After a walk of a hundred yards or so, Liam put out his arm to caution them as he led them to the top of a cliff that overlooked a steep valley. The vista to the east was impressive. Trees dominated as far as the eye could see, and the valley beneath them seemed an impenetrable sea of green.

"Is this the spot?" David held a hand above his eyes, blocking the sun.

"Nah, down there," said Liam, pointing toward the valley.

Justin frowned. "How the hell do you get down there?"

"C'mon, I'll show you."

Again aboard the ATV, Liam started down the hill, driving carefully and slowly. As they neared the trees, David spotted a narrow opening in the forest. Liam steered them through it, carefully negotiating a series of turns and ruts as they drove. The area was dark and damp, with little sunlight reaching the dirt floor around them. Suddenly, they entered a small clearing that featured a creek that slipped and burbled over a tangle of rocks and roots.

"This is the spot I'm thinking of. I doubt anyone has been through here since deer hunting season—and that was me. I'm the only one who hunts here. We used to come camping here when I was little, but since dad started having trouble getting around, we haven't been here in maybe five or six years, except to hunt. What do you think?"

David gazed around the small meadow then walked to the creek. When he came back, he lifted both hands. "Looks great."

"Perfect," seconded Justin. "Great water source, from the

looks of it. Gonna be a bitch to get the jugs out of here, though."

"I was considerin' that. I've been thinking of getting a bigger, more rugged ATV. If I did, it would be easier for dad to get out here, too, which would be good for him. All he does now is sit in the house and watch TV."

"We'll have to test the water." David contemplated the setup. If the water was good, it might be the perfect place.

"I'd be surprised if the water isn't excellent. We used to test it every year and it was then. The springhead is just over there in the trees - nothing to contaminate it before it hits the clearing. But we can test it."

He reached in his pocket for a bottle, rinsed it in the creek and filled it with water, then capped it and handed it to David. "You have a place to test it?"

"Sure do. We should have results tomorrow. We'll need to build a shed for tools and supplies."

"I've got one," Liam told him. "I just cleaned out one of those storage sheds that you can buy at the lumber yards. We've only had it for a couple of years, but we're not using it. I think I can get it over here on a wagon, but I might need some help wrestling it into place. We may have to trim a few trees to get it down the hill, but I think it's doable."

David elbowed Justin in the ribs. "What do you think?"

Justin rubbed his hands together. "If Liam gets that bigger SUV, and doesn't mind the hauling, I think it could work great."

David turned to his cousin. "Keeping in mind what Justin said about the risk, do you think you want to take this on?"

"Absolutely."

David stuck out his hand. "All right then. I believe we're in business."

Liam shook his hand firmly, then Justin's. "Excellent."

David's gaze swept the area. "I'll order the copper sheet

and tubing as soon as we get back to the house. Should arrive in two days if it's in stock."

Justin walked out a rectangle shape in the clearing. "Should fit. Can you haul the metal and the welder out here, Liam? It would be best if we could build the still right here."

Liam pursed his lips. "I don't know why not. You guys staying a few days?"

David shook his head. "We'll head back today, since we've got work to do, but return as soon as the order arrives. The girls might join us too. We can camp in the clearing."

"You don't have to camp," Liam told them. "We have plenty of room in the house."

"But we like to camp," replied David. "It would be a fun outing for us. Speaking of the house, though, what will your mom and dad think about this?"

"Dad'll love it," predicted Liam. "Anything that sticks it to the government is good in his eyes. And, like I said, we could use the extra income. Getting harder and harder to make a living at farming. And we're paying for their place in town now, too, so it's a lot."

"What would you think about growing corn and barley on your land?" The wheels were spinning in David's mind. "Right now we're buying corn and barley from five vendors and paying two dollars a bushel over market. Maybe you could become our sole supplier. That'd be a heckuva lot better for us and would mean a lot more money for you."

Liam blinked. "You'd pay that much? How much do you go through?"

"We get about 50 pounds of meal from a bushel of corn and about 48 pounds of barley meal from a bushel." David calculated numbers in his head. "We usually buy corn meal and barley in 50-pound sacks. We go through four sacks of corn and two of barley a week in Wisconsin and - help me out here, Justin - twice that in Minnesota?"

"Yeah, that's about right."

David nodded. "So, twelve sacks of corn a week and six of barley."

Liam tipped his head from side to side as though calculating. "Yeah, we could handle most of that. I've never grown barley, but some of our neighbors have. That'd have to be for next year, though, since the crop's already in, but we should have enough corn to cover that."

"Done. We'll take all the corn you can grow, and barley next year."

"Sounds good." Liam inclined his head toward the ATV. "Let's head back to the house. Mom's making dinner for us."

"Sounds good." David and Justin followed him and climbed into the vehicle. Justin elbowed their cousin in the ribs. "Seeing anyone these days?"

"Nope. Kind of hard to meet anyone out here." Liam gripped the steering wheel with one hand and waved an arm at the bush around them as he drove.

"Well, we might have someone for you." David leaned forward from the back and grasped his shoulder. "Our girlfriends are recruiting your helpers today, and they're both girls. If they're as beautiful as our two, I don't think you're long for the single world. That's all I'm gonna say for now."

David and Justin enjoyed a fabulous roast beef dinner with their aunt and uncle. They shared what they were up to with Liam's parents, and Liam let them know he was thinking of getting involved. His mother was a little hesitant, but, as Liam had predicted, his dad clapped his wrinkled hands together - a light springing into his eyes. "Finally, something's happening around here. Let's do it. No way to make a living on just farming anymore, what with the cut the damn government takes. Gotta find a way around it—they practically force you to break the law just to survive."

David suppressed a grin. As soon as their plates were

cleared, he pushed back his chair. "I hate to eat and run, but we've got a long drive ahead of us and two beautiful women waiting."

"Say no more." Their uncle pushed back his chair too and stood. He and Liam and their aunt all walked them to the door.

Out on the porch, Liam shook hands with both of them again. "Thanks for thinking of me for this, boys. Looking forward to working with you."

"Us too." David offered all three of them a salute before heading down the stairs to the truck. Justin slid behind the wheel, and they made their way down the long, winding land and turned toward Winona. "Pretty satisfying, don't you think?" Justin rested a forearm on the wheel.

"I don't think it could have gone better." More of the load lifted off David. Everything was coming together. As long as that Rouse and Berzinski kept their noses out of his and Justin's business, everything might just work out fine.

35

BACK HOME, THE BROTHERS WERE ANXIOUS TO TALK TO MADISON and Emily, but neither was home. Justin started supper while David made the call to order supplies for the Iowa still. By seven p.m., Justin was worried. They hadn't heard a word, which was unusual.

"Everything's ready for dinner." He leaned back against the kitchen counter. "I have the chops ready to grill, the potatoes sliced and ready to fry, and broccoli ready to cook. I just need two more mouths."

About 8:20, Madison and Emily walked in, looking happy and smug.

"Where've you been?" Justin planted a fist on his hip. "We've been worried as hell!"

"We had a great day." Emily sashayed over to him and wrapped an arm around his waist. "We have two prospects for you to interview, assuming you had any luck on your trip. The recruitment was done so soon, we decided to go shopping. You should see the things we bought. I think you're going to like 'em."

"Shopping? Where?" Unable to stay mad at her when she was pressed up against him and looking so cute, Justin pressed his lips to hers.

"Rochester." Madison dropped a couple of bags onto a kitchen chair. "And Em had a blast at Victoria's Secret. I think she'll be anxious to show you her purchases."

David raised his eyebrows. "What about you?"

"I might have gotten a few things, too." She winked at him.

"Well, let's eat dinner and then we can see what you bought." Justin moved to the stove, switched on the burners, and soon supper was cooking. As they sat down to eat, they all had a lot to report, but the food Justin put before them looked wonderful and posed a strong magnetic force in opposition to conversation.

As a compromise, everyone ate quickly. Ten minutes later, only a few scraps and bones remained.

"Good thing we don't have a dog, the poor thing would starve." Emily reached for Madison's plate and piled it on hers. She grabbed the other two and carried them all over to the sink. "Tell us how it went in Iowa today."

David filled them in on the visit with their cousin. "He's got the perfect location for a still on his property, and he's more than willing to help out. He's even going to grow all the corn we'll need this summer."

"If your friends agree to go work with him and either is interested, he's a great guy, and single." Justin filled a pot with soapy water and left it on the stove to soak while he joined the others at the table.

"Good looking too, and ripped," added David.

"Geez, Em, maybe we should go." Madison moved swiftly to avoid the sweep of David's hand.

He laughed. "So, tell us about your friends."

Madison launched into a description of the two women.

She told them that Tiffany Rupert was a recent graduate of Winona State. She was using the summer to relax before looking for a job. "Em and I think she would be a great addition to the team. Her major was liberal arts. She's into theater and has done several internships with area companies."

"That's right." Emily nodded. "And Myren Hermundson is a first-quarter senior majoring in engineering with a minor in accounting. She'll be a wonderful addition, because she can help with business details." She nudged Justin in the side. "After all, we are growing by leaps and bounds. I'm gonna need help on the accounting side soon."

Madison crossed her legs. "Tiffany is a handful who is full of the proverbial piss and vinegar, but she also has a great head on her shoulders, and she's careful about how and when she opens her mouth. Myren is quiet, almost shy, but that's just a cover. When she lets her hair down, she's something to behold. I doubt that your Liam will be able to resist falling for one or the other of them. They're both great."

"Which you can judge for yourselves." Emily swiped a few crumbs off the table with the side of her hand. "We're all supposed to go out for dinner tomorrow night so you can meet them."

"Sounds like everyone had a productive day." Justin reached for Emily's hand. "And my personal opinion is that if there is going to be a style show, I'd like mine to be in private."

Emily hopped up. "Let's go."

By the time she had finished modeling all her purchases, Justin didn't even care how much she had spent. They fell into bed together and he was able to prove to her that the new outfits certainly did the job they were designed to do. Afterwards, her naked back pressed to his chest, and his arms wrapped around her, Justin lay awake for a long time, marveling at how much his life had changed in the last few months. Although they were always in danger of being found out and arrested, and the work was long and hard, days—and nights—like today made it all worthwhile.

When David, Justin, Madison, and Emily walked into the restaurant marked by a Viking ship the next evening, two women raised their hands from across the room.

"There's Tiffany and Myren." Madison started toward them and the others followed her. Emily introduced everyone, and David and Justin shook hands with the girls. Tiffany was a gorgeous blonde and Myren an equally beautiful brunette.

"Liam is going to owe us big time," David murmured in Justin's ear as they took their seats.

"Mind if I join you?"

David swiveled in his seat. To his surprise, their cousin stood behind Justin's chair. Justin sent him a sheepish look. "I called and invited him last night—since he and Tiffany and Myren might be working together, I thought they should meet."

"Great idea." David jumped up and pulled a chair from another table over to theirs. "Everyone, this is our cousin, Liam Richards. Liam, this is my girlfriend Madison, Justin's girlfriend Emily, and their friends Tiffany and Myren. We've just met Tiffany and Myren, too, so sit down and we can all get to know each other."

After they had all studied their menus and placed their orders, David poured glasses of water from the jug in the middle of the table for everyone. "Tiffany, why don't you start? Tell us a bit about yourself."

"All right." She clasped her hands on the table. "Let's see, I'm from Rice Lake, Wisconsin - northeast of the Twin Cities. Graduated at the top of my high school class and decided to major in theater at Winona State. I've had a blast this last semester. Did an internship for HBC, a local cable company.

It was great experience, and when I did my final report, they adopted everything I suggested and even offered me a job."

"I guess you didn't take it," said Justin.

"No, I passed. I want to get going on a graduate degree. I can do that here. Then, when Myren finishes her Master's, we can figure out what we want to be when we grow up."

David grinned. "I guess we're all still trying to do that. Myren, how about you?"

She wrapped her fingers around her water glass. "I came to Winona State from Middleton, Wisconsin - a suburb of Madison - because I wanted to attend a smaller school than the U. of Wisconsin, one with a reputation for serious academics. Also, I had to get away from home, where my three younger brothers were driving me crazy."

David nodded solemnly. "I get that."

"Hey." Justin dug an elbow into David's ribs and everyone burst out laughing, which seemed to break the tension. The food arrived shortly after and soon they were all talking away.

"My kind of place." Myren gazed around the room. "Full-blooded Norski, that's me. Wonder if they have lutefisk?"

"My god," said David, laughing, "I guess we chose the right place for Myren. And, yes, they serve lutefisk—whatever the hell that is—on Sundays. So this is your lucky day."

"It's wonderful if fixed right," said Myren. "I'll teach you all to be lovers of it, too."

"Except for me." Tiffany shuddered. "Myren has tried to turn me into a fan, but it's not working. I'll let you all make your own judgments, though."

Her eyes were on Liam, where, David had noticed, they'd been pretty much all evening. Guess Myren was going to have to look elsewhere—it appeared Tiffany had set her sights on their cousin. David studied him discreetly. He was a good-looking guy, 6 foot 4 or so, and rippling with muscles from manual labor. If he and Tiffany ended up together, hopefully it would work out and their relationship wouldn't interfere with work.

As though she could read his mind, Madison slipped her hand into his under the table. David smiled. It had worked out pretty well for him and Justin. He hoped his cousin would find the same happiness with his new co-worker. The server arrived at their table and pulled out a notebook and pen. "I'm having lutefisk, anyone want to join me?" announced Myren.

"Count me in," said Liam, closing his menu.

"I'd love to try it," said Madison, "but I'm not sure I'll like it well enough to make it my dinner."

"Could you bring us one large serving?" David asked the server. "And six small plates so anyone who wants to can try it?"

"You mean like a platter of fish?" she asked. "Lefse, too?"

"Absolutely." Myren took charge.

Dinner was served. The lutefisk got a split decision. Tiffany didn't have any, simply voting thumbs down. Justin, Emily, and Madison had a small helping and liked it. Emily even said she would order it as her entrée next time. David pushed his plate away after a single bite. "Not enough flavor for me."

When they finished eating, Liam shoved back his chair. "I'd be happy to buy an after-dinner drink for everyone. Should we go out onto the patio to enjoy it?"

That idea went over well, and all seven of them headed outside. The sun had sunk below the horizon, but the patio was lit by strings of twinkling lights as well as lanterns on each table that doubled as bug protection.

"So, David, why don't you tell Tiffany and Myren what it is you'd be hiring them to do?" Madison settled onto a chair beside him.

David glanced around, but the patio was empty. Still, he

leaned forward and spoke in a low voice, telling them what he and Justin had been up to the last few months and how rapidly the business was expanding. "Madison and Emily have been incredible, but this thing is becoming too big for the four of us. Liam has agreed to set up a third still on his property in Iowa, so that's where we really need the help. Any chance you might be interested in the job? And before you answer, you need to know that there is risk involved, but there is also a lot of money to be made."

The girls exchanged a look. Tiffany nodded and Myren turned back to the group. "We're definitely in, for the summer at least."

"So," Tiffany rested a hand on Liam's arm, "what would you think of having a couple of roommates for a few months?"

"I'd be the envy of northeast Iowa, that's for sure." Liam smiled. "Two beautiful women living at the house with me. My oh my."

"Do you have room?" asked Myren.

"Will six bedrooms and four baths be enough? It was a two-story, three-bedroom house until Dad and Mom—who used to live there but moved into town a year ago—expanded it when my sisters were little. Too much fighting over the bathrooms. So, yes, I have room. It'll have to be aired out and cleaned, of course. Not really my thing, but I can do it."

"Not to worry," Tiffany told him, squeezing his arm. "Myren and I are no strangers to work. Happy to provide a hand if you'll rent space to us."

"Can you cook?" he asked.

When they both nodded, he covered Tiffany's hand with his. "Forget about the rent. Some cleaning, cooking, and help with the new venture and you have free lodging for however long you want it."

David slapped his knee. "Great. Then it's settled. We'll hire you both for the summer and see how it goes. If you want to stay on after that, we can work something out. In the meantime," he lifted his glass in the air, "to the success of our new venture. May we stay under the radar of the local authorities, in the good graces of the mob, and enjoying each other's company while we see how far we can take this thing."

Everyone laughed and clinked glasses. By the time they left the restaurant two hours later, David was feeling pretty good about their prospects. They had a team in place, now they had to see if the seven of them would be able to produce enough moonshine to keep everyone who wanted it happy. If not, they were all in a lot of trouble.

36

WHILE THE SIX DROVE BACK TO WINONA, A PARTY WAS IN progress in rural La Crosse, where Rick Olson and his wife Peggy were entertaining Al and his wife JoAnne, along with Charlie and Kelly. Rick, a pathologist at Gundersen Lutheran Clinic in La Crosse, had been integral in helping Al and Charlie solve the serial killer case.

The six friends tried to get together at least every couple of months—more often if the opportunity arose—and tonight Al had thoroughly enjoyed the fabulous dinner paired with exceptional wine from Maybach Vineyards in the Napa Valley.

"Don't get too accustomed to the wine," Rick told them as they sipped glasses prior to dinner. "This stuff retails for 189 dollars a bottle. I was damn lucky to pick up six bottles for a song, thanks to a friend. I thought this occasion was the right one to uncork a couple."

"Damn, 189 bucks a bottle!" exclaimed Charlie, quickly doing the math in his head. "That's 33 dollars a glass. Wow, I'll have to suck the napkin dry."

It was that kind of lighthearted evening, and when dinner had ended and dessert wine had been poured, the men retired to Rick's study where the embers of a fire were quickly stoked to life. Rick reached behind his desk and produced a box. "Cigar?"

"Goddamn, right," stated Charlie. "I'd love one. Been chasing rustlers and moonshiners all week, and it's time to relax. How about you, Al?"

"I guess so. I love the taste but hate the after-taste," he told them. "I'll wake up in the morning with a mouth that feels like a herd of elephants ran through it, doing from time to time what elephants on the run are prone to do."

"I think you'll find this better than most," Rick told him. "It's a mild, mild Cuban. Thank god for normalized relations. Now we can get these here. Well, here being mail order."

The three lit up, sat back, and relaxed - Al reveling in the taste of fine wine and great cigars.

"Rustlers and moonshiners," said Rick reflectively. "Sounds like we stepped back a couple of generations. What's going on? I'd love to hear about it if you can tell me."

Al and Charlie took turns enlightening their friend on the current cases they were pursuing. They talked about the amount of illegal liquor they suspected was flowing into La Crosse and La Crosse County, placing it at somewhere around a thousand gallons a week. Charlie talked about the number of beef cattle that had mysteriously disappeared in the south of the county, up to 332 now.

"Any chance it's predators?" Rick bent forward and tapped ashes into a glass tray on the coffee table. "I've heard a rumor there might be wolves in the area."

Charlie shook his head. "We thought about that, but no one's noticed any kill sites or found any carcasses."

Al blew out a puff of smoke. "They seem to have disappeared into thin air."

"The first solid clue we have in the case is a set of unusual tire prints." Charlie leaned back on the couch and crossed his legs, resting an ankle on one knee. "We're following up on that now in the hope that we can bring some closure to this case."

"I'm sure it won't take long, now that the two of you have teamed up. Even the Carbones, with all their power and wealth and connections, couldn't keep you from finding out that one of their own was the serial killer you were hunting last year." He took a long draw on his cigar and blew out a ring of smoke. "I'm sure these rustlers, whoever they are, won't fare any better. Bring me in the slightest bit of DNA, and I'll see what I can do to help you identify the perpetrators."

"Thanks, Rick." Al breathed in the comforting scent of the cigars and relaxed in his armchair for the first time in days. As the three of them puffed and sipped, talk swung to Genevieve Wangen, the serial killing suspect Charlie and Al had helped to nab in Montana. When they had finally caught up with her, she admitted to having taken the lives of 14 young males in La Crosse and the county.

After escaping from the authorities on her wedding day, she hid in a cave and was wounded when she came face to face with Rouse. She died several days later. Al wouldn't have chosen for the case to end that way, but at least the rash of killings had stopped.

"I imagine after the chase to catch her, rustlers and moonshiners must seem pretty tame," speculated Rick.

"Every case is exciting. It's kind of fun to be back in the Old West, don't you think, Charlie?" Al grinned at his friend.

"Not sure fun is the right word. Those rustlers are driving me crazy. And chasin' moonshiners is not for babies, that's for sure."

"Say Al, what do you hear from Julie?" Rick stubbed his cigar out in the ashtray.

Al shot a look at the door. He and Julie were old friends, who had also carried on a brief affair before Al's wife found out and put a stop to it. They'd gone back to being friends, but even though JoAnne had forgiven him, Al didn't go out of his way to let his wife know that he still spoke to Julie fairly regularly. He lowered his voice. "She's doing well. In fact, she's now in charge of all the support personnel at the Kahn Clinic. She loves her new job."

"She still live in the same place?" asked Rick.

"Yep, I think it was gifted to her by Genevieve." Adding to their complicated relationship was the fact that Julie had been Genevieve's niece, which had put a strain on her and Al's relationship since Al was pursuing Julie's aunt in the serial killer case. "Things are going well, and it looks as if her son is going to have it made when he graduates next year."

Julie's son Brody was a star quarterback at the University of Wisconsin in Madison, where he would be entering his junior year in the fall. Rumors were circulating that he could be a serious candidate for the Heisman Trophy. "He's a good kid, a gifted athlete who doesn't let his talent overshadow his quest for a college education and his love for his mother."

"She and JoAnne still talk?" Rick tugged another cigar out of the box.

"They do, crazily enough. If they talk about Julie and me, I never catch a hint of it from either woman. It's almost as if each is afraid to make a wave, lest it upset the ship. It might seem like a wonderful situation, but in reality, it tears me up." Al studied the wine he was swirling around in his glass.

"Hey, ease up," said Rick. "You swirl the drink any harder and it either will be out of the glass or out of flavor."

Peggy Olson stuck her head in the door. "Dessert is served, gentlemen."

Charlie had jumped to his feet before she finished speaking.

"It's amazing," Rick returned the unlit cigar to the box, "that a man as big as Charlie can be on his feet long before either of us can react when food is mentioned."

Still chuckling, he and Al followed Charlie to the dining room.

No sooner had the group sat down to dessert than Al and Charlie's cell phones rang simultaneously.

Al answered first, moving from the table to the den to take the call. When he came back, he was all business. "We just got a call that may be a break in the rustling case. Sure hate to end the evening, but we've got to go. Now."

"Who drove?" asked Rick.

"I did," replied Al.

"How about we take my SUV?" suggested Rick, looking at JoAnne. "Maybe JoAnne can drop Kelly off on her way home, and Al and Charlie and I can head to the crime scene."

The women, not appearing in any hurry to leave, agreed, and without wasting any time, the three men headed out to Rick's Escalade. Al jumped into the passenger seat as Rick slid behind the wheel. "To West Salem, Rick. And step on it if you don't mind. This just might be the break Charlie and I have been waiting for. So the sooner we get there, the better."

37

WHILE JUSTIN AND DAVID WORKED ON BUILDING THE STILL in the shed on Liam's farm in Iowa, Emily led Tiffany, Myren, and Madison into the farmhouse where they gave the old place a thorough cleaning. It wasn't that Liam was a poor caretaker; it was just that the house suffered from the lack of constant attention.

After a couple of days of concentrated effort, the downstairs was spotless. Even the mudroom sparkled under the efforts of lots of soap and elbow grease. Although the addition that contained two bedrooms and two baths likely wouldn't be used much, the women had cleaned it, too.

"Maybe we should have started upstairs?" Tiffany rested her hands on her hips as she surveyed their work. "I'm darned tired, and we still have that whole floor to do."

"Not to worry. Did you see the size of the upstairs windows? If there are things to toss, and I suspect there might be, we can just toss them into the yard and get rid of them that way." Myren's eyes twinkled.

When Emily walked through the upstairs rooms, she was

impressed. Two of the four bedrooms were enormous. The other two had once been the same size, but space had been taken from them to create another bathroom - this one large enough to host a hot tub that wasn't being used but appeared to be in good condition.

"Soap and water, spit and polish," allowed Emily. "We'll get through this in no time. You must be planning to sleep up here, right?"

"I think we'd both like to be close to Liam, but maybe if he decides to pick one of us, his reject will have to move downstairs." Myren, always the humorous one, giggled. "You know, I really like the guy, but he's built for Tiffany—long and lanky. And his jeans suggest he is long in other places, too."

"Myren!" Madison pressed a hand to her chest, clearly feigning shock.

"Oh, c'mon. If none of the rest of you saw it, you're blind as bats in the daytime. That boy's a man—in every sense of the word—if you ask me."

"She's right," agreed Tiffany.

With all four women grinning, Madison shook her head. "Too much information. Let's get back to work and finish this up so the two of you will have a clean room tonight. We're going home, aren't we, Emily?"

"If the men get the shed and still moved into place, that's the plan. After all, we've got work to do, too. We still have commitments to meet every week, and the weekend is coming up fast."

That said, the cleaning resumed. They found no reason to jettison anything through the windows, which Emily found a little disappointing. When Liam returned from the fields at lunchtime, Emily had to poke Madison in the ribs. "You're staring!" she whispered.

With the four women laughing, and the men looking a little confused, Liam headed to the kitchen to make sandwiches for everyone, since it was going to be a busy afternoon.

When they'd finished eating, David asked Liam how he planned to move the shed.

"I think we can use a couple of jacks. We have to raise it enough to slide a wagon under it. Dad and I left it up high enough to fit the jacks under when we brought it here, since we assumed we'd have to move it."

"You farmer types are damn smart." Justin clapped him on the back. "I wouldn't have thought ahead like that."

Moving the shed turned out to be easy, at least compared to leveling a site for it in the woods. Finding a spot in the clearing that would accommodate the wagon was the big challenge. Soon all three men were sweating profusely as they operated shovels. After shoveling for a half hour, and making less progress than they needed, Liam raised the shovel and drove the end of it into the ground. "I'm gonna go get the skid steer. It'll take a little while 'cause I've gotta put the bucket on. One of you want to help?"

Justin rode back with him on the tractor while David continued to work at a spot that was already fairly level. When the two returned, Justin was driving the tractor, followed by Liam on the skid steer.

David stopped working and wiped the sweat off his forehead with a gloved hand. "Geez, lookit that, a real farmer now. Maybe I'll have to leave you here."

"I wouldn't mind, but there's too much work to do at home for me to stay here," lamented Justin. "I must admit, though, I love it down here."

"I think we all do," said David. "But we've got the other sites to run."

With the aid of the implement, the leveling work was quickly accomplished, and by 4 o'clock the shed had been maneuvered into the spot they wanted it. The men then carefully built the base for the still near the head of the spring-fed stream, and moved the apparatus onto it. David fired up the welder and fastened the piping into place while Liam and Justin concentrated on setting up the cooker and the other equipment. By 5, everything was ready to go.

David tugged off his gloves and smacked them together to knock off the dirt before shoving them into his back pocket. "Justin, I think you and I and Madison and Emily should head back to Winona. We have a lot to do to catch up after being away a few days."

Justin pulled the tractor keys out of the pocket of his jeans. "I agree. The women have been hard at work too—we can buy them a nice dinner on the way home."

David gripped Liam's shoulder. "Sorry to leave you all alone with those two beautiful helpers of yours, cuz, but somehow I don't think you'll mind too much."

Liam laughed and climbed onto the skid steer. "Nope, you're right about that. In fact, I don't mind a bit."

38

WEDNESDAY AND THURSDAY SPED PAST WITH WORK AT THE two still sites, and when Friday morning came and Justin joined David, Emily, and Madison around the breakfast table, he suggested they finish up their work quickly so they could drive back to Iowa after they'd made their normal Saturday deliveries.

The next day, the four of them piled into the truck and drove to Wausau. When they strolled into Katie's Bar, Franco and Jimmy sat at a booth. David met Justin's eyes and jerked his head in their direction. "Madison and I will go talk to them if you and Emily want to unload."

Justin nodded and he and Emily went back outside. David shoved back his shoulders as he and Madison made their way to the booth. "How ya doin'?" rasped Franco in a threatening voice. "We need a little... progress report. And it better be good."

"Yeah, we need a little... progress report," echoed Jimmy.

David pressed his lips together to keep from tossing out a smart remark about them being a couple of Goodfella wannabes. No sense in goading the two thugs into a dispute. He slid into the booth across from the two men and Madison joined him.

"Things are going well," David told them. "We think that by the end of the day tomorrow, if we get outta here on time today, we'll have a third still operating so we can increase the amount of liquor to you by two weeks from now. That's if the deal's still on."

"On?" replied Franco in the voice that resembled that of a snake's rattle. "Of course it's on. Don' cha trust us?"

"We haven't done business with you before," David shot back. "So, no, we don't trust you. Until we deliver and see the color of your money, you're just a coupla mobsters to us."

Madison squeezed his arm. David got the message—probably a good idea to tone down the rhetoric a little.

"Listen to 'em, Jimmy," hissed Franco. "They don' trust us. How do ya like that?"

"Not good, Franco, not good." Jimmy set down the mug of beer he'd been sipping from with a thud.

"Is that all you can do? Mimic your buddy there?" Even if Madison's advice was sound, David wasn't quite ready to take it.

"I got my own mind," Jimmy assured him.

"Sure you do," said Madison, her voice a raspy whisper that mimicked Franco's. "Everything you've said since we got here has been a repeat of your partner."

"I'll show you how I can think on my own," exclaimed Jimmy, beginning to rise from his seat, fist clenched.

"Cool it!" rasped Franco, blocking Jimmy's exit from the booth. "I wanna hear what they have to say. But before that, I have somethin' to say. The two of you need to remember that you're just a coupla snot-nosed kids. If you're gonna stay alive, you need to keep your mouths shut and get the work done. This thing better move forward on schedule. You understand?"

Franco's mouth twisted into a grimace and a trace of spittle hung on his lower lip. Altogether, it was the face of someone without a conscience, someone who would kill without a second thought. David shot a look at Madison and shook his head slightly. Should have backed off, like she'd suggested.

"As David was saying," Madison continued in her normal voice, "we should be able to deliver the extra booze you want in two weeks. We're planning to test the new still this weekend. If all goes well, we can shift into production next week."

Franco's face softened slightly. "I like that. Like it a lot. Did ya bring the money?"

"We did," said David, "but let me remind you that us paying you means that your end of the bargain immediately goes into force. We want the extra protection you promised."

"You'll get it. You'll get it," hissed Franco, reaching for the money David placed on the table. Finished with the counting and apparently satisfied, Franco looked at Jimmy.

"You go with 'em. Help 'em unload and make sure all is well. No funny business. Understand?"

"Yeah, boss, I got it." Jimmy's face turned red. Clearly he wasn't too happy about being ordered around by Franco. His jaw tight, he managed to utter, "I'll make sure things go smoothly."

"And don' lay a finger on 'em, got it?"

"Yeah, boss. I said I got it. I'll be back in a few minutes."

Jimmy was as good as his word. Although he grimaced and sneered as David and Madison joined Justin and Emily and helped them move the last few cases of jugs into the basement of Katie's, he even helped carry a couple of cases in himself, muttering to himself the whole time. The few words he caught—"nice boobs" and "like ta get my hands on that ass" and "if you was uner me, I'd show ya somethin'"—tightened up David's stomach muscles, but he tried to ignore them and get the work done as quickly as possible.

As soon as the truck was empty, the four collected their money and hit the road.

"Those guys are freaky." Emily shifted closer to Justin as he steered the truck onto the highway.

"They are," agreed Madison. "But no sense making them angry. We did things just right—unloaded the truck, got our money, paid them, and got the heck outta there. That's the best way to handle those guys."

"I understand," said Emily, "but I hate giving them a cent. After all, they're doing almost nothing to earn it. It's too much, if you ask me."

David shrugged. "It's the price of doing this kind of business. We're paying for protection, and as long as our deliveries aren't stopped, and we aren't hurt, I'm okay with the payment." It wasn't entirely true—it galled him as much as it did Emily to hand money over to those guys. But as he'd said, it was the price they had to pay if they wanted to keep their business growing and thriving - and if they all wanted to stay alive in the process.

39

IN WISCONSIN, AL, CHARLIE, AND RICK WERE FISHING FROM A boat in the backwaters of the Mississippi River near La Crosse. Al didn't say it—although he figured the other two were thinking the same thing—but the spot Charlie had anchored the boat was the same spot from which they had pulled the fifteenth and final drowning victim a few years earlier.

"Hard not to think about finding that body around here." Rick looked thoughtful as he pulled back his arm and cast his line into the water.

"Yep. The beginning of the end right over there." Al baited his hook and dropped his line next to the deadfall lying partially submerged in the water. The same tree they'd found the body trapped under. Hopefully the downed cottonwood tree would attract the panfish they were seeking. "Not sure I've ever said it, Rick, but you did a great job on the case. Without you, we'd still be searching."

"I think your credit is misplaced. Don't forget it was Dr.

Grebin who found the puncture mark in the ear. That was the one piece of the puzzle we all were waiting for."

Charlie had been watching his line intently, having casted into the shadows of the big tree. "But you guys are a team. Everyone played a role. And you were with us when we got the old girl to admit her guilt. That was a big thing, too, wasn't it?"

"Sure was." Al tugged on his line to free it from a branch.

"Kinda slow." Charlie's patience was waning. "Maybe we oughta get closer to that deadfall. It was lucky for us before."

"That's morbid." Rick shuddered.

"Just sayin', we had some luck there before, right?"

"You're right, Charlie," agreed Rick, "but I think seeking sunfish and pulling a murder victim out of the river are two different things, and should be kept completely separate."

"Point taken. Ya know, I'm kinda hungry. Whadda we got in the basket, Al?"

"Charlie, you're always hungry." Al wound in his line. "But I've got you covered today. There are sandwiches, snowballs, soda, beer, pickles, chips. I knew you were comin', after all."

"A guy's gotta eat. Besides, how long's it been since we had breakfast?"

"About an hour," was Rick's wry response. "How the heck could you be hungry? I watched you pack away four eggs, bacon, sausage, toast, and two waffles. That should last you all day."

"Awww, Doc, you know I'm just a growin' boy, right? And I'm chasin' rustlers and moonshiners. Crook chasers need their appetites apprised."

"The word's *appeased*, Charlie." Rick slid across the bench and gazed over the side of the boat into the water. "I should have known better than to take a shot at your appetite. How are those Old West cases going?"

"Not so hot." Al set down his rod, running out of patience

himself. And not just with the fishing. "Charlie and I have little to show for our efforts. We know something about the people involved in the liquor case, and we have a line on the rustlers... at least we think we do. But we have nothing concrete—yet."

Charlie's rod bent and he gave it a yank. A tennis shoe sailed through the air and landed in a puddle of water on the bottom of the boat.

"Good job." Rick had grabbed the net, but when he saw the shoe he put it away and clapped his hands. "Maybe you should nibble on that. Give you a little fiber."

"You guys are mean. If you'll just pardon me, I'm gonna keep on fishin' here and hope to do so in silence."

"You, silent?" Al snorted. "Just who the heck do you think you're kidding?"

"Now, dammit, Al," Charlie turned to him, then spun back quickly when his bobber disappeared twice. Charlie set the hook. Al watched as Charlie played the fish, maneuvering it closer to the boat. As Al reached for the net, Charlie continued to fight the fish. "It's big!" he gasped. "Heavy as hell!"

Al half stood, net ready, until he caught a flash of fins, and dipped the net into the water - imprisoning the fish in the mesh.

"Got it. Nice walleye, that's for sure. I'd say it's at least four pounds. How the heck did ya do that?"

"God takes care of me," announced Charlie smugly. "You guys pick on me all the time and God doesn't like it, so he rewards me in many ways... including with a nice-sized walleye. Eat your hearts out!"

It wasn't long before Rick brought in a sunfish, and a few seconds later Al landed a slab-sided crappie.

"Guess He likes us too, Rick." Al hooked his fish onto the stringer.

Charlie fished in silence for a few minutes then hooked two sunnies in rapid succession. "Guess He likes me better!"

"Say, Rick," Al examined the lures in the tackle box, "Do you remember me saying as we left the dock that the luckiest fisherman gets to host dinner tonight?"

"And I'm prepared to pay off, too," said Charlie. "But we better catch a few more if it's gonna be much of a dinner."

As the sun approached noon, the number of fish on the stringer mounted until finally Charlie suggested it was time to stop. "That's more'n enough. So if I'm gonna cook 'em, are you guys gonna clean 'em?"

"I'm fine with that," said Al.

Rick nodded. "Me too. But back to those Wild West cases. How are you guys really doing?"

"I think we're closin' in." Charlie slid his rod under the seat of the boat. "Al's got a good line on the moonshiners from a friend of his who owns a bar, and one of my contacts identified the tire on a trailer we think was used by the rustlers. We'll have 'em both pretty soon, I think."

"I think so, too." Al piloted the boat back to the landing.

"So where do you think they're located?" Rick reached out and grabbed the dock as Al pulled the boat up alongside it.

"I believe the moonshiners are in Trempealeau or Buffalo County," said Al. "Based on what our source says, anyway. I've been talkin' to the county boys up that way, and they're on the lookout for any activity that seems suspicious."

Charlie tossed a rope over a post on the dock. "We're pretty sure the rustlers are from out by West Salem. We talked to the person we think sold 'em the trailer they're using. Next on the agenda is taking a little trip out that way to visit the guy who bought the trailer."

With the boat loaded and the truck pulled off to the side of the parking area, Al and Rick got to work. There was a cleaning table attached to the dock, and Charlie sat on a bench and crossed his arms as his buddies worked.

"Al, you oughta watch Rick. You can see the doc's touch in how he goes at it. Nice, firm strokes, clean filets. He's got 'er down pat. And you, Al, look like a fish outta water."

Charlie laughed heartily at his pun until Al looked up at him, a frown on his face. "Did you let Kelly know we're coming over?"

His buddy's face turned red as he tugged the phone from his pocket and walked toward the truck.

"I knew he hadn't called her," Al said. "It'll be interesting to hear what she says."

Charlie was back in a few minutes. "Kelly says great. She's gonna batter-fry the fish. She said she'll make a strawberry pie for dessert. I talked to her about French fries, but she wasn't sure about that. She wants me to pick up some of that Fish Shop tartar sauce. I love that stuff. Sure miss that restaurant, too."

Al patted his stomach. "Me too. I haven't had walleye like that since the place closed." All the locals had lamented the shutting down of the Winona restaurant that had drawn patrons from Wisconsin and Minnesota. "Nice of Kelly to agree to have us. You know, Charlie, you have the best wife in the world. If I called JoAnne this late to say we're having company for dinner, she'd probably kick my butt."

"She's special all right, but no more than I deserve. After Charlene, I sure as hell have paid my dues. What a shrew she was. And I'm still payin', too."

"She was a piece of work," agreed Al. "But I'd say you're in good shape now."

"Sure as hell am. Kelly's a dream. Great cook. Great in the sack. Always happy. Never makes fun of me. My kids love her. Life is good. Now if we can just solve those cases…"

As Rick disposed of the fish waste, Al and Charlie started

for the truck, just as Al's radio let out a whoop. As he listened, the dispatcher told him that they had a report of more cattle being stolen in the area south of West Salem.

"Hurry up, Rick!" shouted Charlie. "Rustler case is breakin'. We gotta go. Now."

Charlie jumped into the cab, Al scrambled onto the passenger seat, and Rick, still wiping his hands, vaulted into the back. With lights flashing and siren blaring, the truck rumbled out of the parking lot, the boat bouncing behind them as they went.

The dispatcher led them through the city on Highway 35, and then directed them south and east on Highway 16. The radio crackled as the dispatcher said, "A truck pulling a cattle trailer has just traveled through West Salem and turned eastbound on I-90. State Patrol also pursuing."

As they swept through West Salem at 100 miles an hour, Charlie pushed harder on the accelerator, trying to get more out of the truck as Al turned to check on the boat bouncing along behind. Charlie elbowed him in the ribs and pointed, and Al straightened in his seat to see flashing red lights ahead. As they drew closer, he realized a police car was parked on the right shoulder with the truck and trailer behind it.

Charlie screamed up behind the trailer, silenced the siren, and left the lights flashing as he slid to a stop. He and Al vaulted from the truck and, shields extended, walked up to the officer who was talking to the driver.

"Sheriff's Deputy Charlie Berzinski," Charlie greeted him. "This is Al Rouse, La Crosse P.D."

"Well, Officers, Mr. Peterson here is just explaining to me that we have the wrong guy. I guess you're going to have to be the judge of that."

Charlie approached the window of the truck. "Carl Peterson!" he exclaimed. He turned to the officer. "Thanks a million, but this *is* the wrong man. I've known Carl for years. He's a legit cattle farmer."

"Can I get out?" Peterson reached for his door handle. "Stuffy in here."

Charlie pulled the door open for him and stepped back. The driver stepped to the ground and then, hands in pockets, accompanied Charlie to the rear of the trailer. The tire marks in the dirt behind the trailer put an end to Al and Charlie's hopes.

"Goodyear." Charlie grimaced as he crouched to look at the treads. "We're looking for Otani."

"Then you're looking for Rene Boulon, and I don't want to be around when you find him, Charlie. He's a braggin' sonofabitch."

"That bad, huh?"

Peterson scratched the toe of his boot in the dirt, looked up at Charlie, and said, "Worse. Much worse."

"You've had dealings with him?"

"None that I want to talk about. Sold him a bunch of calves one time, and I've never heard the end of it. Every time I see him, he's bitching about how bad they were. They were purebred Angus. Damn good calves. But he's tough on animals. I'd never sell him another thing."

"Is he well-known?"

"For all the wrong things, that's for sure. If you find him, arrest him and don't ever let him out."

Charlie clapped him on the shoulder. "Thanks, Carl. That's helpful. Sorry about this inconvenience." He let go of Carl and waved at the police car, which was just pulling back onto the road.

"No problem. Happy to help." Carl offered him a salute before climbing into his truck.

Charlie and Al walked back to Charlie's SUV, where Rick was waiting. "Sounds like a real bad guy." Al yanked open the passenger side door. "I don't think I want to run into him when I'm off duty and unarmed. I say we get back to La Crosse and plan to visit Mr. Boulon next week when we have time."

"Sounds like a plan." Charlie stuck the key in the ignition and fired up the engine. "Now let's get home with the fish and the sauce before Kelly decides she's going to kick *me* in the butt."

40

THE COOKER ON THE NEW STILL ON LIAM'S PROPERTY LIT AS soon as Justin flicked the lighter. The flame burned brightly for a moment, while David fiddled with the burner control, calming it into a steady blue flame.

"That's exactly the flame you want for efficiency," he said to Liam. "This is a nice hot fire. It won't be long before we see the mash start to bubble - the first step on its way to shine." He walked around the still, examining it. "The nice part of this set-up is that there's almost no visible smoke. The old wood fires used in the past are gone, and with them the part of the process that most often led to people being caught."

"Yeah." Justin laughed. "All the lawmen had to do was follow their noses."

"Propane is a good substitute. Lots of people have propane grills, so buying the fuel isn't a problem. And the fire burns cleanly—not much flame and little odor. It's perfect," David told them. He stepped back and admired the still for a moment. "Not much is gonna happen here for a few hours."

He glanced over at his cousin. "If you have anything you want done on the farm or in the house, now would be a good time."

Liam grinned. "I always have things that need to be done. If anyone's willing, I need some hay baled and a couple of loads taken to the barn. It will be good for the neighbors to see you working around here. It's not uncommon to hire extra help, so that would explain your presence."

"I haven't hayed for years," David told him. "I'm not sure Justin has ever made hay, have you?"

When his brother shook his head, David grinned and said to Liam, "That means he gets the lousiest job, doesn't it?"

"Sure does." Liam smacked Justin on the back. "We'll turn some of that fat to muscle. You'll be on the wagon, Justin, so you'll have to stack the bales when we toss them up. David, you can drive the tractor. Sound good?"

"Great!" David clapped his hands. "No one ever let me do that before. I'd love to try it."

Tiffany slung an arm around Myren's shoulders. "Guess we'll finish up the cleaning and then make dinner."

Myren wrinkled her nose. "As long as the guys don't get used to us cooking and cleaning for them. I vote they make breakfast."

"You're on." David punched his brother lightly in the arm. "Justin, we're gonna be too tired to drive home. Haying is hard work."

Justin shrugged. "I'm fine with staying over."

The men headed to the fields. It was hard, sweaty work made even more difficult by the temperatures that rose sharply into the high 80s as the sun crossed the midpoint in the sky and began its westward slide.

When the last of the bales were loaded onto the wagon and delivered to the barn, the three men walked to the house, spent from their work. Even Liam appeared to be dragging his feet, although this kind of work was an everyday occurrence for him.

Dinner was perfect—a rolled beef roast made on the grill, baked potatoes, peas and carrots, and apple pie for dessert.

After dinner, Liam proposed a ride out to the still site to see how things were developing. He tossed several rectangular bales on the wagon David had pulled to the barn. Everyone piled on and Liam drove them down the lane along his fence line, reaching the back of the farm in several minutes.

The still was functioning perfectly. "We can probably make as many as 800 gallons a week here." David stirred the pot and replaced the lid. "When that comes on line, we'll be able to fill all our deliveries, including the new order from the mob in Chicago."

David retrieved a quart of the 'shine from the still and capped it tightly before boarding the wagon with the others for the trip back to the farmhouse.

As a nightcap, David fixed everyone shineritas, carefully blending the jar's contents with a bit of sugar, lime juice, triple sec, and ice cubes. Liam took a swig and licked his lips. "David, this drink is terrific—smooth but with the kickback of a shotgun."

"It's great stuff, that's for sure," agreed David. "In fact, it's as good or better than we hoped. Which means our business is probably going to grow even faster than we thought." Liam set down his nearly empty glass. "I've been feeling out several farmers in the area who raise barley, and of course everyone has corn. Most are willing to sell it to me, and no one around here will ask any questions."

"Excellent." David refilled Liam's glass. "We're gonna need a new truck, too - one that's larger than either of our pickups."

"Lots of guys around here drive Ford F-350s," said Liam. "That might be the largest pickup made."

David nodded. "Might be a better idea to trade in all three of our trucks and get three new ones. Em, can we buy three new trucks out of our funds? We're prob'ly talking 120,000 or so, and of course we'll get them from three different dealers."

"No problem." Emily rested her head on Justin's shoulder. "It's a good idea to change up the vehicles we'll be using periodically to throw off anyone who might be watching for them."

"Exactly." David yawned. "I don't know about the rest of you, but I'm ready for bed."

"Me too." Justin stood up and held out his hand for Emily.

David and Madison went up the stairs after the other five. Myren headed to her room at the end of the hall, but Liam followed Tiffany into hers. When David closed the door behind him and Madison, she whirled to face him, her eyes gleaming. "I knew those two would hit it off."

"Yep." David stifled another yawn with the back of his hand. "You called it. Not that I care who's sleeping where at the moment, as long as I have a warm bed to crawl into. It's been a long day."

Everyone else must have thought so, too. Within minutes, silence had draped itself over the old farmhouse.

As promised, the men had produced a hearty breakfast of eggs, pancakes, bacon, and sausages, even though they moaned and groaned the entire time about how sore they were. Fortified by their breakfast, they managed to purchase two trucks, at dealerships an hour apart, before noon. Justin slid behind the wheel of one of them as Emily jumped in from the other side. Liam, Myren, and Tiffany climbed into the other new truck.

Liam rolled down his window when David approached.

"Thanks for everything, Liam. And take good care of that still for us. I'll be in touch soon."

Liam reached through the window to shake his hand. "Sounds good."

David stood back and lifted a hand as Liam pulled the truck forward and onto the road. David got into their old truck, Madison on the seat beside him, and they followed Justin and Emily back home.

Half an hour later, David found himself in the unenviable spot of turning down Madison's advances and trying to wiggle his way out of trouble. "Madison, I agree, your massage was incredible. Unfortunately, I'm still too sore from haying to think about doing anything but sleeping at the moment."

Clearly undaunted, Madison made another attempt to arouse him, but she finally had to admit defeat. "Okay, old man, have your rest," she teased, pulling the blanket up around his shoulders. "But the next time I'm too tired, there better not be any smart remarks."

"Scout's honor," David promised, seconds before sleep overtook him.

Tuesday promised to be a busy day. The sun streaming through the window woke David early, but he pulled a pillow over his head and went back to sleep. Next thing he knew, his brother had flung open the door and was hollering at him and Madison, something about breakfast being ready.

David grabbed the pillow he'd covered his head with and flung it at his brother, groaning at the movement. Madison, normally a light sleeper, hadn't moved, and he nudged her gently with his elbow. "Come on. Maddie. My sadistic brother is ordering us to get up and come down for breakfast."

"That's right." Justin started to pull the bedroom door shut. "If you two aren't at the table in fifteen minutes, the food will be thrown out."

They made it, stumbling down the stairs and over to the table in about fourteen and a half minutes. If David looked as bad as Madison did, the two of them were certainly the worse for wear, in spite of their good night's rest.

"I could have slept another eight hours." David slouched down on his chair. "I still hurt all over. Don't you?" He shot his brother a reproachful glare.

Justin set a bowl of scrambled eggs on the table. "I hurt like crazy, but there's lots to be done. Em and I have to get to our still ASAP, so you two sleepyheads are on dish duty."

David reached for his cup of coffee. "That's fair. Breakfast does smell good," he admitted grudgingly.

"It'll be good to have you two gone." Madison chuckled. "Maybe I can lure the old guy back to bed."

"Well, he is quite a bit older than me." Justin went back to the stove to retrieve the fried potatoes.

When they'd finished, and Justin and Emily had headed out to the still above Minneiska, Madison and David cleaned up the kitchen, then showered and gotten ready to leave.

"Next week we'll have a new truck too," he told her.

He'd barely gotten the words out of his mouth when they hit a pothole and the vehicle bounced wildly. Madison laughed. "Not a minute too soon, I'd say."

When they got to their still, David sensed something was different, but he couldn't put his finger on what it was. He and Madison hauled corn, barley, and sugar to the still, and got another batch ready to cook. He was about to suggest they take a break and cool off in the river when a loud mooing sound stopped him. David whirled around as several head of cattle pushed into the clearing. "What the hell," he exclaimed. "Where the hell did they come from? We own all the land along the river for a mile in each direction, and no one is farming either above or below us. I'm not aware of anyone raising cattle, either."

"David, those aren't cows." Madison touched his arm. "Having been raised on a farm, I can assure you that those are steers. But you do ask a good question. Where *did* they come from?"

David walked up to the nearest steer, the one that seemed the most inquisitive, and petted the animal's head as it nuzzled his hand. "Hi, fella," he said. "Or at least I think you're a fella. Madison says you are."

Madison examined the steer and pointed to a spot on his hindquarter. "He's got a brand. See that? 'Circle E.' Know any Circle E ranch around here?"

David shook his head. "Jeez, this is a problem. It's not like we can call the police and tell 'em. What the hell do we do?"

"I'd suggest we find out how many there are and see if we can round 'em up and move 'em off your land. Is the property you own fenced in?"

"Yeah, after a fashion. But that's more'n a mile in either direction."

She shrugged. "Unless you want to leave them here, we have to move them."

For the next two hours they scoured the property in both directions. The mosquitoes were horrendous, and by the time they finished they had welts upon welts in spite of liberal applications of repellant. They had found ten more steers, for a total of seventeen. The two of them managed to herd the animals into a smallish area at the south end of the property, using several sections of old fence and the river to pen them in. The area had lots of grass and room for the steers to move about.

"Okay, now what?" asked David.

Madison lifted both hands into the air. "I have absolutely no idea."

41

AL WAS GETTING ANTSY SITTING AROUND WAITING FOR something to break on their cases. By 9:30, he'd swung through the McDonald's drive-thru, grabbed a couple of cups of coffee, and stalked into Charlie's office, prepared to take on the world.

Charlie held up a hand as Al walked in. A voice came over the speaker of Charlie's phone, the caller clearly agitated.

"This is George Espelein over near Newburg Corners. I think I've been robbed."

Charlie frowned. "Robbed of what?"

"Steers—seventeen of 'em. I've been across my ranch several times and they aren't anywhere. I've talked to all my neighbors. They say no cattle have wandered their way. There are some funny tire tracks near the corner of the field and no breaks in the fence. I need your help."

Charlie rubbed his temple with the fingers of his free hand. "Give me your address and we'll head right over." He nodded to Al, who set down the coffees, snatched the phone from his pocket, and inputted the address as the man dictated it.

"Gimme an hour. We'll meet you at your ranch house." Charlie hung up, leapt to his feet, grabbed one of the coffees, and headed for the door. For a big man, he never failed to surprise Al with how fast he could move. Al had to almost jog—being careful not to spill his own coffee—down the hall to catch up to him. The two of them headed for the garage to get Charlie's truck. The black-and-white SUV sparkled after a fresh wash.

Charlie climbed behind the wheel, and Al jumped into the passenger seat and did up his seatbelt. They drove in silence for a few minutes, Al admiring the scenery out his window as they drove south along Highway 162 before turning onto County Road PI and following it for a few miles. Just as he drained the last of his coffee, they reached a field that sported a freshly painted board fence.

"I think this is Espelein's land." Charlie set his cup down in the holder. "Should be a break in the fence up here and a road to the house."

"There it is." Al pointed to the opening. Charlie turned up the drive and pulled into the yard. Sitting on the steps was a man with a sunburned face. He was wearing a Stetson hat and he looked anxious, springing from the steps as the SUV drove into the yard and almost sprinting to meet the vehicle. Charlie rolled down his window as the man approached.

"You Charlie?"

"Sure am, and this is Detective Al Rouse." Charlie inclined his head in Al's direction.

"How are ya?" Espelein crossed his arms and leaned on the window frame. His lanky build and weathered face suggested a life of hard work. His jeans were faded almost white in the legs, and he wore a plaid wool shirt with his arms showing through holes in the elbows.

Charlie turned off the engine. "So what can you tell us?"

"About three days ago I moved a group of yearling steers into a pasture at the back of the farm," he told them. "There's plenty of grass and a creek runs through the field—ideal piece of land for young stock leaving the herd. Went back to check on them last night. All but a few were missing."

"They didn't break through the fence, did they?"

"My first thought. I checked the fence around the pasture. All there, and three strands of wire taut and unbroken. Checked with the neighbors to be sure. No one saw them."

Al leaned forward in his seat. "You said you saw tire tracks nearby? Any signs of theft?" "Yep, funny-looking ones. Never seen any like it. I marked up the ground pretty well getting' over there in the trailer. But you can still see the funny marks alongside mine."

"Wanna show us?" asked Charlie.

"Sure. But let's take my truck—it's pretty rough back there." He straightened and Charlie and Al climbed out of the SUV and followed Espelein to his vehicle, so mud-spattered it was difficult to tell what color it was. They drove from the farmyard, turned left onto the road Charlie and Al had arrived on, and proceeded to the next crossroad, turning left again.

"Must be a big farm," Charlie remarked as they traveled along the gravel road, then slowed and stopped at a field road. All three got out of the truck.

"Big farm," noted Charlie again.

"Full section." Espelein nodded curtly.

"Pretty hard to watch all of it, I s'pose?"

"Impossible. But this is the first time I've had trouble. Lots of money gone."

"So are these the tracks?" Al bent over the strange marks in the dirt.

"Those're the ones. See what I mean about different?"

"I do, although Charlie and I have seen them before. They're from an Otani tire manufactured in Thailand."

Charlie crouched down and brushed away the dirt from around the treads. "The same mark has shown up at other rustling sites in the county. We have a lead on where the trailer might have come from. We'd like to think we're close to catchin' the rustlers, but we haven't been able to run down the trailer, yet. We hope to do that this coming week."

Espelein shoved his hands into the pockets of his jeans. "I'd sure like to have those cattle back. That's more'n 125,000 dollars on the hoof. I might have a big farm by your standards, but I'm not big in the scheme of things. Those cattle are the difference between profit and loss for a year. It'd make me damn happy if you found 'em. Can't miss 'em, really. They're all branded with a big E."

Charlie and Al drove with the farmer back to his yard. He went to the barn and came back with a branding iron, the end of which featured a stylized E in a circle.

"We'll let you know if we find anything." Charlie saluted the man before rolling up his window.

He and Al headed back to the road, with Charlie laying out his plan for their next steps. He was adamant about hustling out to West Salem to see if they could talk with Rene Boulon. So adamant, he punctuated his desire with several hard smacks of his palm against the steering wheel.

"I'm all for heading out there, too," agreed Al, "but only to do a little reconnaissance. We need to scout the place out then determine the best way to go about this. I'm not sure that driving into his yard and confronting him is the best way to do it."

"We're on the clock, ya know." Charlie let go of the wheel with one hand so he could tap his watch. "We got two investigations goin' and neither one of 'em is producing many results right now. We'd better get on it, Al."

"He lives at W77867 in rural West Salem," replied Al, looking at the notebook he'd taken from his pocket. "Why don't we drive over there and see the place and go from there."

"I'm all for that," said Charlie, taking a right at the next intersection and driving the back roads toward West Salem. "Can you Google the place on your phone? We can drive past and see what it looks like."

Twenty minutes later, dust billowed into the air behind the SUV as they headed into the hills outside West Salem. At the next intersection, the GPS indicated Boulon's farm was to the right. The dirt road led up a hill into densely forested land. Charlie stopped the vehicle and looked at Al. "What do you think? Looks like a dead end to me."

"No mail boxes or fire numbers." Al pursed his lips. "I say we take a look."

Charlie made the turn, drove slowly up the hill, and said, "Wish we had an unmarked. This damn SUV stands out like a swimsuit at a nude beach."

Al chuckled. "Only you could think of a metaphor about a swimsuit in a situation like this." He gazed out the window, keeping a keen eye on the area as they passed through. *Few signs of life - so a good place to hide out if you're the kind of guy who wants to stay out of the public eye.*

Just as they crested the hill, Al caught the flash of a fire number set back in the trees off a narrow lane, blocked by a thick tree trunk strategically placed across the road. Al got out, strode over to inspect the log and view the number, then returned to the SUV.

"This is it," he said. "Not sure how we get past the log, though. Or how we'd get back out."

"Maybe we should nudge it a bit," suggested Charlie, revving the engine.

"If they went to all this trouble to ensure privacy, maybe

the thing's alarmed." Al hauled himself up into the cab. "Let's go on down the hill and see what we can see."

As they got to the bottom of the hill, a driveway veered off to the left. A mailbox at the road was labeled "Ebersold, S."

"This is Stan Ebersold's place," exclaimed Charlie. "I grew up with the guy. Went to high school with him. Let's see if he's home. Maybe he can fill us in on his neighbor."

Charlie steered the SUV up the quarter-mile-long drive that widened into a spacious farmyard. A giant oak tree guarded the entrance, but the road continued around the tree in an *O*- shape. Charlie rounded the tree just as a middle-aged blonde woman came out the door, wiping her hands on an apron.

"Charlie Berzinski, well I'll be," she said, peering into the driver's side window. Charlie rolled down the glass, extended his hand, and said, "Hi, Beth, how the heck you been?"

Beth took his hand and shook it soundly. "What the heck you doin' around here, Charlie? Don't see much of the cops out this way."

"Just driving around." Charlie held out a hand to Al. "Beth, this is Al Rouse, La Crosse police."

"Aha," said Beth, smiling. "We read a lot about you guys a while back. Got that serial killer, didn't you?"

"We did, ma'am," said Al, smiling back. "We were out driving, as Charlie said, when we saw the log across the road to your neighbor's place. Any idea what's up with that? If anything happened, it'd be impossible to get emergency vehicles back there."

Beth rested her hands on her hips. "You tell me what's with that. Been that way for several months now. We know there are people livin' there, 'cause we hear 'em. But we haven't seen anything of 'em since they moved in last winter. Not very neighborly, if you ask me."

"Sure isn't," agreed Charlie. "Isn't that the old Olstad place?"

"It is." Beth nodded. "Herman Olstad died about a year ago. Place stood for sale until these folks bought it last winter. Went by one day, and the for-sale sign was there. Went by the next, and it was gone and the log was across the road. Never even stopped by to introduce themselves or nothing. Pretty strange, if you ask me."

"We're concerned for their safety," Al told Beth. "If something happened, they'd waste time trying to get vehicles in there."

"You could walk the road, but it's about a half mile back there," warned Beth. "Pretty wild place, too, overgrown with brush. Not very well kept."

"Thanks Beth, you've been helpful. Maybe we'll try hiking back into the property a ways - make sure everyone's okay."

"You do that. Let me know if there's anything we can do. Stan's at work, but I'll tell him you stopped by."

"You do that." Charlie touched the brim of his hat. "Have a nice day now." He put the vehicle into drive and continued around the tree and back down the lane.

"Now there was one hot piece in high school," Charlie said as they left the yard. "When Stan landed Beth our junior year, every guy in our class was jealous. She's a bit heavier now, but still a looker, right?"

"Sure is," agreed Al. "But what're we gonna do about the Boulon place?"

"Do you wanna walk the road?" Charlie swiped the back of his hand across his forehead. "Pretty damn hot out, if you ask me, but if you wanna go, I'm game."

"I think we should," Al told him.

Charlie drove back to the tree blocking access to the Boulon property and stopped the vehicle.

"Let's armor up," suggested Al as they got out of the truck. "You never know what we might find."

The officers put body armor on top of their uniforms, then climbed over the log and began their trek up the road. It was as wild as Beth had told them. Thorns and weeds guarded both sides of the road, and in places the brush hung out over the road, creating an almost tunnel-like feel.

Whatever was going on at this place, whoever was doing it didn't want anyone to find out what it was.

After a quarter mile, Al stopped. His neck had been prickling for the last thirty yards, as though someone was watching them. *This is a bad idea.* "Charlie, I think walking up to this place is a mistake. We'll be sitting ducks. I say we go back, have some official—maybe the clerk of court—call and tell them the stump has to be removed in 24 hours or they'll be ticketed."

42

"**T**HINK THE TREE WILL BE GONE?" ASKED AL THE NEXT DAY as Charlie drove down the road, headed back to the Boulon place.

"If it isn't, we're gonna walk right up this time. My ass feels like it's been though a meat grinder. This damn road is brutal."

Al smiled. "Well, you're the county. What're you gonna do about it?"

"I'm just a goddamned deputy, Al. Not much I can do about the roads, unfortunately."

"That's crap and you know it. Hoop has more clout than anyone in county government. Get him to take some action."

For the next two miles, Charlie mumbled to himself, something about everyone thinking he had power that he didn't have, and expecting him to work miracles when he couldn't, and then getting angry at him when he failed, and he didn't like it.

Finally Al couldn't take it anymore and smacked the dashboard with the palm of his hand. "For God's sake,

Charlie, if you have something to say, say it. Your mumbling is driving me crazy."

Before Charlie could respond, they rounded a curve and began to climb a relatively steep hill. Charlie slowed and said, "Would you look at that?"

Ahead of them stood a neatly stacked row of wood from a freshly cut tree trunk and its major branches. Beside that was a heap of minor branches and twigs.

Al nodded, satisfied. "Looks like we're driving in."

Charlie turned into the laneway, careful to avoid both the stack of wood and the heap of leaves. He steered around the deepest ruts in the road that led through a copse of overhanging branches that nearly blocked out the sunlight.

"Could prob'ly turn on my lights." Charlie ducked his head to peer out the front window. "Damn dark in here. Kind of weird, don't you think, Al?"

"It's spooky, all right. I'm happy I'm armed."

"You got that right." Charlie tightened his grip on the wheel, his gaze fixed on the road ahead. After about two minutes, sunlight glimmered through the trees ahead. When they drove out of the darkness, Al gasped.

"Look at that, will you? What a view," said Charlie.

"It's a five-star vista, all right." Al's eyes swept across the rolling hills. To his left stretched a field of corn, the stalks taller than a man and freshly tasseled. To his right, a field of hay was dotted with bales waiting for the loader. The road traveled between the two fields. As Charlie guided the SUV along, the road suddenly led steeply down through a grove of pine trees. They exited the trees and drove up a gentle incline into what looked like a neatly kept farmyard. Then they rounded a turn and drove up near the house, and the illusion was shattered. The place was a mess.

Standing in the yard, as if waiting for them, was a rawboned man with a ruddy expression and a Stetson

10-gallon hat on his head. At his right hand stood a large pit bull. The dog sported one of those pit-bull expressions that looked like a smile but in reality signaled a readiness to attack. Lying beside the man, to his left, was a large German shepherd. It, too, looked vicious.

Charlie drove up to the man, rolled down the window, and asked, "Rene Boulon?"

"That's me." The response was more of a grunt than anything else. "Who're you?"

"Deputy Charlie Berzinski." Charlie stuck his hand out the window.

The gesture of friendliness was ignored as Boulon rounded the front of the truck, peered through the passenger window, and asked, "And who the hell are you?"

"Detective Al Rouse, La Crosse P.D.," said Al, adopting much the same tone as his questioner.

"What the hell do you guys want with me?" Boulon crossed his arms over his chest. "Did you have something to do with that order to clear that tree off the lane? Caused me one helluva lotta work. Moving trees is a big job. I wasn't ready to remove that one yet."

"Sorry, Mr. Boulon." Charlie propped an elbow on the window frame. "But it's a good idea to have your road open. What if an emergency vehicle needed to get in?"

"They won't," snarled Boulon. "No need for 'em around here."

"I sure hope not." Charlie waved a hand through the air. "But you never know."

Al shot him a look. His buddy was doing an excellent job of staying calm and speaking pleasantly, kind of unusual for Charlie. Al hadn't seen him in professional mode that often, and he was impressed.

Boulon, however, wasn't about to be pleasant in return.

The frown that furled his forehead projected across his face. "Whadda you guys want? I got work to do."

Al scanned the property through the front windshield. Machinery was lined up in neat rows, but most of it was missing one part or another and propped up on pieces of wood. The screen door to the house hung on one hinge, and the barn, what was left of it, canted on its foundation in such a way that it looked ready to collapse at any moment.

Boulon's frown deepened. "I ain't conductin' no tours here, so let's get this over with."

"Sure." Charlie told Boulon about the cattle that had gone missing across La Crosse County.

"Charlie and I have been assigned to find out what happened to them." Al indicated his friend with a jerk of his head.

"Ain't here," said the farmer. "Look all you want. They ain't here."

Charlie glanced at the barn. "You own a trailer with Otani tires, don't you, Mr. Boulon?"

"I do." The man uncrossed his arms. "It's 'round here somewhere if you want to look. Prob'ly in the barn. Ain't used it for months."

"Mind if we have a look?" asked Charlie politely.

"Hell, yes, I mind," snapped Boulon, "but I reckon you drove all the way out here to look, so go ahead."

"What about the dogs? They look kinda mean."

"Hell, yes, they're mean. Ain't been fed in a while," said Boulon. "And they don't like strangers."

"Can you lock 'em up?" Al touched his piece discreetly; wanting to make sure it was still there in case he needed it.

"I can, but I won't," the man snarled. Flecks of spittle flew from his mouth and landed in the dirt. "They live here, just me 'n them and Ma. They have the run of the place."

"We'd like you to pen 'em up while we look around."

Charlie spoke quietly but firmly. "If they assault a law officer, it's as serious as a man doin' it. And you'd be responsible. We don't want to have to put 'em down, but that might happen."

Boulon's face took on a ruddy hue, which rolled up from his cheeks until his entire face looked as if it were burning.

"Who the hell do you think you are?" he snapped. "You come in here, accuse me of rustlin' cattle, and expect me to just step outta your way? You got a warrant?"

"Yes, we do." Charlie tugged the paper out of his pocket and waggled it out the window. Boulon didn't touch it, but his stare grew even steelier. Then he yelled, "Ma, call the dogs so these assholes can look around, will ya?"

A plain-looking woman in a worn cotton dress emerged from the house, a frightened look on her face. She called, "Buster, Prince, c'mon!"

The dogs, snarling and drooling, padded toward the porch. The woman came down the steps and attached the snaps on the ends of two ropes to their collars. Al touched his weapon again. The ropes didn't look strong enough to hold a puppy. Neither he nor Charlie said anything as they climbed down from the SUV and approached Boulon.

"Want to show us the trailer?" asked Al.

"Hell, no, I don't!" snapped the farmer. "Told you where to find it. It's in the barn. Be alert as you're lookin'. Coupla rattlesnakes holed up in there. Haven't been able to find where they're hangin' out, but you'll hear 'em, I'm sure."

Sure enough, as Charlie and Al approached the barn under the watchful stare of Boulon, the sharp buzzing sound of rattlers filled the air. The whir was loud and disturbing, and Charlie and Al drew their guns before walking farther through the long grass.

"Not sure I wanna go in there," lamented Charlie as they reached the barn door, hanging open just wide enough for a person to pass through. The interior of the barn was foul smelling and dark, light filtering weakly through two windows that likely hadn't been washed since the building was erected.

In spite of his words, Charlie reached the door and pushed his head inside. For a moment he didn't speak, likely letting his eyes adjust to the lack of light, then he backed up and looked at Al. "I think I see the trailer at the far end of the building."

Al nodded. He was no more anxious than Charlie to enter the stinking place, but it had to be done. Charlie held the door and Al peered inside. The lane down the middle of the building was strewn with objects and junk, all of it making great hiding places for the snakes that kept up their insistent whirrings. "Looks like there might be an entrance at the back, closer to the trailer."

"Let's go around then." Charlie let the door swing shut. "I sure as hell don't want to walk too far inside that place."

Al nodded and the two officers, weapons drawn and ready, picked their way around the building through what once might have been the cow yard and was now filled with shoulder-high weeds.

Boulon's harsh laughter echoed behind them. "Careful, boys!" he called. "Don't let them snakes get ya. Never know where they might be."

"What a sweetheart," mumbled Charlie as he pushed through the weeds to the other side of the barn. When they got there, Charlie tugged open the rear door. It squeaked loudly, its hinges protesting from lack of use. When it was fully open, the two men stood in the doorway and studied the trailer, half-buried beneath a heap of other items, including cushions from a sofa that slouched off to the side.

"Should we go closer?"

Charlie screwed up his face. "I can see just fine from here."

Al rolled his eyes. "Some tough cop you are. Watch the yard then. I'm going to take a quick look." He picked his way carefully over to the trailer and lifted a sofa cushion, setting it back down quickly when a mouse scampered across it and disappeared in the pile of debris. Holding his breath, Al crouched down, inspected the tire, ran a hand under the bottom of the trailer, and straightened.

He managed to make his way back to the door without encountering any snakes. As soon as he stepped through the opening, Charlie smacked him on the back. "Let's get outta here." They retreated back to the truck and climbed in. Charlie leaned out the window. "Thank you for your time, Mr. Boulon."

The man didn't reply as Charlie started the SUV and drove out of the yard and back down the rutted path to the county road.

"Nice guy," observed Charlie. "About as nice as the snakes he's got keepin' him company."

"He's surly, all right." Al shuddered. "And that trick of hiding the trailer under a bunch of junk didn't fool me. That thing has been driven recently—it reeked of fresh manure."

"How the hell could you tell that?" Charlie grimaced. "The whole place smelled of little use and abuse. Looks like it's been lyin' that way for ages."

Al shook his head. "Charlie, how can that nose, so sensitive when it comes to food, be so numb when it comes to farm smells? There's a big difference between fresh and manure that's laid there for weeks. That trailer's been used recently."

"Shit!" Charlie smacked the wheel again. "Not very anxious to go back there, to be honest."

Al shrugged. "I think he's got plenty to hide. There were a couple of nearly new motorcycles off to the side in the barn.

Bet those weren't purchased legally, either. I do think we are going to head back there—and soon."

The words came out broken up as the SUV bounced over ruts and his teeth clattered together.

"I guess so," agreed Charlie reluctantly. "But I'm bringing the taser with me next time for those dogs. And I might throw on my old jock from baseball too, for good measure."

Al would have laughed, except that both of those ideas sounded pretty good to him too.

43

DAVID STEERED THE TRUCK IN THE DIRECTION OF LA CROSSE. Beside him, Justin was agitated, drumming his fingers on the door handle or slapping his thighs. David gritted his teeth. "I'm getting there as fast as I can, bro."

"I know, but we have to take care of those steers today. This is damn serious. If someone brought cattle way out to the middle of nowhere, they're likely stolen. That means lots of folks are lookin' for them. And whadda think that'll mean for us?"

David repressed a shudder. "I don't even want to think about it. Last thing we want is for a bunch of strangers—especially lawmen—tromping across our property. That's why I called Byrle. He knows everyone in the area, and he's got as much to lose as we do. He said he'd look into it and find someone who can haul that cattle away for us."

"But where's he gonna take them? It's not like he can just drive 'em a few miles up the road and turn 'em loose."

"No, but over a few valleys, maybe? He can find a quiet,

fenced-in place and let 'em go. Maybe Eagle Valley. No one will connect them to us if they find them there."

In a half hour's time, the brothers had crossed the Mississippi and were headed south toward La Crosse and Onalaska. They took the Highway 35 exit then turned left to head into north La Crosse, arriving at Oldendorf's bar in less than ten minutes.

They found the bar owner busy cleaning and stocking coolers. "Gonna be a busy night," he predicted, running a cloth around the inside of one of the coolers. "This time of year, when the college kids start comin' back, we heat up like crazy. Can't be too soon, neither. If it hadn't been for your hooch, it would've been one long, hot summer. Because of you guys, I just got through the first summer since I owned this place without once having to invade my line of credit. Gotta thank you for that."

"Glad to hear it." David settled on a stool at the bar. "So did you find someone who can help us out so we can keep supplying the stuff to you?"

"Asked around. Found just what you wanted," said Oldendorf, grabbing the cooler and hoisting himself up. "Guy's name is Boulon, Rene Boulon. Lives over by West Salem. "Operates outside the law most of the time, I'm told. My guess is that if you let him have those cows, he'll get 'em outa there for ya."

Justin clasped his hands on the bar. "Any idea how we can contact him?"

"Got it right here." Oldendorf paged through a loose-leaf notebook behind the bar. "Here it is. Got something to write with?"

"I'll take a picture." David pulled his phone from his shirt pocket and snapped a photo of the page with the phone number on it.

"I'll call him right now." Justin unclasped his hands and

tugged his phone from the back pocket of his jeans. David held out his phone so his brother could read the number. Justin punched it in and waited a few seconds before shooting his brother a frustrated look. "Mr. Boulon? My name's Justin Freeman. My brother and I have a problem that our mutual friend Byrle Oldendorf thinks you might be able to help us with. If you could call me back, I'd really appreciate it." He left his number before disconnecting the call and shoving the phone back into his pocket. "Sure wish I'd a gotten him," he said, "but no such luck. Anything we can do to help you while we're waiting for a call back?"

"Nope. Help yourselves to something to drink, though. I'll be done here in a minute. Cook'll be in soon if ya want lunch."

Forty-five minutes later, the brothers were just biting into their burgers when Justin's phone rang.

When he answered, David leaned closer, trying without much success to catch snatches of the other end of the conversation. Justin grabbed a napkin and snapped his fingers. David snatched a pen out of his pocket and handed it to him. "Okay." Justin scribbled on the napkin. "We'll be by in an hour or so." He disconnected the call and returned the phone to his pocket. "I've got the address," he said. "We can head out there when we're done eating."

Just short of an hour later, they bumped up the drive to Boulon's house. David eyed the pile of wood at the end of the driveway. He didn't envy whoever'd had to cut up that giant tree.

As David steered the truck into the yard, two ugly, snarling dogs raced to meet the truck. "Shit, we don't want to get bitten by either of them." He grimaced. "That pit bull looks ugly and hungry."

"The German Shepherd doesn't look friendly, either," said his brother.

David held out his arm. "Got your back, bro."

Justin clasped his forearm. "And I've got yours."

As the truck pulled to a stop in the yard, a woman emerged from a house that appeared to be in a great state of disrepair. She limped down the battered steps and approached the truck. David studied her. Might have been beautiful once, but her face was grooved by worry lines, and her eyes looked as if she either suffered from allergies or had been crying. When she reached the passenger side of the truck, she wiped her hands on her plain cotton housedress.

Justin rolled down the window cautiously as the woman yelled, "Buster. Prince. Goddammit, quiet down. Get back on the porch. Now." She waited until the two canines had slunk up the porch steps. "Goddamn dogs are a pain in the ass." She turned back to Justin. "There. They'll be quiet now. How can I help ya?"

Justin explained they were looking for Rene Boulon. "We have to talk to him about a problem we need help dealing with."

"Ah. You're the guys who called from Byrle's place." She stuck a hand through the window, and Justin shook it. "I'm Doris. C'mon in. Rene'll be back in a minute. Just went down to the barn for somethin'."

David wasn't anxious to get out of the truck, and his brother didn't appear prepared to move either. Doris grabbed the handle of the passenger side door and yanked it open. "Oh, fer Chris' sakes, they ain't gonna hurt ya. If they do, they know they'll get one helluva beatin' from Rene."

Justin shot David a look before climbing out of the truck. David sighed and pushed open his own door. Soon the two of them were seated in a surprisingly clean kitchen, and Doris was pouring them glasses of lemonade out of a large pitcher she'd taken from what looked like a brand new refrigerator.

David scanned the room. The kitchen was filled with new

appliances, and from where he sat he could see into an office equipped with a state-of-the-art computer. Above the desk, a 55-inch television set was attached to the wall. Hmm. The unkempt farmyard and dilapidated building had given them no indication that they would find such luxury inside. What exactly did these people do, anyway?

"You seem surprised." Doris set down the lemonade pitcher and rested her hands on her hips.

David's neck warmed. Apparently she'd caught him snooping around the place. "I guess I am, a little."

"We gotta keep up the *poor farmer* image, ya know. We do damn well, as you can see, but we don't dare let the nosey folks around here know."

David frowned. "Why's that?"

"Because our business ain't nobody else's business, 'less we want someone to know. For you, it's different. You're customers, ain't ya?"

"Well, yes, I suppose we are." His throat suddenly dry, David reached for his glass of lemonade and took a swig.

"Damn right we are." Justin straightened in his seat. "We got a big problem we're hoping you and your husband can solve for us."

"Outta my way."

At the sound of someone warning off the dogs, both David and Justin shifted to face the door just as a man—Boulon, David assumed—walked through it and into the kitchen. David swallowed. The man was ugly as sin with his greasy hair and unkempt sideburns. *He* was the one Byrle thought would help them? He looked just as likely to kill them both and toss them onto the front yard as chew toys for those dogs on the front porch. His gaze flicked to his brother. Justin looked as apprehensive as David felt, but didn't meet his eyes. Likely afraid that, if he did, David would tell him they were getting out of there before they could even tell

Boulon what they wanted - which he might have. Did they really want this guy knowing where their property was?

"Doris showin' off her new toys?" Boulon smirked as he jerked his head in the direction of the refrigerator. "That means she thinks you're all right. Not many folks win her over."

"These guys got a problem," she told him. "They think we can help."

"I'm listenin'." Boulon lowered himself onto a chair and flicked a hand at the pitcher. "Pour me some a that lemonade. Damn thirsty."

Doris busied herself at the fridge, pouring two more glasses of the beverage before joining them at the table.

David repressed a sigh. They needed those steers off their property, and they had no one else to turn to. Like it or not, they were going to have to put their trust in this guy. When everyone was settled, David filled them in on the situation with the steers on their property.

Boulon's bushy eyebrows drew together. "Where'd you say this is?"

Justin gave them directions to their place.

"Turn right off Highway 35 after the tracks and before the Fish House?" Boulon scratched Justin's directions on a notepad.

When Justin nodded, the man asked, "How many head?"

"Seventeen," David told him.

"Goddamn, Doris, those're the cattle I dropped off two nights ago. Left 'em penned a couple of miles away at a buddy's place where I could go fetch 'em when things cooled down a little. Must a got out somehow. Guess I won't be able ta use that place no more." He tipped back his head and took a huge swig of lemonade. A trail of liquid dripped down from his mouth and he swiped it away with the back of his hand.

"I'll be goddamned. You want me to re-rustle what I already rustled, is that it?"

David glanced at Justin. This was the guy who'd been rustling cattle in the area? That meant the authorities were after him, which could be bad if they were caught anywhere near him. On the other hand—David drummed his fingers on the table—he wasn't likely to turn them in either, if he did figure out what he and Justin were doing at the property. "I guess that's what we're asking, yes."

Justin nodded. "We're afraid if they stay there, the law is gonna look a little too closely at the area."

David hid a wince. His brother was sharing too much information. Now Boulon would want to know exactly what they were hiding out there. He nudged his brother's shoe with his under the table.

"Why's that?"

David glared at Justin. "We got a little operation of our own going." He left it at that. The less the man knew, the better.

Boulon stared at them for a moment then glanced over at his wife. "Doris, I think maybe we need to get these boys to cut us in for a share of their business, whaddya think? Might help us keep our mouths shut."

Justin shot David a sheepish look, as though he'd just realized he'd said too much.

Before either of them could speak, Doris set down her glass of lemonade. "C'mon, Rene. These two are nice boys. I like 'em. If we created a problem for 'em, I say we solve it. Then we make an agreement—we don't stick our nose in their business, and they don't stick their noses in ours."

He held up both hands. "I was just teasin'. Can I get 'em out tonight?"

The tension in David's muscles eased. "The sooner the better."

Boulon scratched his head. "Doris, where the hell we gonna put 'em? After that visit from the law this mornin', I'm not anxious to bring 'em here."

David looked at Justin, who nodded. "Mr. Boulon, we've given that some thought and have a suggestion, if you're looking to hide 'em for a while."

"Gotta put 'em somewhere, that's for sure. Hope to sell 'em soon, but no tellin' how long that might take."

"Give us a time and we'll meet you up there," said David. "We can help you load 'em and then show you where you can put 'em for a while."

"Midnight sounds about right."

Justin leaned forward. "Where do you sell 'em?"

Boulon scowled. "Pretty damn nosey, ain't ya kid? I ain't anxious to give away no parts of ma business, understand?"

Justin slumped in his seat. "Yessir. Didn't mean anything by the question. Just curious, that's all."

"Well, curiosity can kill a lot more'n a cat around here. Best keep that in mind." Boulon ran fingers through his greasy hair. "Besides, better if ya don't know, kid. Then ya can't get in trouble—with me or the law."

"Yessir," agreed Justin.

"Don't be so damn ugly, Rene," said Doris. "These are nice young men. Treat 'em like that. Hear me?"

"Yeah, yeah, I hear ya." Bulon waved a hand through the air. "Get off my ass, will ya, Doris? Yer getting' ta be a goddamn nag."

"Well, you need nagging sometimes."

Thinking it was best for them to be on their way before the fight intensified—or before his brother opened his big mouth and got them both in trouble again—David rose from the table. "We should head out. Mr. Boulon, we'll see you tonight."

"You'll see me, too," offered Doris. "Not gonna let him at you alone. He can be a bastard sometimes."

"Okay, then," said Justin. "We'll see both of you."

The brothers jounced out of the farmyard and down the drive, eventually turning north onto a blacktopped county road.

"Any idea where you're going?" asked Justin.

"Nope, just in the general direction of home. Need a little time to decompress from that conversation."

Justin's shoulders sagged. "I know what you mean. I couldn't seem to open my mouth without stickin' my foot in it."

"I noticed that." David gave him a wry grin. It was a beautiful day, cool and clear. The dew still lingered on the alfalfa and the corn stalks as they drove along. The popcorn clouds lazily skittered along, seeming to move from side to side as they drove.

Justin opened his window and reached over to turn Garth Brooks up on the SiriuxXM channel.

"Country lyrics are the best, don't you think?"

"I'm not big on country, but Madison loves it, so I'm getting more and more used to it. I gotta admit the lyrics are more like a story than the stuff I listen to." He reached across the seat and punched his brother lightly on the arm as the words to "If Tomorrow Never Comes" drifted through the cab. "Just watch what you say to Boulon tonight, will ya? Really don't want the words of this song to become *our* story if it's all the same to you."

44

BACK IN LA CROSSE, AL GRIPPED THE DOOR HANDLE AS CHARLIE wheeled the Suburban into the P.D. lot. "How about a beer?" his buddy asked.

Al shook his head. "Better not. We could be on the move any minute."

"Not tonight, I hope." Charlie's brow furrowed. "I told Kelly I'd take her out for a nice dinner. We were planning to pop over to Maple Grove."

"Oh, yeah, at West Salem? Guess they've re-done the place to be real nice, huh?"

"That's what I've heard," said Charlie. "You and JoAnne wanna come?"

"Maybe. I'll have to ask her. What time?"

"About seven, I guess."

"If we go, I'll drive."

"Now why the hell do you wanna do that?"

"Because I planted a little bug on Mr. Boulon's trailer, and if it starts to move, we've gotta move, too."

Charlie stared at him for a moment, a frown deepening

the lines in his face. "And you didn't tell me? Why the hell not?"

"I was a little preoccupied avoiding the rodents and snakes to mention it at the time. Then when we drove away and started talking, I forgot about it."

"And you just happened to have one in your pocket? Locked, loaded, and ready to go?"

"I was a boy scout as a kid—I believe in always being prepared. Sorry I didn't tell you, though. By the time we left Boulon's place, I really had forgotten."

Charlie shook his head. "You're not getting senile on me are you, bud? Seems like you're forgettin' a helluva lot of things these days."

"I hope I'm not," replied Al. "That's a nasty disease. You know my neighbor, the one we borrowed the motor home from?"

"Ya mean the one Rick bought?"

"Yep. He was a nice guy. Retired and bought the rig. He and his wife were going to see the country. Then she had a heart attack and died not long after they bought it, and the blow of her death seemed to really hit him hard. He never once took the thing out on the road. Now he's in a home. Doesn't know who he is or where he is. I visited him last week, and he didn't even look at me."

"I'll tell you what, Al, that Alzheimer's is terrible. Every time Kelly tells me about something I forgot, I get worried about that happening to me."

"I know how you feel." Al opened his door. "I'll call JoAnne right away about dinner at Maple Grove. Unless she has something planned, it should work out. See you later."

He closed the door and Charlie sped out of the parking lot on his way back to the sheriff's department. Al watched his vehicle for a moment. *What a good guy. How lucky am I to be working with him?*

Smiling, he made his way into the station and his office. A stack of messages waited for him on his desk. Al drove his fingers through his thinning hair. *Crap, so much for being able to spend a few minutes thinking about the case before quittin' time.*

He dropped onto his chair and reached for the stack to flip through it. Not as bad as he'd thought. Two were from JoAnne, both wondering what he wanted for dinner. That meant they were likely free to go over to West Salem, which was good. Two messages were from Rick. Apparently he was working out plans for the University of Wisconsin football games and wanted to talk to him. The others were from friends, too, just checking in. Nothing of consequence. He tossed the pile back onto the desk and reached for his phone.

JoAnne picked up on the first ring and Al asked her if she wanted to join Charlie and Kelly for dinner.

"Sounds to me like something's up," she said lightly. "You almost never ask me to go out to eat, even though you know how much I like to."

Ouch. That stung. "You're right, hon, I'm sorry. We should go out more often. Nothing's up, though. Charlie and Kelly were planning to go, and he asked if we wanted to join them. I should warn you that we might get called away on that cattle rustling case, though."

"Of course you might." She laughed. "I don't remember the last time we had an uninterrupted night out. I think I'll take the chance though, since it's been too long since we've had dinner with Charlie and Kelly."

"Great. I'll let them know. Be home to pick you up around six."

"Sounds good."

Al ended the call and set down the phone. A minute later it buzzed and he snatched it up. Charlie.

"I invited Rick and Peggy to join us for dinner," his buddy told him. "He and Peggy will meet us at Maple Grove, unless you want to pick them up?"

"We'll pick them up." Al made a mental note not to forget to call Rick to make those arrangements. "We should have two vehicles there anyway, in case some of us get called away."

"Good point. Okay, you make the arrangements with Rick, and Kelly and I will meet you at the restaurant."

When Charlie hung up, Al called Rick and arranged to pick him and Peggy up. He glanced at his watch. Already five. Better head home and have a shower before they went out for the evening.

When the six friends gathered that night, they shared lots of laughs as they discussed home and work. Charlie mentioned the serial killer case had been mentioned in the paper that day. Al toyed with his linen napkin. "That's right. If Genevieve Wangen had lived, the trial would be starting soon."

He gazed at the wine list. Just talking about the case made him want a drink. But if he and Charlie got called out, he needed to have his wits about him.

They finished their entrees, and Charlie had just asked for dessert menus when the phone in Al's pocket vibrated. He grabbed it and scanned the screen. The GPS device attached to Rene Boulon's trailer had reported movement.

Al tossed his napkin onto the plate. "Gotta go, Charlie. Sorry everyone. Rick? Want to join us?" He handed the car keys and his credit card to JoAnne, and gave her a quick kiss. "Take your time. Enjoy dessert. I'll see you at home."

Before she could respond, the three of them were wending their way around tables and exiting the restaurant. Charlie steered the SUV out of the lot, hit the lights and siren, and roared around the curve on his way to I-90. "Where's he headed?"

"He's still near his farm but moving toward the river." Al kept his eyes on the GPS, following the little dot.

"We may lose him in a moment." Charlie pressed harder on the gas. "There's a dead spot in the hills back there, but I'm betting he'll hit Highway 35. We can head toward Minnesota, catch the turnoff near the mall, and be on his tail when he reaches it. Sound like a plan?"

"Yep." Al nodded. "Let's go for it."

The SUV gained speed until the speedometer hovered north of 100, then, with a turn coming up, Charlie slowed a little, passed two cars, and steered the vehicle along the Highway 157 ramp on his way to Highway 53.

"Figure I can use the four-lane to run north for a while?" he shouted. "When they hit the road, we should be waiting for 'em."

Just as Charlie had predicted, the GPS signal ended abruptly a few seconds later, and Al stared at a blank screen as Charlie screamed up the highway, siren blaring.

When they reached Drugan's Castle Mound Country Club, Charlie slowed the vehicle, turned off the siren and lights, and turned into the parking lot. He backed the SUV into a spot between two parked cars so they were facing the road and shut off the engine. "Let's wait here. I don't want to get too far north in case he heads south on us. Okay?"

"Whatever you—" The dot on the screen lit up again. "He's back. And he's coming this way. Charlie, you're a genius!"

"That I am. It's about time you recognized it."

Al let the comment pass as he studied the screen, watching the blip move toward their position as Rick looked over his shoulder. When their target was about two miles away and heading toward them at a steady 50 miles an hour,

Al looked up. "Get ready Charlie, he's almost here." Charlie started the engine but remained in the lot.

The trailer, pulled by a new Ford F-350, passed by the parking lot. Charlie waited a minute, letting two cars pass by before guiding the SUV onto the highway. They settled in behind the second car and drove north as Al watched the screen.

After crossing the bridge over the Black River, the truck turned right, then into the lot of a trailer business.

"Wonder what that's about?" Charlie pursed his lips as he drove by and pulled into a roadside rest area. He turned the SUV around and headed back south. When they got to the trailer lot, the trailer was sitting there, but the pickup and its two occupants were gone.

Charlie smacked the steering wheel. "We lost 'em."

"I'm disappointed," said Rick. "I was looking for some excitement and all I got for my effort was missing out on dessert and a ride through the country with you two jokers."

Al shrugged. "Unfortunately, that's how it goes sometimes. When you're dealing with suspects that can move around, anyway."

Charlie snorted. "Good one, Al. Rick's guys are a little easier to keep track of, that's for sure." The banter continued until the three were back in La Crosse, and Charlie pulled up to the curb in front of Rick's house.

"Tomorrow's my day off." Rick reached for the door handle. The lights in the house were on, signaling Peggy was home. "If you head out then, can I tag along?"

Charlie glanced over his shoulder. "Sure, but you're gonna have to be ready on a moment's notice, and you might have to meet us somewhere en route."

"You're on." Rick climbed out and slammed the door.

Charlie pulled away from the curb. "Since we missed dessert at the restaurant, maybe Kelly would be willing to give me a little sugar when I get home." He elbowed Al in the ribs.

Al shook his head. "Too much information, my friend. Although, now that you mention it, kind of hoping JoAnne's in the mood to give me my dessert when I see her, too."

45

DAVID WAS PISSED. HE HAD JUST TAKEN A CALL FROM RENE Boulon saying that he couldn't make it to the agreed-upon site near Dodge. His trailer had an axle problem, he said, and he'd had to leave it at a trailer repair place near the Black River on Highway 54. If the repairmen there could work on it now, Boulon promised to meet them the next night.

"Dammit! I wanted that problem solved," stormed David in an uncharacteristic fit of temper.

Madison sat quietly. When he finished his tirade, she smiled at him and said, "David, c'mon, sit down."

When he complied, she reached for his hand. "I know how disappointed you are, but there's nothing we can do at the moment to change the situation, right?"

He sighed. "I guess not."

"Then how about we calm down. With an unexpected night off, maybe we can do something fun."

"Like what? I can't think of anything right now that would take my mind off those damn cows."

"Mmmm, you wanna bet?"

"How much can I bet?"

"As much as you want to. Have at it."

He thought for a moment. "Five hundred bucks. How about that?"

"Tell you what, you let me plan the activity and you're on."

"Then, to use your words, have at it."

"Give me a moment, but be ready to go."

David propped his elbow on the table and rested his chin on his hand.

True to her word, she returned shortly to tell him she was ready.

"Where're we going?"

"You'll find out soon enough. Come along with me."

She took his arm and led him out of the house through the front porch to her car. When they reached it, she pulled open the door. "Get in."

David bit his tongue. He wasn't particularly in the mood for games, but they had been working a lot lately. He really did owe his girlfriend a night out. Even if he had no idea what they were going out to do.

She pulled away from the curb and turned left at the corner. She followed Highway 43 along Sarnia Street, crossed Highway 14-61, and went straight ahead on County Road 17.

David frowned. "Where the hell are we goin'?"

"Just relax, Mr. Impatience. This is my deal."

They passed through Pleasant Valley, climbed the hill at the end of the valley, and drove along the ridge until taking Highway 76 toward Houston.

"Maddie..." What little patience he'd had was wearing thin.

"Patience, please, mister." The response was clipped, but when he shot a glance at her, she was smiling.

Two miles later, she took a rutted lane to the left, traveled through the valley to the base of a hill, and stopped. After jumping from the car, Madison grabbed a blanket from the back seat, opened his door, and said, "Time for your adventure, big boy. Let's go!"

David climbed out of the car and followed her down a path for a few hundred feet. When they reached a grove of trees, she spread out the blanket, unsnapped her jeans, and dropped them, revealing she was wearing no underwear. Her shirt came off next, followed by her bra. She flopped onto the blanket, folded her arms behind her head, and contemplated him. "What are you waiting for? Have I lost my charm? Here I am naked, and you're standing there like a bump on a log."

Needing no further invitation, David shed his clothes. When she giggled, he knelt and put a sudden stop to her expression of mirth. Soon they both were oblivious to what was going on around them.

Emily and Justin arrived home to an empty house. Although it wasn't his first choice of activity, she pulled out the Scrabble game and set it up. They'd had almost no time alone the past few weeks, so he agreed to play. He owed her anyway, since he'd promised her a while ago they could give it a try some time.

Justin was trying, but he couldn't concentrate on the letters. When he spelled his fourth three-letter word in a row, cat, Emily let out an exasperated breath. "What is the matter with you tonight? You're moping around like a kid who didn't find what he wanted under the Christmas tree. How about we change this to strip Scrabble? Every time one of us gets a word valued at eight or more, the other has to take off an item."

That got Justin's attention fast. "I'm in, but no loading up with crap like earrings and bracelets. We play like we are."

"That's not fair. In case you hadn't noticed, all I'm wearing is a robe. I have nothing on underneath."

"Oh, I noticed. Look, Emily, either we play like we are, or I don't play."

"Oh, okay, crybaby. I'll get you naked before me anyway. Just wait and see."

She was as good as her jest. Before he knew what was happening, he'd lost his shirt, his socks, and his jeans. As he sat there in his briefs, she smiled at him slyly. "Looks like we're even - just like I said."

He threw her a mock glare. "It's not over until it's over."

She promptly scored a word worth 12 points. "Oh my. Looks like my buddy is going to be exposed."

"I'm not sure I'm your buddy at the moment." He rose and pulled off his shorts, then tossed them on the pile of his clothes.

"I didn't mean you."

Justin glanced down, then back up at her. "Maybe you and your buddy should head upstairs? We've got the house to ourselves."

"But I've got some really good letters here and—"

Justin bent down and scooped her up. Halfway up the stairs, he set her down, breathing heavily. He definitely needed to get back to the gym.

Emily giggled. "What's the matter, big boy? Can't carry a little girl all the way up the stairs?"

Before he could respond, she ran the rest of the way up to the second floor and disappeared into the bedroom.

"Right behind you," he grunted as he stormed up the steps behind her.

After a few minutes of panting and catching their breaths, she rolled to him, teased the hair on his chest, and said, "It's so nice to be home alone. I love you, Justin Freeman."

"And I love you, too, Emily Whetstone. I love you, love you, love you."

The last "you" was punctuated with tickling fingers on her ribs. When she stopped laughing, she propped herself up on an elbow and said, "You know what I'd like to do?"

"No idea."

"I'd like to go drive past the property, see if the steers are still there."

"And I'd like a root beer float," he told her.

"Mmm, that's a great idea. Why don't we go to Lakeview, get extra-large floats to go, and take a drive to Wisconsin?"

An hour later, float in hand, Justin guided the new Ford truck along Buffalo County Highway P. He was glad she'd suggested coming. David had left a cryptic note for him saying that they didn't need to go to the property tonight to meet Boulon after all, and he'd explain why later. Justin was curious about what was going on, since they really needed those cattle gone.

"They've sure improved this road." Emily snuggled closer to him and took a sip of her drink. "The new blacktop makes this a really smooth ride."

"They've also straightened out some of the curves." Justin moved her hand from his lap to hers. "But it's still damn treacherous, so no extra-curricular activities right now, okay?"

She stuck out her lower lip. "You're no fun." To emphasize, she poked him in the ribs, causing the truck to swerve onto the shoulder. She snatched back her hand. "Oops, sorry. I see what you mean. I'll be good, promise."

As they approached the area where the road came to a V, one branch continuing ahead along the Trempealeau River and another turning to the right and crossing the river before entering Dodge, Justin guided the truck straight ahead, eventually reaching the area where the still was hidden.

"They're still here." Emily bounced a little on the seat, obviously more excited about that fact than Justin was.

He stopped the truck, looked carefully around to make sure they were alone, and then turned his gaze back to the cattle. "You're right, all seventeen of 'em. I wonder why Boulon didn't get them out of here like he promised."

He pulled back onto the road and drove along the river. "Something must have gone wrong. David said he'd tell me what happened when he got home, but no idea when that will be."

"Do you have Boulon's number?"

Justin nodded. "I do, but there's no signal here. When we get on top of the ridge, I'll try him."

Twenty minutes later, he pulled the truck to the side of the road and dialed the number. When Boulon answered, Justin pressed the device to his ear. "We had a deal. What happened?"

"Trailer broke. It's bein' fixed."

"Okay." Justin left it at that, not wanting to tip any listener off to the purpose of the call. "I'll check with you tomorrow."

Boulon grunted a response that Justin couldn't understand then hung up.

"A man of few words." Justin shoved the phone into his shirt pocket. "I guess that's good enough, though. Said his trailer broke, and he's having it fixed."

They rode in silence, eventually reaching Highway 95 and turning toward Fountain City. "What say we eat at the Frog?" The Golden Frog, a Fountain City bar-restaurant, was one of their favorites.

Emily bounced again. "Good idea. It's prime rib night."

Which reminded Justin again of their little problem. Boulon better be true to his word and get those steers off their property tomorrow night, before anyone else spotted them and all hell broke loose.

46

SUNDAY WAS A QUIET DAY FOR THE ROUSES. AL AND JOANNE attended Mass at the Cathedral in the morning. Afterwards JoAnne made pancakes and bacon. Al helped her clean up the kitchen and then they settled in with the papers—*The La Crosse Trib*, *The Wisconsin State Journal* from Madison, and *The Milwaukee Journal-Sentinel*.

Al dropped a paper next to JoAnne. "I'm gonna mix a Bloody Mary. Want one?"

"Sure, but light on the vodka, okay?"

As Al returned with the drinks, the phone rang. He set the glasses down on the table. "Who the hell would be calling on Sunday morning?"

"Probably for you." JoAnne didn't look up from her paper. "You can answer it."

Al snatched up the receiver and wandered into the living room. The voice on the other end was so loud he moved the phone away from his ear. Charlie. Something was clearly brewing that was going to end their quiet Sunday. It took Al a minute, but he finally worked out that the trailer was on the move again. "Should we head out?"

"Nah. He might just be taking it home. Just wanted to give you a heads up in case that isn't what happens."

"All right, thanks. I'll keep the phone nearby." Al carried the portable phone back into the kitchen with him.

JoAnne did look up from her paper when he walked back into the room. "Charlie, right? I could hear him from here. What'd he want?"

"That trailer I bugged, the one that might be connected to the cattle rustlers, is on the move. I left the tracker in Charlie's SUV, so he was keeping an eye on it today. He thinks the guy from West Salem might simply be taking it home. He'll watch it, and if that isn't the case, he'll call back."

The rest of the day passed quietly. JoAnne had put a small pork loin in to roast and then paired it with fresh spinach, something they both liked. Al had two big helpings, and when they finished eating, there was nothing left.

He patted his stomach. "I think maybe we should watch a little football and then hit the sack early."

"Football? Again? Can't we find a nice movie?"

"If I do, can we make out like we used to?"

"Maybe." She offered him a coy smile. "You should try it and see."

Al grabbed the remote, turned to the movie channels, found a chick flick, and they settled in to watch. Before long, they were entwined in each other's arms and neither saw much of the movie. When the credits began to roll, Al sat up and leaned back against the cushions. "We need to watch more movies."

JoAnne laughed the way she used to, heartily and a bit seductively, as she reached for her clothes. Holding them to her chest, she asked him, "How much of the movie did you see? Do you even remember the title?"

When he couldn't come up with an answer, she slid forward on the sofa and told him softly, "I rest my case. Care to join me upstairs?"

No sooner were they settled in bed than he turned to kiss her. As she moved to respond, the phone rang.

Al grabbed it before it rang a second time. "Yeah. It is? Where? Hmm, that's right, no signal. Okay, we better be ready. I'll drive to your house. Yep, I'll pick him up."

JoAnne sighed. "You have to go."

"Yeah, sorry." Al threw back the covers. "The trailer is on the move. I gotta pick up Rick on the way to Charlie's. I may not be home before morning."

Although time was tight, Al pulled her to him and gave her a long, lingering kiss before letting her go and climbing out of bed. He hadn't been lying when he told her he was sorry he had to go, even if duty called. A little more time in bed with his wife was a lot more appealing than chasing some guy and a trailer all over the countryside, that was for sure.

Rick was standing on the sidewalk outside his house when Al approached. He leapt into the car before Al had brought it to a stop and then they were off again - racing through the night toward Charlie's house in the hills outside town. When they pulled into the deputy's driveway, Charlie already had the SUV running. Al and Rick jumped into the vehicle with him.

"Belts on tight?" Charlie revved the engine. "We've got a lotta ground to make up."

He wasn't kidding. The vehicle canted dangerously as he pushed the speedometer beyond 80 and roared off Highway 16 on two wheels. They took the 157 connector and exceeded 100 as Charlie deftly steered the vehicle along the four-lane

Highway 53 in pursuit of the blinking red light that marked the trailer they were chasing.

"Let's hope he stays on this road." Charlie gripped the wheel tightly as they roared through the darkness. From the passenger seat, Al glanced from time to time at the GPS screen as the distance between them and the trailer narrowed.

They flew down the incline to the bridge that crossed the Black River near Galesville and sped around several curves. At the stop-and-go lights marking the Highway 53-93 interchange at Galesville, Charlie activated the emergency lights to get them through the red light as they roared down the hill, crossed a creek, and charged up the far side, heading out of Galesville and toward Centerville.

"We're getting' close." Al tapped the small screen. "Better lose the siren and lights."

Charlie hit the switch and the car quieted, although the sweep of the wind their momentum fostered seemed suddenly deafening.

"You can throttle back, Charlie," Al instructed. "He's only a couple of miles ahead now. I think we have him squarely in our sights."

"I stuffed some water in the cooler back there." Charlie glanced over the seat. "Could you open one for me, Rick?"

"Al?" asked Rick.

"Yeah, me too."

Rick dug in the cooler and produced the water that, when he handed a bottle to Al, was refreshingly cold to the touch.

"You sure as heck know how to thrill a guy." Rick mopped his forehead with a hanky. "I haven't been in a car going that fast since high school. Just how hot is this vehicle?"

"I've had 'er up to 130, and my foot wasn't on the floor. She's a goer. Big V-8 and all the trimmings. The sheriff fixed me up real good this time. Last SUV I had was a dud, but this Expedition is a great vehicle."

"I hear the safety equipment is first rate."

"It is. The damn thing sees ahead, tells you what's around the corner, controls speed and direction—next best thing to drivin' itself."

"Not sure how much more excitement I can handle tonight." Rick screwed the cap off another water bottle. "But it sure was a thrill to see the speedometer charge past 120 without wavering."

"I suspect there may be more excitement ahead." Al pointed at the GPS screen, where the red blip was now moving at a 90-degree angle to their path. "Looks like our guy has taken a side road."

"He sure has." Charlie pressed the screen to enlarge the image. "County Road P. Now we gotta be careful."

When they reached P, Charlie made the turn then pulled off to the side of the road after passing a couple of homes.

"Let's let him get a ways ahead," he suggested. "These back roads scare me. Too easy to be chasing and drive up behind him without knowing how close he is. I'd like to figure out where he's goin' before we take off after him."

And so they sat there for what seemed like hours, but in reality was just over twenty minutes. With all three studying the screen intently, the red light took turn after turn, continuing on past Dodge and staying to the west of the Trempealeau River. Suddenly the light slowed nearly to a stop, then turned right off P and proceeded north before sharply angling to the northeast.

"Those roads aren't marked." Charlie punched the display to expand the area around the light. "Looks like a field road. That might be the end of the chase."

He shifted the Expedition into drive and they moved

along P at twenty miles an hour. To Al, it seemed as if they were crawling after their earlier breathless pursuit.

"Where the hell is he going?" Charlie watched the red blip twist and turn, eventually returning to parallel the road they were on. "Unless you guys are really hankering for a shootout, why don't we find a place where we can sort of burrow into the background and wait for him to reappear?"

"I sure as heck don't want a shootout. I don't have a gun, don't know how to shoot one, and don't want to know, either. I want the excitement, I guess, but not quite of the terminal kind." Rick's face had paled in the wake of Charlie's comments.

"Let's wait it out." Al, always the pragmatic one, smiled at Rick as he urged putting on the brakes.

Charlie drove until they came to Alpine Road, turned around, and parked back from the intersection where they wouldn't be seen from the road. When Al looked down at the screen again, the red blip had stopped moving.

"Whatever they're doing here—and I'd bet on it being nothing good—they must be doing it right now. I'd love to catch them in the act, but I don't want us to be the ones who are surprised. That could happen if we try to follow and wind up stumbling into the middle of something before we know it. If we had back-up, we could do it, but at this point I think we're better to wait them out." Charlie shifted to look over the seat again. "What've we got to eat back there. I'm hungry as hell!"

"Makes sense. You probably ate dinner all of an hour and a half ago." Rick rummaged through the cooler and a couple of paper sacks behind him.

Al laughed. Charlie flipped them both off, took a big of chips from Rick, and began to munch noisily.

"Are you gonna share?" Rick leaned forward and rested his arms on the back of the seat.

"Uh, shurrry," mumbled Charlie, his mouth full. He passed the bag to Rick.

Rick took a handful of chips then offered the bag to Al.

"Not him!" protested Charlie. "He'll take the whole damn bag."

The good-natured banter continued then accelerated when Charlie grabbed a two-liter bottle of root beer, opened it, and took a swig from the bottle.

"Jeez," protested Rick. "Aren't we supposed to share that? You've contaminated it now with all of your germs. Didn't we bring glasses along?"

"Oops." Charlie smiled sheepishly then let out a loud burp.

Rick rolled his eyes. "For God's sake, Charlie, we're trying to be inconspicuous. That burp was loud enough to echo off the valley walls." He smacked Charlie on the shoulder. "I know Kelly has taught you better than that. Whadda ya think she's gonna say when we tell her?"

"Why the hell would ya tell her? This is boys' night out. What happens here stays here."

"Small chance of that; if anything happens here, everyone in La Crosse will know tomorrow," said Rick.

Charlie scowled. "And who the hell will talk?"

"You keep making that much noise and no one will need to..." Rick's voice trailed off as the beeping started up again. Three pairs of eyes turned to the screen where the blip was moving slowly but steadily back toward their location.

"Here he comes." Charlie swiped chip crumbs off his lips with the side of his hand and turned back around in his seat.

Al touched his weapon. Thankfully, he did have a gun, and he did know how to use it - something that might come in handy in the next few minutes.

47

None of them spoke as the red dot on the screen approached them. Finally, when he could clearly take it no longer, Rick broke the silence. "What's the plan?"

"I'd just as soon follow him at a distance. He's a surly SOB, that's for sure. I think we find out where he's going and make the stop once we have a better idea of his intentions." Charlie shot a look at Al, who nodded.

County Road P brightened under headlights a few seconds before a truck pulling a large animal trailer came into view, heading toward Highway 35 at a speed no more than thirty miles an hour.

"Treating things gently." Al pursed his lips. "Probably trying not to draw any attention to himself. My guess is there are stolen animals in that trailer."

"Yeah, and keeping them a secret is probably not difficult on the back roads here," said Charlie, "but it's gonna be damn conspicuous once he gets to the highway."

"Not sure about that." Al slid a little lower as the truck passed by, not wanting to get caught in the headlights, although Charlie had hidden the SUV pretty well. "With beef prices up, there are lots of cattle going to market these days. We just have to make certain that if he's carrying illegal beef, we stop him before he has the chance to turn them over to someone else."

When the blip showed that the truck and trailer were more than two miles past them, Charlie started the vehicle, guided it back out to the road, and leisurely set out to follow the truck.

"I'm guessing the next coupla hours are gonna be pretty eventful." Rick rubbed his hands together. "This is darn exciting to me. I'm just a lowly pathologist."

When the red blip reached the junction of County Road P and Highway 35, Al was surprised when it turned right and proceeded north. "What's that about?"

"Confusing, that's for sure." Charlie shrugged. "Let's hope he stays on this side of the Mississippi, or we're gonna have another problem."

The slow-paced pursuit continued for another five miles, until the blip turned to follow the dike road into Winona.

"I was afraid of that," said Charlie. "Shit, now we gotta get the Minnesota guys in on this. Every time state lines are crossed, there's a new set of complications."

"Do we have to let them know right away?" Rick gripped the back of the seat.

"No, but if we're gonna make a stop, they have to know it," said Charlie. "Then we got extradition to worry about and that Boulon guy is a slimy son-of-a-bitch, ain't he, Al?"

"Sure is." Al continued to study the screen. The blip crossed the river, turned left in Winona and then right, indicating the driver was following Highway 43.

"I'm nervous, you guys. We can't chase these folks without the local guys knowin' it. If we do, we could get in a world of hurt."

"Hot pursuit, Charlie," reminded Al.

"Hot pursuit, my ass. That went out with modern equipment and you know it. Plus, in no one's books would traveling thirty be considered a hot pursuit."

Al chuckled. "Good point. Let's see if he leaves Winona. If he does, we can visit the local sheriff's guys. If we call Winona P.D. now, they could screw us up by jumping in."

Charlie nodded, and they drove slowly across the Interstate Bridge into Winona, waited out a red light at the foot of the bridge, then made a left turn and followed Highway 43. The blip crossed Highway 14-61 and continued to the light, where the truck and trailer turned right, taking Highway 43 out of town.

"There, what did I tell you?" Charlie puffed out his chest. "Now can I call the sheriff's guys over here?"

"I'd wait." Al held up a hand. "What if they are going somewhere beyond Winona County? Then we'd bother the guys here needlessly and have to involve another bunch of guys when they get somewhere else."

"That kinda makes sense to me," agreed Rick.

"Aw for Christ's sake, you guys are yankin' my chain." Charlie let go of the wheel with one hand and wiped a bead of sweat off one temple with his fingers. "You know damn well we should be talkin' to the local guys. What if we really need 'em?"

"Charlie, the guy's drivin' thirty miles an hour. He isn't trying to flee or anything close to it. I think seeing where he's headed makes sense."

"Okay, Al, but if I get in trouble for overlooking protocol, I'm sicin' the sheriff on you."

"Fair enough." As they drove through a sleeping Winona, the red blip continued along Highway 43, then turned right when Highway 43 headed out of town. As they followed, they drove through a wide valley that narrowed as they reached its end and began to climb up the bluff. It was a gradual rise, and the gap between them and the red blip remained constant. Boulon, apparently, was in no hurry to get wherever he was going, although he had pushed it up to 45.

They reached the top of the bluffs as the red dot turned right and headed west along Interstate-90.

As they turned down the off ramp toward the interstate, Al caught a glimpse of the headlights ahead of them.

"How about that." Rick smacked the top of the seat. "Looks like we're the only two vehicles on the road."

"Where in the hell is he going?" Charlie scratched his head.

"Not sure." Al lifted his hand. "Could be anywhere. Sure as hell hope it isn't Austin."

"Nah, wouldn't be Austin." Charlie leaned forward to peer out the front window. "That's a pig operation. They even got a Spam museum there."

Rick tapped Charlie's shoulder. "I think Albert Lea still has a packing plant. Wouldn't be going there, would he?"

"I don't think so." Charlie shook his head. "Too much paperwork needed to go to one of the big places. I think he's headed for some farm where he'll drop the load, or a smaller seller who won't mind the lack of paperwork."

They drove steadily along the freeway. After traversing a steep dip, they left the Interstate to take Winona Country Road 29 south. Eventually they crossed into Fillmore County and the road designation changed to County Road 25, which twisted its way through a valley. Then they turned onto State Highway 30 and proceeded west, until the blip turned left and headed south again, this time south on Highway 250. Eventually, they crested a hill and began to twist down again.

"Oh, hell," exclaimed Charlie, "I know where we are. This is Lanesboro—big sales barn here. Bet that's where he's headed."

Shortly, the blip slowed. Charlie pulled to the side of the road.

"Need ta call the Fillmore County boys. And goddamnit Al, don't you say a word."

When no one responded, Charlie keyed in the radio and asked dispatch to patch him through to Fillmore County in Preston. Seconds later, he was telling the Preston dispatcher about the situation and that they now were in Fillmore County and coming into Lanesboro.

The dispatcher in Preston asked for a minute, then came back to say he had cars near Fountain and Rushford, but nothing close to their location. A further conversation led to Charlie being transferred to the chief in Lanesboro. He'd obviously been roused from his bed and sleepily cleared the way for them to continue the chase without the presence of any of his people.

"Guess no one wants to play," grumbled Charlie. "So we're on our own."

Just then the blip stopped moving.

"Well, lookit that." Charlie pointed to the screen. "Where is he now?"

Al glanced around. "Better advance with caution."

"Yeah," chimed in Rick. "This thing'll stand out like a homeless person at a charity ball, all decked out in black and white."

"I wonder," Charlie tapped a finger on his chin, "if we could get kinda close and then let Rick walk up the street. Boulon hasn't seen Rick, so if he spots him he won't connect him to us. Rick could take a quick look around and report back to us."

"It's three in the morning." Al stared at Charlie. "How many people in whatever the hell town this is—Lanesboro, I guess—are gonna be out walking at this time of the morning? Even if he doesn't recognize Rick, he'll know something's up."

"Hmmph, never thought of that."

"He's not far away. How about pinpointing his location? Maybe if we know where he is we can figure out a way to get eyes on him," suggested Al.

"He's outside the Lanesboro Sales Commission." Charlie studied the screen. "Seems to me it's pretty much at the end of the residential area off... umm... Coffee Street."

Al leaned over to see the screen. "Tell you what, let's head up Coffee then take Calhoun. If we keep our lights off, maybe we can pull in among those houses, and I can slip up and take a look at him without being seen."

"Sounds like a plan." Charlie eased the SUV onto Calhoun, a dark street that looped north off Coffee before coming back around to intersect with Coffee again. There were several houses on the street and only one dim streetlight.

"Plenty of cover," said Al as Charlie traveled up the hill and then began the turn back toward Coffee. "Anywhere here would be great, Charlie. Pull 'er over by those trees and I'll walk up the street a ways, see if I can see him."

Charlie did as he was told, and Al slipped out of the truck, careful to close the door noiselessly.

Fourteen minutes later, he emerged between two houses and strode to the side of the vehicle. As soon as he slipped back inside, he turned to his colleagues. "He's parked in the lot in front of what I think is the auction barn. I'm guessing he's planning to sell the cattle here. I suggest we get hold of the county boys again, see if they can meet us here by first light. Hopefully we can take him down before Lanesboro wakes up."

48

AFTER THE PLAN WAS LAID, CHARLIE GOT ON THE RADIO AND talked to the dispatcher, who contacted Fillmore County again. A few minutes later, the sheriff was patched in. Mark Haines sounded sleepy too but all business. "Whadda ya mean I got rustlers in my county?"

Charlie and Al gave him a thorough briefing then explained what they wanted to do.

"Should work. It'll be shift change time, so we'll be above full staff. I'll hold the night guys. We'll wake the day guys and get them in by 6. We'll have them meet you at Sylvan Park about 6:30, and you can take him down right after briefing our guys."

They agreed the plan sounded good. After the sheriff signed off, Charlie called the La Crosse County dispatcher, briefed her, and then asked that Sheriff Dwight Hooper be awakened at 5:30 so they could brief him on their whereabouts and the plan to arrest Boulon.

Then they waited—the worst part of police work but an inevitable component, too. Rick leaned forward and rested his arms on the back of the seat. "What're the chances this will get ugly?"

Al shrugged. "Not sure, Rick. It surely could. Whadda you think, Charlie?"

"I'm hoping when Boulon sees all the law muscle assembled, he'll surrender peacefully. The big worry is whether we'll have enough to hold him. There are lots of alibis he could use that would make it difficult to charge him."

"Like what?"

"Think about it, Rick. He's got a truck and trailer. He could say he is simply transporting cattle to the auction for another party. That's the most likely scenario, I'd guess. Al?"

"Sure, that's the easiest way for him to go. Since we didn't see him taking the cattle, we're going to have trouble making any charge stick. Even if he did, it may be hard."

Rick still looked a little confused, so Al shifted to face him. "If he does insist that he's simply hauling a load for a third party, it could get sticky. If he had help in taking the cattle, he'll have someone he can implicate. Even if not, he could come up with the name of someone he doesn't care if he implicates."

At 5:30, Sheriff Hooper called Charlie on his cell. The deputy put the phone on speaker so his companions could hear. Charlie briefed him carefully, covering all the high points and telling the sheriff the plan.

"So you got a hold of the Fillmore sheriff, that's good. I'm glad he bought in right away. I'm anxious to close this one, Charlie, so I hope you have a live one there. Al, have you called your boss?"

"Not yet, Sheriff."

"I'll take care of it. You boys have enough to concentrate on for the moment. Get Boulon into custody over there so we can begin the extradition process."

Charlie drummed his hands on his thighs, adrenaline

clearly flowing. "We're worried about him saying he's just an innocent shipper, Sheriff."

"If he goes that way, call me and we'll get on whomever he names. The sheriff over there should be able to make a charge stick with the judge - at least long enough to get him back over here where we can really shake him down."

The call concluded, the three men watched sunlight begin to filter over the bluffs surrounding Lanesboro. At 6:30, the first Fillmore County police car drove into the parking lot and Deputy Tim Wilson introduced himself.

Charlie stepped out of the SUV to shake his hand. "How many of you will there be?"

Wilson told him he was part of a two-deputy night patrol. "Craig Loessen should be along in a minute or two. He was over by Harmony. The three day guys should be here very soon."

Just as Wilson finished speaking, three more squads pulled into the parking lot. Wilson introduced them as Avery Larson, Clem Johnson, and Willie Drugsmuth. They all looked tough and fit. Al caught Charlie's eye and nodded, satisfied. It appeared as if they were going to have plenty of muscle to cover all the alternatives. As if to punctuate his point, another squad entered the lot.

Soon a plan was hatched. Two of the deputies would drive east on 16, cross the Root River, and double back to close off that route. The two night guys would seal the west, while Johnson would accompany the Wisconsin group to make the arrest.

Just after seven, Charlie started the truck, and Clem Johnson pulled his squad car into the leadership position as they drove north on 250 before turning right onto Coffee Street. Johnson rolled quietly into the parking lot then positioned his squad in front of Boulon's truck while Charlie pulled his vehicle into a spot blocking the back.

All four lawmen got out and approached the truck. Boulon was stretched across the front seat sleeping. Al rapped sharply on the window, startling the man, who sat up, opened the door, and stumbled from the vehicle, rubbing his eyes.

"What the hell...?"

Johnson stopped him, told him he was under arrest for cattle theft, and read him his rights.

"Cattle theft? What the hell are you talking about? I drove over here last night with a load of livestock to be auctioned this morning. There's no damn cattle theft here."

Charlie jumped in. "Mr. Boulon, we need to check on your load. There's yearling steers missing from La Crosse County, and they're all branded."

"Don't know nothin' about that. Didn't inspect 'em that close when I loaded up."

Charlie walked toward the trailer and peered between the slats. "There it is, Al. The brand is the same as the one Espelein showed us. We got our man."

Johnson cuffed Boulon and directed him to the back seat of his car, calling orders to his colleagues to secure the trailer.

Boulon continued to protest as Johnson shoved his head down and guided him into the back seat. "Hey, listen, I don't know anything about rustling. I was paid to transport those cattle. I'd rather not just leave 'em here."

Al glanced over at Charlie, who looked at Johnson. Johnson pursed his lips. "One of our guys can drive the truck and trailer to the county jail in Preston, where Boulon will be booked."

Boulon slammed his back against the seat. "I told you guys I didn't steal those cattle. I was paid to move 'em to the sales barn. I want to call my lawyer."

Johnson grasped the back door of his vehicle. Just before

he closed it, he leaned in. "You'll get that chance, sir. Right now, we're heading for the jail." The door slammed, cutting off any further protests.

Two hours later, Boulon had been booked into the jail and the on-call judge had taken his seat for Boulon's first appearance. Boulon had called his attorney in La Crosse so the court waited for Gloria Seavey, his court-appointed Minnesota attorney, to show up.

Boulon had already told them he would waive extradition, so Al, seated next to Charlie and Rick in the courtroom, was hopeful that they would be able to transport him home later that day.

By six that evening, everything had been determined. Boulon had waived extradition after being formally charged, and they had driven him back to La Crosse County where his first appearance would be scheduled the next Monday. He was being held without bail. Al would have loved to grill him on the way back, but since Boulon didn't have his lawyer present, he couldn't ask the man anything. Rick, seated beside the handcuffed suspect, looked a little nervous and didn't appear inclined to speak either, so the drive back was a silent one.

It was up to Charlie and Al to collect sufficient evidence to build a case against Boulon that would result in conviction. The man was crafty, and his attorney, Teresa Weinstein, was known for being unscrupulous in her efforts to gain freedom for her clients.

The excitement over, Al and Charlie had dropped Rick at home before heading to the courthouse. Once there, they took a seat on a hard wooden bench in the hallway. Neither spoke for a moment, until Charlie slumped down and shoved his hands into the pockets of his jacket. "Do you think he stashed those cows up there without the owner's knowledge, or did he know the landowner?"

That question had been haunting Al's thoughts since the arrest. "I don't know, but I think we have to do a little snooping. We need to call Buffalo County and see what we can find."

A few minutes later, Al had gotten the number of the Buffalo County sheriff and Jake Reinhardt was on the line. The sheriff had a big, deep voice that thundered across the phone. When Al introduced himself and Charlie, the sheriff became very interested in the situation and promised his help.

"Where'd you say those cattle were?"

"Near the river, north of Dodge." Al had put the phone on speaker, and Charlie leaned in close to answer. "We never actually got to the property. We'd put a tracking device on the trailer, so we know he was on the Mississippi side of the river, about two miles north of Dodge. We waited for him nearby. Al, what was that road we waited on? Remember?"

Al nodded. The name had stuck with him because of its similarity to his own name. "Alpine."

"Know right where that is. The land along the river has lots of different owners. It's not worth much. Prone to flooding, you know? I'll have to walk up to the Register of Deeds office and see what I can find out. Gimme a number where I can reach you."

The conversation over, Charlie bounced one knee up and down. "Maybe we should drive up that way. Talk to a few people."

"Is that a good idea? It's not our territory, so we'd have to let the sheriff know. Why don't we let him call us back first?"

"Guess so. Damn, just can't sit still. I wanna wrap this up."

"I understand. I'd like to have things tighter, too, but we're sorta stuck for the moment, aren't we?"

Al stared out the window across the hall from them, hating the waiting as much as Charlie did. It was a beautiful day. The sun was up, the leaves were turning - many of the trees reflecting bright yellow, red, and orange hues. The temperature was brisk, not yet freezing but brisk. And the smell was unmistakably approaching fall—that crispness that has an odor all its own. Al shifted on the hard bench. "Damn, Charlie, it's a beautiful day. I love this time of the year."

"Me too. That's why I'd enjoy a ride up to Buffalo County."

"Well, let's hope the sheriff calls back soon."

Just as Al finished his comment, Charlie's cell rang. He answered it and put the phone on speaker.

"Charlie, I think I have what you want."

"Let's hear it."

"The land I think you want to know about is owned by two brothers from Winona - David and Justin Freeman. I don't know much about them, but the land has been in the family for nearly a hundred years. About twenty years ago, a Freeman, must be the boys' father, sold most of the farm. I suppose the buyer didn't want the brushy land along the Trempealeau River. The boys have it now, and have kept the taxes paid. Never had any trouble with either of them."

"Sheriff, would you mind if we drove up that way and had a look? We don't know if the rustlers randomly picked out the property to stash the cattle on, or if they had a deal with the owners."

"Tell you what, Charlie, it'd be best if you had a search warrant. I'll see if I can get the judge up here to act quickly, and then I'll have a deputy meet you at the courthouse in a couple of hours. Sound good?"

"Best we're gonna get, anyway. Thank you."

"My pleasure. I want this thing solved as badly as you do. I'll get back to you as soon as I talk to the judge. Give me your number. That way, if you leave, I can let you know the deputy's on his way."

Charlie complied. The call finished, Al sat back, resigned to the waiting game.

Charlie's leg continued to bounce. "Anything we can do on that moonshine case, Al?"

"I 'spose we could head up and see Buck. It's a nice day for a drive. Wanna go to Barre Mills?"

"Anything's better than sitting here watching the paint slowly peel off these walls."

49

David paced the kitchen. The cattle had been removed from their land, which was good, but now they couldn't raise Boulon, who had promised to contact them to give them the all clear. Had something happened? Had he been caught? They didn't know this guy, and David doubted he'd feel any kind of loyalty toward them. Would he tell the authorities where he'd picked the cattle up from?

"What'll we do?" Madison's cheeks were flushed red as she sat at the table, watching him.

"I'm not sure."

"That's not good enough, David."

"Madison, we don't even know what happened to him. It's damn hard to design a plan when you're not sure what's going on with the guy. If we find out, we can think of something."

Madison grabbed a cereal box and emptied its contents into a bowl. "Will you sit down at least? You're making me even more nervous."

David dropped onto the chair across from her with a heavy sigh. "I can't think of a reason he wouldn't have let us know. We told him he could have the cattle. We just wanted them gone."

Justin walked into the room. "Heard anything from Boulon?"

"Not a word. Not one damn word." David reached for the cereal box.

Madison stood abruptly. "I'm going to find Em." David nodded. Justin poured a cup of coffee then sat down opposite his brother.

"There's only one reason he wouldn't have called us, David."

"I know, I know. That's what worries me. How long do you think it would take to clear out the land—remove the still and the other stuff?"

"God, that'd be one helluva lot of work. Couple days maybe. Four or five trips, possibly more."

"Do you think that's what we should do? If Boulon got caught, I'm pretty sure he wouldn't hesitate to rat us out."

"All he knows is that someone dropped a load of cows on our land and we wanted them gone. It was a simple trucking job."

"But we told him he could have them. If they were stolen, he's in deep trouble. And that means he'll talk. That won't be good for us."

Justin tapped his fingers on the table. "I guess you're right. Maybe we ought to get the stuff out of there. We can take it up to Minneiska and stash it."

David shook his head. "I'm not sure that's a good idea. They check the land over in Wisconsin and find nothing, then they'll look at our holdings and come up with Minneiska. They check it out. Whammo, we're in prison."

"Yeah, I see what you mean. Iowa, then? I'm sure Liam would be okay with storing the stuff for us."

"Much better option, for sure. But the trips are way longer."

"What if we rent us a U-Haul truck or trailer? Maybe we can bring the stuff over here by pick-up, load it in the U-Haul, and take it to Iowa in one trip." Justin took a sip of his coffee.

"I like that idea. And we'll get one of the girls to rent it in her name so it's harder to trace to us. If we all work hard, maybe we could have it out of there in a day."

With a plan in place, the load lifted off David's shoulders slightly. He pushed away the bowl of cereal. "Let's go."

By noon they were at the land near the Trempealeau River. David and Justin took apart the still as Maddy and Emily loaded bottles and supplies from the garage into the pickup. By two p.m. the back of the truck was full, but the still was only partly broken down.

"Em and I will take the pickup to town and stash the load in the garage," Madison told David.

Emily nodded. "We can get back here by 4:30 or 5. Will you have the rest of the still taken apart by then? If so, we can load it, clean up before dark, and get back home."

"Sounds good. We'll try to have everything ready by then. Get back here as soon as you can, okay?" David gave Madison a quick kiss and watched as the girls jumped into the truck and pulled off the property. Then he and Justin went back to work, accompanied by far too many hungry mosquitoes.

When the women returned just after five, the still was apart and David and Justin had dragged the pieces to the garage. They loaded up the pickup quickly, but there was still a lot of work to do, clearing the area of any traces of what had been going on there.

Madison touched David's arm. "Maybe Emily and Justin should take the truck back. I can stay here and work with you. Em and I aren't strong enough to handle the still, but I bet the two of them can. We can get things in shape here, wait for them to come back and help us, and still finish up tonight."

David nodded, and Justin and Emily jumped into the truck. Once the vehicle had disappeared, David and Madison went over the area where the still had been, raking and piling until they had a heap of junk.

"Wanna get the wheelbarrow out of the shed, Maddy?"

It took six trips to remove the junk. David piled it on a canvas in the garage so he and Justin could wrap it up and load it on the truck. The still area finished, the two made sure the garage was clean. By 7:30, they were done. Forty-five minutes later, Justin and Emily returned. The two men made short work of filling up the pickup.

Justin tossed a two by four into the back. "Are we taking this stuff to Liam's too?"

David slammed the tailgate shut. "Makes the most sense. Liam's got a dump site, so that's as good a place as any to unload." As he slid behind the wheel and the four of them drove off the property, David breathed a small sigh of relief. If they could get up to Liam's first thing in the morning, maybe they would get away with this after all.

The next day was overcast - the skies threatening.

Behind the wheel of the pickup, Justin, with Emily beside him, followed the U-Haul truck Madison had rented and that David was driving out of the yard at a few minutes past ten. As they drove along the Mississippi and passed through La Crescent, Emily broke the silence. "You're really worried, aren't you?"

"I am. This could be the time we hoped would never come. It spooks me that we can't get in touch with Boulon. To me, that means trouble—real trouble."

"I guess you're right, but you said he's a shady character, and we did tell him he could have the steers. I assume he came and got them. Why would he contact us?"

"Because he told us he would, and he has as much to lose if this goes bad as we do. The fact that we can't reach him is a problem. At least, it could be."

Emily slid across the seat and snuggled against his arm. "I'm sure we'll hear from him soon. And in the meantime, we're doing everything we can. Try not to worry."

Justin let go of the wheel and slid his arm around her shoulders. Emily was right—everything was probably fine and he shouldn't worry. But that was a lot easier said than done.

In the U-Haul, the rhetoric was much the same. Madison was trying to shake David out of his morose mood and stubborn silence.

As they approached Brownsville, she hit the dash with her fist. "Dammit, David, you're acting like an idiot. We've cleaned up the site. What more can we do?"

He sighed and ran the side of his hand across his forehead. "Not much, other than dumping the evidence at Liam's. I just wish Boulon had let us know when he had removed the cattle and disposed of them."

"Disposed of them? You mean like, killed them?"

"No, sold them. There are several auction facilities around, and I was hoping he would take them to one of those. Once they're sold, they'll be a little harder to find. But his silence suggests that something might have happened that we aren't going to like."

"Do you think he got arrested?"

"Quite possibly. And if he's in jail, how long do you think it'll be before we're in jail?"

"David, that would be very bad. I got into this because it

sounded like fun. I know you told us it was risky, but I never really believed we would get caught. If my folks find out, I'm in a world of trouble."

"Madison, if your folks find out, we have much bigger problems, because that will mean we're already behind bars."

"Well, you better figure it out, David. I'm not going to jail. Do you hear me?"

Madison folded her arms across her chest and sat back, her jaw firmly set. David couldn't help but take a jab at the pose. "You look like Little Miss Muffet. My dad used to tell me if I made that face, he'd put a crow on my lower lip."

"If you think that's funny, it's not. I'm scared as hell."

"I'm scared, too. But being scared isn't going to make it better, is it? Let's get this trip over with, then we can think about what we're going to do after that."

The next few miles passed in silence. Finally David looked at Madison. "You know, I've been thinking. What do we have to be worried about anyway? We found some cattle on our property. They weren't ours, and we immediately called a trucker to have them removed."

"But we didn't try to find the owner, did we? They were branded, so if the trucker took them to be sold, aren't we accomplices? Aren't we just as guilty as the man we hired to take them?"

That silenced David, at least for a few minutes. Several miles passed before he shifted in his seat. "I suppose what you say is true. We'd better think of a story."

"But what? If we had reported the cattle to the authorities, we'd be all right, but if the trucker talks, we're in big trouble. There is nothing else to say."

David grabbed her hand and squeezed it. "Still, there's no reason to involve you and Emily. We can say that Justin and I found the cattle and panicked. We wanted them out of there and we called around to find someone to move them."

"Then they'll want to know who gave you the name, and that will link you to Oldendorf. After that it won't take them long to put all the puzzle pieces together and figure out who's been running moonshine in the area."

David sighed. Clearly he wasn't going to convince Madison they would be all right - mostly because he couldn't convince himself of that either.

Justin stepped on the gas, trying to encourage David to pick up the pace. The sooner they got the stuff stored at their cousin's place, the better. "Not much farther now."

Emily rested her head on his shoulder. "Good. Once we dump the stuff, if they do come after us, we can just say we found the cattle wandering our property and didn't know what to do. We were worried about their safety."

He narrowed his eyes. "What kind of danger would they be in?"

"The river? Predators? Remember, we heard those wolves howling on the property not that long ago. We don't have to be livestock authorities; we just have to think of something believable. Can we turn in the trucker?"

"How?"

"We could say that we asked him to move the cattle to a safe place and call authorities, but when we went out there the next day, the animals were gone and we haven't been able to reach him. We don't owe him anything, do we?"

"I guess not. We could probably have a believable tale ready for the authorities. In fact, maybe we should call them before they call us."

"That's a good idea. We could call the police and say we had thought we'd hear from them after the trucker got the animals, but when we didn't hear from him we wanted to call them to make sure the cattle got to their rightful owner."

Justin pulled her closer and kissed the top of her head. "So smart. That—among other things—is why I love you, Em."

They pulled into Liam's driveway in Iowa a few minutes before noon. Liam walked out of the house barefoot, followed by Tiffany and Myren, still in their pajamas. The sun seemed to hit the steps just right, and Emily covered Justin's eyes then rolled down the window and told Tiffany and Myren to "get some clothes on. We can see everything from here."

Five minutes later, Tiffany and Myren re-emerged from the house in jeans and T-shirts.

"Much better."

Justin climbed out of the truck and Liam clapped a hand on his shoulder.

"What brings you guys here?" He shot a quizzical look at the U-Haul.

"We decided you needed another still." David pulled open the back of the rental truck to reveal the still and other equipment.

"But I have a perfectly good still, and it's workin' like a charm. Where'm I gonna put that?"

David told him about things in Wisconsin and their attempts to clean up the site to remove any traces of the liquor operation.

"You've got a place to store it, don't you?" asked Justin.

"Sure, that's no problem. You guys start unloading and I'll get the tractor."

"Great." David clapped his hands before reaching for a piece of equipment. Justin, Madison, and Emily helped him. By the time Liam returned with the tractor pulling a trailer they had a good pile of stuff in the yard. They threw everything from the U-Haul onto the trailer, then Liam started up the tractor and led them down a field road to the woods at the back of his property.

"This area doesn't get any traffic. Let's unload the truck in the brush. I'm pretty sure no one will find it there."

Working together, the five of them soon had the contents of the truck unloaded and tossed back into the brush. They covered it carefully, and a half hour later they were on their way back to the farmhouse. "Come on in and have something to eat before you start for home." Liam waved them inside. Everyone had just settled around the big oak table with a cup of coffee when an insistent knock sounded on the door. Justin's eyes met his brother's. Who could that be? Had someone followed them from Winona? His chest tightened.

"Probably just a neighbor." Liam set the coffee pot down on the table and stood. "I'll check it out."

Emily's hand found Justin's under the table, and she clutched it tightly as Liam headed down the hallway to the front door. Justin strained to hear what was happening. The door opened and a second later, Liam's voice carried into the kitchen. "Hi, Clint. We're just having coffee with friends, c'mon in."

Who is Clint? Justin glanced at Tiffany and Myren across the table. They both shrugged.

The front door closed as a man, Clint, apparently, responded to Liam's invitation. "Don't mind if I do. Things are all right, aren't they?"

Footsteps sounded in the hallway and Justin let go of Emily's hand and wrapped his fingers around his mug. "Be cool, everybody," he whispered just before the two men came into the room.

Liam led the way. "Sure. Fine. We just had some friends from up north drop by on their way south. Clint, this is David and Justin Freeman." He nodded at the two men. "And these two women are Madison and Emily, friends of the brothers. They're movin' some stuff down to Cedar Rapids and thought they'd drop in and say hi. Everyone, this is Clint Roebuck, our deputy sheriff. Pull up a chair and have a cup of coffee with us, Clint."

The deputy sheriff was a big guy, tall and muscular with just the start of a bulge growing around his waistline. Definitely looked as if he could take a crowd in a fight. Justin swallowed. *How did he happen to show up at Liam's right after we did?*

Clint took off his hat and hung it on the back of his chair before accepting the mug Liam held out to him. "When I saw the truck, I was worried that you might have had enough of the farming scene. Glad to hear that you're not leavin'. This place has been in the Richards family for a long, long time."

"Sure has." Liam returned to his seat. "Four generations now, and more'n a hundred years. No way we'd ever let this place go."

"Word around town is that you got yourself a couple of live-ins. That true?"

"Yep, the rumor is true." Liam held his cup in the direction of his roommates. "Meet Tiffany and Myren, the two best friends a guy could have. David and Justin actually introduced the women to me. We hit it off, I asked 'em to move in to help around the farm, and they honored me with their acceptance. Been here for a couple of months now."

"That's what I heard." Clint ran a thumb over the smiley-face on his yellow mug. "You know how the church-goin' crowd picks up on things and moves it around, right? Well, ever since you young ladies moved in here with Liam, the tongues in Waukon have been flappin' overtime. Plenty-a stories about what you might be doin' here, I'll tell ya."

That made everyone at the table laugh. Tiffany tossed her hair back over one shoulder. "Clint, you go back and tell those tongue-waggers that they're welcome here anytime. We'll even show 'em our bedrooms—all three of 'em. We're good friends, is all."

"Not sure you want to extend that invitation to 'em. They just might take you up on it." Clint laughed at his own remark, then sipped his coffee and helped himself to a doughnut from the plate in the middle of the table.

"You gals make these? If you did, I'll for sure not tell 'em or they'll be here tomorrow and every day thereafter. And I ain't gonna say a word about how pretty ya are, either. If I did, the place'd be overrun by men."

The banter continued for another half hour. Finally, Clint drained the last of his coffee and stood. "Best be getting back on patrol." He reached for his hat and held it in both hands. "Ain't many visitors around these parts. The folks back in town will want to know all about it. Well, have a good day, y'all." He tipped his hat and left the house. From his vantage point, Justin could see out the front window, and he watched the patrol car as it traveled down the lane, trailing dust as it turned onto the road.

"He'll be sure to tell everyone what he saw, too." Liam stared into his empty cup, a troubled look on his face. "Out here, if there was an ocean nearby all the ships would be sunk already." He looked up. "Ya better head toward Cedar Rapids on your way home, then cross the river at Prairie du Chien, and drive back up the Wisconsin side. That will lessen the chances of anyone figuring out exactly where you came from."

Justin nodded. "We'll do that. And we'll take it nice and easy, too. Do everything we can to keep from attracting attention." He shoved back his chair. "Sorry if we brought any trouble down on you, Liam."

Their cousin gathered up a few mugs and carried them over to the sink. "I knew what I was doing when I agreed to help you guys. I'm sure it'll all be fine. Clint might be a talker, like everyone else around here, but he's got a good heart."

"I hope so." David returned the cream to the refrigerator

and shut the door. "We better head out before any of your other neighbors *happen* to drop by to check on you."

It was just after three when they left the farm and headed out on the route that Liam had suggested. The trouble was, there was little to see in Iowa. The corn grew tall, and at this time of the year it was dry and ready for combining. With no view to enjoy, and with Emily sleeping beside him, her head resting against the window, Justin had far too much time to think as he drove. Dumping their supplies hadn't relieved him like he thought it would. Likely because the law in Liam's county now knew they had been there. Clint Roebuck might have a good heart, but if he also had a good head, he might hear reports of moonshiners or cattle rustlers in a nearby state, put two and two together, and arrive at the four northerners he'd seen visiting the Richards farm.

50

THE SUN THAT SUNDAY MORNING WAS BARELY UP ON WHEN AL jumped out of Charlie's SUV and followed his friend up the walkway of the jailhouse. Sheriff Hooper met them inside the door. "Glad you're here, boys. I was about to go talk to that Rene Boulon you brought in. He's been yammering his head off about how innocent he is."

Charlie snorted. "They're all innocent, aren't they?"

"To hear them tell it, yes." The sheriff held up a paper cup. "Coffee?"

Al shook his head. "We just had breakfast. We're good."

"All right then. Let's go see what we can find out." The sheriff led the way to the cellblock and stopped at the last cell on the right. Leaning a shoulder against the bars, he took a casual sip of coffee. "I hear you want to talk to me?"

"Damn right, I want to talk to you. I want out of this place and I want out now. What the hell do you think you're doing holding me here?"

"Well, Mr. Boulon, last I heard, we had you on suspicion of cattle rustling. That's a pretty serious offense. We don't let people outta jail here just 'cause they think they deserve to be free."

Boulon drove his fingers through his already-disheveled hair. "Sheriff, I was set up. I got a call from some man in Winona saying that seventeen head of stray cattle had showed up on his property and he wanted 'em moved. What was I supposed to do, turn down the business?"

"At the very least, Mr. Boulon, moving them to a sales barn in Lanesboro was one real bad idea. What did you expect to do? Sell 'em?"

"The guy who called me said his buddy was gonna sell 'em and he would meet me in Lanesboro. None of your guys asked me about that. If they had, they might have caught the real crooks."

"And just who would the real crooks be?"

"No idea, but you could start with the young guy that phoned me. Never saw him. Called me and said that these cows had showed up unexpectedly on some land he owned and he wanted to get rid of 'em."

"Why didn't he call the cops?"

"Look, Sheriff, a lotta guys are afraid of the law. I don't know why he didn't call you. If you hadn't jumped the gun, you coulda asked him yourself."

"So where did you pick 'em up?"

"Some place south of Winona on the Wisconsin side, back in the bush a ways. Not much around. Darker than the inside of a coal mine the night I was there."

"Could you find it again?"

"Whadda ya think I am, stupid? 'Course I could find it again. It was dark as pitch, but I had my GPS set to the coordinates they gave me. Still got a record of that."

"Good. That'll be helpful. And the more you help us, the better off you'll be."

Al studied Boulon. The man had perked up at the sheriff's

words, which was a good sign. Showed he'd likely be willing to turn on whomever it was that had called him, and that guy - one of both of the Freeman brothers, most likely - just might be the one they were looking for. Al's heart rate picked up slightly but he forced his features to stay neutral.

Boulon walked closer to the sheriff. "You offerin' a deal?"

"If what you say is true and the coordinates take us to this property, that can only be good for you. Unless you produce the guy who called you to verify your story, you're in deep trouble. You're in trouble either way, but cooperation will earn you some points with the judge, I suspect."

Boulon scowled. "That's it? A few points with the judge? You gotta be kidding."

"Listen, Mr. Boulon, we have enough evidence to put you away for several years. You were caught with cattle that had been stolen from a La Crosse County farm. Your trailer tire marks were found at the scene of the rustling. Why should we believe anyone else was involved here? Right now, in my book, you're guilty of grand theft, attempt to peddle stolen property, and transportation of stolen property across state lines. What's that worth, ten, maybe fifteen years? Depends on how the judge sees it, of course, but as Judge Batterly has the case, and he's notorious for his zero tolerance policy on rustling, I'd be jumping at any chance to score points with him if I were you."

The color drained from Boulon's face. "Judge Batterly? You sure about that?"

The aging La Crosse judge had earned himself the nickname of "Hangin' Bradley" for his tough stance on crime. If he thought someone was guilty, they would most assuredly get a harsh sentence - likely the maximum under the law.

"You're gonna be in front of him this afternoon so you can see for yourself." The sheriff pushed away from the bars. "Let's go, boys."

Al kept pace with the sheriff as they walked from the cellblock into the main part of the jail. The man had a satisfied grin on his face. He must be pretty confident that he had prepped Boulon for loosening his tongue on the cattle case. If they could only get as good a handle on the moonshine case now, it would be a great day.

He and Charlie followed the sheriff into his office. "Have a seat." The sheriff waved a hand toward the wooden chairs in front of his desk as he walked around to the other side. Al sat down and watched as Charlie wedged himself down between the arms of the chair. "Damn, Dwight, you gotta get some bigger, more comfortable chairs. These damn matchstick ones pinch my ass, crowd my hips, and in spite of the paddin' you're always teasin' me about, hurt my cheeks something fierce."

The sheriff and Al both laughed.

"You know damn well I keep these chairs around to discourage long visits, Charlie. So what are you thinking after hearing Boulon's story?"

Charlie frowned, his forehead furling into tight ridges. "Somethin about this rustlin' case just don't feel right to me. It's too damn cut and dried. I mean, we got Boulon's tire tracks at the scene of the crime. That's pretty damn solid. And we found him with the cattle at an auction barn. That's solid, too. That takes care of seventeen steers. But what about all those other cattle that have been taken? Where are they? Is Boulon the only one involved here? Seems like we'd have picked him up long before now if he was."

"I agree." Al rested his forearms on the arm of the chair and leaned forward. "I'm sure Boulon's involved, but I'm equally sure he's a bit player. A deliveryman more than anything. We still haven't found the big players."

The sheriff cradled his hands across his stomach and tilted back in his chair. "I think you're both right; there's definitely more going on here than we know right now. It doesn't seem likely that Boulon took those cattle off all those ranches by himself, does it?"

Al tapped his fingers on the arms of the chair. "He could be telling the truth about the guy that called him to get the cattle off his property, though. I think we need to talk to these Freeman boys."

Charlie nodded. "Definitely think that's worth checking out."

The sheriff straightened in his chair. "I agree. I'll send our IT guy to meet you at Boulon's truck. If he's got the exact coordinates, we'll know our hunch was right and it was the Freeman property. The two of you can follow up on that lead. In the meantime, I'm goin' back to have a little chat with Boulon. I'm thinkin' that with a little more pressure, he might be willing to cough up a few more names."

"Done." Charlie gripped the arms of his chair and hauled himself to his feet, his face flushed with the effort.

The sheriff shook his head. "Charlie, that new wife of yours is feeding you too well. You were big before you got married, but now you're like a balloon. You've got love handles all the way from your shoulders to your knees. Better think of talking with the employee assistance program about a weight loss effort. Either that, or one of these days we'll be picking you off the floor and sending you to the morgue."

"Geez, Sheriff, you sure know how to make a guy feel good. Kelly is a great cook, but she gives me crap about my weight, too. God, you know how I love to eat."

Al tried not to laugh but couldn't help himself. That sent Hooper into gales of laughter that echoed around the offices of the sheriff's department. Charlie's face grew even redder. When they emerged from the office, Charlie pointed a finger at the receptionist. "Delores, don't you say a damn word... not one."

She twisted her fingers in front of her mouth, as though locking a door. Above her hand, her eyes twinkled mischievously. Charlie threw a disgusted look at Al, who pressed his lips together to keep from grinning. His friend whirled toward the door and Al traipsed after him.

He caught up to Charlie halfway down the front walk. "Good thing we're grabbing those coordinates now, before some lawyer has the truck impounded as evidence and no-touch rules apply."

A few minutes later, the tech guy the sheriff had sent over had coaxed all the information out of Boulon's truck. He handed a piece of paper to Charlie. "Here you go. The exact spot in Wisconsin you want to go."

Charlie grabbed the paper and stuffed it into his shirt pocket. "Great, thanks. Al, let's head out. We'll get in touch with Buffalo County on the way and tell them what we're gonna do. They might want to have one of their deputies meet us there."

"Sounds good." Al hopped up onto the passenger seat of the SUV. The two of them headed north out of town for Buffalo County. It was a bright day, and Al donned sunglasses as they traveled up Highway 35-54, crossed the Black River, the Trempealeau River, and then made a right turn onto Buffalo County Road P.

A half mile later, he spotted a cop car on the shoulder of the road.

"Right where he said he'd be, Al. Looks like the sheriff himself. Must be a slow day up here."

Charlie eased his truck to a stop behind the other vehicle, and he and Al got out. Buffalo County Sheriff Butch Schreiner introduced himself and his deputy, Lawrence Reidt. The sheriff held out an arm. "Lead the way, gentlemen. We're here as back-up if needed."

Charlie nodded and he and Al climbed back into the

SUV. The two-vehicle convoy traveled along the twisty but newly blacktopped roadway, eventually making a sharp left to continue along P and head across the Trempealeau River into the community of Dodge.

As they neared the site, Al instructed Charlie to slow down then turn to the right onto a rutted field road. The sheriff's radio crackled, and Schreiner informed them they were on an unnamed road that would wind back toward the river.

"What the hell did he think we thought? This sure as hell ain't no county highway we're on." Charlie gripped the wheel tightly as the truck bounced over and through a series of ruts filled with water. Eventually the road ended in a grassy area.

Charlie stopped the truck and got out.

Al rounded the truck and stopped in front of him. The sheriff and deputy joined them. "So what's the plan, Charlie?" Al swiped at a bead of sweat that had started down one cheek.

"I think the four of us should head up together, rather than splitting up. We have no idea what we're walking into here, or how many people we might encounter."

The sheriff nodded. "Sounds like a good idea."

"All right then." Charlie adjusted his cap on his head. "Let's go." He led the way to a shed at the side of the road. The doors were locked, but Al peered through the spotless windows. "Looks empty. A little too empty, actually."

Charlie tilted his head. "What do you mean?"

"It appears as though it has recently been cleared out, and the floors swept clean."

"As if someone was hiding something?"

"Exactly."

"Hmm." The big man lifted his hat, wiped his hand across his forehead, and replaced the hat. "Let's see what else we can find."

The men strode down the rutted road along the field. "Lots of tracks," observed the deputy. "Oops, and here's a little hard—or should I say soft—evidence." He grimaced as he raised his foot to show them the manure sticking to the bottom of his boot before hobbling over to the grass to scrape off the smelly, sticky substance.

"Here's some more cow shit." Charlie kicked at the field. "And tracks, too. Both cattle and tire tracks. Bet this is where Boulon loaded them up. Doesn't it look like a truck turned around out here?"

Al studied the area. "I think you're right, Charlie." He pulled the phone from his pocket. After snapping a few pictures of what looked to be the loading spot, he carefully walked the entire area with the other three men.

"Kinda seems like they had the cows fenced in a smaller area." The deputy pointed to the place where the cattle tracks stopped along a line with no fence. "Might have been a temporary fence here." He scuffed the toe of his boot around a small hole in the ground.

As they moved carefully through the entire field and then into the brushy area nearer the creek, it was obvious that some sort of activity had recently been carried out there. The grass was beaten down, and in several areas cleared right away.

Charlie peered carefully at one grassless area. "Not sure what was here, but it looks like it might have been some sort of fire. The grass appears to be burned at the edges of the area, doesn't it?"

Al studied the blades of blackened grass. "You could be right, Charlie."

The deputy had been pacing through the area near the creek, and he stopped now and held up several shards of broken glass. "Any idea what this might be from?"

The sheriff bent down and scooped up what looked to

be a liquor bottle. "My guess is another one of these." He sniffed the opening and blinked. "Whew. Powerful stuff. Moonshine, maybe."

Al shot a look at Charlie. Were their two cases going to intersect after all?

The inspection continued for another hour, the searchers peering into every square inch of the property before they gathered back at the vehicles to debrief.

"No question that something was being done here." The sheriff held up the bottle before carefully lowering it into a bag he'd pulled out of his vehicle. "Anybody got any ideas what?"

"I don't think it was rustling. The area where the animals appear to have been kept looks like it was just a holding area for a small number of cattle." Al kicked at a patch of grass, willing the area to reveal its secrets to them.

"I think you're right," agreed the sheriff. "Know where they were from?"

"Likely the seventeen head stolen from a ranch in La Crosse County." Charlie tugged a notebook from his shirt pocket.

"How do you know?" The sheriff swatted a mosquito on his arm.

Charlie flipped open the notebook. "A few days ago, seventeen head of cattle were taken from a farmer in La Crosse County, a George Espelein. The guy we arrested yesterday was hauling a trailer with steers that all had a brand on them. We're going to get the rancher down to identify them, but unless someone else is using the same brand, we're pretty confident the cattle that were found on this property are the same ones." He flipped the notebook closed and stuck it back in his pocket. "Anyway, thanks for your help here. We'll keep you informed on how the case develops." He held out his hand to the sheriff.

"Please do." The sheriff and deputy shook hands with Charlie and Al before returning to their vehicle.

Al trudged behind Charlie back to the SUV. He would have liked for them to have turned up more concrete evidence there, but if there had been any, it looked as though whoever owned the property had cleared it away. "Which is sort of evidence on its own, isn't it?"

Charlie slid behind the wheel. "What's that?"

Al hopped up onto the passenger seat and closed his door. "I was just thinking about how it looks as though this property has recently been cleaned up. Which looks mighty suspicious to me. I think more has gone on here than we know, Charlie."

"I agree. Especially since we found that bottle and the broken glass. I still believe our two cases are somehow connected, and that discovery makes it even more likely." Charlie turned the AC on high and started back down the rutted lane.

"I think so, too. Now we just have to find out how they're connected, and who is behind both of them."

"Wanna ride along with me over to Lanesboro to pick up Espelein? See if he can confirm the steers are his?"

"Absolutely." Al clicked his seatbelt into place. "One step at a time, Charlie, and eventually we're going to get to where we want to be."

51

AL STEADIED HIMSELF WITH A HAND ON THE DASHBOARD AS Charlie slid his SUV to a stop in front of the steps leading to the main door of the Espelein farmhouse. Seconds later, the door swung open and the rancher hurried down the steps and slipped into the back seat of the SUV. Charlie swung the vehicle around in the front yard.

"So ya think you got 'em?" The rancher fastened his seat belt and rubbed his hands together, clearly excited about what the officers may have found.

"We're pretty sure." Charlie glanced over the back seat as he maneuvered the SUV down the country lane. "We caught a guy we've been looking at for a while trying to unload a bunch of cattle at the Lanesboro sales barn across the river. Through the slats of the trailer, I could see the brand you showed us, but we just want a final, positive ID from you."

"Not to worry. I'll know my steers when I see them, all right. Me and my fellow ranchers started branding all our cattle—something we hadn't done in years—when we began to hear about rustlers operating in the county, so we could identify animals up for sale that had been stolen. Let's hope our strategy worked."

They crossed the river, drove into La Crescent, hooked up with Highway 16, and headed toward Lanesboro. They drove along the Root River, a winding but scenic journey that got them to Lanesboro just after 11 a.m. The sale was already in progress and as they left the truck in the parking lot, Al could hear the chanting of the auctioneer. When they entered the sales barn, a deputy sheriff from Fillmore County headed straight for them.

"Been watchin' for ya," said Craig Loessen as he shook Charlie's hand and then Al's.

Al clapped a hand on Epselein's shoulder. "This is George Epselein, the rancher we told you guys about."

Loessen inclined his head in Epselein's direction. "You lost the cattle?"

"Not sure *lost* is the right word, but yep, I'm missin' seventeen head of young stock."

"And we got seventeen head penned up out back," Loessen told him. "Sure would be nice if you could identify 'em."

"Won't take me but a minute," Espelein told him. "Should have the big E brand on their hindquarters. We're anxious to get these guys, too. The brand strategy is our way to help out."

Loessen led the way around the outside of the sales barn. In the shade of the back of the barn, they found seventeen cattle, all of them content and munching on hay placed in a feeder at the back of the enclosure.

"Sure looks like 'em." Espelein walked closer and pointed to the flank of one of the animals. "That's my brand, for sure."

Loessen glanced over at Charlie, who nodded. "It's his. He showed us the brand when we were out at his place last week."

Al propped an elbow on the top of the enclosure. "Great. So what's next, Deputy?'"

"We need to get some paperwork done. That's the first thing. After that, we gotta get a judge to okay moving those cattle back to Wisconsin to Mr. Espelein's farm. Then, since the guy who brought 'em over here is back in Wisconsin, I'll have to check with the D.A. to see what we have to do to make it your case."

"Can we get that goin' right away?" Espelein reached through the slats and patted the side of one of the steers. "I'm feedin' those out for sale in the fall, and I haven't got much time to get it done."

"I'll do everything I can to expedite the transfer. Based on the fact that Boulon waived extradition and is already back in La Crosse, I'm thinkin' our judge will overlook a few missed dots and crosses on the i's and t's."

"That sure would be helpful." Al caught Charlie's eye and tipped his head slightly in the direction of the parking lot. Boulon had insisted he simply picked up the cattle where they were fenced and took them where the customer wanted them taken. He seemed to be telling the truth, but he was a slippery character, too. That meant there was a lot of work ahead, separating fact from fiction and gathering evidence. And none of it was getting done while he and Charlie were in Lanesboro.

Charlie nodded and held out his hand. "Craig, we appreciate you doing whatever you can to push this through quickly and get those cattle back where they belong." He clapped Epselein on the back. "Al and I'll drop you off at home then we need to get back to work."

"Sounds good." The rancher shook the deputy sheriff's hand too. "Appreciate your help."

Loessen nodded. "I'll be in touch."

Espelein let go of his hand. "When those cattle are sold this fall, you'll be getting' some ribeyes personally delivered. You've certainly earned them."

Loessen touched the brim of his hat. "Not sure I can accept steaks, Mr. Espelein, but the thought is worth nearly as much as the meat."

Charlie, Al, and Espelein strode back to the parking lot and climbed into Charlie's SUV.

"What a nice guy." Espelein leaned forward from the backseat. "You guys are pretty damn nice, too. I can't tell you how relieved I am that those cattle are coming home."

Charlie kept his eyes on the road ahead. "Lotta money walkin' around, right?"

"Lotta money," agreed Espelein. "I was sure they was gone for good. I'd been thankin' my lucky stars that I wasn't missing any cattle, and then it happened. Lot of 'em have gone missing, and I'm the first, that I know of, to get any back."

"Yep, that's a fact. This is the first time we made an arrest, and the first time we got any cattle back. I think our bosses will be happy. Don't you, Al?"

"Absolutely." Al studied the green fields, then cracked the window a bit and inhaled deeply. "Aah, nothing like the smell of newly mown hay to bring back thoughts of my childhood."

Epselein clasped his hands on top of the seat. "You lived on a farm?"

"No, but my grandpa and grandma had one, and I always got to help make hay." A smile crossed Al's face. "You know, as a kid I had terrible hay fever. But much as it hurt me, I loved the smell after we had cut hay. I'd go around snuffling, tears dripping from my eyes, inhaling as much of the smell as I could."

"I love this time of year," said Espelein, "but in my business, winter is the greatest. We get a little rest during the winter months. Calving is over, the ground is frozen, and I get to sit in my recliner and read and snooze. Even get to chase my woman around once in a while."

Al pressed his lips together, unwilling to comment on that.

Epselein chuckled. "You guys prudes?"

"No, sir." Charlie grinned back at him. "Just thinkin' about chasing *my* woman around."

"Me, too," agreed Al.

The three men chatted as they passed through Rushford then continued on along the now lazy Root River on their way to La Crosse.

"This river gets pretty angry in spring," observed Charlie. "But it sure is placid now."

Al's eyebrows rose as he contemplated his friend. *Placid? Kelly must really be doing a first-class overhaul on Charlie's vocabulary.*

When Charlie pulled up at the ranch, Espelein leaned forward again. "Thanks for your great work on this, both of you. Sure am grateful to you."

Charlie shook the hand the rancher held out. "Hopefully we've opened a crack in the scheme that has hit lots of your neighbors."

Al nodded. "Charlie's right. It's nice to crack one case, but think of all the others that are still unsolved. Let's hope this is the beginning of the end for the bad guys."

"Ya gotta start someplace." Espelein pushed open the back door. "I'm glad it was me, but I'm with you. We need to get the whole thing stopped." He jumped to the ground, slammed his door, then lifted a hand before heading up the stairs of the farmhouse.

Charlie turned the key and the engine roared to life. "Well, I got a report to write." He backed up the SUV then swung around and started down the laneway. "How about you?"

"I've got the moonshine case on my mind. I think I'm gonna go see one of our bar owners this afternoon."

"Good plan," agreed Charlie. "Get him to talk, and we

might have a couple of solved cases on our hands before we know it."

"That sounds pretty good right about now, Charlie." Al sighed. "Pretty good, indeed."

52

As Al drove out of the police department parking lot an hour later, he was happy to be away from the bustle of the cattle rustling investigation and, to be honest, grateful to be alone. Charlie was great, and Al loved him like a brother, but brothers get sick of each other from time to time. This was one of those times.

He welcomed the opportunity to be out of the city and in the countryside, and as he drove north on Highway 53, he took in all the beauty around him and marveled at the picturesque nature of the hills and valleys.

The corn had reached its full growth, and the soybeans were beginning to brown a little as the harvest season approached. Overhead, the sky was light blue and dotted with gray-tinged white clouds that scudded across his vision like cotton tree husks in the spring. He passed Drugan's Castle Mound Country Club and pursed his lips. Why had he never learned to play? After all, he'd been a good—some said great—athlete in school. But he had played team sports—football, basketball, and baseball—the kind that banged you up and later in life reminded you that maybe something gentler, like golf, would have been better.

He chuckled as he drove, remembering his father speaking disparagingly of golf as "pasture pool" during his growing up years on the south side of the city. "You play them worthwhile games like football," he could almost hear his father say as they ate dinner. "They'll make a man outta ya!"

Al's mind drifted as he imagined his father bragging at one of the south side bars he frequented when his son became a star for the La Crosse Central Red Raiders, setting a school record for most yards gained in a career that began as a sophomore - a rarity for those days.

He made the right turn onto Country Road T a few minutes after passing Castle Mound and focused his thoughts on the upcoming meeting. He was heading towards Stevenstown and a country bar owned by a guy named Dustin Pearson.

Pearson was a nice guy, but when Al and Charlie had visited him a couple of months back, he seemed nervous and evasive, which led them to classify him as a person of interest.

Al drove into the bar's parking lot and was surprised to see it filled with pick-ups and a few cars. *Now that's unusual for a weekday. Wonder what's going on?*

When he walked into the bar, he almost didn't recognize the place. First, all the dark wood was gone, and in its place were walls freshly painted a light color. That dressed the place up a lot, but it was the bar that captured Al's attention. The last time Al had visited, the place sported an old pine board bar completely devoid of personality. Now a stately bar of polished oak had taken its place and dominated the room. And the restaurant was so full, the only empty seat was an empty bar stool.

The smell of deep fried foods filled his nostrils, and through the window into the kitchen he saw what must have been a dozen burgers sizzling on the grill along with slices of onions. Smoke rose from the deep fat fryer, and sweat trickled down the cheeks of the man tending the cooking in spite of the black band that circled his head.

As Al approached the bar, the cook looked up and used his spatula to reach through the opening between the restaurant and the kitchen and point at the lone vacant stool. "Take a seat," he said.

He turned back to the grill as Al mounted the stool and waited for the middle-aged woman who was tending bar to get to him.

"What'll it be?" she asked sweetly, drying her hands on her apron. "Need a menu?"

"Not necessary. I'll have a 1919 and a cheeseburger with Swiss and fried onions."

"No 1919. We serve Mug." Without waiting for his consent, she opened a cooler, extracted a brown bottle, popped the cap on an opener attached to the bar, and set it on a coaster before him. "Anything else?"

"Nope. This is fine. Dustin around?"

"Not anymore. Heart attack about seven weeks ago. Decided he was workin' too hard, sold the place to me and the mister," she jerked her head toward the man standing at the grill, "and headed for Florida."

"Wow, I wondered what happened. Wasn't this classy a place when I was here last."

"How long ago was that?"

"Two, maybe three months ago," he told her, knowing it was eleven weeks to the day that he and Charlie had first stopped in.

"You missed him then. Not even sure where in Florida you could find him. He didn't seen too anxious to leave a forwarding address. Wanted to be left alone in his retirement, I'll wager."

Or he's hiding from something. Or someone. Al pulled a card from his shirt pocket. "If he does happen to check in and you get a number, give me a call, will ya? I'd really like to get in touch with him."

Someone at the end of the bar whistled, and the woman nodded curtly, shoved the card into the pocket of her apron, and headed for the anxious customer. Ten minutes later, she set Al's burger and fries in front of him. He thanked her and bit into the burger, barely repressing a groan of pleasure. Why were burgers cooked on a grill and served in a bar always better than the ones he cooked at home?

When the bartender walked by a few minutes later, again drying her hands on her apron, she stopped to check his soda bottle. Al agreed to a refill and asked if she had a minute.

"Pretty busy." She set the soda on the bar, but her eyes never stopped surveying the other patrons as she filled his glass from the bottle. "Ya wanna talk, may be better to stop back about three. That's when me and Clay get a little break before the afternoon crowd comes in."

"Great. I'll either hang around, or come back then. Thanks."

Before he could say anything else, a customer a few stools away shouted, "Hey, Shirl, I want somma that good alcohol. You know, the clear stuff?"

The woman sent him a heated look. "Tubby, cut it out. You know we don't sell that anymore. And you know why, too. Just leave it alone."

Her face reddened as the cook called through the opening, "She's right, Tubby. You know we don't handle that anymore. And you damn sure know why. Yet every time you stop, you bring it up. That's enough."

The glasses on the bar jumped when Tubby hit the bar with his fist. "And I damn well told ya to have some o' it when I was in here yesterday. I want some, and I want it now."

"And we don't sell it," the cook said, equally forcefully. He glanced at Al and away quickly. "You know damn well that booze was illegal. So we don't sell it no more. And there ain't gonna be any more of it around here ever. Hear me?"

Tubby stared at the man, then emptied his glass, slammed it on the bar, and stalked toward the door.

"If you come back, just remember, we don't sell it." Shirl planted both hands firmly on her hips.

"And if that's the way it is," announced Tubby, his voice loud and angry now, "I won't be back. You can go to hell."

The big man walked out and slammed the door behind him. The bar had grown quiet, but when the door closed, the murmur started again - quietly at first and then louder. As Shirl came by where Al was sitting, she stopped. "Sorry about that. Some of the regulars have no manners. Tubby's one. He'll be back tamorra all hungry and fine."

"He seemed pretty mad." Al dipped a fry into the pool of ketchup on his plate.

"Nah, he's just full a bluster. He'll be back. Comes in every noon hour."

Al finished his soda, took the last bite of his cheeseburger, and pulled the wallet out of his back pocket. "Great burger, ma'am. I'll be back at three." He tossed a twenty on the bar, then put his cap on and left.

After sliding behind the wheel of his car, he glanced at his watch. Two hours to kill. *Now what?* Maybe he should drive up to Buffalo County and take a look at the recovery site again, see if they had missed anything. Happy to have a purpose, he drove from the valley. As he turned back onto Highway 53, he radioed in and asked the La Crosse County dispatcher to patch him through to the Buffalo County sheriff.

The sheriff was off, but Al talked to the chief deputy, told him what he'd like to do, and asked if that would be all right. He was assured that wasn't a problem.

"We've finished everything we're going to do down there," the deputy told him. "I'll just call the property owner and let him know that you're going to take one more look around."

Al thanked the man, then continued his drive northward into Buffalo County, eventually catching sight of the Mississippi River before it was time to turn right onto Buffalo County Road P for the trip back along the Trempealeau River.

He reached the pasture area, drove across the mowed field to the stand of trees where another owner's property began, and stopped. After climbing out of the car, he grabbed a search rod. Identical to sticks used by those with seeing disabilities, it made a good deterrent for any snakes or other critters he might come across.

Al shoved a pair of gloves and three or four evidence bags into the pocket of his jacket and he was set to go. He approached the stand of trees slowly, carefully searching the ground in front of him. He stopped at the sight of broken glass and nudged a couple of pieces with the toe of his boot. *What is that about?* Filing that away in his memory bank to consider later, he moved on.

He moved through tall grass, finding all sorts of decaying trash but nothing that looked like it could have anything to do with either his or Charlie's case. As he approached the river, Al heard what appeared to be a convention of birds in full discussion. Pushing to the point where the land sharply dropped a few feet to the water, he saw what must have been a hundred crows rise into the air and take flight.

What the heck? That sure was odd. Crows didn't normally scavenge together like that unless there was something large to feed on. The skin on his neck and arms tingled. Was something strange going on here after all?

As he shifted his gaze along the edge of the water, a light

yellow pile caught his eye. Was that corn meal? *Hmmm, corn meal. Or could it be corn mash?*

A small tree had fallen into the river. Al made his way to it and used it as a sort of railing to ease himself down to water level. Once there, he stepped gingerly toward the golden spot on the shore and bent to pick up a piece of whatever it was. It was dry, crusty in spots, and devoid of smell. He took out his jackknife and scraped some of the material into an evidence bag, sealed it, and returned it to his pocket before climbing back up the bank. Although he continued his search for another half hour, Al didn't come across anything else of interest.

He was back at the Stevenstown Bar by three. Shirley led him to a table in the back corner. The bar was quiet now, as she had predicted, with no other patrons in the room. Al hoped that would last until their conversation was over.

"Clay." Shirley hollered at the man still standing in front of the grill. He glanced up and she waved him over.

At first Clay and Shirley were reluctant to say much, but confronted by Al's shield, Clay clearly decided their best recourse was to lay all their cards on the table. "We bought this bar from Dustin Pearson two months ago. It was closed for six weeks as we renovated and cleaned up the place. Since we re-opened, it has done well. But we have a few customers who keep clamoring for some special sort of alcohol that Pearson sold. We don't know what it was, but we have our suspicions."

"And they would be?"

"It must have been hot stuff… hot as in illegal." Shirley lowered her voice and leaned closer to Al, even though no one else had come into the bar. "We've heard about moonshine being available around here, but we sure as heck don't carry it, and we don't know who does or where it comes from, either."

"Do you think Pearson knows?"

"He'd have to." Shirley lifted her shoulders. "These are his former customers, and some of them are downright ugly about whatever it is that he carried that we don't. As you saw before, with Tubby."

Al repressed a sigh. Obviously, the two of them weren't going to be able to supply him with any useful information. "Do you still have my card?"

Shirley nodded and patted the pocket of her apron.

"Good. I'd really like to talk to Mr. Pearson, so please let me know if he contacts you, okay?"

"We will."

"Thank you. And one more thing. Of all the other bars in the area, any rumors circulating about any of them carrying this moonshine?"

Shirley shot a look at her husband, which answered Al's question. He tugged the notebook and pen out of his pocket. "Write down their names, will you? I promise this won't come back on you in any way, except that you will have my gratitude if you assist me in this. And of course, if we can figure out who's supplying the stuff and get them to stop, that can only help your business here. And it'll get any disgruntled customers off your backs."

Clay lifted a hand, palm up. "I guess that's all true. All right, we can give you a few names. Long as you swear no one'll find out they came from us."

"I swear." Al handed him the pen and watched as the big man scribbled in the notebook. When he finished and handed Al back the pen, he pocketed it and the notebook and stood up. He held out a hand to Clay. "I appreciate your help with this, Clay. You too, Shirley." He shook her hand too. "And I'll be back soon, but only to get another one of those delicious burgers. I'll bring a friend of mine next time who will enjoy the food here even more than I do."

Clay walked him to the door. "You're welcome here any time, Detective."

Al nodded and went out the door to the parking lot. He continued his journey through the back roads of La Crosse County, driving toward the city on County Road DD, then turning onto D, before stopping at the Jolly Peddler Bar at the junction of D and County Road W.

Like Clay and Shirley's place, the bar was quiet now at a little before four p.m. Two elderly gentlemen enjoyed a beer while playing cribbage at the bar, the bartender watching the action as he leaned against the back wall.

"Hi, I'm Al Rouse, La Crosse P.D." Al held up his shield and all three men leaned closer to take a look.

"I'm Jerry Knabe, that's Hugh and Steve." The bartender jerked his head in the direction of the older men.

"You own the place, Jerry?"

"Nope, belongs to my uncle, Mike Knabe, but I run it."

"There are rumors about moonshine being sold here. Know anything about that?"

Knabe's face reddened. Al waited. "If you're askin' if we sell it here, the answer's no. But if you're wondering if it's sold around here, the answer is, hell yes!"

Al slid onto a stool. "Tell me more."

He ordered a Pepsi and settled back to listen while Knabe talked and Hugh and Steve listened - punctuating Knabe's words with nods and the odd exclamation of "That's right".

Jerry grabbed a rag and ran it under the faucet in the small sink behind the bar. "Business was good here until about two years ago when Dustin Pearson came by to try and get Uncle Mike to make a commitment to buy an allotment of moonshine each week."

He swiped the rag vigorously over the wooden surface of the bar. "Pearson thought we could sell two to three gallons a week. My uncle told him no, and so did I. He came back about three or four times, and the answer was always the same. I don't think anybody else said no, though, because my business dropped like a stone, and everyone else seemed busy."

Al's forehead wrinkled. "Pearson's gone now."

"But the moonshine ain't. Everyone must still be sellin' it, 'cause we haven't seen any increase, I can tell you that."

"So who's handling it now?"

"Well, we ain't buyin', but Dustin mentioned that he was getting it from a guy in La Crosse."

"Did he mention a name?"

Jerry stopped scrubbing the wood and rubbed the side of his hand across his forehead. "Not sure I can recall it. Something German, I think. Oldenberg, maybe?"

Al's heart rate picked up. "Oldendorf?"

Jerry lowered his hand. "That's it. Byrle Oldendorf. Don't know if he's in charge, but he acts like it."

"That's great information, thanks." Al tipped his glass and drained the last of the cola before setting it down and getting up.

Jerry cast a furtive glance at the door and leaned closer, resting an elbow on the freshly scrubbed wood. "If you want to thank me, just get rid of the moonshine, will ya?"

"I'll do my best." Al reached for his wallet, but Jerry waved him off. Al nodded and headed for the exit. He did intend to do his best to get rid of the moonshine. And now that he had further proof that Oldendorf was the one distributing it, that possibility had just gotten a lot stronger.

53

DAVID AND MADISON PULLED INTO THE FREEMANS' ALLEY IN Winona. Emily rested her head on Justin's shoulder as he steered the pick-up into the alley behind the truck.

"Good day." David hopped down from the U-Haul truck. "It's damn good to be home, and damn good to have that job finished. Justin, maybe we ought to go and return the truck now instead of paying for another day. What do you think?"

"Good idea. We can grab something to bring home for dinner while we're out. Does that work for you two?"

Emily tapped a finger on her chin. "Let's see, you're going to return the truck and pick up dinner while we go in and relax and wait to be served? Yes, I'd say that works for us."

Justin laughed and kissed her before sliding back behind the wheel of the truck. Emily watched the U-Haul and pickup until they bumped out of the alley and disappeared down the street, and then she followed Madison into the house. No sooner were they in than the doorbell rang.

Madison's cheeks paled. "Who the heck could that be?"

She clutched Emily's arm. "You don't think anyone saw the U-haul and figured out what we were doing, do you?"

Emily tugged her arm from Madison's grasp. "Only one way to find out." She strode to the front door and pulled it open. Three men stood on the porch, two of them in uniform and the other in a suit. Her chest tightened, but she lifted her chin. "Can I help you?"

The shorter of the men in uniform smiled. "Miss, is this the home of David and Justin Freeman?"

He had a kindly face that seemed permanently cast in a smile. His voice had a gentle lilt to it. The other two men were also smiling, and Emily relaxed a little. "Yes, it is." She gripped the knob of the door. "How can I help you?"

"Ma'am, I'm from the Winona County Sheriff's Office and these gentlemen are from La Crosse. They would like to talk to one or both of the Freemans. Are they here?"

Emily shook her head. "No, they aren't here. But we live here, too. Can we help you?"

"We'd like to talk to one of them," said the man in the suit. "Will they be home soon?"

"Not for several hours." Emily bit her lip. Hopefully David and Justin wouldn't return until she could get rid of the men. "Can I have one of them call you?"

"Sure, that would be great. I'm Detective Alan Rouse from the La Crosse Police Department, and this is Deputy Charlie Berzinski from the La Crosse County Sheriff's Office. We need to talk to them about some land they own over in Wisconsin. Do you know about that?"

"No, no, I don't. Madison?" Her friend had come up to stand beside her, and Emily shifted to face her. "Do you know anything about land in Wisconsin?"

"I've heard David talk about some property over in Buffalo County. But I don't know anything more than that."

"No problem." Detective Rouse reached inside his jacket

and extracted a business card from an inside pocket. "If you could have one of them call me when they return, I'd sincerely appreciate it."

He handed Emily the card. Her fingers trembled a little when she took it, and she quickly shoved it into the pocket of her jeans. "I will."

"Thank you." The man touched the brim of his hat, and all three of them turned to go. As they walked down the front steps, the bigger man—Deputy Berzinski—stopped and looked back. "If you'd have them call tonight, that would be best. Save us a trip back up here later."

"I'll tell them." Emily closed the door most of the way, leaving only a crack she could look through to make sure they were actually leaving. The men got into a sheriff's car parked at the curb and drove away.

Madison slumped against the wall beside the door. "Oh, god, Emily, it's as bad as we feared. What are my folks going to say? We're all going to jail, aren't we?"

Emily slid an arm around her shoulders and led her back to the kitchen. "Stay calm. The worst thing we can do is panic. When the guys get home, we'll talk this out and figure out what to do."

Madison nodded. "You're right. I'm okay. I just need to stay busy. I'll set the table for supper."

"That would be great. I'll mix us both a drink." Emily headed for the refrigerator. "Besides ..." she grabbed a jug of moonshine from the fridge and kicked the door shut with her foot, "... they seemed like nice guys. Probably just have some questions about the cattle. That's my guess, at least."

Madison set a fork down beside one of the plates. "I never thought of that. You're probably right."

Thirty minutes later, the back door opened and closed and David called out, "Anybody home?"

"We're here. And we have to talk to you, right now."

Emily's voice must have held a touch of urgency, because both men strode into the kitchen.

Justin's forehead wrinkled as he made his way around the island to Emily's side. "What's up?" He touched her arm.

"Just after you left, we had a visit from two Wisconsin policemen wanting to talk to the two of you about the land you own there."

Justin shot his brother a look. "Is that all they said?"

"Yes. I told Madison it was likely something about the cattle. That's all it would be, right?"

"Yes, I'm sure that's it." Justin opened a drawer and took out a knife. "Here." He reached for a lemon and started to slice it.

David set a paper bag on the table. "We brought Chinese food. Let's sit down and eat and we can talk about it."

Madison started pulling boxes out of the bag. "One of the men was from the La Crosse Police Department. He gave Em his card and wants you to call him."

Emily pulled the card from the pocket of her jeans and set it on the island. "I told them you'd be gone for a few hours, so that should give us some time to come up with a strategy."

"Good thinking, Em." Justin stopped slicing long enough to lean in and kiss her on the cheek.

"Yes, good thinking." David took down four glasses from the cupboard and carried them over to the island.

"I hope we can come up with something." Madison sank onto a chair at the table. "All the money and things have been nice, but there's a time to pay the piper, too, and I'm hoping this isn't it."

David took the chair next to her and reached for her hand. "Let's not get ahead of ourselves. We've been careful to cover our tracks, and don't forget that we pay a hefty sum for protection too. That should count for something."

Madison nodded. "That's true. Maybe it will all turn out okay."

Justin filled their glasses from the jug and Emily dropped slices of lemon into them. They each carried two over to the table and settled across from David and Madison at the table. Emily lifted her glass. "To Franco and his ugly mug. May it scare everyone away long enough for us to make our fortune and retire."

The other three laughed, and the tension that had hung in the air since the lawmen showed up at the door dissipated. Emily sipped her drink. One of the guys would have to call that detective soon, but hopefully it would turn out to be nothing. And if it didn't, they would deal with that. If it looked as though they were in serious trouble, they had an awful lot of money in the bank. She'd clean out their account and the four of them could disappear. If not forever, then long enough for the authorities to quit nosing around, looking for a few harmless moonshiners, and get on with the business of chasing real criminals.

David stared at the phone he clutched in his hand. He couldn't put this off much longer. If he didn't call soon, the police would soon be pounding at the door again. The clock showed 9:35. Hopefully this Al Rouse guy would already be in bed, and he could simply leave a message. That would give the four of them the opportunity to do more planning and rehearsing. He was sure the lawmen that had visited were chasing clues to the cattle. They wouldn't have connected them to the moonshine. Would they?

Before he could lose his nerve, David punched in the Detective Rouse's number. The phone rang for the third time. Just as David was hoping to get the answering machine, a brusque voice said, "Rouse."

"Hello, Detective Rouse. This is David Freeman. I hear

you stopped at our house in Winona this afternoon, looking to talk to my brother and me?"

"We did. Thanks for calling. I have a few questions, if you don't mind."

"Sure, no problem." David hoped his voice indicated quiet confidence to the La Crosse detective.

"Mr. Freeman, did you know that seventeen head of stolen cattle were moved two days ago from property you own in Wisconsin to a sale barn in Lanesboro, Minnesota?"

"What are you talking about?" David thought fast. No sense in denying any knowledge of the cattle, in case Boulon had already given their names to the cops as the people who had hired him. "We knew there were cattle there, but we had no idea they were stolen. Are you sure about that?"

David stopped, waiting for more from the detective. When nothing came, he felt compelled to respond. "Mr. Rouse, we own a few acres in Buffalo County along the Trempealeau River. We go there to fish, occasionally, and hunt. My brother and I were there last week and spotted a bunch of steers, but we assumed they had gotten loose from a neighbor or something."

"Well, Mr. Freeman, we tracked the cattle to your land in Wisconsin, and a day ago we arrested the driver of a truck that we had followed from your land into Minnesota and on to Lanesboro, where we believe the cattle were going to be sold."

"Detective, you are catching me totally by surprise. As I told you, we saw the cattle, but there are a lot of ranches in the area, and we assumed they belonged to one of those."

"Well, they didn't. They were stolen, and my partner and I are following up on all leads involving the theft. We're very interested in finding out how the cattle ended up on your property. I'm not accusing you of anything at this point, simply seeking answers."

"I understand, but I can't answer questions I don't know the answers to. And I don't know anything about stolen cows on land we own. If they were stolen, and didn't just wander onto the property, maybe someone realized that we are hardly ever there and decided to use the property to hold the cattle on temporarily. Either way, I don't know anything about them. In fact, I'm as interested as you are in finding out who might have been trying to make my brother and I look guilty of something we didn't do."

"If that's true, I'm sure you and your brother wouldn't mind coming in to sit down with us and discuss the situation to clear things up?"

"If that's what you want, sure. Happy to. But I doubt we'd be any help."

"I understand, but we have to follow up on every possibility. So how is ten tomorrow morning?"

David's stomach churned, but he forced his voice to remain steady. "Ten works."

"Great. I'll meet you at the La Crosse Police Department headquarters. See you then."

"All right." David disconnected the call and sat for a minute before shoving the device into his pocket and running a hand over his face. *Better get some sleep.* If he and Justin were going to be able to think clearly enough to come away from tomorrow's meeting not just Freemans, but free men, they were both going to need to get some serious rest tonight.

54

AS THE BROTHERS DROVE TOWARD LA CROSSE THE NEXT DAY, IT was the kind of morning fishermen and boaters dream about: sunny and bright with just a few white, fluffy clouds scudding across the sky, temperature in the low 70s with a promise of 80 later.

"We oughta be fishing today," said David, looking at his brother, slouched against the passenger door.

"I've never been fishing in my life, and neither have you."

"Well, we better both get good at pretending. When those cops ask us about our land today, we need to convince them we only go there occasionally to hunt and fish."

"What kind of fish?"

"All you fish for in the Trempealeau is bullheads. I'm told they're good to fry up, so that's what we'll tell 'em we do."

"How do you catch 'em?"

"With a pole, dummy."

"Bait?"

"Worms, I think."

"You think? You sure you're ready for this session?"

"Dammit, Justin, cut it out. We need to come across as positive and stupid. Just a couple of good ole boys. That should be easy for you."

Justin crossed his arms over his chest and sank lower into his seat. The rest of the drive proceeded quietly. As they came down the bridge ramp into La Crosse, Justin straightened. "Where the heck is this place?"

"It's that big building, there." David pointed through the front windshield as he drove into the parking lot and brought the pickup to a halt. "Well, here goes," he said, snapping his seat belt off. "Just remember, we have to be cool and nonchalant."

"Don't forget stupid." Justin managed a wry grin, and the knots in David's shoulders relaxed slightly.

He held out his hand. "Got your back, bro."

Justin clasped his forearm. "And I've got yours."

David nodded and let him go so he could push open the door of the truck. They walked into the building and approached the desk.

The young redhead seated behind it smiled warmly, and David smiled back. "We're here to see Detective Rouse."

A moment later, a smiling middle-aged man walked into the lobby, extended his hand, and said, "I'm Al. I have a room reserved right over here." He gestured to one of the doors off the hallway extending from the lobby. "Can I get you anything?"

David looked at his brother. "Water?"

Justin nodded.

The detective picked up the phone and asked for a pitcher and four glasses, then set the receiver back on the base. "We're waiting for Deputy Charlie Berzinski."

David and Justin followed him into the room down the hallway. A long table sat in the middle of the space, with two chairs on each side. The detective waved them to the chairs on the far side and they took a seat. The redheaded woman from the front desk brought in a pitcher of water and glasses and set them on the table. She flashed David another smile, but left without saying anything.

The detective poured them both a glass of water. David's fingers shook slightly when he took it, and a few drops of water spilled onto the table. Detective Rouse didn't appear to notice, and David swiped the water away quickly with the side of his hand. *Calm down. They can't pin anything on you.* He took several deep breaths, willing his heart to stop pounding in his chest.

A few minutes later, later a big guy, maybe 6-foot-5 and weighing at least 220 pounds, all muscle, hustled into the office, took off his hat, sat down, and reached for a glass on the tray.

The deputy downed a glass of water, poured a second, then said, "Sorry to be late. Too much paperwork."

"No problem, Charlie." The detective opened a drawer in the table and took out a tiny microphone. "Do you mind if we record this session?"

"Of course not." Justin sounded calmer than David felt, which helped ease his anxiety a little.

The detective set the microphone in the center of the table and pushed a few buttons, then said, "Please, for the record, state and spell your names."

That done, he followed with, "You are both residents of Winona, Minnesota?"

When the brothers nodded, Rouse said, "Please speak your answers into the mic, as clearly as you can."

"Yes," chorused the brothers.

"And you own land in Wisconsin?"

"We do," said David. "Twenty acres along the Trempealeau River in Buffalo County."

"About two miles from Dodge, Wisconsin?" asked Berzinski.

"Yes, that's right." David wiped his sweating palms on his jeans underneath the table.

Berzinski leaned forward. "Know a guy by the name of Rene Boulon?"

David narrowed his eyes, as if trying to think. "I don't think so."

"Me neither." Justin rested his right ankle on his left knee.

"Hmm, funny. Says he know you." The deputy crossed his arms over his massive chest. "Says you called him a few days ago to come get some cattle off your land."

"Oh, that guy. We don't know him, so I'd forgotten his name. We did talk to a guy in Wisconsin who someone said had a trailer that could move animals. Like I told you last night on the phone, we had gone up to our property to do some fishing and realized some stray steers had wandered onto it, and we wanted them gone."

"Your cattle?" The smile was gone from the detective's face.

David shifted. How many times did he have to say the same thing? "No. As I said, we suspected they were strays. We're hardly ever on that property, so we don't keep animals on it."

"Whose were they?" The deputy, who had seemed friendly enough when he first came in, suddenly sounded as though he was done playing and wanted answers now.

David swallowed. "We don't know."

"Did you try to track down the owners?"

"Yes, we talked to our neighbors. No one else seemed to know whose they were either."

Rouse leaned closer, resting his forearms on the table. "Ever occur to you to call the police?"

"No."

"Why not?"

Justin reached for his glass of water. Had his throat gone as dry as David's? "We were worried you might think we stole them."

"Why would we think that? You hiding something else from us?"

Justin set down the glass with a thud. "Of course not."

The deputy's face had gone hard. If they were pulling some kind of good cop, bad cop routine, David had no idea which of them was pretending to be the good cop. "So you called up Boulon and told him you wanted them out of there and he could just have 'em?"

"Well, it wasn't quite like that, but... yes, I guess so."

Justin uncrossed his legs and clasped his hands on the table. "We've been thinking of selling that land. We were supposed to show it to a potential buyer on Monday, and we needed the cows out of there so we could cut the weeds and clean it up."

David's eyes widened slightly, and he stared down at the glass in his hand to keep from gaping at his brother. How had Justin thought that up so quickly?

"So that's why it looks so good?" Detective Rouse tapped his fingers on the table.

"Well, we always try to keep it looking good. We picnic there once in a while - camp sometimes. But, yes, we went over Sunday, chopped the weeds, cut the grass, cleaned it up best we could."

The detective leaned back in his chair and studied the two of them in silence for a moment. David forced himself to meet the man's gaze steadily. "I suppose you have the name and number of the prospective buyer?"

"Yes, sure. But not with us. I wrote it on a piece of paper and stuck it on the wall by our phone."

David blinked. He'd never suspected his brother of being

such a good liar. The detective contemplated them for what felt like an interminable length of time, but neither David nor Justin shifted under his gaze. Finally the man let out a long breath. "Guess that's it for now. We'll need the name of that prospective buyer. You'll call me with it when you get home, right?"

"Yes, sir." David nodded.

"Okay, then. Charlie, anything else?"

"No, I think we've covered it."

"Okay." Detective Rouse waved a hand through the air. "You're free to go. Since this is still an active investigation, if you're going to be traveling, please let us know. Any trips planned?"

"No," said David.

Justin followed him out the door and back down the hallway. "Do you think—"

David lifted a hand, his eyes on the back of the redheaded woman at the desk as they approached her. "Not here. Wait until we're in the truck and out of here."

Justin nodded and went out the exit after him.

They reached their vehicle and climbed in. Neither of them spoke as they drove across the interstate bridge. They were halfway to La Crescent before David spoke. "Well? How do you think it went?"

"Pretty good. But some of those questions were tough. I was sweating." Justin held up his arms. "See?"

David shot him a sideways glance. "How the hell did you come up with that story about the buyer?"

Justin lowered his arms. "I was trying to keep you from bringing up fishing, 'cause I thought that would give us away for sure. Then I got thinking about how, if they went to the property, they'd have seen how cleaned up it was, and that might have looked suspicious, too. So I was just trying to think of a reason we might have been tidying up around there, and that's what I came up with."

"Impressive, although now we gotta think about someone we can trust who will tell them what we want him to say when the cops call him."

"Liam?"

David shook his head. "Too close. They look into him and should be able to figure out pretty quick that we're related. Plus they may find the operation on his place if they go talk to him."

"Good point."

"Guess neither of us are going to be stupid today." David pressed down on the accelerator. "Let's get home. Maybe the girls will have a suggestion."

"Great idea. But keep thinkin'. We're gonna need to have a name by this afternoon."

David nodded. His brother was right—they did need to find someone to help them out and quick. Which was the problem with lying. He gripped the steering wheel tighter. One lie always led to another and another until you were caught up in 'em like a fly in the web of a spider.

He smiled grimly. Maybe they should have talked about fishing after all.

55

"**SO WHAT DO YOU THINK?**" DAVID LIFTED THE BOTTLE OF beer he'd grabbed from the fridge after he and Justin had arrived back home and took a sip. The two of them had filled the girls in on everything that had happened, and now they had to come up with a plan, fast.

Madison pursed her lips. "You told them that we have a potential buyer for the land, so now we need someone to pretend to be that guy, is that right?"

"Yes. And we promised to get back to them with the name when we got home." David leaned forward from his spot on the couch to set the bottle on the coffee table. "Who can we think of that will verify our story?"

Emily sat down on the arm of the chair Justin had settled on. "Liam?"

He reached for her hand. "Good thought, Em, but we've already talked about that and decided we can't afford to have the authorities visit him. They might find the still."

"Good point." Madison tapped her hand on the arm of the

couch. "What about using one of our liquor buyers? Someone from a ways away, like Eau Claire or someone up there?"

David pushed to his feet and paced the room. "Eau Claire is a good idea. We could choose someone who likes to fish and hunt and make the lawmen believe that he wants to buy the land for outdoor sport."

Justin leaned forward and clasped his hands between his knees. "So who do we know like that?"

Madison's face lit up. "How about Ole Sanerud? He's a longtime customer, trustworthy, and a good friend."

David clapped his hands. "Great idea, Madison. He is a good friend, and he loves Emily." Ole Sanderud flirted shamelessly with Emily whenever the four of them went to his place, which Justin tolerated since the man had to be seventy.

"Yes, he does. Thinks she has a great butt."

Justin frowned. "Not sure I like him admiring my girlfriend's butt, but if you guys think he's the answer, one of us should call him."

Emily's cheeks had gone pink, but she squeezed his hand. "I can do it."

David stopped pacing. "I think that would be best. If you ask him, he'll do it for sure."

Madison jumped up. "I'll get his number." She headed into the office and seconds later returned with an address book that contained the names, addresses, and phone numbers of all the people they delivered to.

David forced himself to sit back down as Emily grabbed her phone and started dialing. During the few seconds she waited for Ole to pick up, his leg bounced up and down until he clasped his knee with one hand to still it.

"Hello, Ole?"

David contemplated Emily. Should they have discussed how much she should tell him before she called? He repressed a sigh. Too late now. He didn't need to worry anyway. Emily sounded cool and confident as she filled Ole in on the steers showing up on their property and how they'd hired Boulon to remove them. When she glanced over at him, David nodded encouragement, and she proceeded to explain to Ole what they needed from him.

"So David and Justin told the police officers that they had a chance to sell the land and cleaned it up so it would look good to a prospective buyer. And that's where you come in..." She explained what they needed and then paused. "Yes, he's here. Just a minute." Emily pulled the phone from her ear and held it out to David. "He wants to talk to you."

David took the device from her. Ole asked him a couple of questions for clarification and David nodded. "That's right, Ole, that's what we need you to do. No, we don't want to actually sell it to you, it's not for sale. I just want you to tell a couple of La Crosse cops that you had made a date to look at it, thinking you might want to buy it. Can you do that?" When Ole responded in the affirmative, David gave his friends the thumbs up. "That's great, Ole. Thanks. I'll give them your number, so expect a call shortly, okay?"

David returned the phone to its cradle and faced his partners. "He's not the brightest bulb on the tree, that's for sure, and he sure as hell has a crush on Emily, but I think he can take care of this." He dug into his shirt pocket and pulled out the card the detective had given him. With a sigh, he reached for Emily's phone again. "Might as well get this over with. The sooner they finish talking to Ole, the sooner we can all get on with our lives."

56

"SO TELL ME AGAIN HOW YOU KNOW THESE GUYS?" Al leaned on the bar, staring the owner of Ole's Bar directly in the eye.

"They just come in here one day and had sandwiches." Ole was visibly nervous—more nervous than someone getting a casual visit from a couple of cops should be. His eyes flicked around the room, barely lighting on Al when he answered his question. Finally his gaze landed on the door, as though he would rather be somewhere else. "We talked a bit about where they lived, and eventually they told me they had some property for sale along the Trempealeau. I told 'em I might be interested. Said I'd drop by on Monday, see what I thought of the place."

Charlie, seated on the stool beside Al, tipped back his head and took a deep breath. "How'er your burgers?"

"First class. People love 'em. Use steers raised in the area, butchered just down the road."

"Sounds good. Gimme the works on a double patty, would ya?"

Al ordered one as well. Seemed only fair to not treat any of the places he was visiting in the line of duty more special than any other. Ole seemed relieved to be busy at the grill, humming as he went about his business, leaving the sizzling meat to serve other patrons from time to time.

As soon as Ole set the burgers in front of them, Al inhaled the aromas of fried meat and onions, and then dug in. Next time Ole passed by, Al lifted his burger. "This is amazing. Might be the best bun I've ever tasted."

"Came from a local bakery. Get three dozen every day. Prob'ly should get more, 'cause we run out all the time."

As Ole pushed meat and onion impediments into the slot at the rear of the grill, a patron walked in. "Need a bloody shiney. Gimme the works."

Ole turned his back to Al and Charlie and leaned over the bar slightly as he reached beneath it, his body hiding whatever it was he brought up and poured into a tall glass. When he straightened, the bottle—or maybe a jug?—had disappeared. Al watched as he added ice, Tabasco, A-1, soy sauce, garlic, and celery salt to the glass. Ole stirred the cubes aggressively, then added some sort of tomato mix and finished the creation with a large mushroom, a stalk of celery, two large shrimp, and a skewer of four different cheeses.

Charlie's eyes widened. "Holy cow, I may have to come up here just to get one of those when I'm off duty. What type of alcohol did you put in there?"

"Special booze." Ole's eyes flitted back and forth between the two men, but nothing more was forthcoming.

Al nudged Charlie's foot under the bar. "Who makes it?"

"We get it from our distributor, but it comes from around here. People love it."

"Can we see the bottle?"

Ole hesitated, but when Al casually pushed open his jacket, far enough to reveal the badge clipped to his shirt pocket, Ole reached under the bar again, eventually emerging with a gallon jug, free of labels and holding a colorless liquid. Al removed the cap, bent and sniffed, then pushed the jug toward Charlie, who did the same.

"Powerful." Al tapped a fingernail on the top of the wooden bar. "That stuff must hit like a mule's kick."

"Not too many folks can handle more than a couple ounces. If they go beyond that, they usually wind up on the floor."

Al and Charlie finished their burgers, wiped the grease from around their mouths with the paper napkins that littered the bar, then thanked Ole and walked out. When they got in the truck, Al smacked a palm on the dashboard.

"We gotta call the ATF boys. If that's not illegal booze, I'll eat my shield. There were no stamps on the jug, and it looked like there were traces of what might have been glue from a label."

"Damn right. Let's give 'em a call. I wanna see the raid."

"As long as we're here, let's drive over to the law enforcement center. Best to let them know first, don't you think?"

"Prob'ly a good idea, Al. No sense pissin' 'em off. After all, we're on their turf."

Charlie maneuvered the SUV through traffic, crossed the Chippewa River via the Lake Street bridge, and pulled into the lot of the handsome brick and stone building. Al followed Charlie into the building. Charlie greeted the receptionist warmly and asked if the sheriff was in.

"Sheriff's out, but the undersheriff, Joel Sweeney, is in. Will he do?"

"Sure will, ma'am." Charlie inclined his head in her direction, and the two men took seats in the reception area.

In less than a minute, a tall man with blond hair,

graying around the edges, entered from the door behind the receptionist. "How can I help you gentlemen?"

"Sir..."

"Oh, c'mon, we're neighbors, aren't we? Call me Joel."

Charlie and Al introduced themselves then followed Joel to his office.

"Nice digs." Al looked around the spacious office area and couldn't help but compare it to the cramped space he and his colleagues fit into. "You share space with the P.D., don't you?"

"Yep, Chief's right across the hall."

Charlie nodded at Al, who leaned forward and said, "Maybe, Joel, you could see if he's in. We have something to talk about, but we aren't certain whose jurisdiction it might fall under."

Joel pressed a button on his phone. "Jerry? Got a couple officers from La Crosse with me. Care to come over for a minute? They want to talk to us."

A few seconds later, Chief Jerry Stanislawski walked into the area and introduced himself to Charlie and Al.

"Let's move to the conference room." Joel got up and led the way before the others could speak. Once in a nearby room, equipped with all sorts of electrical and audio-visual gear, Joel waved them all to chairs and settled onto one himself. "So what's up?"

"We've been following two cases in La Crosse County." Al's eyes shifted from Joel to Jerry and back as he told them about being at Ole's bar earlier and seeing him serve a customer out of a jug with no labels. "We got the owner to give us a whiff. Powerful stuff—we think it's illegal."

Joel and Jerry looked at each other before the chief responded, running his hand over his close-cropped hair. "We know Ole, all right. Always suspected he might be dealing in some illegal stuff, but never have been able to catch him. Since his bar is in the city, I guess it's my deal."

"We thought about calling ATF, but thought we should let you guys know first. Not sure, but it could have implications for a case we're working in our area, since we've been following up on reports of illegal booze showing up in La Crosse and—"

"The county, too," interrupted Charlie.

"Wasn't what we were chasing today, but we stumbled on the booze thing in talking to Ole about another lead we were following." Al ignored the interruption. "We thought we should let you guys know."

"Appreciate that. We work closely with Joel and his officers. We'll take a close look at this."

Al cleared his throat. "This might provide a break in our case, so we'd be grateful if you'd keep us informed. Should the ATF be notified?"

"Probably. If there's a case, it will likely be theirs." The chief reached for the phone on the table in front of him. "St. Paul's office is the closest. I'll give them a shout." After a few seconds, he spoke into the receiver, "Agent in charge." Another pause, then "Hi, Paul." The chief covered the phone and said, "Paul Schumacher—a really good guy." Removing his hand, he continued, "Schu, we're meeting with a couple of officers from La Crosse. They were up here working a lead in a case from down their way and believe they may have found some illegal booze in a bar in Eau Claire. Let me put you on speaker and they can tell you about it."

The chief slid the phone to the center of the table and nodded to Al. Al leaned forward. "Agent Schumacher? This is Al Rouse, a detective with the La Crosse Police Department. We were following a lead in a cattle rustling case down our way and stumbled across what we think might be a moonshine operation at a bar on the outskirts of Eau Claire."

Briefly, Al explained what they had seen at Ole's bar.

When he finished, Schumacher said, "Definitely sounds like you saw some shine. My problem is we're so damn busy over here. I have no one available. In fact, you caught me just as I was leaving the office for northern Minnesota. The Wisconsin team is just as busy. Joel, any chance you guys can handle this one?"

"We can," said the chief. "But I suspect whatever we find will be shuffled your way."

"I know that," agreed Schumacher, "and at that point we'll be happy to take up the case and get it through court."

"So we do the work and you take the credit, right?" The chief winked at Al and Charlie as he leaned forward to speak into the phone, nudging his pistol into a more comfortable position on his hip.

"Works for me." Schumacher chuckled.

"All right Schu, we'll take it from here and keep you apprised of any new developments."

"Sounds good. Thanks Joel."

The chief hung up the phone and leaned back, clasping his hands on his stomach. "There you go. Jerry, sounds like it's you and me." He scrutinized Al and Charlie across the table. "You guys want to be involved in the raid?"

"If you wouldn't mind, Chief. We've been tracking moonshine flowing into La Crosse, and suspect the Eau Claire booze is just part of that bigger network. Charlie and I would love to help take those guys down."

"Makes sense." Stanislawski patted his abdomen. "We'll need some warrants. Problem is, it's Friday afternoon and we won't likely catch anyone today. Why don't the two of you come back Monday and we'll set this thing up."

Al nodded and pushed back his chair. "Now we just have to hope that Ole didn't get spooked enough today to tip off his sources and send them scurrying back down into the holes they've all crawled out of before we can get on this."

57

By Monday at six p.m. everything was set. The Wisconsin ATF bureau had sent two men to Ole's place. They'd been at the bar since 4:30, nursing beers and visiting with each other. Occasionally, one or the other would report to Joel Sweeney, who was in charge of the sting. The last report cited a full bar and a somewhat reserved clientele, apparently still winding down from the weekend.

With Joel and Jerry leading the way in their unmarked vehicles, the small caravan—three unmarked, including the last one in line, driven by Al with Charlie riding, and three marked SUV's—left the law enforcement center. They pulled into the parking lot of Ole's about 6:15.

Four officers, including Al and Charlie, entered through the back, and four went through the front doors after the team leader, Detective Anne Chaney.

Once inside, Anne held up her badge. "We're here to investigate reports of illegal whiskey being sold on the premises. Everyone remain where you are and keep your hands where we can see them."

Ole Sanerud came through the door between the kitchen and the bar, an ugly grimace on his face. Judging by the spatula still clutched in his hand, he'd been cooking at the grill when he heard the commotion. Now he set the spatula on the counter and wiped his hands with a towel. "We're gonna do as ya say." Jerking his head in the direction of Al and Charlie, he said, "I shoulda known those two jokers would be back."

"Okay, Ole," said Chaney, "you know why we're here and what we're after. Are you gonna show us, or do we take the place apart?"

"I'll show ya." Ole's voice was indignant and sharp as he moved toward the front of the bar. "Better come back here. What yer after is below the bar."

Chaney gestured for Al to come around the bar with her. After he'd joined her, she bent down and grabbed the two gallons of clear liquid Ole pointed out, set them on the bar, and followed that with two more.

"How many others?"

"That's it." Ole's eyes darted from one lawman to another.

"What's in the basement?" Chaney casually rested a hand on her weapon.

"Nothin'."

"We're gonna take a look. Show us the entrance." She turned slightly to nod at two of her officers, who headed for the basement door. She turned back to Ole. "What about the shed? You own it?"

Ole's nod was barely perceptible.

"Is it locked?"

Another nod.

"Where's the key?"

Ole reached into his pocket and produced a ring filled with keys.

"Why don't you take me out there?" There was more than a hint of insistence in Chaney's voice as she let go of her weapon and took Ole by the left arm to lead him to the back door. Al and Charlie followed the two of them. They were joined by another deputy, this one looking as if he could play linebacker for the Green Bay Packers, who took Ole's right arm.

They followed Chaney and Ole to a metal shed about fifty feet behind the tavern.

Ole opened the lock without being asked, then flipped a light switch and attempted to step back.

"No, after you," said Chaney, pointing into the shed.

As they entered the dimly-lit building, Chaney whistled, and her deputy said, "Whoa, the mother lode, it would appear."

Al's heart thudded against his ribs. *This is it—our big break, finally.* He elbowed Charlie in the side and his friend nodded, his eyes reflecting the excitement coursing through Al.

On the concrete floor sat several dozen plain cardboard boxes, devoid of markings. "Open one, Ole," ordered Chaney. The bar owner knelt on the concrete and pulled one of the boxes toward him. "No real reason to do this," he said softly. "You know what's in it."

"All moonshine?" asked Chaney, her arm sweeping the room.

"All of the blank boxes, yeah."

"Whadda ya do with this stuff?" Her forehead wrinkled. "Surely you don't sell all of this at your bar."

"Guys com'n get it," mumbled Ole.

"Speak up. What did you say?"

"Guys come and get it." The words were louder this time, easier to understand.

"So you also wholesale the stuff?"

He nodded, his gaze fixed on the floor.

"Where do you get it? Who do you sell it to?" Chaney propped a foot up on an unopened box of moonshine. As if to emphasize her questions, she kicked at the box. But Sanerud just knelt there, mouth closed.

"Okay, Ole, if that's the way you want it. Stand up." Chaney cuffed him and read him his rights. "You guys get him down to the LEC," said Chaney, nodding at two deputies. "He'll start singin' when Joel and Jerry start in on him."

"I want my lawyer," said Sanerud.

"Sure, Ole, we'll contact your lawyer," offered Chaney. "S'pose it's that crooked Wesley Arneson." When Sanerud didn't respond, Chaney said, "Really, is that who it is?"

A nod from the bar owner confirmed it. Chaney looked at the petite deputy and said, "Janet, call the creep when you get in, but keep Sanerud away from him until I'm back."

Chaney waved a hand and two officers led Ole away. The big deputy stayed in the shed to inventory boxes as Chaney, Al, and Charlie went back inside the bar.

"Eight jugs back here, two half gone." One of the agents who'd stayed inside pointed to eight gallon jugs sitting near the end of the bar.

"A dozen more down in the basement." The two officers who had headed down there appeared behind the bar, clutching jugs in both hands that they set on the bar next to the others.

"Let's get 'em loaded." Anne met Al's gaze and held out a hand toward the jugs. "You two have put in all the work on this—you want to do the honors?"

Al nodded. "Sure, thanks." He and Charlie carried the jugs out to their vehicle and loaded them inside. It was thoughtful of the lead agent to allow them to take in the goods, recognition that the credit for the raid belonged to them. Frankly, at this point Al didn't particularly care who got the credit. He just wanted whoever had supplied the stuff to Ole Sanerud brought in so he could go back to sleeping at night.

58

AL AND CHARLIE WALKED INTO THE EAU CLAIRE LAW Enforcement Center just as Sheriff Rolf Cranstrom strode into the outer office area. "There you are." His voice, friendly and welcoming, boomed out across the area. "I thought I'd come see if you were here. We're just getting to the fun part with Ole, and I thought you'd like to be in on it."

As the two La Crosse lawmen joined the sheriff, he asked, "Do you want to participate or observe?"

Al shot Charlie a look. "We're happy to start as observers. If you aren't making any headway, we're happy to step in and give it a shot."

The sheriff nodded. "All right then. We'll see how it goes. Likely won't need you. Joel's the best interrogator we have, and our friendly barkeep appears ready to spill what he knows. But we'll see." The sheriff walked them back to the cellblock.

Before reaching the cells, the sheriff gestured to a room. When they entered, Al could see Ole Sanerud through the one-way glass, seated on a chair and talking to Joel Sweeney.

They were just in time to hear Sanerud say, "Tell me what you need. I'll do anything if there's a way to make this go away."

"Ole, you're in deep shit," said the interrogator. "This isn't going away, not completely, anyway. But we might be able to cut you some slack in exchange for help."

"What kind of help?" Sanerud straightened on the chair.

"Things like, who's your source for the booze? How do they contact you? Or anything else you can tell us about where the moonshine came from."

"I'll tell you what I know, but you gotta promise to go easy on me if I do."

"I'll tell you what," Joel said. "If you answer all of my questions forthrightly and honestly while hooked up to a polygraph machine, I promise full consideration."

"Sure, whatever you need. I ain't got nothin' to hide."

Joel exited the room. Ole fidgeted with his hands and seemed relieved when the deputy walked back in with another man who was carrying a machine that he set on the table. Carefully explaining what was happening to Ole, the man connected him to the machine. Then he asked a series of questions, easy ones at first such as his name, birth date, and where he lived.

The baseline set, the more meaningful questions started. Among them were those that were of critical importance to Al and Charlie. Several bottles of water sat in the center of the table in the observation room, and Al reached for one and unscrewed the cap.

"You are both a retailer and wholesaler, right?"

"Well, yes, I guess. I sell some in my bar and I sell some to other folks, too."

"Other people who operate bars?"

"Yeah."

"Who are they?"

"Aww, do I have to tell you that?"

"Only if you want to get any kind of deal from us."

Ole bowed his head, sat there for a few minutes, then looked up and began to tick off the names of bar owners. Al set down the bottle of water, snatched the notebook from his pocket, and scribbled them down as Ole spoke. When Ole finished, Al had a list of sixteen names. Joel pressed a palm to the table. "Any others?"

"Those are the only ones I supply to. Can't say if anyone else gets their own stuff somewhere else."

"And who do you buy from?" The question came spinning out of the deputy's mouth without special emphasis or fanfare. Even so, it sent Al's heart rate soaring again. Were they about to get to the bottom of this case? Charlie shifted his weight from one foot to the other beside him.

Al picked the water bottle up and took a swig.

Ole appeared to recognize the importance of the question too. He turned white, hung his head, squirmed, then said, "Haven't I told you enough?"

Joel crossed his arms over his chest. "I guess you've done enough to shorten whatever sentence you get by a few years. But you haven't done enough to earn any significant benefits yet."

"If I tell you, do I avoid jail time?"

"I can't promise that. But if you don't, that won't even be a possibility."

Ole swiped a few drops of sweat from his forehead with the sleeve of his shirt. "Okay, I buy from Byrle Oldendorf, and he gets if from a couple of guys in Buffalo County."

"Names?"

In spite of his efforts, beads of sweat slid down Ole's face and down his neck. "Well, umm, their names are David and Justin Freeman. Used to be them all the time, but now a coupla women sometimes make the delivery."

Al almost spit out the mouthful of water he'd just

taken. The Freeman brothers were the ones making all that moonshine? Heart pounding, he screwed the cap back onto the bottle and set it on the table. He'd figured they messed around making a bit of the stuff, since they'd found corn mash and pieces of broken bottle on their property. But now they had a credible witness to the fact that those two young guys weren't simply messing around—they were the primary source of the hundreds of gallons of illegal booze flowing into the area. Charlie punched him gently in the arm and Al grinned.

"And they are?"

Al shifted his attention back to the interrogation. Would Ole give up the women's names too? It was likely the two women who lived with the Freemans, but Al would love to hear the bar owner confirm that.

Ole hesitated, until Joel started to get up, then he held up a hand. "Okay, okay. Emily Whetstone is the one I deal with most. She comes with a friend, Madison... something. I think it starts with a D."

"So the main two suppliers are brothers, David and Justin Freeman, right?" Ole nodded, perspiration continuing to trickle down his cheeks. "And this Emily Whetstone and Madison whose last name starts with D, make the deliveries?"

"Yep, that's right. That's all I know. Now I gotta answer to them."

The two officers asked a few more questions, then the one who had come in with polygraph machine disconnected Ole, and Joel brought him a glass of water and a towel.

Ten minutes later, Al, Charlie, the sheriff, the police chief, and the undersheriff, Joel Sweeney, were gathered in the chief's office.

"Your guys did great." Al nodded to the three men seated across the table from him and Charlie. "David and Justin Freeman came onto our radar a few days ago, in connection to another case. Now that we have a positive ID, we should have enough to shut down the supply to La Crosse and wherever else those guys were shipping."

"So you two will make the arrest?" The chief clasped his hands on the table.

"If it's all right with you, since they're in our jurisdiction. We'll keep you updated on developments, though."

"Sounds good." The chief unclasped his hands and stood up. "Let us know if we can help in any way."

Charlie nodded. "Sure will."

The rest of them men stood too, and Al and Charlie shook hands with the other three. "Good working with you gentlemen."

"You too." The sheriff led them to the door and pulled it open. "Good luck on the takedown. It'll be good to get those guys off the streets."

"Yes, it will." Al went out the door and turned back. "So you know, we'll be heading to the Freeman place in Winona first thing tomorrow. These guys have proven to be pretty slippery, and we'd like to see them behind bars before they hear we're closing in and disappear. With the money they must have been making, that's a definite possibility, and we have no desire to start from scratch in trying to track them down."

59

THE NEXT MORNING, THE SUN WAS BARELY BRIGHTENING THE sky when Al and Charlie and Winona Assistant Chief Tom Williams, warrants in hand, approached the Freeman house. Charlie parked the black SUV at the curb, and the three men jumped out, strode up the walk, and knocked on the front door.

The same beautiful blonde woman who'd greeted them the last time opened the door. When she saw them, her chin lifted. "Can I help you?"

"Emily, isn't it?" Al pushed back his jacket to show her his badge. "Detective Al Rouse."

"I remember."

"May we come in?"

"I guess." Emily's response was less than definitive, but Al stepped through the doorway anyway. Emily stepped back, and Tom and Charlie came inside to join Al. "Are either David or Justin here?"

"No, neither one."

The three men walked into the living room where a tall,

auburn-haired woman sat on an armchair in the corner. She rose when they entered, but didn't speak.

Al walked toward her. "Are you Madison?"

She swallowed but nodded. "Yes. Madison Danielson."

Al tugged his handcuffs from his belt. Madison's gaze fell on the set and her face blanched. Al took another step forward. "Emily Whetstone and Madison Danielson, you are both under arrest." He quickly outlined the charges and read the women their rights. "You'll have to come with us."

"Wha... where?" sputtered Emily.

"See, I told you..." Madison's words came out almost in a wail.

"Madison, shut up," snapped Emily, quieting her friend.

Charlie had cuffed Emily, and he took her elbow as Al directed Madison to the door with a hand on her back. Once the women were in the back seat, Al and Charlie climbed into the front. Al had expected the women to protest their innocence as they drove, but they remained silent until they reached the law enforcement center.

Tom Williams met them at the door and led the group to a conference room. As soon as everyone was seated, the questioning began.

Al studied the two women. Emily crossed her arms and glared at the men, clearly not about to tell them anything. Madison, on the other hand, was noticeably nervous, rolling her hands in her lap and gazing around furtively.

As the questioning droned on, Madison asked if she might use the rest room. Williams ushered her out the door.

"I'll be right back." Before Charlie could question him, Al strode across the room and out the door. He caught up to Williams and the young woman in the hallway. "I can accompany her if you'd like, Tom. Let you talk to Emily for a few minutes."

"Sure, thanks." Tom nodded and headed back into the interrogation room.

Halfway to the ladies' room, Madison stopped and faced him. "Detective Rouse, what kind of trouble are we in?"

"Big trouble. You're implicated in an illegal liquor operation. You could be looking at serious prison time."

Her lips quivered. Al gave her a minute to compose herself then asked, "Madison, is there something you want to tell me?"

She shook her head but not very emphatically.

"Are you sure? If there is, it may help you with your situation."

She sniffled. "What does that mean?"

"Depending upon your role in all of this, the judge will take any help you give us into consideration when it comes to sentencing."

"So I might not have to go to prison?"

"Maybe not. If your information leads to the arrests of people more involved than you."

She stood silently for several moments. Finally she met his gaze - her eyes rimmed red. "I'll tell you anything you want to know, but Emily can't be there. She can't know."

"Let me see what I can do." Al walked her the rest of the way to the restroom, waited outside until she came through the door, then escorted her back to the interrogation room. After she'd gone in, Al stuck his head through the opening. "Talk to you for a minute, Tom?"

"Of course." The assistant chief came out of the room and closed the door. He wiped the side of his hand across his forehead. "That girl isn't about to say a word."

"She might not, but I think Madison's willing to share what she knows. She just doesn't want Emily to know she's turning on them. Any chance of questioning the two separately?"

Tom blew out a breath. "I'm willing to try anything at this point."

"Good."

"I can keep working on this one," Tom jerked his head toward the door he'd just come out. "Why don't I set you and the roommate up in the other interrogation room?"

When Al nodded, Tom opened the door again. "Ms. Danielson. Come with me, please."

Madison's face was ashen when she came out into the hallway, but her shoulders relaxed a little when she saw Al. *Good. She must feel comfortable with him. Might be more willing to talk if she did.*

Al followed Tom and Madison down the hallway and into another room. "Detective Rouse has a few questions for you," Tom informed her as he directed her to a seat on the far side of a small table.

Madison slumped down on it. Tom left the room as Al took the chair across from her and smiled. "Look, Madison, I think you got into this whole thing without realizing the gravity of what you were doing. But you're old enough and smart enough to understand now that this is a serious situation, one that could impact you for the rest of your life. You're in school, right?"

She blinked at the sudden switch of topic then nodded. "Yes."

"And your parents, they're supporting you in getting your education?"

A tear slid down her cheek and Madison swiped it away. "Yes, they are."

"You don't want to tell them you're going to prison, do you?"

She let out a choked sob. "No, I don't. Like I said, I'll tell you whatever you want to know if you can keep me out of jail."

"I'll do my best." Al moved his chair closer to the table and propped his elbows on the wooden surface. "Where are the Freemans?"

"At the cave. We have a cave up near Minneiska that also has a still. We've used that since taking down the still in Wisconsin."

"Can you tell us where that is exactly?"

"I can, but it would be better if I showed you, because there are two entrances." She closed her eyes.

"Something the matter? Do you need a drink?"

"No, but... the thought of taking you there. Of seeing David and Justin ... They're going to hate me."

Al sighed. "David and Justin should never have involved you and Emily in all of this. It was cruel of them to do so. They knew what they were doing, and that they were breaking the law, and now they will have to pay the price for that. Whether you help us or not, we will find them and bring them in. But if you help, it will go much better for you."

Madison drew in a shuddering breath. "I suppose."

Al pulled the notebook out of his pocket. "All right then. Let's get started."

60

AL ASKED MADISON SEVERAL QUESTIONS, ABOUT HOW LONG THE Freemans had been in business and who they delivered the booze to. The names she gave him lined up with the bar owners Ole Sanerud had listed, which boosted Al's confidence that she wasn't lying about anything else she'd told him. She confessed her part in the scheme too, as well as what part Emily had played.

After an hour of questioning, Al pushed back his chair. "I'm going to talk to my partner about organizing a group to head to Minneiska. I don't want you to have to face Emily, so wait here and I'll come back for you shortly, okay?" He reached across the table and touched her arm lightly. "You did the right thing, Madison. I know it's tough, but now chances are good that you can move on with your life. Get your education and graduate and start living out your dreams. Assuming, of course, that you never get involved with anything like this again,"

She shook her head. "I won't. Not ever."

"Good." He pulled back his hand. "I'll be back soon, okay?"

She nodded, and Al rose and left the room. He'd managed to stay cool and collected in there, but as always when a big case was breaking, his heart thudded and enough adrenaline coursed through him he was pretty sure he could lift a car off the ground at the moment. *Calm yourself, Rouse.* They still had a couple of big hurdles to cross. They needed to find David and Justin Freeman, and they needed to bring them in to face justice, preferably without anyone getting hurt in the process.

An hour later, a raiding party, comprised of officers from Wisconsin and Minnesota, had been assembled, and Al and Charlie were briefing them. Tom brought Madison into the room. Her eyes darted from officer to officer like a frightened deer seeking an avenue of escape.

Al rested a hand on her shoulder. "You're going to be fine, Madison. We just need you to show us the cave and we'll take over from there."

"When... when I do that, can someone bring me back here? I don't want to be there when you arrest David and Justin."

"Don't worry. We'll be sure to keep you clear." Al squeezed her shoulder before letting go. "You can ride with me in the vehicle with Deputy Charlie Berzinski." He guided her to the exit of the building and they stepped out into the sunshine. Al glanced at his watch. Almost 2 p.m.

"They'll still be at the still, right?"

They walked past a horse trailer, and Madison's attention shifted to it. "Are they going with us?"

"Yes. Since you said there were two entrances to the cave, one on the bluffside, we need officers mounted who can move fast if the men try to escape on foot. But I asked if they would still be at the cave."

She nodded. "They said they had lots of work and wouldn't be back until after dark."

"Good." Al directed her into the backseat of Charlie's SUV, then went around and climbed into the passenger seat. "I didn't cuff you," he said, looking back, "because I trust you."

Charlie, who'd been waiting for them in the vehicle, turned the key and fired up the engine. When the caravan pulled out of the parking lot, their SUV led the way. Al looked back over his shoulder. Through the rear window, he counted eight vehicles, including a tank-like one with the letters S.W.A.T. emblazoned on its side.

Madison looked back too. "All those to arrest two people?" Her voice shook.

"Yes." Al spoke gently, hoping to keep her calm so she wouldn't change her mind about helping them. "A greater show of power makes it less likely that David and Justin will resist, which is their best hope of staying safe."

Her face went even whiter and she slumped against the seat. Hadn't she considered the possibility that the Freemans could get hurt in any sort of takedown? *Keep it together, Madison.* Al took the notebook out of his pocket and scribbled on it. Then he set it down on the seat between him and Charlie. Charlie glanced down at it, scanning the words before nodding.

Get there as soon as you can, or I'm afraid we're gonna lose her.

Madison fidgeted with her fingers as they drove. When they passed Goodview and entered Minnesota City, she asked, "Which way are you planning to go?"

"Which way do you recommend?" The deputy met her gaze in the rearview mirror.

"I'm not sure." Madison frowned. "One entrance is on a

blufftop between Minneiska and Weaver, the other on the bluffside about a quarter mile closer to Minneiska."

The two men in the front conferred quietly then the detective grabbed the microphone and asked for all caravan members to listen up. "We're going up through Rollingstone," he told them. "We'll drop half the group at the cave entrance along with vehicles, then the other half will proceed to the second entrance off Highway 61. That group will include the mounties."

Several people answered "roger" before silence descended in the vehicle. The sheriff turned left onto Highway 248, drove into Rollingstone and headed out Broadway, picked up County Road 25, then on Madison's command turned right onto Mount Vernon Township Road 2, a gravel surface but smooth enough, given the time of the year. They drove in silence until bumping onto a blacktop surface.

"This right?" The deputy was focused on the road ahead, both hands on the wheel.

"Yes, this is the way we went. I'm sure about that." Madison scanned the passing scenery to make certain they were on the right route. Her stomach lurched and she pressed a hand to her abdomen. She hated what she was about to do, hated turning on David especially, after everything they had shared. She pushed back her shoulders. But the detective was right—they never should have gotten her and Emily involved in anything as dangerous as this. She had to protect herself now, and her future.

They rolled along County Road 28, and when it ended at the junction with County Road 31, Madison pointed straight ahead. They drove several miles, the deputy looking back for reassurance every now and then. Each time, Madison said, "Yes, this is right."

When County Road 30 rolled to the left, Madison leaned

forward and stuck out a finger to indicate the road ahead. "Stay on this. We're getting very close."

After about a mile, the road began to turn sharply downhill. Again the sheriff looked back. Madison nodded and said, "Yes, down the hill but go slow, we'll turn soon." Two miles later, Madison pointed to a dirt road that ran steeply uphill.

The detective studied a screen on the dashboard. "According to the GPS, this is where the vehicles going to the other entrance to the property should break off." He twisted in his seat to look behind them. "Yep, there they go." He turned back. "Better put it in all-wheel drive, Charlie."

"Good thought." The deputy hit a button on the panel between the two front seats then eased the rig right onto the dirt road. Slowly—very slowly—he powered the vehicle up the hill. Twice they bounced over fallen limbs, the large oak trees that lined both sides of the path creating a canopy that shaded the vehicles.

Madison could hardly breathe. *What am I doing?* She shoved the thought away. Too late for second thoughts now. After a few more minutes of bouncing around on the rutted road, she leaned forward. "Stop here." A dirt path led up the hill.

"Take that path until you get to a farm field, then go through the field a couple hundred feet until you see red and white strips on a birch tree. You go up that log road, through a clearing, find a dirt road, and take the right fork up the hill. You'll see the cave entrance in a clearing."

Her fingers shook and she clasped them in her lap. "I don't have to go with you, do I?"

The detective shot a look at the deputy, who shook his head. "I think we can take it from here. Stay in the vehicle and keep your head down. You should be safe here." The two of them climbed out of the SUV. Madison heard a click and tried the doors—she was locked in. Fine with her. She had no desire to go anywhere, and her legs were trembling so badly she wouldn't get very far anyway.

Through the side window she watched as the team formed. The detective and deputy were joined by three others - two men and a woman on horses - and two other men driving ATVs. The detective pointed up the hill and Madison watched them as long as she could, until they disappeared over the crest. Then she rested her head against the glass as tears slid down her cheeks.

What will happen now? Will I ever see David and Justin again? And what about Emily?

61

AL AND CHARLIE FOLLOWED MADISON'S DIRECTIONS AND within minutes came across a white pick-up. Al opened the front door and pulled the handle to release the hood. Charlie tinkered away for a minute before straightening, several spark plugs clutched in his fist that he tossed into the bushes.

Al nodded to Sheriff David Brand, who had dismounted at the entrance to the property where they had agreed to leave the horses and ATVs. He gestured for the officers with him to take up their positions at the mouth of the cave.

Al and Charlie joined them, taking cover behind a couple of trees near the entrance. "Look at that, brand new steps," Charlie hissed.

Al studied the mouth of the cave, his heart rate accelerating like it always did at the start of a takedown. Charlie was right. Stairs made of what looked to be new lumber dropped from the entrance into the cave.

The sheriff strode to the opening, scanned the area for a few seconds, then turned back to the group. "Okay, we're going in. I'll take the lead. Except for the two guards at the entrance, the rest of you follow me. Everyone loaded and ready to go? Avoid shooting if possible, but be prepared to be met with firepower." Everyone nodded.

The sheriff gave the go-ahead. Al's chest tightened. This was it.

"Did you hear something?" All of David's senses kicked in. He straightened up from stirring the mash and pressed a finger to his lips. Justin nodded. David crept away from the still and ascended the first set of stairs. He pressed his back to the cold, damp wall and peered up. His heart jerked in his chest. The entrance was crawling with police.

He stumbled back down the stairs and into the cavern. "The whole damn clearing is filled with law enforcement, Justin. There must be twenty of them. We have to put the emergency steps into place and get out the back way if we still can. Hurry."

"But what if they're out there too?"

David drew in a calming breath and held up both hands. "Let's not worry about that yet. We knew this could happen, and we've prepared for it. You connect the overhead cord, and I'll set the surface bobby traps. Once that's done, if there are cops out the other way, too, we'll retreat to the grotto. Be sure to bring the plunger with you."

Justin nodded curtly and headed out of the cavern. David made his way to the corridor and armed the traps. *There, that will seal the ends. We should be plenty safe if we're hidden in the grotto.*

Pushing back his brother's question about what they would do if the police had found the back entrance too, David moved stealthily, turning sharply into the grotto as he reached the natural bend in the cavern. Was there any chance the two of them would get out of here without getting caught? The idea of being locked up in a cave sent cold chills coursing through him. *I'm not going to jail. I'll do whatever it takes to avoid that.*

When he reached the cavern, Justin was already there, waiting for him. David jerked his head back toward the corridor. "All the surface traps are armed. You get the others?"

"Yes." Justin held up the plunger. "Good to go."

"Great. Then let's get out of here." David started toward the back entrance, Justin falling into step beside him. They rushed through the cave, careful to avoid tripping over any loose rocks or debris. When they reached the lower entrance, Justin made his way to the opening and glanced out. Seconds later, he flung himself back into the cave, nearly knocking David over. "There's more of 'em out there. Maybe another ten or fifteen. Damn, we've had it, David!"

David flung up a hand. "Quiet for a minute. I need to think." Blood pounded in his ears, so loudly he had trouble forming a coherent thought.

Justin grabbed his arm. "How could they have found out? Somebody must have told them where we were."

David met his brother's gaze. "It had to have been Madison or Emily. They're the only ones who knew."

The color drained from his brother's face as he let go of David's arm and slumped against the side of the cave. "If one or both of them talked, the police have to know they were in on it too, so now they're in trouble." He looked at his brother, his skin gray. "What have we done?"

David swallowed. His legs shook and he lowered himself onto a rock. "We already lost all our family. If we don't have the women in our lives anymore, and we don't have this business or our other jobs, we have nothing."

Justin sank down beside him. "If we go down in this cave, maybe they'll go easy on the girls, figure they've suffered enough."

David ran trembling fingers through his hair before turning his head to meet his brother's eyes. "Might as well dig in here and fight then. Either we die or everyone out there dies. All I know is there is no way I'm letting them lock me up."

Justin shoved back his shoulders. "Me neither."

He held out his hand and David clasped it. "Got your back, bro."

Justin smiled grimly. "And I've got yours."

The cave wound its way back and forth but steadily downward. In less than a minute, Al, Charlie, and the officers with them were in a grotto, this one lit by natural light. Al nudged Charlie in the ribs. "Can't be that big a cave. We must be getting close to the other entrance."

The sheriff walked back and stopped in front of them. "We're getting close to the rear entrance, and the other group is there, in position. We should have these guys trapped between us. I'm going to move ahead and call on them to surrender."

Al nodded. The SWAT leader had crawled ahead and was crouched behind a boulder at the start of a bend in the cave. The sheriff carefully crawled to him and peered over the rock. He must have seen the brothers, because he held out his hand and someone gave him a bullhorn, which he lifted to his lips. His voice boomed out of the cavern, bouncing off the damp rock walls. "David and Justin Freeman, this is Sheriff David Brand. You are under arrest for the manufacture, transport, and sale of illicit liquor. Surrender immediately." When the words died away, silence draped over the cave. Al strained to hear something, anything, through the dim light of the flashlights around him.

Finally, a voice broke the stillness. "This is David Freeman.

We are not going to jail. Do you hear me? We are not going to jail."

"Mr. Freeman, the choice isn't yours." The sheriff spoke loudly but without the benefit of the bullhorn. "If you force us to move in and you are armed, someone will get hurt. How about you make it easy on all of us, including you and your brother, and give yourselves up. We have both entrances covered—you're not getting out of here. Trying to break free would be madness."

A shot rang out and a bullet ricocheted off the sandstone walls of the cave, cutting channels in the rock where it hit. Instinctively, Al ducked.

"That's a dangerous ploy, Mr. Freeman," said the sheriff. "If you continue that, you'll give us no choice but to come in firing."

"C'mon then." The elder Freeman brother's voice held a note of mockery. "We're ready for you. We have you just where we want you. Guess you didn't notice the booby traps along the walls of the cave. A very dangerous oversight, Sheriff."

Several raiders flashed their lights over the walls. Al followed the thin beam emanating from his. Above their heads he spotted a wire. But what was it connected to?

The sheriff made his way back to Al and Charlie. "We need to get everyone out of the cave in case they're not bluffing about the booby traps. We'll monitor both exits—they'll have no way out. You guys start back. I'm going to notify the other team to get out but to stay near the mouth of the cave and then we'll be right behind you."

Charlie and Al retreated the way they had come, until they reached the stairs. Seconds later they were back on solid ground. After taking up position behind the trees again, they waited for the sheriff and the rest of the officers to emerge. Five minutes later they did. The sheriff came straight over to Al. "Those boys are digging in, and it looks as though the place really could be rigged. We need to end this right now before someone gets seriously hurt."

Al pulled his weapon from the holster. "How about we lay down a barrage, maybe scare them into offering themselves up, then you move up when we quit shooting?"

"Sounds like a plan. Give me a couple of minutes to get everyone in place." The sheriff gestured for the rest of his team to join him. "Stay back until the firing stops then we'll move up and lay down our own barrage, make sure those two know we mean business."

On Rouse's count, the team with him opened fire, carefully avoiding the cave mouth as they shattered the silence that had fallen over the wood. Dirt, sticks, and rocks flew into the air as bullets hit all around the entrance until Al raised his hand and the firing stopped.

Silence.

Before anyone could move, all hell broke loose. A loud boom echoed off the distant hills of Wisconsin as dirt, boulders, and logs whistled through the air, spewing debris in all directions.

When the echo stopped and quiet again took over, Al looked around. Charlie was lying in a heap about twenty feet away, his clothing stained with blood.

Crouched low, Al sped across the distance and rolled his partner over.

Charlie's eyes were closed, and although the front of his clothing was dirty, there seemed no problem there. But when Al looked down, his hands were stained with blood. "I need help over here," he yelled.

The sheriff jogged over and crouched down beside him. "I've called for the medics. They'll be here soon."

Al continued to search Charlie for the source of the blood. "What about the Freemans?"

"There's so much crap between us and them - I have no idea."

A man carrying a medical kit dropped to his knees beside Charlie. He grasped Charlie's wrist, listened for a few seconds, then nodded to Al. "I've got him. You go check for the fugitives."

Reluctantly, Al left his friend to the man's care and followed the sheriff to the dirt mound that once was a cave entrance. The sheriff motioned for his team to join him. "Let's clear out this opening, see if we can get in there and find them."

"The hole's just big enough to let me in," called a team member, a woman. "I'm going inside."

On her hands and knees she began her climb into the cave, twice stopping to move large rocks out of her way.

Fifteen minutes later, her voice drifted up through the hole. "No sign of either Freeman. Either they're buried in the rubble or they found a way out of here."

The sheriff frowned. "Let's hope they didn't get away, but it would nice to bring them in alive."

Two officers jogged to the ATVs and retrieved shovels. When they returned with them, the sheriff signaled for four people to take turns shoveling and put the rest of the team to work clearing rocks from the blast area.

"We must be close to breaking through." Al peered into the gloom of the cave, but the dust from the explosion still hung in the air, making it difficult to see.

A few seconds later, one of the shovelers said, "We're through."

The sheriff started forward. "Good, let's get down there and see if we can find those guys."

Al followed him down the dust and rock covered stairs. Several officers joined them at the bottom and continued to dig. After several minutes, the sheriff held up a hand.

"Stop." He jerked his head, ordering the men who had been working to step back. Al tagged along after him as the sheriff grabbed one of the shovels. "Somethin' here. Let me look."

The sheriff attacked the pile, slowly uncovering a tennis shoe. He lifted his head and his eyes locked with Al's. "I think we just found one of them."

The shovelers went to work in the area, digging very gently. Slowly the body of David Freeman was exposed and then, a few feet from him, they found his brother. It took several minutes of careful work, but finally they had unearthed both of them.

The sheriff shook his head. "Such a waste of life." His voice was tinged with sorrow, which only increased Al's respect for the man. He took a deep breath. "Okay, let's try and wrap up here. Larry, Dennis, stay with the bodies until the BCA evidence boys arrive. Should be any minute. The rest of us can head on back to the LEC and spend some time debriefing."

Al trudged back to the road where Charlie was sitting in a sheriff's car after having his wound field dressed by the man with the medical bag.

"Caught some flying debris in the explosion. It's not a bad wound, mostly flesh—or in this case, muscle. This guy is all muscle." The medic tapped Charlie on the shoulder. "Get to the hospital and get that wound looked at. Make sure your tetanus shot is up to date, too, okay?"

"Sure will." Charlie grabbed the man's hand. "Thanks for helping out. I appreciate it."

He clambered out of the car and leaned heavily on Al as the two of them made their way back to the SUV. Al sighed. The day had not gone as he would have liked - not by a long shot. They might have solved the moonshine case, but the resolution had come at a high cost—two young men dead and the lives of two women pretty much destroyed. Not nearly worth the money they must have made, no matter how much it was.

The acrid smell of dust and explosives clung to their clothing. It would take a while for it to fade, even with washing, But it would take a lot more for the images in Al's mind to fade—of two kids, buried side by side under rubble and gone forever.

62

THE NEXT MORNING, AL WOKE AT FIVE A.M. AS USUAL. HE wasn't tired. In fact, he was anxious to begin the day. He scrambled out of bed over JoAnne's protests, jumped in the shower, and was ready for work twenty minutes later.

He thought about stopping in at Ma's but passed on the idea. Charlie would still be sleeping, because the doctor had given him pain pills after seeing him.

Al had dropped him off at home where Kelly was waiting to snuggle him and make him feel like a king. Al smiled at the thought of the two lovebirds, happy that his friend had finally found love.

He made a quick stop at Fayze's, picked up two dozen assorted pastries, and headed for the office.

Al was soaking his second doughnut in his second cup of coffee when a shadow fell across his desk. He looked up to see his boss. "Hi, Chief." Al nudged the bag of pastries closer to the other side of the desk. "Help yourself."

"Don't mind if I do." The chief sank onto the chair in front of Al's desk and reached for the bag. "Good smells coming from this office. And you had a good day yesterday, I hear."

Al set down his doughnut and leaned back in his chair. "Depends on your definition of good. We did manage to wrap up two cases."

"But ..." The chief cocked his head.

Al ran a hand over his head. "Can't quite get the picture of those two brothers buried in debris out of my mind. As the sheriff put it, it's a terrible waste of life. And all for the sake of running a bit of illegal booze and making a few bucks."

"More'n a few, I'll wager. But your point is well taken. While it's good to get those two off the streets, no one ever really wants to see a case end this way." The chief took a bite of his pastry and chewed thoughtfully. "How's Charlie?"

"I'm pretty sure he's sleeping in, but I think he's okay. He got hit by some flying debris. Suffered a few cuts across his belly. Which isn't surprising, I guess, since he's such a big target." The chief snorted. "That's true, he is." He shoved the last bit of pastry into his mouth and brushed the crumbs off his hand. "'Course, you keep bringing in treats like this, and they'll be sayin' the same about me."

Al grinned. "Don't worry. You've got a ways to go before you can compete with Charlie."

The chief crossed his arms over his belly. "Maybe this'll make you feel better. I know you think you solved two cases, but it was actually three."

Al's forehead wrinkled. "Three?"

"Yeah. Moonshine case solved with the Freemans and the two women. So that one's all but wrapped up. And not only do we know that Boulon was involved in the rustling, but when the sheriff started questioning him, he spilled his guts. Gave us the names of the big wigs signing his paychecks. Four more arrests made this morning, which looks like it's shut down that operation, so we can put that case on the books too."

Al wrapped his fingers around his paper coffee cup. "Really."

"Yep. And that's not all. Dan and Bill have been working another case. Reports of the Chicago mafia moving into the area. They hadn't made a whole lot of headway, until yesterday when I got a call from Byrle Oldendorf, owner of the Handy Corner bar, shortly before things went down with the Freemans. He tipped me off that a few members of the Chicago mob were about to get involved. Apparently the Freemans had been paying them for protection and the mobsters were actually planning to keep up their end of the bargain.

"I took a team over and we intercepted them, brought them in for questioning. The leader, some brute named Franco del Gotto, is wanted in Chicago and a few other cities for a long list of outstanding offences. Don't expect he'll see the light of day any time soon, if ever. So that's a pretty good day's work, I'd say."

Al sagged against the back of his chair. "Wow. I had no idea. I guess, even if I don't like the way things went down, we did go a long way toward cleaning up the county yesterday."

"Yes we did, thanks to you and Charlie. The two of you make a pretty good team, you know? In fact, if you guys are lookin' for something to do, I was thinking I might talk to the sheriff, see if he'd be okay with loaning Charlie out to us again, once he's feeling better. I thought you guys could take a look at that old, unsolved kidnapping case."

Al straightened in his chair. "The Sovereign case?" That one had always piqued his interest, and he'd spent a lot of his spare time looking over old files and newspaper clippings, looking for a lead.

"That's the one. Been thinkin' about it for a while. That the kind of thing that would interest you and Charlie?"

The cloud that had been hovering around Al since they'd recovered the bodies of the Freeman brothers the day before lifted slightly. "Yessir, it would. It'd be a different kind of challenge, that's for sure. I'll bet Rick would be interested, too. Okay if we involve him?"

"Whatever you need. Go for it. But, Al..."

"Yes, Chief?"

"Take a few days off, okay? Maybe take that beautiful wife of yours somewhere nice."

Al reached for his doughnut. A few days off did sound tempting. And he and JoAnne were way overdue for some alone time. "You know what, Chief? That's not a bad idea at all. In fact, I think I might just take you up on that."

CPSIA information can be obtained
at www.ICGtesting.com
Printed in the USA
BVHW032310090321
602184BV00011B/95

9 781733 182645